I0594769

TESTIMONY

THE SOUL MONGER:
BOOK THREE

MATILDA SCOTNEY

Copyright © Matilda Scotney 2020
All rights reserved.
National Library of Australia Registered

No part of this publication may be reproduced, stored in a retrieval system, offered as a free download on any website, or transmitted in any form or by any means, electronic, mechanical, photocopied, recorded or otherwise without the prior written permission of the copyright owner. Short passages of text may be used for a book review or discussion in a book club.

This book is a work of fiction. Any similarity between the characters and situations within its pages, or places and persons, living or dead is unintentional and coincidental. Matilda Scotney has asserted her moral right to be identified as the author of this work.

Testimony: The Soul Monger Book Three
ISBN: 978-0-6487545-0-3

Cover design by Beehive Book Design.

"Out beyond the ideas of wrongdoing and rightdoing,
there is a field. I will meet you there."

- Rumi

CHAPTER ONE _

They say that sleep is never dreamless. Is it a dream when there are no images? Where there are no characters, no frightening scenarios played out, no long-wished-for romance, no need for joyful remembrances to quicken the slumbering heart? Just perfect peace? Laurel dreamt only of colours, vibrant and vivid, that streamed in threads around her unconscious body, slowed the blood in her veins, and even though they had no form, caressed her lightly, soothing her, their whispers…their *whispers?* Laurel winced at the sudden, clattering urgency in their breath, a touch, firm against her arm. The gentle colours retreated as a fresh voice cut a path through her awareness.

"Mom, *wake up!*"

A voice so dear, so unexpected, she willingly left behind the peacefulness of the colours and opened her eyes, and for the second time in her life, Laurel woke to the sensation of variance fluid sucking at her back and thighs. As the unfamiliar cold air startled her body, Laurel snatched her first newborn-from-variance breath. This time, unlike the first, it was gentler, more humane, thanks to the Chaese scientists' inventiveness. Now, the voice she heard was not that of a Soul Monger, waking her as a slave, but of her beloved daughter.

"Go slow, Mom. I'll help you sit up."

Laurel attempted to connect with the sides of the variance chamber and felt the warmth of Ava's hand as she supported her mother's struggles to rise.

"*Ava?*" Laurel needed to say her daughter's name, to tell her how comforted she felt at her presence; she and Ava readily shared thoughts, even muddled ones such as these, but it wasn't the same as saying her name aloud. To utter it made it real.

Laurel struggled to whisper through her tightly clenched teeth, and her mouth rewarded her persistence by abruptly opening wide, with the ensuing deep draught of air into her lungs bringing on a fierce fit of coughing.

Laurel blinked. At least she supposed she did. It was difficult to tell if the shrouded vision was Ava or an afterimage, although she was positive the patch of warmth on her shoulder was her daughter's hand. She had no idea at this point as to the passage of time, and the hazy image of Ava offered no clue. A second familiar voice came from over her shoulder, the voice she heard the first time she woke from variance. This time, it was friendly, concerned.

"Is she okay?"

"Yes, Uncle Darlen," Ava replied. "I'll look after her."

"Okay," Darlen called back. "I'll wake Marcel. Harry's in the common room with Scarlett. She's hounding him with questions, so one of us needs to rescue him."

Harry? Once more, Laurel felt gratitude for having someone she loved making it through the Transcender safely. Ava slipped a gown over her mother's head, encouraging her to locate her arms when her mother appeared at a loss. Then, as the last of the variance fluid slurped its path onto the floor and into nothingness, she gently encouraged Laurel to stand.

"Can you take your weight, Mom? You need to move."

Laurel tried to nod; she abandoned any attempt to speak in favour of protecting her long-unused throat and lungs. She knew that difficulty would reduce rapidly and that the turmoil of her bodily sensations—she wasn't sure of her head's location—were likewise short-lived side effects. Even with that knowledge, it dismayed her to discover she was moving her hand up and down instead of her head in response to Ava's question. She tried to step forward, but the movement caused nausea to swell in her gut. Laurel never thought she would anticipate dry bapth and the cloying thick pink variance antidote fluid, but at this moment, she looked forward to it.

Accepting Ava's arm, Laurel's feet contacted the cold metallic floor, and she tried to plant them both firmly, although she found herself lifting and dropping each in turn before they settled. She felt the floor firm beneath her—that was a tick for her feet—but the disorientation made her less assured about the position of the rest of her body. She found her neck and rotated her head to peer at Ava, her face still veiled by the half-light. Laurel blinked again. Once they were outside in the corridor, she would see her, look into her eyes, see how she'd changed these…however many years it had been. *"Please let it not be too many"*, Laurel pleaded silently, *"let me not have missed much more of her life"*. The thought crossed to Ava, who answered with a gentle squeeze of Laurel's arm.

Variance needed purging, Laurel knew this, and she knew that movement was essential to void its effects. To stand upright and walk a few steps was all that was needed. Once she mastered that, she knew from experience, it became easier, but her knees wouldn't straighten and raising one foot resulted in it flapping down too hard in the same spot. She couldn't take a single step. Ava drew her forward, poised to catch her if she fell. Laurel carefully drew in her breath; this feeling was not as baffling as the first time, and she urged her body to respond to her commands. In the moments she wobbled halfway to the door gripping Ava's arm, she had become steadier and more upright, her vision returning and her eyes demanding only a couple more blinks as they acquainted themselves with the intense light of the passageway.

Safe now from the effects of variance and assured each part of her body was where it should be, Laurel turned to her daughter. Reaching up, she touched Ava's face, searching those brilliant violet eyes. Ava seemed taller, more lovely, her raven hair pulled back into a loose ponytail, but not much older than the nineteen years she had been when they entered the Transcender. Laurel tilted her head and smiled. Only now did she whisper that all-important name.

"Ava."

Ava smiled and gripped her mother's hand, holding it against her face. "I'm fine, Mom, everyone's fine. I missed you. You'll feel better when you've had the antidote."

Marcel's bewildered voice rambled in the background as Darlen woke him from variance. Soon they would all be back together. Ava arranged her arm about her mother's waist, keeping her close as they gradually progressed towards the Canaa's common room. Laurel thought briefly about the first time she woke from variance, aboard Darlen's original ship, and the greasy patination that covered the bulkhead, the appalling stench, the sad, bewildered gazes of the other whole souls, the Soul Monger's contempt and intimidations and their alarm when he told them they had woken to a life of slavery. So different now. This time, they were all family.

Harry had taken the antidote and was reclining in a soft chair. He looked quite himself, even though his attempt to rise and greet Laurel proved an effort. Laurel wanted to run to him and hold him, but she'd likely end up sprawling across the floor, and land at his feet in an untidy mess. Instead, she waved at him to remain seated and allowed Ava to help her sit beside him, where they contented themselves with a loving squeeze of each other's hand. Scarlett knelt on the other side of Harry, her arms around his waist, her young face lit with smiles. Her family were back together. She came around to Laurel to kiss her and hug her in welcome before sitting between her and Harry. Marcel was close behind Laurel, his far-too-short gown dangerously close to an embarrassing revelation. Darlen was busy holding a second gown around Marcel's lower regions, but Marcel was still too disorientated to co-operate, not yet having got around to discovering there was a body between his feet and his head. Darlen sat him down, exhaling a noisy sigh of relief as he covered up the parts of Marcel he felt

Scarlett didn't need to see at her age.

"I told you that you needed longer gowns," Laurel smiled as Darlen set the antidotes in front of them.

"I know," he grinned back, "but I never expected to use them again." Darlen jerked his head towards Marcel. "He hasn't lost any muscle mass in variance. In fact, I swear he's grown."

Marcel leaned back his head. "I feel terrible," he said, clearing his throat and trying his voice for strength. "I don't want to do this again. Next time, I'll walk."

"Drink this," Darlen held up the pink liquid, "just half of it, eat the bapth, then drink the rest of the liquid. You'll have no troubles with your voice, and it will get rid of the disorientation."

"I didn't think this would be so welcome," Laurel smiled as she sipped on the pink antidote that Helen—when Darlen first took them from Earth—had erroneously assumed was a McDonald's thick shake. Darlen had doggedly refused to disclose its constituents, and Laurel guessed she'd never need to know, hoping it didn't contain Darlen's saliva, like in the variance fluid. Whatever it was, it did the trick.

"The last time," she said, releasing Harry's hand and disengaging her arm from Scarlett's grasp, "we had shocking sore throats. This did little to ease it."

"Didn't stop you talking, as I recall," Darlen chuckled.

"Could you blame us?" Laurel choked a little on a laugh. "You kidnapped us and told us we were slaves!"

"Did he actually tell you that?" Harry said, surprised.

Laurel nodded, "And copped a mouthful from Helen."

Darlen grinned. "She was crazy about me, even then."

Laurel grunted a reply and closed her eyes. She missed Helen, missed her dry wit, her friendship, but she would have been proud of Scarlett, who looked to have grown some and was now very like her mother, dark-haired, petite and not just a little sassy. Laurel supposed that much wouldn't have changed. Ava and Darlen were as they left them. Mer was the same; in fact, there was little difference from before they went into variance. But first, the antidote, get rid of the nausea, the gravelly voice and brain fry, then ask questions.

"Two years," Harry blurted out, answering the first question that had entered Laurel's head.

"We've been asleep two years."

"I suppose it stops us ageing," Marcel answered, handing out a surprisingly insightful response despite his heavy eyelids and croaky voice. It was clear the antidote was not to his taste. "I didn't feel like this after stasis," he grumbled, holding up the beaker and peering into its depths. "What the hell is in this?"

"Apart from spit?" Laurel said, half-joking.

"Ugh," Marcel pulled a face. "Well, I hope it was Scarlett's."

Darlen hid his grin by turning away. Yes, Scarlett provided some of the enzymes, but she was just a little girl. It needed reinforcing. Laurel would have known. He glanced at her, and she was looking right back, her fearful suspicions confirmed. She shrugged a "what the heck", and Darlen lifted his eyebrows. He knew she'd keep his secret.

"I told Harry just before we went into variance," Laurel said, switching the subject from bodily fluids. "If we keep having to be suspended, I'll end up younger than Ava."

Ava laughed. "Well, as you like to observe the day of our birth, Scarlett and I kept that up, and just to make it a bit of extra fun, we gave Mer a birthday as well. He has one whenever we want."

Mer made a few munching sounds and cackled as his eyes glowed red.

"He says it's his favourite thing to do," Scarlett giggled, clambering into Laurel's lap as best her lanky seven-year-old legs allowed and curled up against her. Ava gave the girl an affectionate poke on the arm.

"You forget I can understand him too. He said we gave him no choice!"

Marcel sighed. "It's good to see not much has changed around here."

"Life carried on as normal," Darlen said, dragging up a chair. "Ava and I kept Scarlett up to date with her education, but we included flight simulations, ships ops, engineering, stuff that has a practical application, better suited for her life in space."

"She's only seven," Laurel pointed out.

"I could pilot a ship at seven," Darlen said. "Engineering, understanding sensors and gathering data have mathematical applications. Knowledge of those subjects can often be a matter of life or death."

Darlen had cared for Ava for years while they were in stasis before, and he did a fine job. Scarlett couldn't be in better hands; he would make sure she had all the skills she required to help her make the right decisions in a crisis.

"I don't want to fly an axispod, Auntie Laurel," Scarlett said. "But I like the engines and the tech things. Mer lets me take him apart."

Mer munched some sounds in response, and Scarlett glanced up before looking back wide-eyed at the group, admitting, "Only his arm, I can't take his head apart because most of his transceivers are there, and he wouldn't be able to tell me how to put him back together."

Marcel gulped down the final swallow of the antidote and pulled a face, sticking out his tongue with a "Gyah!" sound, the noise soliciting an enormous grin from Darlen.

"Hits the spot, doesn't it?" he chuckled, amused by Marcel's facial contortions.

Harry shrugged. "I thought it was rather refreshing."

Marcel's head and shoulders tensed and shuddered before he admitted. "I do feel better, but that stuff is revolting!"

Seeing he'd made sufficient recovery, Scarlett, the budding engineer, robotics specialist and pilot, vacated Laurel's lap to cuddle Marcel. He allowed her to climb carefully onto his knee and kiss him noisily.

"Did you miss me, Marcel?" she said.

"Umm, of course, all the time," Marcel frowned. "I thought of nobody else."

"Daddy let me reprogram all your holoenemies so I could practise my programming skills," she told him proudly. "You'll love the new ones."

"That's clever. So, you didn't have time to get bored in the Transcender?"

Scarlett shook her head gravely. "Only Daddy got bored."

Darlen nodded. "At first, but it's different from the Transcender that leads from the League to Laurel's universe. There was so much action; it gave us a lot to consider. I never really analysed what kind of purpose a Transcender might provide other than to get us from one universe to the other. It also did something else I didn't foresee; when the journey ended, this Transcender spewed us into the nebula and then just vanished."

"The nebula?" Laurel said, puzzled.

"Yes, it's still here. Some of it anyway."

"Across dimensions?"

Darlen pulled an "evidently so" face.

"What about the dimensional shifts?" Harry longed to return to the flight deck to study the data on their new location, but while he felt fine just resting here, he wasn't confident about applying too much brain power.

"As expected," Darlen said. "I observed dimensional slips throughout, but the Transcender directed our course." He looked at Ava. "I took some convincing it wasn't the ship that was moving. Ava recognised that from the outset. Either way, I had no idea where we would end up. The Transcender delivered us here."

"And we don't know where here is," Ava added. "But I'm sure it's where the Transcender wanted us to be."

"Any co-ordinates?" Harry asked idly, then rubbed his eyes and grinned. "Brain fry. I know we can't have co-ordinates. Sorry, I mean, relative position?"

"To what, Harry?" Darlen gestured through the

viewport. "We've got a nebula, and that's all we know. I'm positive it's the Miran Forin or at least a fragment. We've been holding position since we exited."

"So you can look at it one more time, Auntie Laurel," Scarlett said.

"You're very thoughtful," Laurel smiled. "When my legs feel stronger, we'll go together to the observation deck and admire the view."

Marcel gave Scarlett a peck on the cheek and eased her off his knee with a gentle nudge. "My brain seems to be recovering at a different rate than my body," he said, squeezing his eyes shut tight then opening them wide. "I'm not even sure my body parts are in the right place yet."

"Your bodily functions were directed by variance for two years," Darlen said. "It'll take a day for you to feel normal again."

"I'll take your word for it, Darlen. Is there anywhere we can put down if need be?"

"The sensors are still populating the star charts, Marcel." Darlen scratched his head. "I've had more than one occasion to speculate why the Chaese are no longer spacefaring. I can't work out why; it's certainly not their technology. These sensors have a reach I have never seen before. Of course, we won't know the designations of any systems, but from what I can see, the sensors are compiling an index and a celestial map for us. I suppose it presumes we're morons."

Harry concurred with the ship's assessment. "In this universe, we are. Are we definitely in a different universe, or are we simply in another sector of the old one? I mean, if the nebula is here…"

Darlen didn't have the answer, just conjecture. "A universe is a big place. We could be just in a different sector because I didn't see a dimensional fold open as we exited. I only have experience of one Transcender before this. It might be that each Transcender—if there are more than the two I've encountered—behaves differently. Perhaps this one doesn't bridge universes."

Laurel's intellect was still too syrupy to have to comprehend multiverses, even if she knew there were at least two and even if Harry had recovered enough to ask intelligent questions. She'd take simple answers for now.

"Ava, what was so impressive about the Transcender?" But of course, she was inquiring about a transdimensional phenomenon. How could the answer be simple?

"Mom, it's unbelievable!" Ava stood, taking the floor, her arms reaching out as if to gather them all into her wonderment. Clearly, the Transcender had had an effect.

"As soon as we entered the curlew," she began, "the ship simply stopped!" Ava made a chopping action with her hands and a theatrical side-to-side movement with her eyes. "The instrumentation continued to register the passing of ship's time and perceived distance, but it didn't produce positional data." Ava paused; each day, she had marvelled at her adventure in the Transcender, and she wanted to depict the experience just as she saw it.

"The ship doesn't move. It seems to become absorbed into the void. I didn't sense movement even though Uncle Darlen believed we were moving. There were no signs of widespeed precipitation. At first, the outside darkness pressed against the ship, and even though I'm used to being in the nebula core, I found it stifling." She looked at Darlen. "Uncle Darlen said it was typical, but then he'd never encountered what happened next."

"I used to kill a lot of time sleeping and reading," Darlen admitted, "I probably didn't notice, but I don't recall any kind of celestial event in the other Transcender."

Ava rolled her eyes. "I don't know how he missed the fireworks! A yellow spiral blasted through the darkness. It revolved slowly, like a vortex…" Ava demonstrated the path of the spiral with her index finger, "and it had a tail that seemed to stretch into infinity. Seconds afterwards, another followed, and the tails flicked together. Then they passed over us and disappeared." Ava raised her hands, her eyes shining with excitement. "They were moving, but not in a physical sense. It was like watching 'Time' flow. We saw other bright flares of light, quickly followed by blackness, and then showers of flashes, like fire—which isn't possible in space—but it's the only way I can describe it. I could detect the nebula, but it was distant, an echo, just glimpses, really. I sensed we weren't sharing the same space. It appeared shortly after we saw the first galaxy forming."

"How do you know that was the formation of a galaxy?" Harry asked.

Ava sat down. "I don't know how I know." She looked up, puzzled. "I just know. We saw so many things, worlds, distant stars."

"Ava has the theory the Transcender is an arm of a greater stellar nursery," Darlen said. "She called it the quintessential dimension."

"That sounds impressive."

"I didn't just make it up, Marcel," Ava said. "Uncle Darlen told me about scalar fields, and the concept of quintessence and this substance called ether, but as these theories originated in your universe, Mom, there's nothing in our database. If the Transcender harbours dimensions, it's possible galaxies and universes are being established within those dimensions. Even Darlen doesn't know how many dimensions we travel across. I think once we enter the Transcender, we are in a fold between dimensions. But I saw the gateways to others."

Gateways? How curious. "What do they look like?" Laurel asked.

"You've shown us books, Mom; when they're closed, the pages all join in a block." Ava pressed her palms together. "But on closer inspection, you can see each page is a fine line. That's a dimension. And between those lines is Time. Time is bright. Some phenomena we saw slipped between those pages into the brightness."

"So why did two years pass? Why not an instant?" It made little sense to Laurel. At least not yet. But from someplace, a memory was nudged.

"In my experience," Darlen said, "Time has a kind of pre-ordained chronology. Laurel's Earth is part of a spatial pattern but covers several timeslips; we've talked about how Earth has a unique time sequencing. The dimensional interchange isn't defined, but the Magen allowed me to slide into the dimensional crossroads, locate the whole soul and slip into the time I require. But the Magen's power seems to stop at me moving around dimensions at will. Isilia is the only other planet I've ever seen this kind of Time arrangement."

"But if the Miran Forin nebula was present within the Transcender, how did that cross dimensions?" Laurel had studied all the conclusions by the League scientists about the time situation on Earth. Adding in dimensions seemed to have somehow not been considered.

"I'd like to know the answer to that," Darlen agreed.

"So would I," Ava said, "but there was no sign of the extent of the nebula, no sign of the core, just the coloured strands. After we exited, it was more like standing in a rainbow. It's far less dense here..." Ava frowned, devoting her thoughts to a later episode.

"When the Transcender tossed us out," she said, "and closed behind us..." she looked at each of them in turn, as if they could bring insight to the experience, "the nebula...was *waiting*." She angled her head from side to side, uncertain that she'd explained herself well enough. It sounded rather absurd. "Darlen said there is invariably a sense of momentum at one end because you aren't plunging into a picot, and I was prepared for that, but it was like we were—" she held out her hands and looked up, "—caught."

"It *was* unexpected," Darlen agreed. "As soon as I spotted the shift in the Transcender, we all prepared but...nothing. The progression was smooth."

"I don't think the Transcender occupies space the same way as the nebula, Mom," Ava said. "It's like the buttonhole on that Earth garment you manifested on Isilia when you got cold; you know, the overcoat. We just slip through from one side to the other. If we had some control over Time, though…"

"You just reported a lot of goings-on for a button-hole."

"I know," Ava admitted, "and time passed, but it shouldn't have. I wish I knew why I feel this way." The mystery had bothered Ava almost from the point they entered the Transcender, but for Marcel, Harry and Laurel, it was probably a little soon to join in seeking out the nuances of Time, and Harry turned his attention to more practical matters.

"Maybe we should go to our beds, recover, then get underway once we're all functioning. We'll gain nothing by sitting here and blitzing our brains. What's the priole precipitation, Darlen?"

"Only seventy-five per cent of that in League space. It'll get us where we want to go, though."

Harry shrugged and looked around, lifting his eyebrows quizzically as his eyes settled on Laurel. "Which is where?"

Laurel struggled to her feet to check the sensors, which were still busy populating the starfield.

"First star on the right and on till morning?" she offered with a grin.

Darlen saw that Peter Pan film on one of his visits to Earth. "I think you mean 'second star to the right and straight on till morning'?"

Laurel smiled. She'd never seen the film, only ever heard the saying. "It's as good a direction as any."

CHAPTER TWO _

The following day, fully recovered from variance and after once more waking happily beside Harry and enjoying breakfast together, Laurel found some time to be alone with Ava. They stood on the observation deck, arms about each other.

"I missed you, Mom," Ava smiled, hugging her mother tight. "These two years took a long time."

"I feel like I've aged, honey," Laurel said. "I wonder if there's a way of changing my molecular structure, so I don't need to go into variance again."

Ava laughed. "Maybe if we find who we're seeking in this universe, they might know the answer to that."

Laurel watched the filaments of the nebula reaching out to her. Ava was right. It was smaller, more distant, and despite the colours that defied definition, it brought Laurel a sense of closeness. To her, it was like being a child, looking up to the clouds and seeing part of the rainbow, glittering through raindrops and sun.

"I hope we get to see it again," she breathed. "There's so little of it now."

Ava shared a little of her mother's sadness. "It's been a backdrop for most of my life." Inside the Transcender, despite the unbelievable things they saw, she had been glad of its familiarity.

For a moment longer, they stood until the ship veered and the nebula slipped from sight. Laurel sighed. "How can we be sure we're heading in the right direction?" She lovingly tucked one of Ava's dark curls over her shoulder. "You had such an understanding when you felt we were getting off course. Are you still so certain?"

"I don't *not* feel that way, Mom. It may mean that we've arrived, and it doesn't matter what heading we take now; we'll discover our destination, anyway. Or be discovered."

"Of course, I recognise nothing the sensors show," Laurel smiled, "but this morning, I feel…I'm uncertain, nervous, excited even."

Ava nodded. She and her mother seldom disagreed with their shared thoughts. If one thought it, then rarely did the other contradict. On this point, they were in complete accord, but she had a question that bothered her while her mother was in variance. Now she had been patient while she recovered. She didn't want her to dredge up memories while her brain was still undergoing the effects of variance.

"Do you recall once suggesting the nebula was an artery," she said.

"I do." Laurel recalled the discussion immediately. "We just need to determine where that heart is."

"Well, I can't answer that, but while we were in the Transcender, with a front-row seat to all that…that galaxy building and observing the dimensional variations and those columns that represented Time, I thought about what you said."

"You think maybe the Transcender is a nucleus of some sort? Or perhaps another artery that leads to the heart of the universe?" Laurel quickly caught Ava's thoughts.

"I need further information, but all those dimensional corridors go someplace, Mom. They are a journey leading to a destination, and Time is attached to them. I considered the possibility of the Transcender being the heart, the centre, the birthing place of the cosmos, but it seemed to fall short. I sensed there was a common…" Ava turned and grinned. "Listen to me, rambling! Would you believe I took a visual and let it run? Guess what?"

Laurel shook her head, although she already knew.

"It didn't record a thing," Ava laughed, "just blackness and static as though my eyes were tricking me."

"But they weren't?"

"Uncle Darlen and Scarlett saw everything I saw, and Mer tried to record it himself, but he got nothing either. As you know, he stores everything in his memory, but not that, Mom, not that."

"Maybe you were witnessing something outside technology's capability to produce a cohesive record."

"I don't think it's that basic. As I considered the probable explanations, I also made room for the improbable."

"And you came up with…?"

"What I saw doesn't yet exist. Or at least it won't until it enters one of those dimensional folds. I think that goes for life as well."

"Do you think the Transcender fosters some kind of pre-existence?"

Ava shrugged. "Humans from your world believe in an afterlife and spend their lives preparing for it. What about what came before life?"

Laurel nodded. She didn't have an answer for that even when she lived on Earth, and now, after all she'd seen and experienced, she still didn't.

The sensor array was still busy compiling star systems but offered a fair summary of their current position relative to the collection of planetary bodies it had so far identified. Besides the fact the array was still cataloguing, there was an unsurprising mix of worlds, stellar clouds, asteroids and a few distant pulsars that the sensors were feverishly categorising. This space appeared to yield nothing out of the ordinary and lent substance to Harry's suggestion they may simply be in a remote and unexplored part of their own galaxy. Laurel felt strongly this was not the situation.

"The Transcender from League space crosses dimensions, Harry," she said, seeking to pick up on an elusive sense of familiarity as to where they were.

"But Darlen said he didn't detect a dimensional fold when the ship left this Transcender." Harry glanced at Darlen, encouraging him to respond. Harry didn't especially relish the dimension and Time conundrums they'd encountered; they made his head reel. He preferred leaving such puzzles to Laurel and Darlen.

"That's right," Darlen said. "I didn't, but I also wasn't the one to discern the Transcender. Like I say, they may not always behave the way we predict."

"Baii and Ilivi claim their people arrived from another

universe," Marcel said as he marvelled at the sensor's scope to index the strange star systems and join the dots of their present course, even though the ship had no prior data upon which to draw. "If we find Riynea, then we'll know for sure. There's no point in second-guessing." He brought the coordinates out for everyone to study, sprinkling the flight deck with a graph of the most local star system relative to their position.

"The system we're approaching appears empty of any human civilisation," he said. "The atmospheres of all the worlds are too rich in methane to sustain human life unless the inhabitants have somehow adapted."

Ava shook her head. "We should just keep going."

"Okay," Darlen said with a grin. He would not argue. Ava's intuition had got them this far, wherever "this far" was.

The system they found themselves in may have been uninhabitable, but it was spectacular, even more so than the Massienes cluster. Moving through its colourful, bright stellar clouds and planets kept Scarlett entertained for hours and was quite a distraction for the rest of the crew. Like a scenic Sunday drive, Laurel thought, through unfamiliar countryside so charming to look at, but if they landed anywhere, it would be deadly to human life. They left the navigation to Mer and sat up on the observation deck with lunch, like a picnic in the country.

Laurel still found considerable magic in space travel. She hadn't truly ever got over the novelty. Too often, space just whizzed by at widespeed, its grey swirls revealing nothing of the passing spacescape, so she savoured the times when she could quietly enjoy the beauty it presented. The precipitation was less here, and as it was all so new, inadvisable to simply zip through. There was time to take advantage of a relaxed pace, enjoy the scenery, and take an unexpected vacation. They were likely to be within the system for at least a couple of days, and it wasn't as if they knew where they were going. Laurel and Ava just knew their destination would reveal itself soon.

The circular raised area in the centre of the observation deck gave breathtaking, panoramic views of space in all directions. The planets seemed closer together than the crew expected, considering the size and atmospheres. A delightful spectacle of two tiny nebulas, almost mirror images of each other, touching nose to nose in what looked like a tender kiss, brought much commentary and hilarity. Ahead lay a green planet, peeping through thundering grey clouds, the single sun casting sombre rays across the atmosphere to add majesty and splendour. Mer drew their attention to two impossibly small moons, too spherical to be mere asteroids, spinning in orbit around a gas giant, minuscule twin mobile pimples against a vermillion surface.

Skirting a mottled pink and green world encircled by mineralised rings that sparkled in the reflected light from the planet's daylight, the crew marvelled at the jewel-like brilliance. Darlen named it "Scarlett" and logged it into the sensor, the only named planet amongst billions of computer-assigned numbered spheres.

There seemed no reason to hurry. They all agreed; where would they hurry to? The "first star on the right" quote from earlier appeared to have returned a manifestation of good instinct. It was as if now they expected to stumble across what they had been searching for all this time, or perhaps, as Ava and Laurel both thought together without declaring openly, for someone to show up, looking for them. Marcel didn't share their optimism.

"My lady sister," he said to Ava days later. "I think we're lost."

The earlier expectancy and excitement of finally being out of the Transcender and the unscheduled holiday was wearing off, leading to concern they may not be at journey's end. Ava folded her arms and looked through the viewport. As they'd departed the star system in which they'd spent a few rather pleasant days, she felt a transformation. That shift also affected her mother, and Marcel's enquiry coincided with an impression of something more definite. She didn't answer Marcel's question, instead instructed Mer to make a course correction. The rest of the group had an instinct of what it meant, but only Scarlett voiced it.

"Are we there yet?"

CHAPTER THREE _

"Look at the size of that thing!" Darlen's awe reduced his voice to a whisper as the immense ship filled the viewport. Before them, the vessel drifted in space. so vast and intimidating they had no view of open space at either side from their position on the flight deck. The size of a city, with no visible engines, no markings, the ship was as high as it was wide. Assuming its firepower corresponded to its size, any attempt to fly above or around it would undoubtedly prove suicidal.

Darlen brought the Canaa to all-stop and put his hands to his head in confusion as he viewed the instrumentation. "Why the hell aren't the sensors picking it up?"

"They're still not," Harry confirmed, watching the sensors for any signs of change, but they showed normal space ahead. Harry had seen almost as much of their own galaxy as Darlen, encountering many configurations of space going vessels, but nothing came close to this mammoth, not even cargo carriers, which were several times the size of a consular ship. He wondered what kind of race could build such a colossus. Laurel listened to his thoughts and observed, then caught Ava's eye, verifying that her suspicions were correct.

"It's not real," she declared.

Darlen and Harry turned. "Not real?" Harry looked from Laurel to the ship outside, his face creased in bewilderment.

"It looks real," Marcel replied. "How are we looking at something that's not real?"

"I get it," Darlen said, slightly regretting the fact the vision had hoodwinked him. He should have been a little more space smart than that. "It's a manifestation. We must have found the Riyneans."

Laurel nodded. "Looking back, at first sight, we didn't realise the palace on Isilia was a manifestation," she reminded them, "albeit a rather elaborate one, like this." She gestured towards the viewport, where the object pretending to be a menacing ship remained. "We are either close to Riynea, or there are others like the Riynea with similar manifesting abilities."

"It looks tough," Marcel said unconvinced, even though he trusted Laurel and Ava's instincts. Manifestation or no, it was too immense for him to see in its entirety from the flight deck. "It might be just the façade. There could be a squadron of warships behind it."

"I can't see a weapons array," Darlen said, "even a manifestation of one, but yes—" he acknowledged Marcel, "It could be hiding battleships."

"I don't get a sense of aggression from who or what is causing it," Laurel said, glancing at Ava, "but we can't be sure. The Riynea have incredible telepathic ability. They could easily deceive us."

"Baii and Ilivi gave no sign their people were warlike,"

Harry pointed out. "And if it is a manifestation, any weapons would be pointless."

But Darlen wanted to examine the possibilities just a little further; they were in an unknown region of space, and anything was conceivable. "What about those two thumping great tunnels under the wings?"

Mer joined in, making munching sounds as his eyes lit red. He seldom pointed or gesticulated, but in this instance, he did.

"He says they're just useless passages," Ava translated. "He can see space through them."

Darlen studied the ship. "Mer's eyesight is a darned sight better than ours. Maybe they're fashioned on external cargo bays or landing ports."

Laurel pointed to the sophisticated pattern-work on the massive central hull. "Do you remember the gates to the palace on Isilia? The birdlike emblems with flaming wings, talons and tails? Doesn't this ship remind you of them?"

"Crimson and gold, as I recall."

"Yes, Harry. They're not a display of aggression; they're a token of nobility and strength."

"If they respect that," Darlen suggested, "perhaps we should power up our weapons, display *our* strength. At least let them see we would defend ourselves."

"There's not much point, Darlen," Laurel said. "What would you fire on? It's not there. It's testing us, and any act of aggression on our part might just send a fleet of warships, if they have one, on the defence."

"Well, whoever they are—" Harry shifted his attention back to the sensors, "they're scanning us, so I would say that hidden in that manifestation, or at least nearby, is at least one ship."

A low hum momentarily filled the flight deck. Seconds later, a clatter on the counter behind them made them turn. Marcel scooped up the flat, grey object deposited there and peered at the unfamiliar rectangular device. He handed it to Laurel.

"There are many strange symbols, Laurel. Do you understand them?"

Laurel turned it over in her hands. She hadn't seen one in years. Not since Earth. "It's a computer keyboard," she said, the nostalgia of the object bringing a smile to her lips. "These symbols are English letters. They're used to construct words and sentences."

"A communications device?" Harry took the keyboard from Laurel, and he too turned it over in his hands. Something from her world. Fascinating. And out here.

"In broad terms," Laurel answered, "yes, but whoever is on that ship must have manifested it from my memory. It seems—I don't know—extraordinary, and given the technology on the Canaa; out of time."

They all looked again towards the ship barring their way. Scarlett suggested they went around it, her seven-year-old child's logic not grasping the concept of the ship not really being there. Just in case a monster was lurking outside, she stepped a little closer to Darlen to place her hand in his.

"I think it would just have to sniff, sweetheart—" he smiled, acknowledging her fear but not reinforcing it. She would meet all kinds of strange things in space, "—and we'd finish up sucked into one of those great big tunnels, manifestation or not." Darlen looked around. "Could it be a projection from a planet? There are a few systems up ahead."

Harry was inclined to wait and see what transpired with the artefact in Laurel's hands before theorising further. "I think we should just stay and see what they want. Laurel?"

Laurel put the keyboard on the counter. "Remember when I was trying to analyse the woven fragment?" She looked up; they remembered. "Ava mentioned a keyboard she saw in my mind. While it didn't precisely translate, I used the mental display as a kind of physical medium so that by mentally touching symbols, they transformed into cohesive patterns for me. It wasn't ideal, but I did finally get somewhere." Laurel ran her fingers across the keys. "Like a crystal ball or a seer's stone," she said, more as a whispered thought: no-one else on the flight deck, perhaps except for Darlen, would have any clue as to those objects.

"So why would whoever that is out there manifest this gadget?" Harry said. "We can't assume that ship belongs to the Riynea, and we have no idea of the species in this region of space."

"I'm convinced that ship is a display of power," Laurel said, "designed to intimidate until whoever is controlling it knows who we are and what our business is."

"And they would have analysed our weapons capabilities for sure," Darlen said.

"The Riynea are telepaths, but neither Baii nor Ilivi were invasive," Ava pointed out. "I wonder if those people also think this is a communications device and are giving us a prompt. I saw it in your mind; maybe they did too."

Ava's appraisal brought a consensus of agreement.

"Okay, so tell them 'hello'," Darlen suggested.

It sounded so simple, all this technology, all this distance they'd crossed, and now, it might hang on one simple Earth greeting. Laurel tapped "hello" in English and waited. She scanned the keyboard as if willing the keys to depress themselves with an answer.

Nothing.

Marcel suggested a Seeran or a League hail.

Laurel tried a standard Seeran greeting. Still nothing. There was no reason to expect anyone out here to understand these languages, but it gave Laurel an idea. Closing her eyes, she rested her fingers on the keyboard, and taking a deep breath, brought all her focus to finding the right word. She pushed the keys. Not English. Not Seera.

"Shalom".

Seconds later, the vision of an elderly man materialised on the flight deck. His facial features appeared to be Riynean. Long, drab and worn garments hung on his slight frame but folded neatly in a ritualistic fashion about him. His hair was coiled in a tight bun on top of his head, wispy strands hanging limp and grey across his shoulders and dropping almost to his waist. He surveyed them for the briefest of moments, then his voice burst into their minds, powerful and assertive, with a deep, urgent resonance that contradicted the man's diminutive form.

"Cover the vessel!" he ordered, and although the connection was telepathic, Scarlett covered her ears. *"You emerge from Sheerguhd. You cannot remain here. Return with me. The masters must not discover you."* The man faded from view,

leaving only the echo of his warning buzzing in their minds.

Stunned by the sudden appearance of the man and the shortness of the exchange, Harry checked with Laurel. "He spoke Seera, right?"

"I'm not sure," she shrugged, "but I understood. Onoth on Isilia could make us understand him using telepathy. He was Riynean."

"Sheerguhd?" Darlen puzzled over the old man's meaning. "Does he mean the Transcender or the nebula?"

"Sheerguhd was mentioned on the weave," Laurel nodded. "I don't know if it refers to the nebula, but that man wants us to hide the ship."

"And he spoke of the 'masters'," Marcel reminded them.

Harry agreed. "We must be on the right track, but it doesn't sound as if we will get much of a welcome. Was he a manifestation, Laurel, or had he somehow teleported onto the ship? He looked pretty solid."

"A manifestation, like the ship."

"Do you get anything negative from him?"

Laurel shook her head, there was something she couldn't put her finger on, but it wasn't strong enough to say she had doubts about following the man's directives. "Not specifically," she replied, "his concern is genuine. Follow him. If the masters are out there, I'd rather it wasn't just us meeting them on our own."

***

Despite all the evidence pointing to the ship having no actual substance, Darlen couldn't work out where the little man's real ship might begin or end. If the vessel were tucked away somewhere within the manifestation, it would be prudent to keep a safe distance until he had more information, but obligingly, the colossal ship dissolved in a shimmer; in its place, a small-scale runabout, a fraction of the size of the Canaa. It had neither weapon nor widespeed capability. The little ship turned and levelled its flight fins but didn't proceed.

Laurel swallowed hard; she knew the man was waiting for something she nor Ava had so far accomplished. The thought filled her with dismay. "He's standing by for us to cloak the ship."

All eyes swung to the two women, and there was complete silence on the flight deck. Even Mer watched for the outcome of this turn of events. Laurel looked at the tiny speck of a ship replacing the imposing warship from a moment ago. The man's urgent insistence they hide the ship suggested he knew the ability of a whole soul to conceal objects. The problem was, it was a technique that neither Ava nor Laurel had up to now mastered, even though they had tried. As it stood, only Helen had ever concealed the ship.

Harry turned to the sensors and carried out a few short-range scans. "His ship is about as basic as you can get. It's not much more than a hull with minimal instrumentation and not even as advanced as a level one axispod. I doubt it would be much good if the masters turned up. I'm surprised he's flying about without defensive capabilities."

Darlen disagreed. "He doesn't feel under threat for himself; his fear is for us."

"Darlen's right," Laurel said. "I suspect this guy knows a lot more about us than we probably know ourselves. He assumes we would know how to cloak the ship, but…" she rounded suddenly to Ava, who lifted her hands, stretching them towards her mother. Slender tendrils of violet-coloured vapour drifted from her fingertips.

"Mom?"

"I see it. It's happening."

"How will we know if we hide the ship?"

"We will, I promise."

"I can't move."

"I think it took Helen a while to learn to operate while she was in this state. It's okay."

Then the Riynean ship moved. Laurel nodded her encouragement to Ava; seemingly, they'd fulfilled the old man's urgent request. The Canaa followed, matching the small ship's limited speed.

"I wish I knew how this was happening," Ava said, smiling, looking inward to gain confidence in this new energy.

"Helen mentioned strong emotion played a part."

"I feel energised!" Ava agreed, *"but I'm petrified of moving in case I break the connection."*

Steadily, the intensity of maintaining the ship's cover relaxed, and Ava felt able to shift her position, although slowly. Harry recalled Helen's exhaustion on Semevale 8 after her first experience with this phenomenon, and he insisted Ava sit, not knowing how long this journey might take. Hours afterwards, Laurel felt moved to take over the mantle of the ship herself. She saw the aura of violet relax into Ava's body and became aware of the comforting flow of her own essence. The Riynean ship continued leading them, proof the Canaa was still concealed.

"*On Earth,*" Laurel sent to Ava, "*there would be people saying prayers over us and calling for us to be exorcised.*"

Ava grinned. "*It's ignorance, Mom. You once said we were human, just not like other humans. There are probably many more like us on Earth, maybe on other worlds, with their abilities undiscovered.*"

"*When Darlen brought the six whole souls to the League,*" Laurel sent, "*I often wondered why there was no real fear, that we so calmly accepted everything set before us, even the war. League space seemed more like home than Earth, and the closer I got to the nebula, the more 'at home' I felt. I thought the nebula would have had a lot to do with explaining the whole soul question. Now we're leaving it behind; I guess the answers lie somewhere ahead.*"

"*At least we've found a Riynean, but if he's representative of the people we're going to meet, he's scared.*"

"*He's definitely scared for us,*" Laurel agreed. "*I can't believe that even after all this time, the masters are still in control of this universe.*"

"*Maybe it's not 'after all this time',*" Ava suggested, the phrase reminding her of the Time paradox both in the nebula and the Transcender. "*Maybe we cut across a Time threshold or even moved into another dimension when we exited the Transcender. Remember the Time inconsistency in the nebula?*"

"*I remember.*"

"*If we've stepped into another time, we may be closer to the events of the war Baii spoke of. That would mean he is in the future now, or even a corresponding universe.*"

CHAPTER FOUR _

Darlen couldn't overhear Laurel and Ava's conversation, but he'd been busy coming to a few conclusions for himself, some of them not unlike Ava's. His father had told him the Magen was an instrument for hopping between the strange Time and dimensional slips surrounding Earth. Clearly, his father's knowledge was restricted to Earth and the League, but Darlen wondered, even though a single hop through a slip was attainable, the Magen was like a dimensional key, and it had to be assigned to someone of his species. In other words, he was a tool. He grinned at a sudden image of Helen in his mind. It was one of her favourite descriptions of him in their many arguments, but he saw now, the word had a practical application. He recalled that Laurel sensed something about Time in the nebula core. Perhaps the Magen had not cleared a dimensional portal. Maybe the Transcender had sent them back in time. He turned to Harry and was disconcerted to find he was studying him.

"Are you thinking what I'm thinking?" Harry said.

"You're too shrewd for me, Harry, so I'd say no."

"If the masters were part of Baii and Ilivi's history, it's fair to assume there would have been some progression or even resolution of the war since then."

Darlen nodded slightly. "But the old man's anxiety suggests otherwise. It could be a centuries-old impasse."

"I don't think so," Harry said. "He knew Ava and Laurel were significant. What if we passed through some Time vortex, a shift, and maybe missed out the dimensions altogether. Even you said the Transcender didn't act as you anticipated."

Darlen had to agree, but all they had were theories. "You know that stuffy old discourse about the movement of Time on Earth?" he said.

Harry nodded. "Laurel quotes from it now and again."

"Yes, it's tedious. You should never have told her about it."

Harry produced a thin-lipped grin in response.

"Never mind that now," Darlen continued, "Whole souls have a sequential life on Earth, but whatever timeline they inhabit intersects at some point with that of other whole souls."

"You mean, they eventually cross paths?"

"Yes, other humans exist in more than one Time. Shadow existences. They're all actual, but there is only one physicality. The Time movement distorts their perception."

"You think the whole souls know of this?"

"Innately maybe, but I have yet to meet a whole soul who had this shadow reality."

"This would imply they have some influence over time."

"If they have this skill on Earth," Darlen said, "I dare say they'd have it here. Even if they don't know it."

"Laurel and Ava are bound to have a few ideas."

"Laurel recognised an accord with Time in the nebula. Ava is still considering her belief a single dimension held us within the Transcender. They'll nut it out, Harry." Darlen slapped him on the shoulder. "Don't worry. Hey, they figured out how to hide the ship, didn't they?"

Harry conceded they did. And he knew the two women would "nut it out". He wasn't a whole soul, but he'd picked up a little of his whole soul dad's intuition. The immediate future, he was sure, was about to become very large. Very large and very dangerous.

As the little ship leading them possessed no widespeed capability, it shuffled along at such a pace, the Canaa felt as if it were at full stop. Darlen calculated the Riynean ship travelled at around a quarter of the speed of light, so he and Harry assumed either widespeed prioles had yet to be discovered in this universe or technology had not progressed to a degree to harness them. The old man made no further contact with them, and even though Laurel was sure she and Ava were still hiding the ship—otherwise, that might be a reason for the man to hail them—she suddenly lost confidence and despite her earlier reassurances to Ava, wished she could see some actual evidence for herself. She said so to the others.

"Helen wasn't confident either," Darlen said. "But it always worked."

"She had a bit more practice than we have."

"Have faith in yourself, Laurel," Harry said confidently. "You have remarkable abilities—" he looked at Ava, "you both do. We all trusted Helen, and we trust you too."

CHAPTER FIVE _

"Looks like some sort of array or hub. Harry, what do you think?" Darlen pointed at the sensors. They'd travelled at least three days with no further contact from the little ship. Harry drew out a facsimile of the massive object looming ahead for them all to view. No doubt their destination.

"Another manifestation?" Harry said.

"No," Marcel shook his head. "The sensors are picking it up."

"Monkey bars," Laurel said softly.

Scarlett brightened. "Monkey bars?" She knew what a monkey was, a curious Earth creature. Laurel had told her about them. She would like to meet one.

"Monkey bars are a kind of climbing frame for children," Laurel explained. "That's what this looks like, pipes woven at right angles to each other, but this one extends out into space."

"It's embedded into that moon," Marcel said as he walked through the starfield emission, checking out the object from all angles. "How does it maintain orbit of that planet?"

"I think it's a Terminal, a Space Station," Darlen said. "They've used the moon as the base plate. It's probably a warehousing complex with a transit port, maybe servicing that world." He pointed to the planet below, its northern hemisphere obscured by a murky mist so thick, even sunlight couldn't penetrate. Around the equator, the fog displayed an odd delineation between north and south, not typical of a weather system. "They may have moved certain services off-world because of the pollution in that weather front."

"You've seen something similar to this station?"

"Well, not on this scale, Marcel, but there's a planet, Ioin, close to the Gartyran homeworld that operated a resource like this. Several planets brought their goods to store, trade and ship; it was the neatest and best-kept trading post I've ever seen. But it wasn't as impressive; that thing has got to poke out at least seven kilometres from the moon." Darlen turned to Laurel. "A lot of climbing, even for a monkey."

"I never left Gartrya except to go to League space," Marcel said. "I didn't know of Ioin."

Darlen waved a hand to dismiss the debate. "The people weren't friends with the duke." That was a chapter of his life, long ended and, for him, best forgotten. "The Riynean ship is slowing," he said, "so it would appear the monkey-bar moon is our target. According to the sensors, there are four planets in this system, all with industry and infrastructure remnants but no signs of dynamic technology. The fourth looks like it has only scant vegetation, mostly rock with a few oceans." He studied the sensors. "Three of the four look to have undergone catastrophic events, low population, non-functioning technology—destroyed most probably. Only the barren planet has power output." He looked at the others, although he didn't expect a reply. "Maybe a sentient non-human species? Definitely life there. The large planet with the bizarre weather system has major ecosystem degradation. Something had a major effect on the biosphere. What population is left will be in poor shape, starving most likely. The atmosphere is contaminated, more noticeably in the northern hemisphere. On the other two worlds, sensors show nitrogen/oxygen atmospheres, vegetation and a reasonably healthy ecosystem but only scattered signs of life. The fourth planet seems unaffected by those catastrophes." Darlen pointed to the polluted planet, announcing grimly, "Welcome to the war zone."

Laurel directed the sensors to analyse the planet's atmospheric conditions; they struggled due to the unknown toxins but managed a partial result, showing forty per cent analysed had between seventy-eight per cent and ninety per cent match to toxins known by the Chaese. The rest could not be explained. One thing was for sure; whoever released those pollutants into the atmosphere meant business.

Laurel rubbed goosebumps from her arms. "Someone must have detonated a nuclear device in the far north of that planet." This felt bad. This was not just a war; someone was trying to annihilate a civilisation. "What we're seeing is a nuclear winter, or something similar."

"I've never heard of a nuclear winter," Harry said.

"No-one dropped atomic bombs in the League," Laurel pointed out. "I can't be sure, but I believe whatever it is they detonated was constructed to produce a controlled result, confined to a segment of the planet at first, then slowly creeping into other parts. See?" She pointed to a sensor-extrapolated progression of the polluted cloud. "My knowledge of this stuff is only from science at school but check out the origin; it was detonated around twenty years ago, I would say at low altitude, and apart from the toxins and dust that developed from the ensuing destruction of industry, buildings, soot from fires and so on, I suspect they'd already added in a few poisons for good measure."

"How would they control the speed the cloud dispersed," Harry asked. "It's dense, but even so, it would get caught up in normal weather conditions, surely?"

Laurel shrugged. She knew little more than he did. "I have no idea, Harry. Earth has never experienced a nuclear winter. Localised nuclear disasters on Earth resulted in a myriad of health and ecological issues in the vicinity, but this, well, this is cataclysmic. The device was obviously calculated to wipe out part of the population and the ecosystem, then allow the fallout to take out the rest."

"Something the masters devised?"

"Who else?" Laurel had no choice but to attribute this form of devastating warfare to them. "They're clearly not in a hurry. Even though the sun is shining on the Southern continent, it's not likely to be that warm there, and without arable soil, no crops will grow. The ground will probably be poisoned even where that cloud hasn't yet covered. Like Darlen says, the people left there will probably be starving. This process can take many years, and when all life is wiped out, it will be uninhabitable for decades."

"At these levels," Harry said, making his own worried

calculations, "I dread to think what condition the people are in; starving would only be one issue."

"Would we be able to help?" Ava asked.

"We don't know the level of medical treatment possible here," Harry said. "They may have already tried to ease suffering and failed."

Laurel nodded. "This must be the masters' plan, to wipe out humankind, but it seems they want to inflict the maximum amount of suffering while they do it."

"What about the unaffected planet?"

"Humanoid readings as far as I can see, Marcel," Darlen said, creating a few sensor sweeps. "And it seems to have technology, possibly as developed as whoever built the Riynean ship. But not as advanced as us." Darlen looked at Harry. "And that doesn't auger well for advancement in medicine. The rest of the system has a couple of planetoids, nothing else."

At that moment, the Canaa powered down and stopped. Mer interfaced with the ship but indicated an override on the controls, and he would need a few seconds, declaring the mechanism holding them to be a primitive traction beam. Darlen shook his head and told Mer not to do anything. The old man had steered them here for a reason. Instinctively, Laurel and Ava knew they were no longer hiding the ship but were now concealed within the space station's massive structure. Their vantage point provided a good view. The barred segment of the Terminal was octagonal, roughly ten times the dimensions of a League consular ship and jointed neatly to maintain the shape. A platform ran through the centre, entirely cased within the bars. Random shelves, with the appearance of docking ports, were dotted around the exterior. A helix-type arrangement connected the structure to the moon below. Negotiating the array of bars would probably take some skill given the size of the Canaa in relationship to the Riynean ship.

"What do you think this is?" Marcel had been watching the ship's sensors while the others were checking out the array. An object appeared in synchronous orbit over the northern pole of the polluted world. Only the shape and mass of the object had been assessed at this point. No other data was available.

"Some kind of mechanism?" Darlen looked from the sensors to the viewport but could see nothing at this distance. "The one that delivered the incendiary that caused the devastation?"

Laurel's blood ran cold. "That's the master's ship."

Harry drove the sensors to deliver further information, but they had little to offer while they remained focused on the object. "That thing is massive," he declared. "No wonder the Riynean manifested that huge ship when he contacted us. He must have assumed we were more masters or other hostiles and didn't want us to see him as a soft target."

"Is the ship aware of us?" Marcel asked.

Mer munched a few sounds.

"He says no incoming scans or probes," Ava said. "The old man wanted us to hide the Canaa, so I'd say he planned on us arriving undetected."

"Maybe," Darlen agreed, "but unless the array is

shielding us as well, how can we be certain?"

"Is the Canaa still covered?" Harry said.

Laurel shook her head. "Not since the Riynean ship stopped."

"So, the masters' ship detecting us depends on what type of sensors they run." Harry looked but found no evidence of any scans, "Unless they've got great eyesight and can see us at this distance."

"Don't disregard it," Darlen said. "We know nothing about the masters. I would have thought they were far more advanced than the Riyneans but looking at the ship on the sensors…" Darlen fell silent.

"Looking at the ship…?" Marcel prompted.

"They're no further along than us." Laurel finished the sentence for Darlen.

Darlen nodded. "That would likely make them look very powerful if all the civilisations in this system are as technologically backward as our new friend."

"Then they're not going to want us showing them up for what they are," Harry said.

Laurel held up her hand. "Let's not be too certain it's the technology that makes them powerful. We might match them, even though we are considerably smaller. We don't know what other attributes they possess that may be stronger than developing better machines than these people. Earth's scientists could produce bombs like the one devastating that world, and they have only scraped the surface of technology compared to the League."

"Mom's right," Ava cut in. "These masters could be psychic or have the ability to perform bizarre phenomena.

Look at Mom and me, we've never been able to hide the ship before, but suddenly, in this universe…" Ava didn't need to finish. They got it.

Mer munched an alert as an electronic communication hailed them from the space station. The sudden pull of the traction beam drew them closer to the station's outer hull, wresting with the size and angle of the ship to fit it into a docking port. The automated aperture and Mer eventually worked out a suitably accommodating position, with the opening extending its seals according to Mer's specifications. A couple of shudders shook the ship, followed by a slurping sound as air filled the accessway. Then all became quiet.

"I guess we've arrived," Darlen said. He slapped Mer on the arm and pointed to the array. "Looks like you made a friend." Mer's eyes lit up, and Ava and Scarlett laughed at his reply.

"What did he say?" Laurel asked.

"He said the array doesn't have a sense of humour," Ava chuckled.

"It's probably not configured for a ship like this," Darlen said. "That's why there was so much pushing and shoving to make us fit. The Riynean ship is a strange shape, and it's ugly." He opened his hands and raised his eyebrows. "You've got to agree."

They all suddenly found something else to do. The Canaa was the oddest and ugliest ship they'd ever come across, but to Darlen, its architect, she was a work of art.

CHAPTER SIX _

"What do we do now?" Marcel looked around. They'd been waiting for more than an hour. "Just stand by for orders?"

"Seems logical," Harry said. "We have no idea what comes next."

Laurel turned her head to listen. "It's okay, the Riynean is coming for us."

"Is he alone?"

Laurel nodded. Scarlett wasn't sure about this turn of events; for someone so brave in the face of such a spectacle as a Transcender, now she preferred the safety of her father's arms. She reached up to him as they heard the hiss of the airlock.

The old man approached them with a smile and none of the Riynean formality they received on their first encounter with Baii and Ilivi on Isilia. The man reached out first to Laurel, then to Ava, and encouraged the men to come closer as he touched each one on the shoulder in greeting. He spoke again through their minds.

"I am Sedar. I apologise for my earlier, hastened, and afraid demanding welcome, but if the master's had identified you... Please come with me."

They followed Sedar through the pipe-like maze of

passages; he didn't communicate telepathically again, allowing Harry, who had wisely brought along a hand-held version of the pandroscope the Chaese had helpfully provided in the field medic pack, time to scan him.

"Elevated heart rate, adrenalin. That calm is a pretence. He's terrified," Harry murmured to Laurel.

"He didn't expect us, Harry," she murmured back. "Our presence might have exposed them to more danger or made matters worse."

"We don't yet know what those dangers are," Darlen said, checking his voice so the man wouldn't hear, although he appreciated the Riynean could read his mind if he pleased. Darlen hoped he'd done the wise thing in bringing Scarlett with him onto the station instead of leaving her with Mer, it was just that the planet side of the spaceport looked exposed, and from here, too apparent to what they supposed was the master's ship. He was glad the Canaa was tucked away on the far side. If any masters were lurking, well, he preferred not to consider the possibilities. "Have you got any sense of what's going on?" he said to Laurel.

"Not yet, but Ava and I can sense apprehension. You could cut the atmosphere with a knife. I think there are quite a few people on board this station."

Darlen nodded. Considering the size of the master's ship, he shared their concern.

Four corridors branched off a mezzanine floor, leading south, east, north and west. The mezzanine was cold, filthy, and barely furnished. It looked set up for as much comfort as possible, with the conspicuous inclusion of half-dismantled machinery converted into chairs and surfaces.

Sedar invited them to be seated on the jumble of metallic benches arranged in a semicircle. Scarlett still clung to Darlen, peering at Sedar suspiciously from under lowered eyelids.

Sedar once again spoke into their minds. "*These…*" he gathered five pins from a tray, "*…will help you make sense of our language. There is a sting as you insert them.*" He demonstrated the location at the back of the neck, "*but they are old technology. As our species integrated and we shared and learned our languages and culture, they became unnecessary. There are few left now. We do not need them.*"

Harry took the appliance and examined it. Little more than a miniature pin with a spherical head, he would have preferred more information before he implanted it anywhere. Laurel nodded her understanding as he flicked a glance towards her.

"We have to trust these people," she said. "I fully believe that what we came to find is here—" she looked around, "someplace." Laurel studied the pin. Harry embedded a Fobel node under her ear when she was first aboard the consular ship just after her arrival, to promote language assimilation between treaty planets, but this mechanism was many times larger.

"A Fobel node?" she asked Harry.

Harry nodded. "I would say so, although a Fobel node is a fraction of the size. No-one really knows for sure where the original model for Fobel nodes came from; they're attributed to a few dozen different experts." He leaned in towards her with an enigmatic grin. "Ancient experts, I might add."

"Well then," she smiled as she prepared to insert the pin into her neck, "we may get some answers to a few more ancient questions."

Darlen was possessed of an ingrained caution about blindly agreeing to anything an alien species asked of him. So even though Laurel and Ava telepathically assured him of Sedar's intent, he was nevertheless the last to comply. They introduced the pin as instructed, quickly learning that Sedar's remark that it would sting was a monumental understatement. Laurel and Harry knew several nerves passed through the area, and the ensuing headache made them all glad they were seated. However, the initial sting didn't last long, and Sedar smiled as their discomfort eased, and each, without exception, breathed a sigh.

"That really hurt," Marcel said, rubbing the insertion site of the pin, much of which had quickly burrowed under the skin, leaving only a slight, barely detectable mound.

"It was necessary," Sedar said. "I can speak inside your mind, and you will understand, but the Kalmeddi and the Farisee are not telepathic races, and I am a weak interpreter."

The vocal receptors in the pins were highly acute, and they understood Sedar clearly. They glanced at each other to confirm they all understood.

"It's keener than the Fobel node," Harry said to Laurel, impressed. "It took you a few days for Seera to enmesh itself into your auditory cortex."

"The Fobel node was less aggressive in its incorporation, though," Laurel pointed out. "I don't remember any pain, and its effects were more subtle. I wonder how much we'd retain if we withdrew the pin."

"That would be an interesting study. With a bit of luck, they'll let us take one with us when we leave. There's…"

"Sshh," Laurel put her finger to her lips as a group of individuals approached the mezzanine area from the northern corridor. As Sedar stood, they followed suit. The first two to arrive were Farisee; Laurel recognised them from her vision of the ark shown her by the Diri wraith and by Ilivi when they were on Isilia. They—Laurel made an unchecked assumption they were female as they had rather ample bosoms—were striking in real life, with deep brown skin, wide eyes and generous lips. The hair was braided and expressed in individual styles; on one Farisee, the braid draped over her shoulder; on the other, the braid was looped around her head. They were humanoid, slightly shorter than Laurel, and similar in stature, but their arms and fingers seemed longer and more tapered. The two females wore breastplates and knee-length skirts fashioned from a tanned material. Their lower limbs were dressed in a similar fabric, much tighter and which covered their feet. As they walked, they made a slight slapping noise as their feet contacted the floor, causing a slightly thrusting gait as they stepped forward. Laurel had the thought the armour-like garments were insurance against something other than enemies, for they carried no weapons.

The Farisee stood aside to allow the other two members of the group to enter the mezzanine. The first, an unsmiling Farisee female, taller than her counterparts and more elaborately dressed, the brown skin of her face decorated in exotic dark blue tattoos, stopped to appraise the guests through yellow eyes. Colourful beads sat close to her throat and upper arms, with gold bands at each ankle. She had no hair to speak of, just a soft fuzz at each side of a bald centre section.

The second person, a stooped, besieged-looking human male, wheezing and pale, struggled to keep up. His clothes were old, his hair stuck up in little white tufts, and his face carried a careworn expression, his eyes moist and only half-seeing. But he smiled and reached out to welcome them, especially delighted to see Laurel and Ava. Both women felt something constrained in his greeting; they could have probed to gain some understanding but agreed now was not the time. It was enough that the man's intent was pure, and even though the Farisee seemed less welcoming, more guarded, their intention was also sincere.

"When we saw your ship, we didn't know what to think," the man laughed, not joyously, but somewhere between sadness and relief. "Perhaps," he struggled to take a deep breath, "at last, we will be liberated." He took Laurel's hand and gave it a limp squeeze, then held it as if he were reluctant to let her go, perhaps prevent her from retreating at the burden his words implied. Then he smiled and dipped his head. "I am Jadren, reluctant ruler of the Kalmeddi," he grunted, "for what it's worth. I was a lowly government agent, and they had no-one else." Jadren blinked his rheumy eyes. "Even in times of disaster, people need a figurehead, even one such as I. It does my tired heart good to see you." He didn't let go of Laurel's hand as he turned to his sour-faced colleague. "This is Olyo, Ascendant of the Farisee people."

The group acknowledged Jadren and Olyo, but the Farisee made no acknowledgement, turning her solemn gaze instead to Scarlett, fixed like a limpet to her father. And there, Laurel saw her expression change to one of curiosity. The two Farisee escorts, upon seeing Scarlett, commented quietly to each other on her presence. Sedar had not issued Scarlett with a speech device, so Darlen, unsure how he should handle this scrutiny of his daughter, instructed her to say "hello". Scarlett wasn't keen, but she lifted her hand in a modest wave. The Farisee escorts regarded the salute with amusement. Waving was plainly not common, but the two women each raised their hands, their bemused expressions dissolving into broad smiles. Laurel also noticed a softening in the Ascendant's features, but still, she stopped short of granting her mouth approval to smile. Harry gave silent praise to Laurel's description of the Farisee. He recognised them on sight, fierce-looking, strong, but the apparent leader seemed suspicious, cold to their presence, perhaps even icy.

Ava remembered the Diri wraiths vision of the ark and the Farisee vividly, and she thought about it often over the years. Now, allowing her thoughts to circumvent the border of one escort's mind, she instantly backed off. These were good people, possessed of a spiritual zeal she had never before met in her limited encounters with other species. The Farisee were immersed in a culture of ritual, idols and tradition. It was more intense even than she remembered from her vision experience with the Diri wraith when she stood with her mother and Helen, and it felt strange and new and deeply intimate. And somehow chilling. A place not meant for intruders to pry. Immediately, guilt engulfed her. Had she asked, she knew she would not have been embraced in there. Ava looked across at her mother, who picked up on the swift rush of guilt and guessed what she had done. Ava wondered if Sedar knew, but thankfully, he gave no such signal. Just in case, Ava deliberately and carefully cleared her mind.

Jadren, with some reluctance, finally let go of Laurel's hand and shuffled towards a blanketed couch, sinking down thankfully and wearily. Laurel and Harry both recognised in him the symptoms of impending cardiac failure, and if the occasion arose, they would offer their help, but from his appearance, it was likely there would be little they could do.

The two Farisee escorts remained at the junction of the entrance. Olyo, who still had not spoken a word, preferred to stand. If they required further confirmation that Sedar was of the same race as Baii and Ilivi, they saw it when he knelt, tucking his long, tattered robes under him in a ceremonial sweep, skillfully arranging the folds around his person; the process delivering a pang of remembrance to Ava of the first time she saw Baii and the elegance and serenity he brought to the simple act of kneeling. She pushed away the momentary longing in her heart.

CHAPTER SEVEN _

"I could not reach out to you across distances," Sedar said, "thus the deception. I have never seen a ship such as yours and desired to come close to confirm your origin and purpose. I sensed Hebre—" he looked first to Laurel and Ava, then to Darlen, Scarlett sitting quietly in his lap, "and of Legion." He shook his head. "Never have I seen a Legion female." Sedar smiled at the little girl. "She is fond of these creatures?" Several grey kittens appeared on the floor beside Scarlett, who, whooping with delight and forgetting her caution, slipped from her father's lap to gather up one of the balls of fluff. A Farisee escort came to kneel with Scarlett and scooped up a second kitten. Scarlett's childlike trust returned in the common language of playtime.

"A memory of these creatures is close to the surface of the child's mind," Sedar explained. "They bring her joy, and she is in unfamiliar surroundings."

"Thank you, Sedar," Laurel said. "We are hoping to find some answers as to the origins of what we call whole souls, but what we believe you call, Hebre. We know from contact with survivors of your race on the other side of the Transcender, that the Hebre became outcasts from their world."

Sedar raised his hands, delight and shock on his face transforming his wrinkled features, widening his eyes and lifting his lips into an extraordinarily broad smile, revealing worn down mostly rotten teeth. "Other members of my race? They are safe then?"

"Why, yes," and while it delighted Laurel to be the bearer of such good news, she became mindful of a pervading sense they had entered a time not so far removed from when the Hebre left Eden, but right now, Sedar was far too stunned to answer her questions, so she would elaborate for him on their discovery of the Riynea on Isilia. "They live a peaceful and pleasant existence on a beautiful world," she explained, also noting Jadren's more restrained jubilation at the news. "Many others of your race continued on a longer journey that took many years. I believe they reached my home planet too."

Sedar was so busy sighing his satisfaction and relief at her message, Jadren took over the conversation.

"This brings light to the darkness. Where is your home planet?"

"Earth. It's…" Laurel discovered that explaining widespeed might be more complicated than she imagined, so she settled for something more pre-school. "It's in another universe."

Jadren's old eyes shifted around in their sockets as if giving Laurel's comments some thought. His mind was very open, and his thoughts were available, but they seemed confused to both Ava and Laurel, with various scenarios popping out and replacing the one before. Jadren's mind was a tiring place.

"I have never heard of a planet called Earth," he frowned, "nor of this Transcender of which you speak. Is it a heavenly phenomenon?" He angled his head towards Olyo as if she might have an answer.

But Olyo didn't reply, and Darlen took up the explanation. "It's a portal between our universe and yours."

"Ah!" Jadren slapped a trembling hand to his forehead, understanding. "Sheerguhd. Throughout history, a superstition. A terrifying beast capable of lashing the universe with its poisonous tail, displacing star systems and destroying worlds. A fiction that sprung from the superstitious minds of the ancients. We became too confident. Only the Farisee—" Jadren deferred to his Farisee companion, "had the wisdom to fear its power."

"Did the masters arrive through Sheerguhd?" It felt strange to Laurel to say that word. It had meaning now. For so long, she had believed it was an ancient reference to the nebula. But before Jadren could answer, Olyo suddenly commanded the floor, holding forth in a strong, clear voice.

"The Eye of Sheerguhd opened—" she announced to her astonished audience, her arms raised like a hellfire preacher, her clenched fist shaking at the viewport towards empty space, "…to look upon its servants. And there, in the heavens, it stretched forth its mouth, for all to witness its might and anger." She made a fierce intake of breath, her voice thundering in bitter triumph, validating the truths of her beliefs, absolving her religious passion and proclaiming prophecies of Sheerguhd written by her Farisee forebears and the perils of turning from God. There were no tears, she displayed no grief, but her words were as a lamentation.

Olyo's arms fell to her side, and her voice dropped in intensity, her words contacting her shocked audience in a tone of awestruck fear; she leaned forward, swaying, her eyes gleaming with fervour, a sob of anger catching her voice. "It held us in thrall," she whispered, clenching her teeth and raising her fists in a grasping, clutching movement, "while from its bowels…" Her assertive, angry voice returned and she called out, again pointing towards the viewport, "it spewed forth the serpent, come to lay waste to Eden!"

The group sat in dumbfounded silence. Jadren and Sedar less so, but Olyo's outburst had given Laurel some clues. From the lips of a witness, she heard the definition of that phrase, "out of Sheerguhd". It literally meant that, and it made sense now they knew what Sheerguhd represented, notwithstanding the impressive delivery. The masters came from another universe or perhaps another dimension. Either way, to have been inside the Transcender—inside Sheerguhd—they had to possess interdimensional travel capabilities, presumably owing to the possession of the Magen star. That raised concern for Laurel; they had unwittingly brought back a Magen star within Darlen. She knew the Hebre had taken all the Magen stars with them when they left; if so, then it was possible their return could provide the means for the masters to leave Eden. The prospect made Laurel uneasy. Having the masters reaccess the Transcender didn't sound like an attractive prospect. Jadren leaned forward and caught Olyo's hand to calm her. For a moment more, she gazed towards the viewport, then regained her composure, her large eyes still shining.

"The Farisee have deep convictions," Jadren said, his voice mild and drained, as though even speaking was a burden he would lay down at the first opportunity.

"Olyo's words gave us clarity," Laurel assured him. "On our journey here, we encountered the word 'Sheerguhd'. We didn't know what it meant, but now, it may be what we call a Transcender."

Darlen addressed Olyo. "You say Sheerguhd opened above. Do you mean you could see it with the naked eye from a planet?"

Olyo lifted her chin. "It scattered the stars. We saw only its thunderclouds," she continued calmly without further gesticulating. Even so, there was power in her words. "The wind was mighty and terrible. It destroyed buildings and crops on Eden. The people cried out in fear and trembling as it struck them down."

"Sheerguhd opened above Faris," Jadren explained, "but it was visible from certain parts of every planet. I was on Eden, and it was truly horrifying. Then it was gone. And the heavens were silent once more. The wind to which Olyo refers came after the masters' ship established orbit. An explosion caused earthquakes across the globe, a rare event on Eden, and we recorded massive fires burning in the north. Routine medical tracking of individuals showed them as deceased. Millions of men, women and children perished. We were unable to determine how many, as our sensors stopped functioning soon after."

"And the masters?"

Sedar, reclaimed from his joy at learning his people survived, and sobered by Olyo's discourse and the ensuing conversation, drew their attention. He cupped his hand, and a diorama, similar to that which Ilivi presented on Isilia, climbed into the air between them and dispersed into an exact representation of the events that took place. Having looked into the yawning gateway of a Transcender, Laurel understood seeing Sheerguhd would have been terrifying to the uninitiated and to those who regarded it as a myth. At least she and the others had the benefit of Darlen's education.

As they observed the churning, terrifying storm in space, they were attracted to a movement from the curlew—the centremost eye—a silver light emerging into the surrounding space. The light increased until a distinctive shape loomed. A ship, ovoid but with a flattened brow forward and aft, advanced slowly from the void. A long tail, made up of a ragtag assortment of smaller ships, followed in its wake, snaking a path towards Eden, uncaring of the panic it had created on Faris. Sheerguhd, its work done, closed behind its deadly cargo, instantly restoring normal space.

"I would say, looking at that, Sheerguhd can open out into any part of the universe," Darlen said as Sedar's diorama hovered, waiting. "When we arrived, it opened into the nebula."

"Unless it's unstable or random," Harry suggested.

Darlen shook his head. "The one that leads from League space has been the same for millennia, Harry. League space to Earth's system. Earth to League space. But that doesn't mean it's not subject to cosmic laws."

"We can't add to your knowledge, friends," Jadren

said. "This is the first documented record of a sighting of Sheerguhd. The second sighting was when Sedar witnessed it opening at the Miran Forin nebula the day you—" he stopped himself to collect his thoughts, reminded of an earlier conversation with Sedar, just prior to him bringing the strangers on board the station, "—when Hebre escaped."

Harry leaned forward. "Wait…did you say, 'Miran Forin'?"

Jadren looked at each visitor. Why was the name of the Miran Forin so significant?

"In our universe," Harry said, stunned that two separate universes would give the nebula identical titles, "we call the nebula by that name. It means demonic, hostile."

Jadren smiled and shook his head. "The Miran Forin nebula is anything but hostile. The Miran Forin gave us Hebre." He smiled again at Ava and Laurel. "It sent us the deliverers."

There, that tantalising word. Deliverer. We are the deliverance. Laurel pondered on its significance. But does that mean they meant the Hebre to deliver them? Save them? If so, from what? The masters? Plainly that hadn't happened, or so it seemed, so what did it all mean? Laurel knew she was in danger of besieging her hosts with demands for information, so she took a breath, and a leaf from Harry's book, who apart from his outburst about the nebula, was allowing his understanding to increase at a more sedentary pace, extracting data as he went.

"We emerged from Sheerguhd at the nebula," Harry said to Sedar. "Did you think we were masters? Is that why the elaborate manifestation? As a deterrent?"

Sedar swept aside the diorama. "Would it have worked?" he grinned.

"If we didn't have whole souls on board, yes."

"Whole souls?"

"It's what they call the Hebre in Harry's universe," Laurel explained. "On my world, there is a race called the Hebrew. I discovered evidence of their language in archives on Harry's world. I have been a student of languages in the past, and I recognised the symbols. There are records to show the Hebre settled on a remote planet which later became part of the League, but the masters followed them, causing them to flee into the Transcender—Sheerguhd, the one in League space. This knowledge led us here. We also recognise that if we—" Laurel gestured to Ava, "are Hebre, we may not be fully human, but that the masters somehow gave us human form."

Sedar closed his eyes. "The masters brought only death and destruction. Not just to us, but Hebre also." He allowed Laurel to sense the rush of emotion in his heart, and when he opened his eyes again, he smiled. "The masters did not clothe you in flesh. That you took a mortal body was by your own generosity and sacrifice."

Laurel's thoughts swirled. She felt the confusion of the others; this wasn't an explanation. "How did we make ourselves mortal?" she said, raising her hands in a gesture of puzzlement as another thought struck her. "Does it have something to do with the nebula?"

Sedar had no doubt these two women were Hebre, but where they came from was a mystery, and in a ship with no known configuration. Were these Hebre the leaders who left fifteen years ago, pledging to return, to deliver the people from the masters? Could they be descendants perhaps, from a time far distant? It would be difficult for him to enter their minds to probe. The Hebre turned the hearts of the Magen Bearers and Legion, striking a decisive blow to the evil masters by stripping them of many of their most prized warriors. But it was merely part of the deliverance; the masters continued to reaffirm their evil domination and slaughter. The liberators the Hebre promised would return, appeared to have no remembrance of their vow.

"The child has the air of Legion," Sedar said suddenly to Darlen, turning his attention to Scarlett, leaving Laurel's question about the nebula hanging between them. "Yet…I sense you bear the Magen, do you not? And you are for us?"

Darlen didn't understand the question and responded on instinct. "I've always rather been for myself."

Sedar had shaped his question as a test to determine if the Magen Bearer also had no recollection. Darlen wasn't ready to trust the man yet, despite Laurel's measured suggestion to co-operate. He liked and respected the other Riyneans he met on Isilia, but his time with the Chaese working on the ship brought him into contact with many ordinary Riyneans, and he learned they were skilled at prevaricating when they thought it would serve them. No doubt, the telepaths among the Riyneans were every bit as accomplished.

Sedar nodded serenely. "Ah, I see, until you had people to cherish and safeguard." Sedar turned back to Laurel without waiting for a response. "And the communications mechanism," he said, "An extraordinary and unsophisticated means of contact?"

"It had several functions," she replied, wondering why he'd deflected her question before. Empathically, she felt he had only delayed responding and decided he required a moment to consider an answer, or maybe there *was* no answer, so she went with the flow. There was no way he could have fully understood the keyboard, so she answered him honestly. "In this case, I sensed the greeting that was called for and transmitted it using that physical medium. I applied the same technique before when I was still gaining mastery over my empathic and telepathic abilities. Shalom is a greeting used by the Hebrew race on my world. I wondered if the Hebre are ancestors of the Hebrew people."

"This expression, Shalom, is not native to Hebre," Sedar said. "This greeting belongs to the Edensai."

"Edensai?"

"The native civilisation of Eden. The Hebre have no language of origin—" Sedar looked to his associates and lifted his shoulder slightly, "of which we are aware. When they arrived, Hebre embraced the Edensai way of life, their culture and their language."

"We've never heard of Edensai," Laurel said. "We thought the Hebre might have originated from the nebula, and the masters were their oppressors, clothing them in flesh and condemning them to a life of fear and subjugation on Eden." She gestured weakly. "I will admit, much of our information comes from fragments of cloth, archives and conjecture. The only substantive knowledge we gained was from the descendants of the Riynea who escaped, and it would seem their information is not totally accurate either."

"From our perspective," Olyo said, still undecided about these women. She knew Hebre, and these women neither spoke nor acted as such, "that would be remarkable indeed that you would have offspring. The arks entered Sheerguhd only fifteen years since. We—" she took in both Laurel and Ava with her cool glance, "were close allies, yet you know us not." She then considered their faces. "And it appears age did not settle upon your brows."

Laurel guessed that meant they didn't look any older than the women who'd left years before, giving weight to the theory they had somehow traversed time. Olyo had likewise concluded that Laurel and Ava were not the Hebre women she expected to return, although Sedar seemed to perceive and understand more. She sighed inwardly. She was not intuitive, her expectations had not been met, and she felt discouraged. Judith, who now called herself Laurel, had been a friend but were they one and the same? Sedar had urged her to not expect too much from the newcomers, but it was painful. Olyo still felt the loss of Judith's companionship.

"I'm sorry," Laurel said, gaining a sense of Olyo's feelings. "I feel we have disappointed you. When we were inside the nebula, we discovered that while we linearly measured time—mainly because we knew no better and relied on our instrumentation—it seems time had its own agenda. We didn't influence it or change its course, that we know of anyway. And we have no memory of ever having been here before."

"The Riynea, from your time. Do they still have their powers?" Sedar asked.

"Yes, some can manifest objects," Laurel said. "Those with this ability are regarded as a ruling class nominally on the planet. But we don't know if they're from our present or our past."

"I never quite got the point of this power," Darlen said, shaking his head. "It seemed…superficial…if I can describe it that way. They manifested a few practical objects and a few playthings—" he pointed to the reasonably accurate replicas of the kittens, "but nothing that had any enduring practical benefit. The people we met were good, decent people but their manifestations to me were little more than parlour tricks." He grinned at Sedar. "Although I will admit your warship was pretty sensational."

"I'm glad it impressed," Sedar grinned right back, allowing himself a measure of pride in that manifestation. "I can tell from your thoughts the meaning of this 'parlour trick'. The power of manifestation is far more than this; it is a discipline of the mind. There is a fundamental difference between our species, my friend. We are both human, but Riynean brains allow psionic abilities. We channel this for serenity, to direct our thoughts. The manifestation of objects is purely a side effect, although I grant one we do use. We can also levitate and shelter ourselves from rainstorms," he added with a chuckle.

Darlen remained underwhelmed. At one time, before Helen, before the others shared a ship with him, a good rainstorm was an ideal way of getting showered and cleaning your clothes all at once.

"Are you able to tell us the history of the Hebre? How we..." Laurel smiled at Ava, "...fit into all this?"

Sedar hesitated. Perhaps the account would be better coming from the Edensai remnant on the planet, or even the converted Legion who'd turned from their evil traditions and now lived and suffered along with the Edensai. But he knew as much of the Hebre history as anyone, and the woman was impatient. He didn't need to be a telepath to understand body language. Her amber eyes were anxious, her upper body leaning forward in anticipation. He looked around. They were all impatient, and he was here, now; perhaps for his sins, this was meant to fall to him.

CHAPTER EIGHT _

"The story of the Hebre and the masters have become part of the oral history of the Edensai," Sedar began. "I know many of the stories, heard of the traditions spoken in the Places of Peace by the Trah, the Holy Word Keepers. Since the advent of the masters and the destruction of the once magnificent Places of Peace, the Edensai have rebuilt the ruins into houses of sanctuary, insignificant enough to be disguised from the Legion destroyers."

"Perhaps at least some of this saga has endured to your Earth?" Jadren said to Laurel, he also knew the stories, but Sedar had walked among the Edensai for decades and knew their traditions well "—or perhaps even to this League of which you speak?"

"I'm just matching up Hebrew and Hebre in my head because of the language and similarity in name," Laurel told him. "Hebrew text on Earth doesn't speak of an invasion by aliens but does speak of persecution and slavery."

Sedar thought of Judith, the Hebre woman with amber eyes who left with the arks. He saw those same eyes in this woman, a destiny yet to be completed, a promise made but still to be kept. Perhaps in the telling of the history, a memory might be stirred.

Sedar manifested a diorama of the star system. "For centuries, our four planets lived together in a spirit of co-operation. We traded, shared knowledge, and existed in complete accord. We knew only peace; we had social conventions, our own customs and our own belief systems, but we were tolerant of one another's differences. There was never conflict."

Sedar then began his extraordinary and chilling narrative of the discovery of an injured, pregnant woman, taken pity on by a farming couple on Eden. She claimed no memory of her past, and when her child was delivered, she disappeared, leaving the infant in the care of the farmers. The child, a boy, seemed normal apart from his eyes, which were without colour.

Within a year, the farmer's two other, previously healthy sons had perished, leaving the clear-eyed child as the lone child. This situation was echoed on several occasions in remote areas on the planet and not initially declared to authorities, only coming to light when other parents lost children. It was then records documenting the clear-eyed child phenomenon were established. In ten years, thousands of these children were born, both male and female. It was a mystery; the so-called clear-eyed children developed as normal boys and girls, but in all cases, the parents either never produced other sons and any they had died. Post-mortem examinations gave no answers.

"Was there any kind of genetic mutation noted? DNA or RNA sequencing anomalies?" Harry asked.

"There were a few inconsistencies," Sedar conceded. "Detailed physical examinations of the children from infancy revealed those differences. I am not a physician and will not presume to advise you further on this point, but apart from their eyes, those distinctions were not noticeable to the ordinary person. A transformation took place at around the age of twelve…"

Sedar then returned to the narrative, revealing that the children became rebellious, first in their homes, then in their education and the community. Other children were injured, beaten and terrified within their communities and the clear-eyed children often gathered to spread fear and mayhem throughout the municipalities and cities. Danger from the children lurked everywhere, around every corner, and the people called upon the authorities to stem the carnage.

"And did they?" Laurel asked. It sounded like Earth. Nothing could be accomplished there either to totally control youth gangs and crime.

"What could they do?" Sedar said helplessly. "These were children, but they aimed to make mischief and create havoc. Their behaviour earned them the title of 'imp'. By the time each imp reached the age of fourteen, they had abandoned their homes, lived wild and roamed in gangs. Parents of younger imps came to dread when their clear-eyed child reached the age of chaos."

"Perhaps you could have initiated a cull," Darlen said, thinking how such culls were often used for wild, out-of-control animals on many worlds in the League and Independent systems. He would classify out-of-control kids as the same thing. "Sounds like you needed a few weapons well before the masters arrived."

"Weapons?" Sedar was taken aback. "To destroy

children? We did not know of weapons until the masters came. The Edensai could not destroy a child. They could not take a life. In desperation, they reached out to the government to help but not once did they consider harming the imps." He looked about him, to the quietly wheezing Jadren, to the stoic Olyo. "Why would they?"

"To save themselves?" Darlen offered, quite reasonably, he thought.

"To inflict suffering or harm to another living being is an affront to the gods of Eden." Sedar looked at Olyo. "To all gods. On Riynea, even though we do not bow to any deity, our conscience forbids us to do harm."

Laurel felt she knew too little to question cultural differences at this stage, but Harry was less sensitive.

"What about disciplining these 'imps'?" he asked, but Sedar's understanding of that word didn't mean punitive measures. His frown showed he thought Harry meant something else. "I mean," Harry tried to make his meaning clear, "did anyone lock them up to stop their behaviour. Inflict some pain?"

Sedar understood then, but to the Edensai, going to such extremes would have been altogether alien. "Again," he emphasised, "Eden is—was, a place of harmony. They have never restrained their citizens."

"But as a means of preservation?" Harry pressed, although he knew this was all history now.

"The Edensai came to the belief their God sent the imps as a trial," Olyo cut in before Sedar could answer. "If he would not defend his people, then it was his will."

"I have never seen a planet that doesn't suffer some

kind of lawlessness, regardless of faith and spiritual beliefs," Darlen said. "I've been to a lot of worlds; humans everywhere need to have their behaviour directed in some form or other, rules, limits on freedoms, conventions to live by, that type of thing." He was getting a strong feeling this was a pacifist society. Little wonder the masters were still here having a party.

"The Edensai do have conventions to live by," Sedar said, "taught to them by their Holy Trah, the keeper of the word of God. My people adopted some of those standards. They made for a peaceful society. We—" he spread his hands and looked down. "We were content."

"Did they ever find the woman who gave birth to the first clear-eyed child?" Ava asked.

"Those imps are the offspring of Lilith," Olyo cut in again, her voice rising in excitement. "She is the mother of the masters. She walked on Eden in preparedness for their arrival. She left her spawn in readiness to receive their brothers."

"Lilith? The goddess of death?" The reference stunned Laurel, and Olyo regarded her in confusion. Judith would know the story of Lilith.

"Who's Lilith?" Harry whispered.

"She's a myth from Hebrew culture," Laurel whispered back. "I'll explain later."

"Let me show you some visuals. It might help you understand the advent of the Hebre," Jadren said as he shuffled over to a desk with a white vase-like object positioned centrally. As he approached, a night-time view of the heavens appeared from the perspective of someone standing on a planet. This was a physical file rather than the diorama manifestations Sedar used to supplement his story.

"Here," Jadren began, "we're looking towards the West, the direction of the Miran Forin nebula. The sky has all the celestial bodies relative to the planet's rotation. See the next night? This…" Jadren pointed to a flowing cloud, dense enough to obscure the stars. Laurel held her breath. The cords and tendrils of the nebula, so familiar to her, so reassuring. Without even noticing, she smiled.

"This took place around eight years before the masters arrived," Jadren said, "about twenty-five years after the first imp was born. At first, our scientists assumed it was some type of plasma stream but couldn't identify its origin. When it was first detected, this was the position of the sun." Jadren enlarged the images to provide relative position.

"It couldn't have been anything from the sun," Harry said, "but it looks like the nebula residue."

Jadren nodded. "We've flown close to the nebula, but we've never seen colours such as these. As you can see, many are indescribable…" He lay his hand to his forehead. "My mind cannot comprehend them, others…" he looked at Ava and Laurel, "the colour of your eyes."

Laurel thought of Eli, who had brown eyes like many humans. Helen's eyes were blue, sapphire blue, yes, but not unique, yet looking at the colours wafting as a wave through space, the brown and the blue were as she saw them in the nebula, vivid, beautiful, familiar.

"The wave of colours drifted into the view of the naked eye," Jadren continued, the exertion of speaking causing him to take a moment to find a suitable perch near the table for fear his frailty would see him on the floor. He waved away Olyo's offer of help.

"At night, the western sky turned into a spectacular aurora of colours. We took ships up to investigate, but there was little to see or measure. It was as simple as flying through a rainbow."

"But it had significance?" Laurel and Ava already discerned what this visitation meant, but Harry, Darlen and Marcel would need to hear it.

"Deep significance," Jadren said, a thin smile on his blue lips as he clenched his fist to add emphasis. "The lights blazed in the heavens for many days. Ah, they were spectacular!" he grinned, his tired eyes twinkling. "One night, we looked, and it seemed they had left us. We examined our sensors, regional scanners, even obsolete telescopes, but there was no sign. And that night, there was no imp activity reported on Eden anywhere. The next morning, each imp returned to its home, even the older ones, or submitted itself to the authorities."

"And it was no longer clear-eyed?"

Jadren nodded, confirming the accuracy of Laurel's statement. "Each imp's eyes had taken on one of the colours in the aurora. In most cases, they seemed like natural eye colours—" He glanced at Ava, "except for one, a girl not yet at the age of chaos, her eyes were vivid, extraordinary, like yours."

Sedar took up the story, allowing Jadren to rest. "The imps worked hard to correct the destruction of their communities," he said, returning to the diorama, "to repair their societies and families as a whole. And months later,

Edensai parents of an imp child once again started to give birth to normal, healthy children."

Marcel was sceptical. That all sounded very neat and tidy, even for a passive race such as the Edensai. "They were very trusting to receive the clear-eyed children back into their families," he said. "Were they so certain the children would not return to their evil ways?"

"The Edensai have large hearts. They forgave," Sedar said simply. "The parents welcomed their prodigal children with joy, and the imps proved themselves worthy of the Edensai's trust. After the change, the imps took on great physical stamina and speed, and became possessed of telepathic skills; as such, they developed a close relationship with Riynea. Some had capabilities that were far beyond anything witnessed by any human on our worlds."

"How did they earn the name Hebre?" Laurel asked.

"It is what they call themselves," Sedar said. "In Edensai, Hebre means 'to pass over' or 'flow', because Hebre crossed space to save Eden from the imps."

Harry shook his head. "I'm sorry, you all seem to be accepting that these lights in the sky somehow possessed the bodies of these teenage criminals and altered their mentality." He turned to Laurel, his voice loaded with scepticism. "Laurel, c'mon, you're a physician. This kind of metamorphosis is not possible, not to mention this implies you and Ava come from these imps. I know for sure you are as human as I am."

Of course, Harry would challenge, but Laurel knew right to her very core what Sedar and Jadren said was true, but Harry was likewise correct; she just had to join the two halves of the truth. And it should disturb her to learn she had been part of a demonic race that wrought devastation on honest people. It was incredible, flying in the face of all she believed to be good and right, but as Sedar waited, the trauma that went with such a revelation didn't materialise, not for her, nor for Ava, who also knew there was far more to this truth than Sedar had described.

"I don't know, Harry," Laurel answered. "If these imps were human, the only visible anomaly was the lack of eye colour. It could have been any number of conditions. Sedar, you spoke of a few other characteristics?"

Sedar opened his hands in apology. "I'm sorry, I do not trust my recounting of this knowledge to be solid. We have a physician who is visiting a community on Eden. He arrives back here at sunrise and is far more proficient with the imps' physiology than I."

"Okay, we can wait for that," Darlen said. "So, they lacked conscience until they had a change in eye colour? Am I right?" He waited for Sedar, Jadren and Olyo's agreement. "You are convinced these colours in the heavens somehow distilled themselves into these imps?"

"Hebre confirmed the truth of our belief," Jadren said.

Laurel found the explanation moved the pieces of information into a better position than she had before. "That must be what was meant by us being clothed in flesh. We are human, but with an element of the nebula that imbues whole souls with these extra powers. Ava and I have seen this essence in each other."

That part at least made sense, but if the essence of the powers came from the nebula and possessed the imps, how did it possess their posterity? This was a question Laurel would need explained but doubted she would receive it in this company. It was clear to her now they had somehow ended up in the past. The masters still held Eden in its 'thrall' as Olyo so eloquently put it. Laurel's excitement at learning this much was overridden with dismay that the conflict was not yet over.

"And how long did you say it was between the two events?" she asked. "Between the changing of the Hebre and appearance of the masters?"

"Eight years," Jadren said. "In that time, peace reigned on Eden."

"Do your people believe the masters knew of the existence of these imps and planned to use them to conquer Eden?" Laurel asked Olyo, who dipped her head.

"They seemed to know of at least one."

"Wouldn't that have outraged the masters to see these imps changed?" Marcel said, "No longer causing terror?"

"The masters' came to unleash their rage on the humans," Olyo replied. "The discovery of the imps turn from evil would not draw them from their intention. And they do not wish to conquer; only destroy."

"So, after these children changed," Laurel continued, "after the masters arrived, there was a mass conversion of these Legion soldiers; these servants of the masters?"

"That is correct," Sedar said. "A Hebre woman captured a Magen Bearer and two of his Legion soldiers. They have cloaking technology on some of their ships, but Hebre sees all. The woman overcame the three men and returned them to her community. They never left. They wept and thanked her for rescuing them, telling her they were weary from the demands of the masters and the bloodletting that had been their way for centuries. They embraced the sanctuary and stillness of the Edensai spirit, and even though now they suffer hardship alongside their chosen people, they do not falter."

"When did all this mass conversion take place?" Laurel asked.

"The first of the proselytes joined the Edensai only three years after the masters arrived."

"And others followed?"

"Many thousands with their hearts changed, and all but a single Magen Bearer took shelter with the Edensai mountain folk, condemning themselves to a life concealed in the labyrinths of Eden, where the masters would never find them. The masters heaped great trials upon the heads of the Edensai, but they did not give up the Magen Bearers. Soon, as is the way, both Magen and Legion took Hebre and Edensai women to wife. A few older Hebre, male and female and the humans had already united in marriage."

"Interesting," Harry said. "Did they reproduce?"

"Children were born, yes," Sedar answered. "A few of the Magen Bearer/Hebre unions produced an infant with Magen Bearer qualities, but in most cases, they produced a normal, human child. Hebre/human unions would, infrequently, produce a Hebre child. But never did the very few purely Hebre unions bring forth children. Not once. We maintain it to be impossible."

Laurel knew that it was not impossible. Ava sat there, absorbing every word, living proof.

"How many Hebre are left on the planet?"

"Not one." Jadren shook his head. "They all left. Their task was to stop the imps."

"Who gave them that task?"

"It would have been the God of Eden," Olyo said with authority. "He saw the destruction on Eden and sent Hebre to save its people."

Ava lifted her hand. "But didn't the Edensai think their god had sent the imps in the first place? And ultimately, the Hebre didn't save them; they left."

Olyo's conviction and fervour gave way to a passion that showed in her voice. "Lilith spreads her seed through Sheerguhd. Hebre follow. If she has spawned imps in other kingdoms, they will turn them to righteousness. Even without the masters, the imps can disrupt and lead to decay in society."

Marcel had listened attentively to the revelations. It was painful for him to imagine his gentle father and grandmother, and even his dear lady sister and Laurel had ancestors who had been a menace to society. "If the masters are on a quest to wipe out humanity," he said to Olyo, "why does this matter to you as a non-human?"

"It is an affront to all that lives," Olyo said. "The Farisee gods teach that all life is precious. We must preserve life. The gods so ordain."

"Even if that life is out to destroy your own life?"

Olyo gave Marcel an impatient sideways glance as if he were a fool to ask. That was what she meant.

He ignored the disdain. "Are the masters' lives more precious than the Edensai? Surely, one must weigh up one against the other. Humanity against a marauder?" Marcel looked to Laurel, then to Ava, and lifted his chin in defiance. "I would not hesitate to destroy the marauder to preserve the lives of the righteous."

Laurel had encountered religious zeal on Earth, and she knew that once a person was under its influence, it was a difficult thing to go against, even to the point of sacrificing one's life to its laws. She would explain to Marcel later that throughout history, many have died defending their beliefs. To him, it was a classic case of kill or be killed, but when a culture steeped in tradition, worship and obedience to faith depart from that path, the consequences can be far-reaching. She fired a silent thought at him. *"We cannot challenge an ancient mindset just because it doesn't make sense to us. We're the newcomers here, remember?"* He made no response that he heard her.

"Sedar," Laurel said, shifting the conversation away from Olyo, who was not fond of any challenge to her faith. To her, killing was killing. "The Riynea showed us a record of a Hebre woman using teleportation to bring your people to the surface of a planet called Isilia. The Hebre…I don't know how to describe it…reset time to preserve the planet."

"Reset time?" Sedar frowned and tapped his finger against his lips. "Hmm. To preserve history?"

"I don't know the specifics. It had the effect of restoring much of the planet and saving the civilisation."

"Hebre protected the Edensai, and us when we cried out for help," Sedar said. "There are some who say Hebre has an extraordinary affinity with Time, one far beyond our understanding. Magen Bearer…Darlen," Sedar's expression suddenly lifted, a look of hope lighting his old features. "Look out to the world below, tell me, is time stable?"

Darlen barely flicked a glance before answering. "There are no separate timeslips if that's what you mean. I can't distinguish even a single portal. If they really are like this woman on Isilia, Laurel and Ava would have no capacity to turn back time to prevent the masters from arriving. If that were the case, I would have thought the original Hebre would have done it."

Sedar's flash of hopefulness ended, and his shoulders sagged slightly. "Your report of the Hebre woman presented cause to hope. Hebre has a strange power, and to see you again, I thought…" His voice faltered and he looked up at Laurel and Ava with sad eyes before falling to silence.

"How can it be that you have no memory of us?" Olyo's curiosity got the better of her, but her demeanour was softened, and Laurel felt the earlier ripple of estrangement and suspicion falling away.

"As I said," Laurel shook her head, "we have no memory of ever being here before. I am from Earth, and Ava was born on a planet called Mentelci. The Riyneans we met before had very little history to offer; it mainly dealt with their time on Isilia and gave few details of what went before their arrival. They seemed certain of the teleporting incident."

"The ancestors may have been protecting their heritage," Sedar said, "perhaps to not commemorate the loss and carnage. We have never encountered a people who wish us harm. It would be a painful legacy."

Although she ached to know more about the Hebre,

the decimation of the planet below and the general sadness suggested the war still raged, and that was where Laurel knew she must direct her questions. They were all part of the answers she sought anyway, even though it had not been in her plans to walk into yet another conflict. In her heart, she knew that was why she was here. She nodded towards the planet.

"Can you tell us about the masters? About that ship?"

Once again, Sedar brought up the diorama story of the Transcender, continuing from where he left off earlier. The serpent-like ship headed towards Eden as the evening sun's burnished orange light turned the world into a splendid, shining jewel in the heavens. Finally, the masters' ship reached the planet's north pole, gradually forming a circle with its evil head coming to rest, face turned towards Eden. With its tail draped protectively over its neck, it looked like a coiled snake watching its prey.

"The chariot that bears the instruments of annihilation," Olyo whispered.

Laurel turned her attention to the viewport at the ravaged planet below. "And that is Eden?"

"It *was* Eden," Sedar said. "See, the southern continent is all that is left now of the most glorious world in the heavens."

It was hard for Laurel and the others to reconcile the splendid vision they saw in Sedar's diorama with the desolation of the atmosphere evident before their eyes. Laurel stood and walked to the viewport; there was a peculiar pull to the world, a desire to see it for herself. Ava felt it too and came to stand beside her mother.

"They're killing it, Ava," Laurel said, her heart filled with sadness. "The masters are killing that world."

Sedar watched them. He sensed their desire to go to Eden. It gave him hope they would remember their purpose, the promise of Hebre.

"Death creeps upon the surface," Olyo said as she joined them at the viewport and planted a dusky-skinned hand on Laurel's shoulder. She smelt of musk and spices, and it kindled a memory in Laurel of pain and loss directed at her, but Olyo's gaze continued towards the planet. "Vegetation, forests, plants, crops, even the water is tainted," she said. "The masters do not allow warmth, even from the sun. Already, many have starved to death and countless others, societies, provinces, massacred at the hands of Legion."

Laurel turned. She hadn't thought of it before, but Jadren and Sedar would also be suffering from lack of food, and they both looked as if they could use a good meal. The Farisee women seemed to have fared better, but then, Laurel had no idea of their metabolic or dietary needs.

"Have the masters visited your world, Sedar? Or yours, Jadren?" Laurel asked.

Both men nodded. "They set up a command post in every region," Jadren said. "Every person who came under the mantle of scientist, including physicians and engineers, was ordered to register with Legion. To ensure their co-operation, they took one of their children or a close relative as a hostage. They all complied."

"What happened to the scientists? The hostages?"

"Dead. "He waved a hand, almost dismissively, but his

eyes showed deep pain. "Slaughtered by Legion. And on the planet, all power hubs, access to technology, power, heating, artificial light was denied, and Legion systematically destroyed the sources. It would be an impossible task to rebuild. And our wives and daughters—" he put his hand to his heart, "those of childbearing age, they took them. We never saw them again. My own family—gone." Jadren's voice faltered, the pain still so raw. Fifteen years they said, since the Hebre left here, this could have taken place years before that. How would you ever recover from such a tragedy?

"And the same on Riynea?"

"Yes," Sedar nodded. "Jadren and I were both on Eden when it happened. I was a government researcher, invited to study the Serpent Ship phenomenon—we adopted the name given by the Farisee—and the destroying cloud above the northern continent. There was to be a conference, and the Edensai government called us to attend. The serpent was in a stationary orbit then, and there appeared to be no activity. A day after we arrived on Eden, we saw movement in the heavens, and many of the smaller ships that made up the serpent's body spread out, some to Kalmed and some to Riynea. We were not allowed to return home." Sedar hung his head for a moment, the weight of the awful outcome of that day still fresh in his memory.

Marcel was incredulous. "I cannot accept you just stood by and let them do this to you."

Sedar opened his hands in supplication, willing the young man to understand. "What can I say. We are peaceful. We did not know war. We did not know cruelty. How could we fight back?"

"Instinct surely," Marcel exploded, "in the protection of those you love. Of your homes. Your heritage. Do you not have a desire to preserve your lives?"

"A few of us got through the Legion blockade and returned to Riynea," Sedar said as he tried to defend his people but unwilling to speak of what awaited him back on his home planet. "They didn't force us to register, instead…"

Jadren placed his hand gently on Sedar's shoulder. "It is not necessary to recount this, old friend." He gave Marcel a patient but cautioning stare. "Not now."

Sedar shook his head as if trying to dispel a horrifying thought, but he took Jadren's advice and didn't continue.

"These four planets are all we know," Jadren said. "What lies beyond interested our forefathers for a moment but now, we have lived together in such harmony…perhaps we were unwise, as it seems it blinded us to evil."

"But the Hebre had powers," Laurel reminded him. "Couldn't they have taken on the masters?"

"Hebre lived as the Edensai," he told her. "We believed it was not in their nature to kill, at least until the early news of the devastation on Kalmed and Riynea filtered through to Edensai. After that, all Hebre gathered together."

"How many?"

"In total, one hundred and forty-four thousand," Jadren said, "not including the children born to them, who were too young to fight. The Edensai trembled at the fury of the Hebre but allowed that their creator gave each person the will to follow that which was in their heart. The Holy Trahs warned Hebre that to kill was against their laws, but many of us believed a different authority governed Hebre."

Those words reminded Harry of Laurel's proficiency as a fighter during the war with Gartrya, her bravery, her strength. Hebre angry? He could believe it, even while being compassionate. He'd seen Laurel become a killing machine when she saw good people exploited. But he couldn't understand why the Hebre didn't do something when the detonation occurred. Laurel watched him, and she wondered the same thing.

"At last, someone showed a bit of common sense," Marcel snorted. "Hebre defended the Edensai and all the other people left on the planet?"

"Those banished from Riynea and Kalmed became exiles," Sedar said. "I said before that we all respected, and to a significant part, embraced many Edensai laws in our own governments. Hebre inhabited imps born of Edensai women but were not Edensai, nor were they Kalmeddi, nor Riynean, and when the masters attacked us, Hebre laid aside the ways of the Edensai. They fought the masters and afterwards filled the arks with as many people as possible. Then they left Eden. We do not know why they did not attack the masters when they first arrived and released the winter cloud."

"Did the Hebre read the minds of Legion? Or of the masters?" Ava asked.

"Neither Hebre nor Riynean can see the minds of the masters," Sedar told them. "Legions thoughts are not hidden, but they are as automatons; their actions guided by the singular evil thoughts of the masters."

"What about the Farisee?" Harry asked. "Were your people taken?"

"We are not human," Olyo said. "The masters' journey is to destroy human life. They say they will cleanse the scourge of human life from the face of creation."

"We know there is more than one universe," Harry said. "It's futile to try to measure the scale of human life within a single galaxy, let alone the almost eternal nature of a universe. My people are advanced in interstellar travel, but we have only explored the tiniest fraction. These masters have set themselves an impossible task, surely?"

"They appear to have little concern in how long it takes," Jadren said. "We know they have already attained it in what they call the first kingdom. We are the second. Sheerguhd provides them with a portal to travel wherever they wish to go."

"And you continue to help the humans?" Laurel asked Olyo.

"We are traders and merchants. We built the arks," Olyo said. "Many Farisee were on Eden when Sedar and Jadren attended the forum. The masters have never blockaded our ships nor visited us on this station. They do not regard us as worthy of their interest."

"That's good news for you," Harry said, "and good news for the Hebre. Without you, without your ships, without the arks, it seems they would have never left Eden."

Olyo turned to face Harry. "You are simplistic in your appraisal, human," she said, an edge to her voice. "The preservation of life, all life, is at the foundation of the

Farisee. We could not let them perish. To do so would have caused a scourge to come upon my people. Our gods would not have tolerated such a sin, so we did that which was in our power to accomplish. But we had no power against the cloud."

"I meant no disrespect," Harry said. "I would like to know how, apart from converting Legion to a life of peace, how Hebre went about fighting the masters and the remaining Legion?" Laurel was a hell of a warrior, and Harry remembered Marcel and Ava's father willingly laid down his life to end a war. "From my knowledge, Hebre would gladly sacrifice themselves to save another."

Olyo bowed to Sedar to allow him to proceed with the history lesson. She struggled with understanding how these women had forgotten them, their sacrifices, and the revelation they had somehow travelled through time. She simply had to trust all would be revealed as the gods willed. But Sedar shook his head.

"We have been speaking for many hours without offering refreshment," he said, "and I fear we have exhausted the child." He smiled at Scarlett, now fast asleep in the Farisee escort's arms. "We have little to offer, but we would be glad to share what we have."

Marcel stood. "We have enough on our ship, Sedar," he said, glancing at his crewmates, even though he already knew their answer. "We would be honoured if you would join us."

Sedar hesitated. He felt a sense of embarrassment at the meagreness of anything they could share; were it not for the Farisee, the refugees on the station and on Eden would have starved. He bowed. "We gratefully accept your offer."

Olyo declined, but for the first time, a smile highlighted her striking features. "The Farisee do not partake of human food, and I will take my leave." Without another word, her escort passed the sleeping Scarlett to Darlen before sweeping out in procession behind the Farisee Ascendant.

CHAPTER NINE _

Later, after Jadren and Sedar retired to their quarters on the space station, and after having picked up more understanding of the history of this star system, its co-operatives, its governments and its impressive lack of crime and violence prior to the imps, the crew of the Canaa sat in the common lounge, their brains sparking off with too much new material to allow sleep.

"If there's twenty-five years between the first of the imps and the arrival of the Hebre—" Laurel was doing the math, "then another eight before the masters turned up, I wonder how long it took the Hebre to get the people together on the arks and leave. And how did they decide who they should take?"

"It sounds like the Hebre somehow took on the masters," Harry said. "I note Sedar sidestepped details. Besides that, Lilith sounds to me like a massive spaceborne virus."

Laurel was inclined to agree. She pulled up a few snippets of history from her memory. "Lilith is mentioned in Hebrew mythology. She stands for the emotional and spiritual aspects of the darkness. Terror, sensuality in its darkest form, unchecked freedom. She sounds like the imps.

To the devout, I can see how she might represent some manner of supernatural event. Have you ever heard of any children being born with clear eyes, Harry?"

"Actually…" Harry searched his memory for a text he'd once read. "There was a physician who researched and collected ancient reports of macabre birth abnormalities. It took him about eighty years to assemble a single volume, but the records were so old they couldn't be substantiated. Still, it made impressive reading. I can't remember exactly, but some women on…some planet or other gave birth to children with clear eyes, all stillbirths. It could have happened in other systems as well and just not been documented."

"How long ago?"

Harry blew out his breath. "Wow, I don't know, hundreds of generations maybe. I wouldn't mind checking out the medical records of one of the original clear-eyed children born here. Either way, I can't explain the connection between the lights and the shift in the children's behaviour, nor the fact they inexplicably developed eye colour either."

"Well, if Lilith is a spaceborne virus," Laurel said, "I'm not sure we're going to explain away that connection so simply."

"What about Mom and I being descendants of these imps?"

"You're human, Ava!" Harry scoffed. "I have reams of pandroscopic records to verify it."

"According to Sedar," Laurel reminded him, "so were all these children of Lilith, with just a few distinctions. I would be interested to see if those differences included extra ribs and vertebrae." She smiled at Darlen. "And I'd be willing to bet Soul Mongers are descended from Magen Bearers."

"I knew the proper name for what Soul Mongers call 'hopper' in my ribs is a Magen," Darlen agreed, "although I'd never heard the term Magen Bearer before now. Sedar's story bears out what all Soul Mongers believed; that we can only produce a Soul Monger child with a whole soul, so that's got to be Hebre or those imps. That alone adds strength to the theory whole souls descended from those little buggers."

"It's fascinating," Harry grinned, the mystery of it all making his eyes gleam. "Do these imps exist elsewhere? How did the Magen Bearers propagate their species prior? Unless they've got wives or a stash of females somewhere on that ship. I can't see how the only beings they can reproduce with are human aberrations arising from a pathogen."

"The whole concept of procreation here is compelling and worrying," Laurel said. "Sedar told us a few Hebre children were born from Hebre/human unions. Are they born with clear eyes? What is the aetiology of that pathogen? Does a nebula entity inhabit these newer arrivals from birth? How did I come to be Hebre? And Ava? And the rest of the whole souls? Ultimately, the only explanation possible is we are descended from the Hebre who left here and finished up on Earth. After Hebre arrived there, what are the circumstances of conception…"

Laurel paused mid-sentence, a long-forgotten memory.

Her mother always called her "little alien" because her eyes were such a strange colour. Her aunt had told her they were amber, and Laurel still held to that, but amber possibly didn't go far enough, and she didn't remember ever meeting anyone with violet eyes like Gabriel and his mother, nor Ava's.

"I wouldn't want the masters to know we have a Magen Bearer here," Ava said. "They might attack us to get to him; then they could get through the Transcender."

Darlen shook his head. "The Farisee seem sure the masters won't bother them here. The masters' ship isn't scanning us."

"I hope they're right," Marcel said. "Part of me wishes we'd taken a different direction."

Ava pushed him with her foot. "Then we wouldn't have got answers."

"My lady sister, we still haven't."

"We have some," Laurel said, "unfortunately, we've also got more questions."

"I don't know why the Farisee worship that Lilith," Marcel said, pulling a face. "She brought nothing but ruin."

"They don't worship Lilith," Laurel told him. "They follow the rituals because they fear her. She appears to be a recent addition to their gods, and from what I learned from the Diri wraith, the Farisee observe strict obedience. Some religions on Earth are just as intense. They won't change because of your point of view; it's their job to make you think like them."

Marcel snorted and punched a fist into his palm. "That will never happen! I will let no harm befall the people I love.

I will fight to preserve them."

Laurel smiled. Marcel didn't understand his own zeal was as much a conviction as the religious zeal he so roundly rejected.

Ava rubbed her eyes. "If we're going to go on chewing it all over, I think we could all use some coffee." As she rose from her seat to head to the galley, mugs of steaming liquid appeared in everyone's hand, including Scarlett's and Mer's, the contents slopping out over the rims as the recipients jumped in surprise.

"What the…? Ava looked down at the beaker in her hand, hot liquid stinging her wrist and pools of brown liquid dripping onto the floor. She put the cup in her other hand and wiped her arm on her slacks, glancing up at her equally bewildered, coffee-stained colleagues. A delighted Scarlett handed her cup to Mer without even taking her eyes from Ava.

"You magicked it, Ava," she said breathlessly.

No-one moved. This would take a few moments to process. Ava took several slow deep breaths before announcing, "We don't need this coffee." Instantly, the mugs and the spilt coffee on the floor vanished.

"Not magic," Laurel said. "A manifestation."

"I didn't have any control," Ava said, inspecting her hands. There was no sign of the redness on her wrist from seconds previously. "Scarlett could have been burnt."

"I'm okay." Scarlett wiped her hands just in case any residue of coffee remained. She hated the stuff.

Ava stepped away from the group. "I'm going to try it again. This time, I'll adjust my intentions."

Scarlett was right in her observation because the wait was a little like waiting for the culmination of a magic trick. Ava held out her hand, made her request more specific, and a steaming beaker of coffee appeared. She sipped it.

"It tastes just like coffee," she announced, surprised.

"Baii said manifested food has no nutritional benefit," Harry said.

"That's because he didn't know what went into Big Macs," Laurel laughed. "Ava knows what's in coffee, but the point is that Ava manifested it at will."

There followed an experiment of manifesting small objects. Both Laurel and Ava successfully manifested kittens, much to Scarlett's delight, and a collection of minor everyday utensils used on the ship. Ava eliminated the items quickly. For Laurel, it required focus. She got the hang of it, even though neither of them felt ready to tackle anything more substantial.

"I didn't realise at first I manifested that hot tub on Isilia, nor the vision of Helen," Laurel said to Harry as they got into bed, weary but still with some sleepy and vague formulations of new questions to ask of Sedar and Jadren when they next met. "The overcoat incident on Isilia didn't make sense; that was an accident, a bit like the coffee. Until today, it hadn't happened again. Perhaps we need to be close to a Riynean for the ability to make itself known. Maybe they're a catalyst, but now I know for sure we can manifest; perhaps we can use it to our advantage."

"It's amazing," Harry agreed, his brain still reeling from the fact the two people he loved most in the world could make objects he could see and touch appear out of thin air. "I can't wait to see what else you can create. It's a shame you have to be close to your creations though. Imagine how useful it would be if you could manifest, say, a chair and then walk away, and it stays where you left it?"

"If that were the case, the common lounge would be littered with cups of coffee and a bunch of tools and appliances." Laurel giggled at the thought. "Perhaps it is better this way; it's certainly more controlled."

"The three representatives we met seem to have interesting social constructs," Harry said, changing tack. "You said the Farisee are steeped in idol worship and dogma, but I didn't see any of that with Olyo, apart from her discourse on Sheerguhd. They seem prepared to put their own safety aside to help the Edensai."

"I saw those rituals on the Farisee ship the Diri wraith showed me," Laurel said. "Ava did peek into one of the escort's mind; she shouldn't have, I know, but she says what she found there was, as you put it 'steeped in dogma'. I don't think the Farisee feel as secure as Olyo maintains. These masters, they have their own agenda and could just as quickly turn on the Farisee."

"You might be right, but Laurel—" Harry had to ask; he already knew if these people needed Laurel's help, she wouldn't hesitate, but for him, he wasn't so sure; their luck might have run out. "We came here to discover the origins of whole souls, and I know you are human. I have always believed a whole soul's power is a rare, naturally occurring phenomenon. I still have doubts that an alien influence is giving you empathic and greater physical capabilities." He sighed. "And do we really want to be involved in another war?"

Laurel snuggled her head against his chest. All this time, she believed she was on a quest to find her whole soul ancestors. Even the prospect of the masters had seemed remote, consigned to the distant past. To find that somehow, the Canaa had moved them to a time close to the exodus, she wondered how she could abandon these people to their fate. The task of defeating the masters wasn't finished. She peeked up at Harry.

"What?" he smiled, feeling her eyes on him.

"We started out looking for my ancestors," Laurel said, "and now, we're here because we made a promise."

Harry rolled onto his side and waved on the interior light. "What are you talking about? I didn't make any promise."

"Sounds ridiculous, doesn't it?" Laurel said. "I know I haven't been here before, but there's a part of me that remembers, and it's at the forefront of their minds, Sedar's, Jadren's and Olyo's. I couldn't miss it."

"Anything specific?"

"No, just out of reach, but I bet it's got something to do with 'deliverance'."

"What's telling you this? Intuition? Is it the nebula entity, the part you and Ava seem so accepting of but makes me raise my eyebrows with healthy scepticism?"

Laurel propped up on her elbow. "I think maybe that is the part that's remembering. Harry, ordinary human beings don't have the power to manifest; they don't read minds or have strong telepathic senses. Even your society recognised them as different. The League built entire social conventions that compared normal humans to whole souls."

"We did at that, but none of us believed you to be supernatural. And what about the Riynea? Sedar scans as human."

"Okay, I accept the Riynea and Hebre seem to have something in common, so why can't the entities from the nebula be naturally occurring? It seems that originally, they merely enhanced a physical body that suffered some kind of ocular albinism and caused certain autonomic functions of its brain to be reactivated to allow it to conform to normal society."

Harry nodded sagely. "A side effect of which is empathy, telepathy, enhanced speed and enhanced physical strength? Sounds all very naturally occurring to me."

"It sounds silly put like that, but it brings into question religion's belief in souls."

Harry tapped his finger on her forehead. "In there is a busy place," he laughed softly. "Your human side, this soul thing *and* the entity. I'm surprised you've got room for me!"

Laurel gave a breathy snort and turned over, dragging his arm over her waist to keep him close. Harry tried to be open-minded, but what made sense to her on the inside would appear to others as fantastic. But Sedar, Olyo and Jadren spoke of the Hebre as a fact, lauded their abilities and lamented the loss of the brave Hebre who sacrificed themselves to save the Riynea, Edensai and Kalmeddi on Eden. Laurel reached out to Ava but was glad to find her daughter sleeping peacefully. Then she checked on the rest of the Canaa before pushing her mind beyond. In the quiet of the station, it met Sedar.

"*Rest now,*" he said. "*When you wake, we will give you answers and then find more questions.*"

CHAPTER TEN _

"Do you have any physiological data on the clear-eyed children?" Harry asked Sedar the next morning. "From before the change and then after the lights arrived?"

"We have excellent records," Sedar said, "and the physician has returned. He will guide you through them."

Scarlett happily agreed to spend time with the Farisee escort from the day before, provided she remained on the Canaa close to where Mer and Darlen would be speaking with the only two Kalmeddi engineers left from an entire civilisation. These engineers had gathered data on the masters' ship while they were on Eden. It lacked detail, but Darlen felt it would give them more than they had at present and might even provide a foundation on which to work. Even at first glance of the data, Darlen knew the Canaa's sensors would contribute more practical and specific information, provided they could obtain it without the masters discovering who was probing their ship. Ava and Marcel went to meet Olyo to learn more about the cultural development of the four planet alliance. As the crew had met that morning, there was an unspoken agreement that they would be staying, at least for now, to take stock of the situation and see what they could do to help.

Beril, the physician, was pleased to share his knowledge of the clear-eyed children and grateful for the diversion from the monotony of life on what was basically a system of corridors meant for storage. For years, his only companions were the few dozen or so other ragtag refugees who'd left the surface of Eden to face their prolonged death from lack of nutrients and monotony, a condition he believed would kill them before starvation. As a Kalmeddi physician who regularly worked on Eden before the invasion, he'd met many clear-eyed infants' parents during their formative years, including the period following the transformation by Hebre. Edensai parents in populated areas were diligent in the regular health checks of their progeny as they grew. These children were outside the parameters of what was considered normal, so he and other physicians had been conscientious in their record keeping.

Beril, very elderly, with a kind and gentle manner, shared the same heavy weariness Laurel saw in Jadren. Beril also gave Laurel that same flash of recognition she'd received from Sedar, something beyond recognising her as Hebre. Sedar introduced Laurel and Harry as physicians, a presentation of great satisfaction to Beril, a man of eloquence and superior education by any standards and well versed on the subject of the clear-eyed imps. Knowing the visitors were medical people meant he could confer freely, without resorting to language and medical terms suitable only for laypeople. He trusted the language relay pin would suffice with medical terminology.

Beril's extensive records were held on transparent, rectangular sheets he raised to eye level and which, with a slight nudge, delivered a clear wall of data. The sheet expanded until it produced a comprehensive summary of findings and accurately indexed data alongside a clear, life-size image of a male child aged around four years. Laurel and Harry were impressed. The record didn't exhibit the depth of detail of a pandroscope, but the display was clear and thorough.

"Human," Harry and Laurel said together. "Yes," Harry continued, "but with two extra ribs and two extra vertebrae—" He looked at Laurel. "Like you. If the imps were born of Edensai women, then your human ancestors might originate from here."

So possibly, one mystery was out of the way, but they still had to consider the imp and Hebre element to the whole souls' existence. Laurel studied the optical data. "I see no explanation for the lack of eye colour," she said. To Laurel, the eyes looked normal for a child of that age. The child was also possessed of other characteristics which, while not un-human, needed further study. The child's lungs were slender and, as a result, had diminished capacity. This particular child would almost certainly have suffered breathlessness upon exertion. The heart was enlarged, possibly as a result of respiratory issues. The circulatory system was missing several venous branches. Nerve bundles were out of place, the liver too small and the kidneys little more than rudimentary.

"In many ways, it looks like a failed human clone," Harry said.

Laurel nodded. "But it isn't. Check out the blood chemistry."

Harry folded his arms and took his time. At length, he said, "Either there are a few terms we're not understanding, or this is highly abnormal."

"Your language pins should interpret the bloods for you," Beril said. "The records are Edensai, and your pins calibrate automatically to your language. If it's easier, you may study the body fluid samples yourself."

Harry's eyes lit up. "I would love to. Do you have a hormonal profile? Biochemistry? Genetics?"

Beril smiled and clapped Harry on the shoulder. "All of them, my friend."

The second sheet attached itself to the first, and the data unfolded in front of the child's image. All three doctors stood watching as the story told in the blood of the child unravelled.

"What do you make of that?" Harry said, pointing to an apparent anomaly present in the blood.

Laurel shook her head. "I've never seen anything like it. A pathogen, maybe?"

They viewed the solid hourglass-shaped protein in the sample. It made up a tiny per cent of the other irregularities, but it seemed the most sinister. "I wonder if you've seen many space-borne viruses?" Harry asked Beril.

"We have never encountered any diseases that we could absolutely say came from space," Beril admitted. "We were unable to identify this particular irregularity, nor indeed, explain any of the others either."

"I believe we can," Harry said as he calibrated the data stream to the palm pandroscope. It handled the information efficiently. "That is definitely a pathogen. I can't be sure whether it exists in the female body before conception or if it simply targeted the foetus. The other mystery is how it had such an adverse effect on its siblings."

Beril let out his breath in relieved surprise. "Then you do not accept these children are born of the goddess Lilith?"

Harry suppressed a compulsion to explode into laughter. "No, I don't!" he spluttered. "I can't believe you do either."

Harry's restrained mirth was not lost on Beril. "I don't, but I haven't yet had a better explanation."

"Well, let's see if we can give you one. You say you have extensive records on the older clear-eyed children? May we see?"

"I have this child's records until the age of ten," Beril said. "He is one of the original imps. There is a gap during its chaotic years until he became Hebre. He went on to father a child with an Edensai woman. The child was also Hebre."

"Would you happen to have the records of his offspring?"

Beril smiled. Of course, he did. Hours passed. Image after image was overlaid, data following data was analysed and explored. Although Beril believed there was nothing left to discover, they retired to the Canaa's medical bay, where more advanced equipment in the shape of the full body pandroscope's analytical programme provided volumes of new insight.

Sedar, Olyo and Jadren returned with the others to hear the findings. This new information that Lilith was a pathogen and not a demon wouldn't go down well with

Olyo, but that really couldn't be helped.

Harry loved research, especially medical research, and to see him so inspired, finding such a unique subject, Laurel was happy for him to take the floor. The pandroscope had extracted the information about the clear-eyed children, going from the first examination findings and blood pictures to the period that followed the changing by Hebre. A separate file was created for the subject in adulthood and then one for his child; a human with Hebre characteristics, and even though Laurel had been part of that day's research, to see it all together now and share it with the others helped her make sense of so much more.

"This is the first subject we're using," Harry told the assembled group, displaying the image of the little boy. "Beril has records for him right through to adulthood and fatherhood, plus records for his child. He and his family were part of the exodus from Eden."

Harry explained that one way of identifying whole souls in the League was their extra vertebrae and ribs. The imps had identical skeletal additions. He then pointed out the peculiarities of the child's physiology; his lungs, kidneys, liver, and anomalies in his circulatory system and heart. He then overlaid it with the data from the boy's growing years. Growth took on a typical childhood pattern, and even though the internal viscera remained functional and grew accordingly, the overall shape changed little. Harry took care not to bore the non-medical members of his audience with the problems these children would probably face. This child, after transformation by the Hebre, appeared to suffer few ill-effects from its poorly evolved internal organs, although Harry had no doubt the pre-Hebre version would have faced many difficulties. That they even survived was baffling. The only variation after the transformation by Hebre was a change in the definition of the corpus callosum between the two hemispheres of the brain. In the changed adult, it was larger and less defined. They agreed this was due to the entities' habitation and reason for the Hebre hosts heightened telepathic, empathic skills and physical strength and speed, factors not impeded by the subject's compromised physiology.

But for Harry, the most intriguing part was the child the Hebre fathered. Beril insisted this child was the imp's offspring, and it did have the skeletal additions to support that theory. The infant also had near normally developed lungs, heart and kidneys. Its circulatory system was more robust than its imp parent. The nervous system, although again not entirely normal, was better developed. In summary, it was a more normal human than the original clear-eyed imp who fathered it. Curiously, the infant's blood retained the strange hourglass pathogen.

"So, there was an evolution of some kind?" Marcel asked.

Harry grinned broadly. "Yes, in a single generation. Amazing, isn't it? And look…" Harry then brought up a pandroscopic image of Laurel from when she first arrived on the Consular ship. She was fully human, and there were no signs of the hourglass pathogen. She exhibited the skeletal extras, but the brain was typically configured. Ava's scans were very similar.

"You must have come to some conclusion?" Darlen

asked.

"Yes," Laurel joined in then, taking their attention away from the view of her innards. "We think the children suffered a congenital abnormality as a result of the pathogen. What we have worked out is that it infects males and is attracted to the xy chromosome. When an infected man impregnates a woman, the pathogen is transmitted. According to Beril, there has not been another clear-eyed child born since the arrival of the Hebre. Any Hebre child born has an eye colour from birth. Also, this pathogen may have been the reason male siblings of the imp died; it could be some males were susceptible to a yet unidentified component of the virus."

"Are you saying the nebula entities gave whole souls their abilities?" Darlen said. "And the children their eye colour?"

Laurel was convinced, but she allowed Harry his non-committal lift of the shoulders.

"And what of the story of the woman, Lilith?" Marcel avoided giving a "told-you-so" glance to Olyo.

"The theory of a spaceborne virus is not new, and I am grateful for this clarification," Beril said. "The Edensai are deeply spiritual, and the existence of their god is a constant in their lives. They do not necessarily share the Farisee beliefs—" he made a slight bow to Olyo, "but also, they do not wholly reject the possibility the children were sent as a punishment. Lilith could be a name for either a plague or a god."

"How can they, anyone, believe these children changed their behaviour and became psychic the moment a multicoloured cloud entered the atmosphere?" Darlen asked.

"I am a man of science," Beril replied, "from Kalmed, where my people are not given to religious fervour, yet I cannot deny the evidence of my own eyes. I saw the imps only hours after the colours vanished from the heavens, and though it may not have a basis in science, I believe the entities descended from above, took over the bodies of the imps and changed them. We may have unravelled biological facts, but we have yet to discover a different truth to explain a phenomenon science cannot."

Darlen didn't respond. He could be convinced that the whole souls he'd encountered over the years were possessed by a power not easily explained. This was the first time he'd come close to learning where that power came from.

"Beril," Laurel asked, "would you have any data on the masters' physiology? We might find a vulnerability we can exploit, somewhere to target them physically as opposed to their technology, which we also know little of, and I would be interested to see if we can establish any parallel between them and the imps."

Beril hesitated, then took a deep breath, flashing a hesitant glance at Sedar, who realised the inevitability of this moment as soon as he knew Laurel and Harry were physicians.

"We have one," Sedar said, "a youth, here on this station, brought to us by a former Legion soldier for us to study. Of course, we could not be the instrument of his death, so we keep him in a confinement field, but he is still very dangerous. We were going to release him on Eden where the masters might recover him, but we could not destroy him."

"Even though he would destroy you?" Marcel kept his thoughts to himself, but he regarded Sedar's attitude as an inconceivable apathy towards his duty. Marcel didn't go as far as mentally calling Sedar, his people, nor any of the people from these planets, cowards, but when he searched for a word, right now, he couldn't find a better description. It seemed that none would defend themselves against a growing evil. He thought about his father, who had given his life to save him and his world. To Marcel, to give your life to save your people was noble, was right. Laurel warned him telepathically not to judge, that it was not cowardice to stand by one's convictions. He heard her and felt ashamed, but not before he realised another had also listened to his thoughts. Sedar nodded slightly,

"Even though he would destroy us."

CHAPTER ELEVEN _

They held the young master in the corner of a cold cargo bay. A low bed, too short for his angular frame, took up most of the confinement beam cell. As soon as the boy realised he had visitors, he stood and turned his back to them. Standing tall in his nakedness—forsaking any covers, he ignored Sedar's request to look at them, only glancing over his shoulder at Laurel's voice. When she spoke a second time, asking him to turn, he obeyed, slowly revealing his sublime and terrifying beauty.

Throughout his upper body and arms, sculpted musculature rippled under his light copper skin. His eyes were a cold icy blue, and his hair a cap of gold curls. His soft lips were a perfect cupid's bow, his shoulders broad and graceful. In Earth's mythology, this boy would have been considered an Adonis, the god of beauty and desire. He was exquisite. Perfection.

Harry, Beril and Laurel followed the palm pandroscope as it compiled a study of the boy.

"He presents as human," Harry said, "but the face…the bone structure…" He looked at Laurel. "I don't understand. All humans have inconsistencies throughout their bodies—nobody's perfect—imperfections are natural.

But this boy?" Harry considered the pandroscope findings. "It's as though the skull went through many prototypes to arrive at this degree of precision." He shook his head in disbelief. "This is the most perfect skull I have ever seen. And his teeth…" Harry's voice trailed off as more startling data about the boy added to their wonderment.

Laurel had to concur. The boy's skeleton appeared to possess not a single bony irregularity. He was a textbook example, without flaw in feature or structure. Except for one. Two extra ribs and two extra vertebrae. Laurel's blood ran cold; this was unexpected and unwelcome. Harry and Beril saw it but chose to make no mention.

"This is interesting," Harry said, moving on quickly when he heard Laurel's understandable and quick intake of breath. He displayed a small section of the boy's reproductive system image lifted from the pandroscope. "His gonads are immature," he said, "and his genitalia is infantile, prepubescent." At that, the entire group, including Ava, Marcel, Darlen and the still somewhat disturbed Laurel, peered at the boy's penis.

Beril had noted this. "The only anomaly you will find apart from the obvious correlation between his and the imp's anatomy, is the disparity between his apparent age and his reproductive age. But I bid you review this…"

Beril had set up a real-time chart tracking the boy's digestive process.

"Milk-fed. Interesting," Laurel said. "And he could be anything between eleven and twenty."

Harry agreed. "There must be something in the mother's milk to explain that musculature. I've only ever seen this kind of lactation persistence in a spikit; they feed their calves almost into adulthood."

"We do feed him milk," Sedar said, glancing at the boy with unconcealed contempt. "He likes it not."

"We came to the same conclusion as you," Beril said. "Since he's been here, on the formula we devised and which has been kindly provided by the Farisee, we have measured a three per cent loss in body mass." He showed Laurel and Harry the reconstituted milk formula, not constructed of anything they recognised. "We cannot synthesise adequate nutritional supplements for our own people, let alone…" Beril glared at the youth. There was part of him that would have gladly allowed the boy to starve were it not for Olyo and Sedar's consciences. "Suffice to say his needs are not that of a normal human child. And we do not have the means to wean him."

The boy chose that moment to set up an ear-shattering hiss through his clenched teeth, distracting Laurel and Harry from asking the obvious question of what those means of weaning were. Once he got the group's attention, the boy screamed, "Hebre!" his voice mocking, "Hebre who fled before us in terror!" He thrust his chin high so he could look down on them, even though he was roughly Marcel's height. Laurel knew he meant to intimidate, so she stepped closer. To her surprise—to everyone's surprise—the boy fell silent and took a half step backwards, despite the dividing force field between them. Laurel studied his face. He stared back, resolute, defiant. "You're not particularly terrifying now," she responded quietly. Laurel sensed she had stood in such a place before, in front of a master. She snatched at the memory, but it was fleeting, slippery, and she could not make it stay. On attempting to enter the boy's mind, she found Ava already there, but there was little of value, only a ponderous sense of self, weighty and negative. His contempt for humankind was as much a part of him as his flesh. Neither Ava nor Laurel could learn anything of significance from him.

The boy then turned his loathing on Harry and Marcel. "Primitive. Useless. Usurpers. *Small!*" He spat to make emphasis, then sniffed the air. "Third kingdom. I smell it upon you." He looked suddenly at Darlen as if registering his presence for the first time, and Sedar, Ava and Laurel sensed a moment's confusion. It was fleeting, then inhaling deeply, the youth folded his arms and closed his eyes, dismissing everyone in the room.

"He needs to dominate the situation," Ava said. "He's attempting to be fearless, but he feels alone. Hatred, loathing, anger; they're all he's got."

Harry agreed. "I thought the masters would be fierce, terrifying, but he's like a little boy, all bravado."

"Do not underestimate him," Sedar warned. "Even a master of this age can have a crushing effect upon a man. I have witnessed the power of a single adult master; this..." he gestured to the youth, "...is but a child. Even so, you should learn his strength."

"He looks harmless," Harry shrugged.

"He is not harmless." Beril's voice carried the same warning. "Sedar, a demonstration...?" He turned to the group and gave a slight bow. "With your permission, I will take my leave. I have had one encounter, I believe my advanced age would not contend with another. Sedar, you have the two Hebre women here if he needs to be suppressed. Perhaps the younger man—" he pointed to Marcel, "—also needs to leave."

"Subdued?" Ava said.

"There are several of us," Darlen said, "plus two women with superior agility and strength, not to mention Marcel's predisposition for fighting. One lad can't take us all on."

"He will not 'take you on'…" Sedar began, but Beril held up his hand.

"A short demonstration will offer more than words," he stated, then headed for the exit.

Darlen pulled a small sidearm from his jacket. He'd already decided he wasn't going anywhere without a weapon. "If he acts up, I'll shoot him."

Sedar opened his mouth as if to speak, then closed it again. He didn't want to kill anyone on the station, because he would never hear the end of it from Olyo and the Holy Trahs on Eden, who knew of the young master's presence here.

The young man watched, a hint of a sneer on his perfect mouth. Harry, Marcel and Sedar stood to one side, flanked by Darlen holding his weapon at the ready, and Laurel and Ava to the other, awaiting the "demonstration". Sedar deactivated the containment field.

The effect on Harry and Marcel was almost instantaneous, with Marcel being the first to fall to his knees as an overpowering stench like rotting meat streamed from the young master. Marcel's head jerked back; his fists clenched tight as the veins in his neck and temple stood out blue and throbbing against his flushed skin. His eyes were squeezed tight in a torment of overwhelming physical and mental ecstasy as sweat drenched his dark hair and soaked into his shirt. In a speedy move, Laurel prevented Harry from taking up a likewise position, using her body to shield him from the boy.

Laurel and Ava were unaffected, as was Darlen, who obeyed Laurel's tacit "wait" as he stepped to protect Marcel. Sedar restored the confinement, and Marcel fell forward onto his hands, gasping for breath. Harry sagged against Laurel, spared from the worst effects by the barrier Laurel created. Sedar also appeared to have been affected, his wrinkled old face bright red and covered in beads of sweat. The entire exercise took less than twenty seconds.

Laurel helped Harry to a bench. "That was some hit of pheromones," he gasped, taking a deep breath. He mustered a painful grin at Sedar. "Going by your appearance, it doesn't get easier."

Sedar shook his head and dabbed at his face. "I believe my age provides some protection from the sensual component of the effect."

"It didn't affect Ava and me at all," Laurel said, checking Harry's vital signs with the pandroscope, "but we picked up the wash of emotion from you and Marcel and the smell from the boy. It seems Darlen is immune."

Darlen gave a slight shrug. He'd felt nothing.

Harry blew out his breath in a whistle. "That's a hell of a weapon, subduing an enemy with nothing more than a glance in the right direction."

Marcel had collapsed face down on the ground. Ava checked him out and proclaimed him "okay" as she helped him to sit up.

"The boy is still too young," Sedar said. "In the adult male, the stench can kill the victim, but death does not come quickly, nor without pain. It takes many minutes as the body drowns in its own fluids."

Harry's mouth went dry. "That's unbelievable. How can we defeat a weapon like this?"

The boy proudly studied the effects his overpowering stench had on the group. Once again sealed within the confinement beam, he allowed their response to be entertainment. He had brought a grown man to his knees and profoundly affected two others. Once more, Laurel looked into his mind but still, despite his obvious glee, there was only darkness. It was like trying to read the mind of a dead man.

***

Back on the Canaa, a recovering Harry sat with the pandroscope, going over and over the readings taken during the "demonstration" and rechecking Marcel for residual effects.

"It's not just a question of sexual arousal," he said, keeping his voice down so Scarlett, playing dress-up with Mer, wouldn't overhear. "At the initial rush, I would have signed up to anything, even if it went against my good sense and morals."

"A weapon that can shape a person's behaviour," Darlen said to Laurel. "Even you and Ava can't influence another's thoughts."

"The boy didn't appear to trigger any process to deliver the pheromone," Laurel said. "It took effect almost immediately the confinement field went down, and it didn't vary in intensity."

Marcel was also reflecting on the experience. "I can't believe how it affected me; I was helpless. The whole time I was terrified, awed, I even felt…" he shook his head, "like I wanted to touch him, physically, in a sensual way. I've never felt like that towards a man before."

"This is a weapon, Marcel," Ava said with a faint flicker of a smile. "He's trying to gain power over you, not have sex."

"It felt that way…" Marcel replied, clearly still uncomfortable about the whole experience. "And I was utterly paralysed. What if he'd made demands? I mean demands like releasing him or surrendering ourselves to the masters? How would we have resisted?"

"I think he's too immature to have gained full control over the power yet," Laurel said, "but now we know about that ability, we may be able to develop a countermeasure."

"Another thing in our favour," Ava said. "Earlier today, Olyo told me about the masters—she showed me an image of a full-grown male—he was gigantic!" She shook her head. It was an incredible image. "But Olyo told me a hard enough blow to the side of a master's skull can kill."

"Olyo told you that?" Harry said, surprised.

Ava raised her eyebrows; that morsel of intelligence from the passionately religious Farisee surprised her too. "Yes, but the blow has to be delivered by Hebre."

"Well, it wouldn't be by anyone else," Harry declared,

"everyone else seems to be slaves to their conscience, or are you suggesting that only Hebre possesses the strength to kill the masters? I suppose if they're unaffected by the scent, they'd be the only ones able to get close enough. Apart from Legion, of course." Harry looked at Darlen. "And I suppose Magen Bearers."

Ava shook her head. "No, the Legion converts aren't fighting back. Those who've defected have taken up the ways of the Edensai; pacifists, somewhat backward, quiescent, accepting of their fate."

"Ava's right," Darlen said. "The two Kalmeddi engineers, if you can call them engineers," he added ungraciously, "showed me their propulsion schematics. Harry, they're barely further developed than the League's Griel interplanetary protocol."

"What!?" Harry had never seen a Griel system; they'd been obsolete for centuries. In their time, they provided only the most laborious mode of space travel. It would have been quicker to push a ship through space than use Griel harmonics.

"It's not just their technology," Marcel added. "The way Olyo spoke, it was as if the society on all the planets came to a standstill, socially and technologically, well before the arrival of this Lilith sickness."

"That's what she said," Ava nodded. "No expansion, not even strong population growth, on any of the planets apart from Faris."

"Arrested civilisations?" Darlen said. "I can understand that on Eden after the imps began causing trouble, but before? Why?"

"I think the four planets, between them, became complacent, comfortable," Ava replied, "and they gave up any desire for development. Perhaps their spiritual convictions stunted them, and they were content in the pursuit of spiritual devotion. I don't know. I'm just guessing."

"But the Kalmeddi and the Riyneans don't worship gods in the same way as they do on Edensai," Marcel pointed out.

"I know," Ava said, "but they did the same. They just stopped developing."

"Well, it seems they haven't made any attempt to resist the invasion," Laurel said, "and I'd like some more information on the masters; how that boy would be weaned, for example. Sedar would know, but I've noticed he's started to keep his thoughts concealed. We'll have to ask the physician. Harry, we should go to the surface, see what's going on there."

Harry agreed. "Shall we take the Canaa?"

Darlen didn't like the idea of taking chances with their only mode of transport. "The Canaa is our way out," he said. "It's too much of a risk."

"We could ask Olyo to take us in her ship," Ava suggested. "She might let us if we conceal it, so Mom and I aren't detected."

"I know why I won't be invited," Darlen said. "Either way, I need to check out the Kalmeddi engineers' data on the masters' ship again before I go probing it myself. Hopefully, I may find a weak spot within their defence and strike capabilities and come up with something we can use.

Laurel," he grinned, "I gather we're not turning tail and flying out of here just yet?"

Harry had asked her if she wanted to be embroiled in another war. She didn't, yet somehow, this *was* her war. She looked at each of her crewmates. "I—no, I don't want to turn tail and fly out. But it's not just my decision."

Marcel looked up but didn't respond; he'd go wherever his family went, fight where they fought. Ava also glanced around, waiting for a reaction to her mother's statement. No-one answered, and after a moment, Darlen tossed his sidearm to Harry.

"Mer and I can reproduce a few of these," he said. "I have the Gartryan knuckle weapon the duchess was using before she died. I can crank up its power, but we must consider the resources here. I doubt they have anything that resembles a production line, and materials are likely to be an issue. I'll see what I can scrounge. It's a shame we've only got that one master. I'm curious to see if a single sidearm blast would drop him." Darlen grinned at Laurel. "I suppose you might want to study him further?"

"He might be useful," Laurel agreed, "so don't shoot him just yet. I wonder if we can mobilise those converted Legion and organise an insurgency; that's if they'll trust us. Sedar mentioned a few communities on the surface, so he may give us an introduction. Harry, we should take a full medpac to the surface; perhaps if they see we want to help, it might make a difference."

Olyo responded favourably to using a scout, which had only enough room for Harry, Laurel, Ava, Marcel and a single pilot. The pilot performed several rituals as she prepared the vessel for departure, bowing towards several icons and lifting beads to her lips at specific stages of the flight sequence. The rituals were like those Laurel had observed in her vision with the Diri wraiths and quite fascinating, but while she enjoyed watching this cultural activity, she sensed Ava's distraction.

"What is it, honey?"

"Mom. The masters. I think they know we're here."

CHAPTER TWELVE _

Olyo offered Darlen a Farisee servant to care for Scarlett and keep her entertained in a section of the station where she might be whisked away in a small Farisee ship if the masters changed their plans and attacked. Darlen conceded the Farisee knew the situation far better than he, so he accepted, thanking Olyo for her consideration. It occurred to him privately that his strong-willed, though somewhat impressionable daughter, might end up indoctrinated into the religious rites and rituals of the Farisee. Still, this would be a small price to pay for her safety. The Ascendant, ever pragmatic, assured him that should the crew of the Canaa die during their endeavours, she would personally care for the child, embrace her into Farisee society and keep her well-hidden underground in the unfortunate event the masters were ultimately victorious. Olyo herself would then nurture her according to their customs, so Darlen need not fear. Unsurprisingly, Olyo's reassurances fell a little short of their mark.

It was only the second time Laurel and Ava had concealed a vessel. The exercise provided a welcome distraction from the sudden realisation there was at least a possibility their presence was known to the masters. Cloaking, or mantling as Helen used to call it, was still so new to them.

"I'm divided between feeling how natural this ability comes to me and astonishment that I can even do it at all," Ava grinned.

"I was in awe of Helen when she did it," Laurel said, "but she and Darlen got into all sorts of scrapes—not that I ever got the full story—so I bet she had plenty of practice in cloaking the two of them. She got a bit anxious when it came to cloaking the entire ship for the first time, though."

"Mom, why do you think none of the history of the Hebre and Edensai was left with the Riynea on Isilia?"

"Maybe it was, Ava. Knowledge gets lost and added to over time, quite often distorting the fundamental truths. I'm learning we can't count on anything contained in ancient documents. History seems to be a hotchpotch of truth and fable."

"The woven fragment from the prison planet about the serpent from Sheerguhd seems accurate enough," Ava pointed out, "and if the Hebre came up against the masters, it might seem like they were cast out of Eden."

"I'm not so sure anymore they were cast out. They may have escaped or left of their own accord. Besides, all those snippets of information were just a trail of breadcrumbs for us to follow. I think we were meant to come back."

Ava didn't answer, just nodded slightly; she'd always been polite with her telepathy, but her empathic senses, like her mother's, were always switched on. Intent was strongly linked to the subconscious mind, so for the few people she'd met, she didn't need to go searching, seeing the recognition behind their eyes and the realisation she and her mother were long-awaited.

Laurel watched the approaching planet loom ever larger until they grew into a speck hurtling towards its surface. The pilot steered away from the devastated northern hemisphere towards an area which for now remained unaffected by the ominous cloud, and where bright sunlight reached the planet below. Eden. Paradise. Laurel's heart skipped a beat as the planet's terrain loomed into view. Everywhere was devastation. Where there should have been rolling hills bathed in sunlight, there were just vast wastelands. Even the majestic mountains reaching ever upwards seemed sad and dark. *What have the masters done?* Laurel whispered under her breath, the pain of what she saw not from her mind but from somewhere even more buried, somewhere in eternity. And she didn't understand.

"Do you think we should be concerned that the masters know of us?" Ava's voice moved across Laurel's thoughts, distracting her from the sadness of the view before her.

"Are you positive they do?"

Ava blinked. *"Almost, but for some reason, it doesn't frighten me. That boy on the station, I felt…well, kind of that he had been abandoned. That he suffered a terrible loss, that whatever made him evil was out of his control."* She shivered. *"Something ancient."*

Laurel agreed. *'I don't understand how the masters know. Darlen found no evidence anyone other than Sedar observed us unless the masters' sensors are more advanced, possibly subtle and not discernible, but from what we know, that doesn't seem likely."* She glanced towards Sedar, seated next to the Farisee pilot, his mind as closed as ever, but then he appeared very practised at keeping his own counsel. Laurel raised her eyes to Marcel, who met her gaze, then she looked at Harry as she communicated a silent thought to them both, allowing them a fleeting glimpse of Sedar's possible betrayal as she consigned the thought deep into their subconscious mind. Ava listened in, and all the while, Sedar gave no indication of being aware he had fallen under suspicion.

The ship steered towards a highland area close to the southernmost continent's borders, slipping down through low flying, sun-brightened clouds and well away from the encroaching fog. Tears pricked behind Laurel's eyes as they passed over a desolate landscape, deserted cities and abandoned farms. Rusted and dismantled barge-like transports were broken up to use as shelters. Smouldering fires, which bilged black, probably toxic smoke into the streets, were surrounded by large groups of individuals who used the fire as a focal point for a pitiful assembly. The buildings were mainly too damaged to offer safe accommodation; the gaping holes throughout their uniform, gabled roofs would be a threat of collapse to anyone foolish enough to enter. The slightest movement would likely bring what was left of the structure down on any head desperate for sanctuary. Each city was in the same state of ruin and decay, and as they passed unnoticed above the people, Laurel felt as if she were looking at a civilisation just a solitary gasp away from death.

"What are we feeling?" Ava asked, shifting restlessly from one foot to the other.

The Farisee pilot prepared to land the ship. "You are possessed of the nebula," she said, "and you sense the despair and sorrow of the world." The woman looked over her shoulder. "Such sadness touches all our hearts, makes us all empaths."

The pilot flew across a stagnant lake, the stench of which, as soon as the pilot switched from recycled air to external, instantly assaulted their nostrils. Sedar and the Farisee pilot ignored the pong, but Laurel had to fight against gagging. Stinking vapour covered the filthy water's surface, and the pandroscope warned of toxic gas bubbles bursting from its depths. So close to this marsh was not a good place to live, and Laurel was glad the few ragged children, who watched the spectacle of them uncloaking with a mix of fear and interest, kept their distance from the bog. Laurel held up the palm pandroscope, which flashed a warning not to approach the polluted water or its marshy surroundings, but that warning came too late and had to be ignored; besides, most of the area suffered pollution.

Several shed-like structures stood in a circle a few hundred metres from the marsh, not far enough away for the smell to dissipate. To one side of the sheds, the city's remnants were either in a state of crumbling disintegration or entirely flattened. There were no discernible plants or vegetation. The Farisee pilot explained that even though the masters didn't investigate Farisee scout ships, she felt it prudent to place it where it was not so easily seen, particularly as she'd noticed the use of fire on their approach, a comfort that invited the wrath of the masters and Legion if a patrol was in the area. The outbuildings were so dilapidated and broken down, it would be easy to miss a small ship slotted neatly between the stinking lake and the rubble, and their destination was just a little too far distant to keep the vessel cloaked.

Sedar ushered them towards the sheds. Each shelter's outer wall had been built up with an eye to reinforcement and with some skill, and each shelter had a complete roof. A single rear wall provided some protection, but the rest of the structure was open to the iciness of the day, with the sun offering little warmth. Each shelter faced inwards, creating a large, central courtyard where people with sad, haunted eyes assembled in groups. Inside the shelters, tattered sacks fastened to posts offered privacy to the many people lying on the floor. The stink of death and misery competed with the smell of the lake. Laurel felt her steps falter, her senses overcome by the grief and suffering of these people who had built what could be described only as a ghetto from the ruins of their home. Some people turned with listless interest to look at the newcomers, and those that looked a second time raised a finger to point. Ava and Laurel both felt the quickening, the flicker of hope as people spread the word.

"Hebre!"

Harry touched Laurel's arm. "They know you. Even I can feel a sense of trust."

Laurel nodded, humbled as weary face after weary face turned to them. No-one crowded them; not one soul pushed to get closer, even though it seemed that every person in the compound able to walk gathered around as their presence was noticed, even some whose legs could not carry them were helped by others so that they may behold Hebre. The small children who followed them from the ship were less interested in the group than they were the Farisee pilot, who didn't accompany them into the yard but remained on the perimeter, most likely on the lookout for Legion activity, which she told them had become rarer as the humans died out. The pilot gave each child a small, round cake which they grabbed without a word and jammed into their grateful, hungry mouths.

"Mom," Ava sent to Laurel, *"I can hear people's thoughts. They are calling us the deliverers."*

"I hear it," Laurel sent back. *"I think we're about to find out what we really mean to them."*

The crowd parted respectfully, and a frail, ancient woman, supported between two men, made slow, painful procession towards them. The tallest and elder of the woman's escorts was a broad-shouldered man with a serious expression, vivid blue eyes and a massive beard. Laurel guessed him to be around fifty years of age, with a demeanour that put Laurel in mind of Darlen. A converted Legionnaire, perhaps? The other man, underweight on an already slim frame with a pale, gaunt face hidden under a matted beard, would probably have been in his early twenties. Between them, they tenderly supported the woman as she came close to Laurel. Both men wore the tatty, ill-fitting gowns that seemed to be the only clothing available, and like everyone else, these men were shoeless.

The old woman nudged the two men away as she reached Laurel, hobbling those last few steps painfully, but with pride. Her feet were swathed in filthy bandages, her hair equally dirty and matted, and the skin on her feeble, trembling arms hung loosely as she reached for Laurel, who stepped forward, fearing the frail woman might lose her balance. The woman's weary eyes almost slipped back into her head, and her pale skin puckered into a wreathe of wrinkles over her forehead and cheeks as her slack mouth widened into a toothless smile. She tried to place her hands on each side of Laurel's face, but the effort was just too great, so Laurel reached down, took the woman's hands and completed the gesture. She held them there as the old woman's pale eyes shone with tears. Intuitively, Laurel bowed her head, touching forehead to forehead with the ancient dame. Unprepared for the onslaught of intense emotion, a sob broke from Laurel's throat, and tears splashed helplessly onto her cheek. She took the woman's hands from her face and held them in front of her, barely able to see through her tears.

"Hebre." The woman's mouth worked at the words, but her soft voice became entangled in the labyrinthine maze between her weak breath and ancient gums. "The deliverers."

"Mother," Laurel whispered, not knowing where the words came from, but feeling that her heart would burst with emotion. "We have not forgotten you."

The woman nodded slowly and took her hands from Laurel's, once again soliciting the two men's support, allowing them to help her to a circle of stone seats where she sat and awaited Laurel and the rest of the group to join her.

Harry watched the emotional scene in mute

admiration. Laurel believed she had been guided here or that their arrival was no accident. What he just witnessed confirmed that whatever Laurel's purpose, he would be beside her all the way. At some point, as they observed the hushed welcome from the old lady, Marcel had sought Ava's hand, a need to connect and show his love and allegiance to her. He wiped away a tear as he too felt the hope the two women's arrival had inspired.

"Mother?" Ava asked Laurel as they accepted the invitation to sit. "Do you believe she is related to the mother of the original imp? Your ancestor?"

Laurel shook her head. "When she touched me, I knew that was how I must address her. She has knowledge, wisdom. She guides these people. It's in that way she is their mother."

"You said we hadn't forgotten her?"

Laurel looked about her at the sea of curious faces, "I didn't mean only her. I meant all these people. We haven't forgotten, Ava. We just haven't remembered yet."

Harry sat beside Laurel and squeezed her hand. "You okay?" he said, checking out her face, still a little blotchy from the unexpected bout of weeping.

"I'm fine," she smiled.

"These people seriously need our help," Harry said, glancing around the shelter. "I don't need the pandroscope to know they are all malnourished and diseased."

Laurel agreed. "That will be the short-term fix, Harry. I don't know how, at least not yet, but our priority must be to save them from the masters."

With the group seated and the elderly woman safely propped between her two escorts, Sedar stood and introduced the visitors, then placed his hand on the shoulder of the man Laurel thought might have once been part of Legion.

"My friends, this is Abel. He has been part of this community for almost eighteen years; Hebre turned his heart, and now he abides amongst the Edensai, content to share their suffering. Yosser," Sedar turned to the younger man, "is Edensai, orphaned by Legion. He and Abel care for the weak and vulnerable in this community." Sedar looked about him. "As you can see—" he nodded towards Laurel, "—all within this compound."

"Are there other communities such as this?" Harry asked, closing off his senses to the stench of unwashed bodies and disease that rose and mingled with the smell from the lake, driving away any fresh air foolish enough to come close. He wondered about the infection rate here, the close living quarters, and how so many had survived. The smell would be the least of their worries.

"There are other communities," Abel said. "As far as we can tell, around twenty, each with up to one thousand Edensai. The few Riyneans and Kalmeddi left on Eden during the purge have been absorbed into the tribes."

"Is that the sole number of people left on this planet?"

Abel saw upon first sight his questioner was not Hebre. Such colour hair, like sand, was not seen amongst them; besides, he had never seen these men before. When they arrived, Sedar had privately told him the two women would confound him with their likeness to Judith and Esther, but that he must be prepared that they would not know either him or their surroundings, that all they encountered would be new and shocking.

"There are those who live in the mountains and those in the ruins of the cities," Abel said. "They scavenge to live, as we do. They would live here in the compounds but are only admitted when one of our number makes room for them. We do not know for certain how many are left on Eden."

Harry knew that even with Abel's dispassionate delivery, he got the idea that "making room" would be a regular occurrence.

"You have arrived on a dying world," Abel continued sadly, the weight of his contribution as Legion to its demise clear to Ava and Laurel. "Soon, there will be none of us left to mourn, and the masters will declare another victory."

"This isn't their first invasion?" Laurel said.

Abel shook his head; the woman looked so like Judith, her hair, her eyes, the softness of her mouth. He knew she was Hebre, that she could enter his mind if she so chose, perhaps find out why his heart skipped a beat when he first laid eyes on her. "They overthrew and destroyed the first kingdom," he said, keeping his emotions level. "They wiped out every trace of humankind in accord with their objective and work. In the first kingdom, the humans were brave, but there were no Hebre, no-one to deliver the promise you gave to our mother..." He laid a gentle hand on the old woman's shoulder. "That she would yet live to see her people delivered."

Laurel looked about her at the deplorable conditions.

She could provide practical help, but besides a sense she had an obligation to fulfil, precisely what that promise might be eluded her. These people were placing a good deal of faith in two women to deliver them where thousands of Hebre before had seemingly failed, merely leaving them with a vague promise they would return. Perhaps it was arrogance to assume the pledge made to the people fifteen years ago applied to them.

"There are only two of us," Laurel pointed out, "but we have considerable expertise in weaponry." She waited for Abel to declare he would not join a fight, knowing he'd adopted the principles of a non-combatant people, but he seemed at ease with her words.

"Hebre didn't say how many would return," he said softly.

"I'm sorry," Laurel answered, doggedly resisting the urge to read this man's mind to get the information. "It's just that we genuinely don't recall making any promise. We have never been here before. We believe we may be descendants; from the future."

Laurel's proclamation did not affect Abel. He knew of Hebre's perception of time. He didn't doubt they could have returned from a point far distant. But without memory? That was harder to understand.

"Kingdom?" Marcel asked, wondering at the use of such a word. "Do you speak of a galaxy or something more?"

Abel recognised the air of Hebre in the young man. He'd seen this in the human children born to Hebre but in whom the nebula entities chose not to invest. The man with the sand-coloured hair was likewise comforted. "I speak of neither," he said. "A kingdom would be a single point in a galaxy, and a galaxy a single point in the whole of creation."

A cryptic reply worthy of a place in scripture, Laurel thought. It wouldn't satisfy Marcel.

"We have been inside Sheerguhd," Ava said, extending a double-take at Yosser's intense gaze, and shifting her body slightly, so she didn't have to look at him. "Does Sheerguhd lead us to another dimension where these kingdoms reside?"

Abel frowned. Sedar had not mentioned the ship came from Sheerguhd; he said it came from the nebula. To emerge from Sheerguhd would mean…

"Sheerguhd is the beginning and the end," he said after a moment. He would not yet voice his realisation that a Magen Bearer must be among their number. "Sheerguhd *is* eternity. It is where stars are born, and it is where galaxies die. It is the birthplace of all living, the resting place of all that has been and all that will be. Within Sheerguhd, the kingdoms are created."

"Do you have a way of defining it?" Marcel asked. "My lady sister believes Sheerguhd led into a stellar nursery, a single element of a greater whole that lies between universes. Are you suggesting Sheerguhd *is* the universe? We understood it to be a gateway, a corridor between universes."

"I think you are deceived, my young friend," Abel said. "Sheerguhd *is* the universe. There are not multiples." He blinked slowly, wishing them to grasp his words fully. "And Sheerguhd opens his eye only to a Magen Bearer."

Laurel considered it. So Sheerguhd was separate to the Transcender and the Transcender merely a portal *within* Sheerguhd, and they called it the "eye". Abel awaited Laurel's response; he knew she heard his pointed comment about the Magen Bearer, but she was not forthcoming with a reply, so he looked to Ava. None of the group made any indication they knew to what he referred. That was prudent of them, Abel thought. The return of a Magen Bearer would need to be hidden zealously from the masters.

Laurel and Ava took a moment to weigh this information together. Abel said there was only a single universe, alluding to separate kingdoms and dimensions within that universe. The Transcender was just another name for a movable point between these places. It would take some study, and Laurel's brain was already compiling a diagram for later analysis. And they both knew Abel realised a Magen Bearer was among their number, but now was not the time to confirm Darlen's presence.

The old lady pulled on Abel's sleeve to draw his attention, and he bent his head close, listening attentively, nodding his understanding. "Hagar—" Abel held the woman's hand affectionately to his chest, "our mother says that God will make his wishes known to Hebre."

"Well, I'd better pay attention because I have no idea," Ava sent to Laurel. *"Right now, I feel a little overwhelmed."*

"We just need to be patient," Laurel replied, *"We were expected, so that makes me sure of our connection to this place, these people. It will become clear. Meanwhile, let's see if we can learn something about the current situation and offer some practical help."*

"At this point, we're still considering what we can offer

in terms of medical aid," Laurel said to Abel. "It is evident your people are suffering." She indicated to Harry. "We are physicians. We have diagnostic tools and medicine, and we can ease some of their pain. Perhaps…"

Abel held up a hand to stop her. He understood Sedar's cautionary words better now; this woman didn't know her own strength. To offer succour and aid to the sick was not her purpose. He had stood with Judith when she vowed that she would not abandon the people, that she would return.

"In all communities throughout the Southern land…Laurel," he stumbled over the curious name, "sickness and death are without mercy. You cannot save those upon whom death has already laid his finger. To renew the flesh once the carcass has begun its decay is against natural law. This I know. Hebre are good and compassionate," Abel's smile was gentle, "but you are not here to preserve the hopeless; you are here to deliver the hopeful."

Laurel knew Abel was telling them not to waste their time unless they could offer something more abiding. She saw there was still fight left in him, an unwillingness to lay down and die before his former masters. As they spoke, a second Farisee scout arrived and a few people left the gathering to arrange themselves expectantly in rows, but many were too sick even to stand.

"The Farisee," Yosser said, "bring bread to appease hunger. So that while we starve to death, our bellies feel full."

Laurel asked how often the Farisee brought the bread.

"Every few days," Abel told her. "We also forage for a fungus that thrives in the stinking lake. It provides a protein but also has high toxicity levels, so eating it might kill us, but we might also die if we don't. A few plants, bitter and virtually inedible, have defied the ground's poison to grow in the forest, but those Edensai outside the compound usually strip those. Former Legion—the Sons of David, are less affected by the toxins."

"Are there any other sources of food?' Harry asked, even though he knew the answer. He'd never encountered malnutrition; it was a condition unheard of in the League.

"No," Abel shook his head. "Without the Farisee, we would not have survived this long." He looked at Laurel, trust in his eyes. "For many of us, it has been our wish to endure only to see Hebre return."

"We analysed the weather front in the north," Harry said. "We know the masters detonated a device in the atmosphere, although we can't narrow down the chemicals specifically. Is it something that poisons the water and soil even though the cloud remains in the north? Do you have any knowledge of it, how it can be stopped, or if the cloud can be dissipated?" Harry activated a datacache. Abel seemed familiar with the technology, but Ava and Laurel sensed his discomfort at describing the desolation his kind had brought to this world. Even after all these years, even after acceptance by the Edensai, they could see his conscience tormented him.

"A single device has this reach," Abel said, highlighting the vast area affected by the explosion. "The damage to human, animal and plant life is impossible to measure. The cloud settles low to the ground and is slow-moving, taking years to compromise a world. Once the canopy is laid, it cannot be undone. The masters design it thus to extend their bliss in the torment of their victims."

"In that case, why do they kill so many at the start?" Marcel asked.

"Sacrificing part of the population on a world such as this is of little concern," Abel explained. "The masters will bide their time, content in the knowledge the suffering of the people endures."

"Is this why they don't apprehend the Farisee ships?" Harry said, truth dawning on him, "because by feeding the people rations of questionable nutrition, they are prolonging death?"

Abel dipped his head once, acknowledging Harry's wisdom.

"Do the Farisee know this?" Laurel asked.

"They know," Abel said, "but they are people of passion, of conscience. They cannot stand by and watch children starve."

"I know you believe we have a greater purpose," Laurel said, "but will you let us treat the sick amongst you? As Harry has outlined, we have analysed the cloud, and though it hasn't reached here yet, its effects must have been carried by underground water, in the air, and the soil is polluted. Your people are starving, yes, but there are other diseases."

Laurel turned to Hagar. "Mother, let us help the people, let us alleviate their suffering while we find a solution."

Hagar's mouth moved in her silent speech, then she

smiled her gummy smile, reaching out her bony hand to Laurel and pushing Yosser from his seat beside her, suggesting that Laurel sit in his place. Yosser grinned. "Hagar gives you her permission," he said, "and God will guide your hands. Hagar is our word keeper, our Holy Trah," he explained as he made room for Laurel. "She has kept the ancient oral traditions passed down through generations of Edensai in this region. Joshua, her student, left on the arks. He was forty, too young to have learned all, so Hebre recorded our laws on stones, lest they are lost."

Ancient stones, oppression, suffering, a promised land, even the feeding of the people by the Farisee, which could take on the biblical manna's appearance, all the similarities seemed to have roots somewhere other than the world upon which many of the Hebre and Edensai finally created a home.

"Stones?" Laurel said. "Like this?" She took the datacache from Harry and showed Yosser an image of the stone she found in the League vault.

"The same," he said, surprised. "We don't know where Hebre came by these artefacts, but once closed, they open only to Hebre. You have seen them?"

"Well, not the records of your people," Laurel had to admit, sorry she was unable to confirm the desperate delight in Yosser's and Hagar's eyes, "but an account of a people who fled persecution by a race they called 'masters'. I'm convinced those people were the descendants of those who escaped on the arks. I also believe the masters who pursued these people were crushed when they attempted to enter the Eye of Sheerguhd."

Hagar nodded, her smile so wide much of her face disappeared into her mouth. She leaned up to whisper in Laurel's ear, but all Laurel could hear was the faint sound of wheezy air whistling past Hagar's gums, but in her mind, the words were clear. *"I told my people Hebre would protect them,"* Hagar whispered as she placed Laurel's hand over her heart. *"Hebre promised deliverance."*

"Hagar speaks of Judith," Abel said, and Laurel heard deep emotion in his voice. "Judith told us she would not forget, that she would not abandon her people."

"Judith said she wouldn't abandon you? Or Hebre?"

Abel was silent for a moment. He remembered Judith's words. Had he misheard her?

"When you said to Hagar you had not forgotten us, was this not your meaning?" he said. "That you had returned to be once more among us, to stop the masters entering Sheerguhd and to end their reign here?"

"Hebre took all the Magen Bearers," Laurel said. "So the masters can't enter Sheerguhd."

An expression of confusion came over Abel's face. "The Magen Bearers whose hearts were turned, left Eden with Hebre. A faithful Magen Bearer pursued the arks into Sheerguhd, but there is another, still here, who remains loyal to the masters. When the destruction of Eden and the other worlds is complete, and all human life extinguished, the masters will re-enter Sheerguhd."

The news came as a surprise. Ilivi had told them Hebre took all twenty-seven Magen Bearers, but even she admitted her history was sketchy. They'd been foolish enough to accept its accuracy, and now, in their ignorance, they'd

walked into something that far outpaced their assumptions.
How much more was there to this story?

CHAPTER THIRTEEN _

"We understood the masters were stranded here," Harry said. They'd assumed, mistakenly so it seemed, that only a single Magen Bearer remained, and it was he who took the masters and Legion into Sheerguhd to follow the arks.

Abel shook his head, "My friend, that is not so, there is still one who abides with the masters, and he has a child who will take the Magen when his father dies. The masters will not leave until the humans in this system are dead. If they become tired of their play, they will merely send Legion to eradicate the rest. It would be easy for them to accomplish this. The Farisee estimate there are less than two million souls left on Eden and a handful each on Riynea and Kalmed."

"Abel. Mother," Laurel said, unsure how she would accomplish it, but she would protect these people with her dying breath. "We will not let them leave this system. We will defend you, as Hebre in the past tried to protect you. We will find a way to defeat the masters."

"Those of us whose hearts have changed will stand beside Hebre," Abel promised. "If you are to make war—" Laurel felt Hagar flinch at Abel's words, "then I need to tell you there are three more arks, on a mountain further north.

Perhaps there is hope," he said softly, a bitter half-smile on his lips. "Better that we die alongside Hebre than under the heel of the masters."

"The Edensai, the Riynea and Kalmeddi amongst us revere Hebre," Yosser chimed in with such youthful vigour, he seemed more like a hopeful teenager than a jaded man in his early twenties. "Where once there were imps, gifted only in destruction and despair, with the changing by Hebre, you became demigods who brought benevolence and succour."

Laurel had the grace to be humbled by such an accolade, even though she felt it went too far. However, Ava showed less restraint and burst out laughing, causing several people to turn from their cakes of bread.

"What!" she exclaimed. "We're just people, everyday people. Granted, we have these extra abilities, but really, we're just *normal!*"

Where most would have thought such an outburst in the face of Yosser's discourse, despite the solemnity behind the words might offend, it seemed to amuse some of those gathered; even Sedar managed a smile.

"Normal?" Abel gave a small laugh. "On your world, would a phenomenon such as the turning of the mischievous imps not be regarded as miraculous or divine? And if strange lights in the heavens preceded such a change? Or when two women stretch forth their hands to command the elements to bring rain and make crops grow?"

Laurel had to agree that on Earth, such events would have been deemed inexplicable or to those so inclined, miraculous, so she added, "On my world, Earth, many ancient people believed that gods visited them from the heavens. There are thousands of books written on the subject, cave paintings, ancient texts. I'm afraid we're undeserving of this admiration. We're still learning how the nebula entities influenced Hebre of earlier times and how they influence us now. I'm not even sure Ava and I can call ourselves Hebre."

"I see the spirit of Hebre in your eyes," Abel said, and as he spoke, Laurel felt a strange draw to him, a memory that slipped away as her mind tried to hold it. He felt it too, and the moment passed between them, unnoticed by anyone else. Abel didn't allow her to explore the vision; his next words were to the gathering, forcing her to put the thought away for later analysis.

"A Hebre woman," Abel continued, "who did not speak of family and not known to the Edensai, came from the East. She sought the wisdom of our Holy Trah, our mother, who embraced her and loved her." He looked down fondly at Hagar, who nodded at the memory. "And it came to be that the Hebre looked upon this woman, called Judith by her own word, as their leader. It was she who bade Hebre live by our mother's teachings." A soft murmur rose from the people and the esteem in which this Judith was held sent a tingle into Laurel's spine.

"When the masters split Sheerguhd," Abel said, "Hebre suffered beside the Edensai, the Riynea and the Kalmeddi. Legion swept across this land with murder in their hearts, and none could stand against them." His voice softened as he spoke of the woman he loved more than life itself. "Judith commanded Hebre to hold fast the customs of the Edensai, but as the blood of more innocents stained the land, so Judith's anger grew. When the masters attacked Riynea and Kalmed, she gathered Hebre to her. They would resist the masters, but she did not ask the Edensai to bear arms, nor kill."

"And would they have? Killed, I mean," Ava asked.

Hagar pulled Abel down to whisper into his ear, to help him tell the story she could not.

"Edensai love Hebre," Abel said, translating Hagar's breathy utterance, evoking the same tenderness in his voice that Hagar communicated. "In flesh, many Edensai are their children, returned to them from evil, but their spirits were of the nebula, and they had no more authority over the choices of the Edensai than they had over the masters. Our mother tells us in the events that followed, many people came to believe God himself sent Hebre."

"Did the Hebre engage the masters or Legion in battle?" Marcel asked.

Hagar nodded, but Abel was her voice. "They did fight but without weapons. Hebre's speed allowed hand to hand combat, but their greatest weapons were their words. Judith and her companion, Esther, forced low altitude Legion transports from the sky, using nought but their minds. Legion was unprepared for this resistance where before, there had been none, and the soldiers were overcome. Judith offered peace, and so many confessed they had become weary of their duty. They joined with the Edensai in tradition."

"What happened to those who wouldn't be converted?"

"Hebre executed them," Abel said matter-of-factly.

Harry shouldn't have been surprised. He'd seen Laurel in a fight; she didn't take prisoners, but that didn't stop him blurting out, "They didn't return them to the masters?"

Abel made a slight shift with his shoulder as a question, and Harry didn't pursue his comment; it made sense not to send them back to swell Legion ranks.

"It sounds like the Hebre were not against killing then?" Ava sent to her mother.

"So it seems,"

"Can you tell us about the masters?" Ava said. "We know nothing of their history."

"The masters claim descent from Benjamin," Abel replied in a matter of fact tone, "the first-born son of the creator of the universe. Legion is descended from David, the defender of the heavens and the creator's second son."

"This creator is a lone man?" Ava asked.

"Male, yes, not a physical being. The masters say no mortal can behold him, that his majesty and magnificence would rob the light from their eyes."

"You are, were Legion. You evidently didn't believe that?" Marcel said, trying to mask his irritation with all this religious jiggery-pokery. He had no time for superstition. He preferred facts, but his sister picked up his thoughts and frowned at him. *"Can't you be a little more open-minded for once?"* Marcel shrank a little at her unspoken admonishment. She was right. Maybe some mysteries defy explanation. His sister's abilities were a mystery, and he accepted her.

"This creator had two sons?" Harry asked. "Was there a female creator as well, or was that not necessary?" It occurred to him someone with the skill to create a universe might not need the opposite sex to procreate. Although he wasn't convinced all this was anything more than myth.

"The mother of Benjamin and David was Lilith."

"The plague?" Ava blurted out.

All eyes swung to Ava, who put her hand to her mouth in mortification. "I'm so sorry," she said, "I hope I didn't offend. I know very little about such things."

"I feel like an idiot. How could I have been so insensitive? Again!" Ava sent to Laurel.

"It doesn't seem to have done any harm. I'm surprised it was you that said it and not Marcel."

"I just told him to shut up a minute ago and not be narrow-minded."

Laurel bit back a grin, *"Oh well, there goes your example."*

Marcel was still deliberating over Abel's earlier remark. "You said 'defender'. If there is only one universe and everything in it belongs to this creator, why does it need defending?"

"It is a story told by the masters' to satisfy themselves and to control Legion," Abel said. "It is not the truth; it is a lie."

"Do you know the truth?" Marcel pressed Abel for an answer, but Laurel sensed hesitation in the older man.

"We have myths and legends on my world," Laurel said quickly, seeing he needed time, and perhaps trust to answer Marcel. "And we have scripture which many believe is the word of their god."

"And do you believe this scripture?" Abel asked, grateful for the reprieve.

Laurel shook her head, causing a few fair curls to come

loose from her scarf and drift down onto her shoulder, an action he recognised and loved, but he kept his emotion deeply suppressed. If she sensed his reaction, she gave no indication.

"I have learned that truth is often found in the most unexpected places," she answered, because lately, that had been her experience.

"This creator the masters believe in. Do they worship him as a god?" Marcel asked, finding the whole concept unbelievable and primitive. It was all rubbish as far as he was concerned, but he would try not to sound judgemental.

"They would be angry to have him so diminished," Abel said. "Humankind apportions human attributes to their gods; anger, generosity, love. They maintain a god can be urged to intercede for man in matters of war, fear, even love. To the masters, such a god would have all the frailty of the humans they despise."

"So why do they hate humans, but not species like the Farisee?" Harry asked.

"They tell us their almighty creator gave in to lust and discarded his mate Lilith in favour of Eve. It was from the union with Eve that humankind was born. With Lilith, he could not create such beauty and perfection. This created enmity between Eve and Lilith."

"What did Judith teach that changed your people?" Laurel knew this was the same question that Marcel had asked moments before about truth, and she felt Abel would answer her, if only in part.

"Judith had remarkable wisdom," Abel said. "She knew things of the universe that many did not. She told us the truth; that the masters were not divine, that we were a creation in a decaying world."

"Created by whom? Not this god you mentioned?"

"Judith did not say who created the Menwora," Abel answered, "only that it was a world with a dying sun. Their end of days had begun. The Menworan ruler lost his children in one of the natural catastrophes befalling the planet. In his grief, and perhaps in his selfishness, the Menworan ruler called the physicians and holy men to restore their lives."

"Did they succeed?"

"They did," Abel nodded, "but Judith did not tell us how this was accomplished, only that the Benjamin who returned from the realm of death was not the gentle man who departed this life. The likeness who rose from the grave was evil, cruel, exacting harsh punishments in the name of Lilith. He killed his father, and the ruling council sought to banish Benjamin from Menwora."

"And the ruler's other children who died?"

Abel shook his head but hesitated long enough for Laurel to guess he knew more than he cared to tell. "I am not certain. I do know that Benjamin was able to procreate after he was resurrected and founded his own tribe. The ruling council sought the help of spiritual advisors, the Sons of David, to find a way to stop the evil."

"The Sons of David—your forefathers," Laurel smiled. From somewhere deep inside, she felt the pieces of the puzzle reorganising themselves.

"Yes," Abel said, "but none of the tribes on Menwora were space going, so there was no way to banish Benjamin.

The Sons of David were men of great physical strength, men of intellect and science, but they were also cloistered and reclusive. Several among them were custodians of a powerful fragment of a star said to be forged in creation. This sacred task was handed down through generations to a certain few who knew its power."

Laurel saw the connection; the Sons of David were also the Soul Mongers' forebears, and the sacred star was the Magen.

"The Sons of David rallied but were subdued by the Sons of Benjamin," Abel continued. "Judith told us some families of the Sons of David were taken hostage to ensure the Sons of David's compliance, then Benjamin plucked a ship from the sky and fled into Sheerguhd."

Laurel was confused how this planet, Menwora, would exist in isolation. If a passing spaceship could be "plucked", one would have to wonder about its crew's capabilities to detect life on the planet.

"So there were other, space-going species in the area?" she said, "perhaps studying the dying sun? Not realising Menwora was inhabited?"

"Perhaps."

"Just men? Only sons?" Marcel asked. "No females?"

"Yes," Ava said. "Are there female masters?"

"No," Abel gave a short reply, the subject of the masters' procreation was not for this forum, "but Judith did speak of the high status of women amongst the Menworan."

Laurel quickly found Harry's thoughts and deflected his next question of how the masters perpetuated their race, sensing Abel's reluctance. "What has happened to the Sons of David since they've been here?" she asked.

"Since being welcomed on Eden, some have taken wives," Abel said, once more sidestepping the subject of procreation. "As Legion, they were as all humans, but no women are among their ranks."

Laurel understood now the curiosity when Sedar saw Scarlett. A female Legion and a possible future Magen Bearer.

"If this Benjamin was brought back from the dead, is he immortal?" Marcel asked, the idea making his flesh crawl. That would be a formidable foe indeed. "And the others who were resurrected, if there were any? Are we dealing with something that cannot be destroyed?"

Abel folded his large, calloused hands over his knee and looked down. "No, Benjamin did not continue," he said quietly. "He dwelt amongst the living only long enough to found an army of unnatural beings and to corrupt the noble Sons of David. Judith offered no more of the story, only to say that reparation will always be demanded from those who violate natural law. Some believed Judith's account to be a fabrication to distract Legion and bring them to the side of the Edensai. We'd never heard of Menwora, and some questioned how she could know of such things, but those who followed her didn't doubt." Abel paused. "She was wise."

"Is it any different to the Farisee believing in gods they've never seen?" Laurel said. "Or the Edensai's obedience to their faith? You found her words an inspiration."

"Until the conversion and the rebellion," Abel

explained, "neither Legion nor the masters were aware of Hebre amongst the Edensai. When Hebre resisted, the masters hunted them and took those they captured as hostages, but Judith, Esther and one other, Jonathon, escaped to Faris in a scout, hidden from the sight of the masters. They returned with three arks, undetected by the masters and made ready for the exodus.

"Their fury at the change in so many of their soldiers caused the masters themselves to visit the source of the betrayal. They tortured the Edensai below the north with their stench, massacred the people in the villages and towns, murdered men, women and children and left their bodies to rot where they fell." The gathering listened in sadness and silence; for some, it was history; for Laurel and the others, it was shocking and new. Abel bowed his head. "There is nothing in the central lands now but a mass grave," he said sadly. "The masters vowed a swift end to the Edensai if the rest of the Hebre did not yield."

"And did they?"

Abel nodded. "Some, but they wanted Judith, believing it was she who rallied Hebre against them. As the Farisee boarded the refugees on the arks, Judith went to the masters' ship."

"Alone?" Laurel was warming to this Judith. She had plenty of spirit.

"Judith was unencumbered by fear," Abel said, as if fear were a thing that came with a choice. "She taught us death is simply the shedding of the mortal; it is the spirit that endures. But she knew the day to part with her mortal body had not yet come, her purpose not yet fulfilled."

Her purpose not yet fulfilled? Laurel frowned. That's what Helen spoke of that night on the terrace on Isilia. Did the entity return to the nebula when its physical life was over, its purpose fulfilled? Was Helen in the nebula? Xavier? Gabriel and his mother? All whole souls? What about whole souls who died on Earth, far from the nebula? Did they even die on Earth, or did they somehow continue? Too many questions, and right now, Laurel was keen to know what happened next.

"Did Judith rescue the captive Hebre?"

"She did. And never told us what came to pass on the masters' ship," Abel said. "We know she was there, but how she got there is a mystery. The Farisee helped with the evacuation, and none of their scout ships were where Judith could have accessed them. Judith returned with the Hebre and didn't speak of the experience."

"That's a puzzle," Laurel sent to Ava, *"no way of getting from the surface. Unless… I wonder if Judith possessed the skill of teleportation like the woman in Isilia's history. Could that be a possibility?"*

Ava gave a secretive flick of her eyebrows, not wanting to give away she and her mother were chatting privately. *"Yes, that seems reasonable, but she may not have advertised this skill to the Edensai, so don't say anything."*

Hagar pulled Abel's sleeve once again to whisper in his ear, and he recited Hagar's words to them. "Our Mother says the greater mystery is the sudden cessation of all activity from both masters and Legion after Judith returned here."

"Do you know why?" Marcel wondered how Judith even managed to get off the ship alive if the masters were looking for her and how she brought other Hebre with her.

"I wish I could tell you, friend," Abel said. "I know only that the exodus continued, and apart from one incident with a Magen Bearer who was returning from Riynea, the arks entered Sheerguhd. As Hagar says, it is an abiding mystery. When the Eye of Sheerguhd opened to welcome the arks, not a single Hebre nor Magen Bearer was left on Eden."

Laurel thought about the words Ilivi showed her on Isilia, "Let my people go", which she said were written in a language her people had not understood. Thinking back, Laurel believed those words to be Hebrew because she recognised them so quickly, but now, she had doubts. Maybe they were Menworan. Is this what Judith said to the masters? Did the invaders respond to a request from a lone woman? This Judith fascinated her; Laurel even felt a kinship and decided she would ask more about her if the opportunity arose.

"You say the arks left unhindered," Harry said, "but didn't the masters and Legion follow them?"

"Aye, one hundred and sixty masters," Abel told him, "more than a hundred Legion and one of the two remaining Magen Bearers. This was no match for so many Hebre, and they did not start their pursuit for many days, but they were arrogant, determined. We cannot explain their delay."

Laurel's head snapped up! Abel was lying! He knew what took place! This was the fairy story part added to placate a superstitious people. Laurel was about to send him a solid psionic communication to ask him what he thought he was doing, but she found her way barred. If she pushed, she could have navigated the barrier, but he would have his reasons for maintaining his silence. She settled for widening her eyes to let him know she knew. He answered her with a slight flick of his eyebrows, then looked down at the old lady propped wearily against his shoulder. "I fear Hagar is tired now," he said, indicating to Yosser to help the old woman to her rest. "She seldom leaves her bed, but today—" he smiled at the visitors, "is a special day."

<hr>

The evening had drawn in, and most people retired to small groups as Abel concluded his story of Hebre and Judith. Laurel, Sedar and Abel sat together in one group and Ava, Marcel, Yosser and Harry in another. Laurel felt a draught of warm air from above, causing her to shiver. She hadn't noticed the cold until the warmth hit her shoulders. Abel pointed to an array of pipes above their head.

"It's powered by solar energy," he explained, "but because the solar collector on the roof is limited, it is not easily seen from above. Unfortunately, the sun's rays are weak at this time of year. This single pipe offers some protection against the cold. It also powers a small evaporation unit which produces some drinking water."

Laurel was impressed. The central tube was similar in design to an air-conditioning conduit. It had a tacked together look about it, but still, she admired innovation in the face of adversity. "Did you construct it?"

Abel gave a breathy laugh, his bushy beard puffing out rhythmically. "No, I'm not an engineer. The Farisee placed one of these in as many shelters as they could, but the units are fragile, overuse causes them to breakdown, and they aren't replaceable."

"I saw groups of people lighting fires when we arrived," Laurel said.

Abel sighed. "Legion will strike if they see, although some would prefer a quick end than the misery and starvation planned by the masters. They have lost hope."

"We would like to learn as much as we can," Laurel said, "But I—" she took a deep breath, "I find it so hard to believe these people accepted you. Your conversion to their ways must have been indeed profound."

"Hebre accepted us," Abel acknowledged that truth with a simple raising of his hands. "Magen Bearers, Legion, all those who turned from the masters were accepted, without suspicion, without enmity." He nodded sagely. "Hebre knew our hearts. It was time to make peace, and although we have adapted to the Edensai teaching of peace, we have not yet sworn ourselves to it."

Later, Abel walked out to the ship with them. The stench of the lake seemed less in the evening, and Laurel supposed the hours they'd spent at the compound might have offered some immunity from the smell, or perhaps it competed with the aroma of unwashed bodies they encountered in the compound itself, but it still made Laurel's eyes water. Harry felt like someone had stuffed the smelliest parts of a dead animal's offal up his nose. Seeing Marcel's aghast expression, he clearly felt the same. Harry was eager to get back into the ship and recycled air. Next visit, he'd bring a desensitising mask.

"If you require us to summon other Sons of David, if

you find a way to defeat the masters, I pledge we will stand in defiance beside you," Abel told Laurel, making clear his commitment to Hebre. "The Farisee communicate with us and will transport my people from the outlying communities; they can take the word back to their people. Our will drives us…" Abel clenched his fists and held them up in a show of strength, "and our bare hands will be our weapons. It is all we have to offer."

"Leave that to us," Harry said. "We can supply weapons, but first, may we return to set up a clinic to help your people? I had hoped to do something today."

"I fear you might be overwhelmed."

Harry grinned. "Abel, we are fortunate to have advanced equipment, and we will bring Beril to help. I believe we will manage."

Laurel waited until the others were on board, holding back to ask one more thing of Abel. She wanted to know why he lied. "The Benjamin and David story wasn't the only truth Judith told you, was it?"

He clasped his hands in front of him. "There are many versions of the truth."

"You've got one that has no variations."

He smiled. "That certain Hebre hold a unique bond with Time? And that's how they managed to evade the masters?"

"I knew you were keeping something back,"

Abel gave a slight nod. He knew she knew.

"Will you tell me more? About what happened when Judith went to the masters' ship?" Laurel said as she stepped onto the ship's ramp.

Abel's answer only added to the mystery. "There is much of the story that is not mine to tell."

Abel watched as the ship morphed into invisibility, and he remained there even as the night deepened. In the distance, he heard the community preparing to sleep. Yosser came out to stand with him.

"You didn't tell her?"

"What would you have me say, my young friend?" Abel replied with a smile.

"The truth," Yosser said levelly, "that it was her who brought you from darkness."

"She doesn't remember me, Yosser."

"She must remember," Yosser scoffed at the idea. "She is Hebre. You saw her eyes! How can she forget?"

Abel looked up at the stars. Judith was not like the other Hebre, and even though fifteen years had passed, he still mourned. They all knew her story; she appeared from the east, no explanation of family, no identity, just her name. When she left on the ark, Abel spent many long hours just watching, hoping she would return. As years passed, he almost gave up. Seeing this woman, so like Judith in every way, even after Sedar's warning she had no memory of them, threatened to send him roaring to his knees at the unfairness. But he didn't. Instead, he looked down at his companion.

"I believe centuries have passed for her."

Yosser shook his head at his friend's unwillingness to accept his words. "I do not understand you, Abel. She loved you. Even when I was a child, I knew this truth. She was your wife!"

"*Judith* was my wife, Yosser. This woman? Perhaps somehow, the spirit of Judith has endured, or her likeness passed down through many generations." He grinned and placed a hand on the younger man's shoulder. "Esther also seems to have descendants."

Yosser gave a little snort in response, reflecting on his astonishment at seeing Ava. The young Hebre woman, Esther, had welcomed the little boy Yosser into her home and heart when he lost his parents to Legion. Although less than a decade his senior, she had been a light amongst all the chaos and sadness as he grew up. And alongside Judith, Esther proved one of the most powerful of all Hebre.

"Did you see the mountain who walked beside her and whom she called brother?"

"I did see him," Abel said. "Her protector, I think."

CHAPTER FOURTEEN _

During the trip back to the station, Ava, Marcel and Harry engaged in general conversation about their meeting with Abel. Laurel's empathic senses told her Abel would be a strong ally, but she replayed that moment repeatedly in her head, that moment earlier when she felt she recognised his smile, had caught a faint hint of spice; smoky, warm and intimate, and his sigh, a murmur against her hair, their tears mingling as he held her. She'd whispered words to soothe him so long ago…

Laurel brought her attention back to the conversation, feeling disloyal to Harry to have shared such an intimate image with Abel, even one so fleeting. She turned her attention to Sedar, who appeared to be deliberately steering clear of any telepathic link with her or Ava. If he were a spy, he would have been well placed to see their thoughts, so it puzzled her initially as to why he chose not to at least try. It occurred to her that if he was being coerced somehow by the masters, then the least he knew, the least knowledge he could impart, but it was still risky. For now, they would not include him in any strategies or decisions regarding the masters.

As soon as they were back on the Canaa, they told

Darlen of everything that had gone down on the planet.

"Two Magen Bearers remained, not one," Marcel said, "the one who went into Sheerguhd to follow the arks and another. I did wonder about that when Ilivi told us; the masters stranding themselves didn't seem much of a strategy."

"It changes the game a bit," Laurel agreed. "It means that at any time, they could just blitz Eden and head out towards the Transcender. Then what?"

"They'll get into the next kingdom," Darlen ventured. "League space, I'd say."

"Would that mean they'd encounter Baii and Ilivi?" Ava felt she would do anything to protect them. "Hopefully, the masters would encounter a species like the Ferle first."

Laurel thought for a moment; naturally, Ava would be concerned about Baii. "I'm not sure," she said, "perhaps it depends upon where Sheerg….the Transcender opens out." She shook her head. "Calling it Sheerguhd feels strange. I felt we had shifted in time when we arrived on Isilia, so they might miss them altogether, but I don't plan on speculating on what they might do. We need to stop them. There were quite a few men there who didn't speak but who I think were former Legion, and there are more in the outlying communities. If Abel is representative of them, they will fight, but they all look tired, even Abel, and no doubt most are suffering the effects of toxicity and hunger."

There was a treatment they could offer the community to ease the effects of malnutrition, treat the bone cancers Harry had surreptitiously diagnosed with the palm pandroscope during their visit, plus synthesise a nutritional supplement for the Farisee cakes. They would need Mer to process the supplements and treatments on the surface, and Darlen assured them he could cope without him for a day or two. Improving health would lift the people's spirits, and if the Sons of David fought, they needed to be in the best condition possible. Laurel and Harry knew they could never get to the other communities, not if their priority was stopping the masters, and that was where their focus had to lie. Fixing the numerous health conditions was pointless if there was no future, but for now, they didn't have a strategy, and they needed to see if Darlen could manufacture weapons and gain further intelligence about the masters' ship. Treating the ailments in the community would be a productive way to pass the time.

They turned their attention to discussing several possibilities of assault on the masters and discarded each one as unworkable, even if they had a substantial army. None of the group could come up with a solution that would even the odds between them and the murderous Legion that remained loyal to the masters. The Edensai had never waged war, the Kalmeddi and Riynea had never borne arms and the Faris…well, little point in looking to them as combat partners, and right now, they had no idea of how many former Legion would join the crusade.

Laurel changed the subject; they needed a break from thoughts of conflict. "They knew us," she said to Darlen. "Not just as any Hebre—" she pointed to her eyes, "but as people they once knew."

"I peeked into Yosser's mind," Ava said. "As he was younger, he…" she scrunched up her face.

"He what?" Marcel asked.

"He definitely thought I was someone else. Someone he was fond of."

Laurel nodded. "I got that. Abel was very good at keeping his mind singularly focused. I suspect he has had much to do with the Hebre. I must admit, every way we look, what we believe is turned on its head. I thought it was the Hebre who were the original inhabitants of Eden."

"So did I," Ava said. "If we have really stepped back in time, it would explain why they believe they know us. If not, we must be uncannily similar to the Hebre they did know. Is it possible that we, or perhaps all the whole souls who made it to Earth, were never meant to remain there?"

"Maybe Soul Mongers are just couriers," Laurel suggested. "If Hebre can't access the nebula from Earth, they would need a Soul Monger—a Magen Bearer to get them through the Transcender. Perhaps our journey here was somehow written in the stars."

"Mom!" Ava laughed. "How poetic."

But Laurel wasn't trying to make a romantic statement. She was serious. "The merging of Edensai imps and Hebre came about because of a virus; a virus with origins we have yet to discover. It would take more research, but as the children of the imps were better developed than the imp parent, I can't help but wonder what transpired when those children grew up and procreated."

Darlen laughed out loud. "The Farisee think you're some kind of fantastic creation from the loins of a goddess!"

"Yes," Laurel pulled a face at him, "well, that's far-fetched, but still, how did Hebre entities come into being?

And why haven't the nebula entities entered the masters and turned their hearts like they did the imps? We also learned, Darlen, that the so-called Sons of David are your forebears, custodians of an ancient star said to be forged in creation. The forerunners of the Magen Bearers. Abel told us your ancestors were men of intellect and science. What do you think of that?"

Darlen gave her a wide grin. "Not much has changed, has it? No mystery there," he laughed.

"And while we're on the subject of mysteries," Laurel continued, "there's something else."

Realising the joke about his intellect was over, Darlen listened to Laurel's thoughts about Sedar. "What possible reason could he have to sell us out?" he said, but the others had nothing to contribute. Only Laurel had a suggestion.

"Leverage," she said. "Sedar's careful to avoid entering our minds—" she gestured to Ava. "He lets us into his, but he has a threshold we can't get beyond. He's deliberately not listening to our thoughts now. I think the less he knows, the less he can tell the masters. They've got something over him."

"They've got something over everyone," Darlen said. "What would be the point? They all seem resigned to their fate."

"I don't know," Laurel shrugged. "Hebre resisted the masters and rescued thousands of people. If the masters know we're here, we could all be in danger."

"In that case, we should shoot him."

"Darlen, we can't kill Sedar," Harry said, although he didn't wholly disagree, not if Sedar was likely to put them all in danger. Still, "He might be useful."

"You mean like that young master?" Darlen practically read Harry's mind. To Harry, both Sedar and the young master were potential threats, but they could offer further insight.

"Stop talking about killing," Laurel scolded them. "We don't know anything for sure yet. We need to find out more."

Happy he'd rattled up the atmosphere, Darlen turned back to the conversations the others had on Eden. "Did you get any more background on the masters? The war?"

"Some," Laurel said. "A Hebre woman, Judith, seemed to possess specific insight about the masters' history; she used it to convert the Legion and Magen Bearers."

"What specific insight?"

"The masters claimed to be divine, but she knew their claims were lies." Laurel then related the story Abel told them about how Benjamin was restored to life but fabricated a creation story to elevate their prestige.

Darlen whistled. "Wow, does this mean the masters are immortal?" Then he gave Laurel a mischievous grin; she would be the only one who knew what he meant when he laughingly said, "Are they zombies?" the statement drawing a "be serious" glare from Laurel. Marcel had no idea what Darlen was talking about, or even saw the humour.

"Well, I asked if they were immortal," he said, "but Abel said Benjamin died again a few years later."

"I think Abel knew this Judith," Laurel said, their shared moment still fresh in her mind. "He said Hebre have a unique relationship with Time."

"So, could we sneak up and take the masters unawares?"

Darlen shook his head. "I told you, Marcel. On Eden, Time is stable, but Laurel and Ava could cloak a battalion and sneak up on them that way."

"We haven't got a battalion," Marcel said. "Not yet, anyway."

"Neither do we have all the facts," Harry pointed out. "Abel did say there are more arks. We may be able to mount another exodus."

"I wonder how the masters managed to keep their species going?" Laurel noted Abel carefully avoided being drawn into any conversation with the strangers about procreation. "It would appear Legion have procured human females before for breeding, and the converts have taken Hebre and Edensai wives. I can see this is where the whole soul lines have continued, but the masters…"

Harry wondered about that too. "We'll have to ask Beril. I'd like to know why they don't have the means to wean that boy either."

Darlen stood and yawned. He, for one, would be sleeping on it. "Let's not get too distracted. Better we pull together a battle plan, take it to this Abel, beat the crap out of the masters and get the hell out of here. Then no-one will have to worry about them producing more of the little bastards."

CHAPTER FIFTEEN _

The following day, Laurel and Harry sought out Beril, whose demeanour and facial expression gave them a quick heads up that he found the subject of both the masters' reproduction and weaning distasteful. However, he knew he would have to impart the knowledge, so he cautioned Laurel and Harry about the graphic nature of both practices, reluctantly accepting their assurances they were prepared for anything. Beril knew better. What he was about to show them was beyond their imagination. He produced two slides. Lifting the first, he thrust it into view.

"We have no way of confirming the accuracy of this report," he said. "This is an extrapolation from the information of a Magen Bearer. However, no Legion nor Magen Bearer has ever witnessed this event; it appears to be at best hearsay, and at worst, a falsehood handed down from their forefathers. There is a theory the ancestors of the masters, the Menworan, reproduced in this way, even though I would have to question how any human species would have this ability. Legion, who now once more call themselves the Sons of David, have faint memories, fragments of the oral traditions that say the woman was made from the rib of a man, but we have no way of verifying from them if this brutality is fact or not. We are speaking of possible truths lost in centuries of lies."

The first slide showed a graphic illustration of an adult master removing one of his own lower ribs. While there was little in the way of physical description, and the focus was mainly on the actual procedure, it was easy to gain the view this was a huge man with a robust skeleton. Beril had composed the slides, and his sole interest was producing an account of the reproductive process as told to him by the Legion soldier. He'd used some data from the captive young master to project bone density and size.

The graphic depicted surprisingly little blood, with the master appearing to simply reach in through his skin and snap off the lowermost rib. The extracted rib was unusually thick and looked more of a density than one would find even in a thigh bone. The master lifted the bone to his mouth, where he held it at a distance of a hand's breadth. From his mouth, a torrent of milky fluid poured forth from two open glands inside his cheeks, saturating the bone and creating a sac that swelled until the liquid ceased discharging. Beril halted the presentation.

"The masters call this fluid 'bane'," he said. "Contact with it can paralyse."

"Bane?" Laurel had heard that word before. "It's an old term used on Earth for something that causes death."

Beril inclined his head. "I have not seen it kill, but I can't be sure."

"I think it looks like variance fluid," Laurel said, looking at Harry to see if he had come to the same conclusion. "Darlen has owned up to it containing bodily fluids."

"I shudder to think," Harry grimaced at the thought, "but you're right, it does, although Darlen isn't a master, and he doesn't have these glands in his mouth."

"No, but think back to Abel's story. It might be a naturally occurring enzyme on the Menworan homeworld. The two races could share a common ancestor."

"It is my opinion," Beril said, "as basically the only physician left, that the broth the master produces can influence the molecular pathways and hormonal structure of the bone. We have been fortunate enough to study the remains of one of their females. There is little to distinguish her from any female. The boy we have here has not produced this broth; he may be too young. I haven't been able to get close enough to examine the glands and see if I could stimulate production, but the Magen Bearer who brought me this information cautioned me the broth contains paralytic agents. Unfortunately, our instruments are inadequate for the task of such an examination. Even your pandroscope gave no further information."

"I could examine the glands," Laurel said thoughtfully.

Beril and Harry stared at her.

"You could," Harry responded slowly after a moment. He didn't want to encourage such a venture.

"It would be unsafe," Beril said. "He is powerful."

Harry knew his caution would fall on deaf ears, so he grinned proudly despite his caution. "So is she."

Beril dipped his head to acknowledge Harry's appraisal of Laurel's abilities before returning to the slide. "What follows is a maturation stage. The rib remains protected within the broth, similar to an amniotic sac, until it reaches term. I saw no point in guessing what transpires at this stage, as from what the Magen Bearer told me, it sounded almost identical to human gestation in that the foetus remains within the sac until it is ready. There the similarity ends." Beril displayed the second slide. "The female is never 'born'. She simply begins to exist, to fulfil a purpose once the sac ruptures." The slide showed a girl of around fourteen emerging from the sac.

"And that purpose is to procreate?" Laurel asked.

Beril nodded. "The female we examined would have had normal internal organs but, interestingly, a bifurcated uterus. Copulation, a once-only act by the male, is vicious and results in significant injuries that never heal. Conception results in a twin pregnancy."

"What do you mean by 'vicious'?" Harry looked at the life-sized version of the female; even by human standards, she was small and slender. A man the size of a master could do severe damage.

Beril overlaid an image of the young master and displayed it next to the adult male. "While you see that the youth has small sex organs, the adult male does not. We have not had the opportunity to study an adult male medically, but modesty is not a characteristic, and as they are surprisingly impervious to heat and cold, they often go naked. It is reported that their penis size is entirely proportional to their physical size. The women, as you can see, are diminutive, perhaps to make them easy to dominate. Pregnancy occurs at the first and only mating."

"The story of a woman being fashioned from the rib

of a man is one I've heard before," Laurel said.

"Where did you hear it?" Harry knew for sure Laurel hadn't heard it in the League.

"On Earth, it's just a line in a book, supposed to be ancient texts," she told them. "I've mentioned the book before, Harry, the bible."

"A record of your people?" Beril did not welcome the news that Hebre encountered these practices elsewhere.

Laurel saw her comment had rattled him. "Some say it is, Beril. I have found a few things here with parallels to that book. I can't explain it."

Beril gave her a long look. He was sure Hebre would have seen much in their travels since leaving here. He continued with the presentation.

"We believe the resulting pregnancy lasts around seven months, and the twin infants are of equal size to newborn humans of good weight. We assume the duration of the labour and attributes of childbirth are the same as for any human."

"Beril," Harry said, "you mentioned you didn't have the means to wean the young master here. Why is that?"

Beril swept away the slides of the masters and displayed a breastfeeding woman. Quite unlike the peaceful maternal bonding between mother and child any human woman would have been entitled to, the alarming spectacle showed two violent infants tearing at the breasts of a screaming female, her milk blending with blood. It was graphic enough for Laurel to know the birth would have been equally traumatic.

"I will greatly multiply her sorrow and her conception.

In sorrow will she bring forth children," she said quietly to herself, quoting a passage from the bible. Harry looked at her but didn't comment.

The woman seemed designed only to suffer, to endure pain. The two male infants bit and ripped at her, and she bled from several wounds. The fact it was a simulation did nothing to mitigate its shock value.

"The infants grow far more quickly than human children, as you have seen," Beril said. "In this next image, we have true images of the remains of the mother recovered by a Son of David. He told us she and one twin had died, but of course, we suspect he helped that process or there would have been nothing of her left. The other twin is the one held here; they were in the process of weaning."

The slide showed a partially decapitated body. The interior of the body cavity was more or less devoid of viscera, one arm mutilated, and the rib cage crushed and splintered. What bones remained intact were covered in bite marks. The genitalia was missing. The woman's other arm was twisted and flung above her head, but most of the digits gnawed away. Jagged tears covered the arm, and subcutaneous fat bled out onto the skin. Beril waited as Laurel and Harry took in the image.

"They eat their mother?"

Beril understood their horror. "They seem to reach a point where the mother's milk is either inadequate or where they no longer require her to nurture them, so they turn on her and rip her to pieces, feeding on her for several days. Mutilation is their initiation into adulthood. After this, their diet is of protein only; we know they eat the flesh of animals, but..."

"But what?" Harry prompted.

Beril bowed his head. "We believe it is the reason some people were left on Kalmeddi as a source of food."

Laurel placed her hand gently on Beril's arm; this was too distressing for him. "We should stop now. You've given us a lot of information."

Beril recovered himself quickly. He had a part to play here, and he would not let his sadness take precedence over his chance to help. "I believe, if you are to fight these beasts, you need to know everything we know."

"You always say know your enemy," Harry reminded Laurel of one of her oft-quoted sayings during the Gartyran war. Possibly, it was never more apt than now, and Laurel still believed in its importance.

"Do you still have the female?" she asked Beril.

Beril indicated that they follow him, but Laurel hesitated. "You know, Harry, you go. I'm going to find Darlen and visit the young master."

They found the boy sleeping on the floor, shunning any "human" comforts Beril and Sedar had provided. When he turned, Laurel saw he rallied his contempt, but she also felt a sense of defeat. Laurel felt empathy, but she knew it was the natural compassion of one viewing a feral kitten that would one day grow to be a destroyer of wildlife. And like the kitten, this being was a killer, and she would not choke on the feeling that allowing him to live would be a disservice to all humankind.

"I've come to examine you. I won't hurt you," she lied.

She would hurt him if he attacked her.

The boy got to his feet in a single graceful movement, standing as close to the containment field as his body allowed. He glanced once at Darlen, weapon at the ready, then returned his gaze to Laurel. As before, when Laurel entered the boy's mind, she found no ordered thoughts, just a focus of blind rage, anger and hostility. Apart from one thing. Laurel tilted her head thoughtfully when she encountered it, taking a moment to unravel the sensation. Not mourning, nor regret; it was *hunger*. An insatiable need for flesh. The image of the woman he and his brother were devouring when he was captured lingered in his mind.

"Your mother?" Laurel ventured.

"It provided meat," the boy spat instantly as if anticipating her question. "I am stripped of my birthright."

"And that is why your people abandon you?"

The boy didn't need to answer. Without that rite of passage, the savaging of his mother, the symbolic destruction of Eve, he could not join the ranks of the masters. He was immature, inadequate, still requiring milk, not yet fully weaned. He knew his people would not come.

Laurel lowered the containment field. The boy didn't move, just watched her, hissing softly, causing her to again liken him to a feral kitten, unsure of the approach of an unknown, bigger cat, but he made no move to attack. Laurel didn't doubt if it came to it, she would prove considerably stronger than this boy, both physically and mentally, but with that prospect, she wondered how she would compare if she met one of the adult males. She held up the palm pandroscope, and the boy followed the instrument's movements as it built detailed images of his body. The pandroscope showed dense bone minerals, the signal so strong that the rib cage was virtually steel. It made Laurel wonder how much protection the contents of the chest needed. She touched him, and still he didn't move. He ceased hissing when her fingers contacted the skin on his neck, smooth and distinctly chilly. At her request, he obediently opened his mouth. Focused imaging with the pandroscope and physical examination revealed two glands at the back of the mouth at either side of the tongue. Laurel applied external pressure at the site of the glands, hoping they would yield at least a drop of the bane for analysis, but none was forthcoming. Laurel guessed these were tied to the boy's sexual maturity and reproductive system, still undeveloped, but she had nothing by which to compare. It would be likely only adult males produce the serum able to turn a rib, even ones such as these, into a human female. Disappointed that she could not extract a sample, she signalled to Darlen to reignite the containment field, but as she stepped back, the boy lunged, his teeth bared, his exquisite features transformed into the face of a demon. Too quick for him, and even for Darlen to react with his sidearm, she instinctively soared high from a standing position and kicked the boy to the side of the head. Several teeth flew out of his mouth with the impact, one eye protruded from its socket, and his body hit the bulkhead with considerable force.

Laurel drew a deep breath as the young master's lifeless body slid to the ground, both arms twisted behind him and his head at an odd angle. The boy's demonic face relaxed as death claimed him. Darlen stared at Laurel in surprise. He stepped forward and touched her arm.

"Are you okay?"

Laurel nodded and checked her clothes for blood. Then for a full minute, the two stood contemplating the contorted body of the young master. Laurel looked up at Darlen.

"I think he's worth dissecting at some point," she said without emotion, dismissing the scene with a flick of her hand as she turned towards the door, leaving Darlen to clean up.

———

"You did what?!" Harry yelled. Ava and Harry had met up with Laurel and Darlen later on the Canaa. Marcel stayed on the station to continue searching for suitable materials with which to make weapons.

"I killed him," Laurel shrugged. "He charged at me, and I retaliated."

"With her bare hands," Darlen grinned, then corrected himself. "Foot, I mean foot."

"You kicked him?" Harry struggled with his surprise.

"Yes, a broken neck, according to the pandroscope," Laurel said, "but I'd like a closer look at his internal organs. Maybe take him apart. Darlen put him in storage."

For a disturbing second, Harry was left speechless by Laurel's nonchalance, but then, this boy was the enemy, and he'd seen Laurel up against an adversary before.

"Uh, well," Harry said, a little disconcerted. "At least we know the kick to the side of the head works."

"Shooting him would have worked too," Darlen

grinned, equally detached about the death of the boy. "Laurel was just quicker than me. You know? That stench of theirs is a powerful weapon. I hope we're not biting off more than we can chew. Laurel against a boy is one thing, but Laurel against a master…" Darlen opened his hands to invite comment. They all knew Darlen had every confidence in Laurel, but they were up against an unknown enemy, and their first line of defence seemed to be only Laurel and Ava.

"If we can get the Sons of David—the former Legion to fight with us," Harry suggested, "then I believe we have a chance. They're immune to the stench."

Darlen scratched his bald head. "We can assemble a few weapons using the duchess's sidearm as a template, but they have limited range." He produced a schematic for them all to consider. "Perhaps it would be more a defensive weapon rather than for direct engagement. Mer and I worked with the licks; again, not so effective without a triconomic interface, but there's not much we can do about that. Mer reproduced a dozen with scrap metal the Kalmeddi engineers had on the station. Incidentally, they weren't squeamish about making weapons, not like the Farisee, who won't help with the manufacture, but I bet they've got at least some of the technology."

"We have the Canaa's guns and cannons," Ava reminded them.

Laurel wasn't keen on placing Darlen on the masters' radar, assuming he wasn't already.

"That would mean revealing ourselves," she said. "If our suspicions about Sedar are correct, he might have told them about the weapons capabilities on the Canaa, assuming his initial scan registered our weapons. It's possible, though, if none of these civilisations have armaments themselves, the scan probably wasn't calibrated to search for them. Where is Sedar, by the way?" They hadn't seen him at all that day, although Laurel knew he was on the station. She reached out but couldn't find him, although she did find Marcel, his head filled with angry thoughts about the elderly Riynean. He jogged up moments later, looking suspiciously agitated.

"Where've you been?" Ava asked.

"I just caught Sedar on that gadget the Faris use for their ship-to-ship communications," Marcel snarled.

"What was he doing?"

"Reconfiguring it! I saw the same calibration we used to decipher the data on the masters' ship. He was delivering a message. It was a carrier wave, a bit crude, but it was a message."

"What did it say?"

"I don't know," Marcel admitted, forcing himself to calm down, "but I assumed any contact with the masters was probably not in our best interests. We don't want them knowing Darlen is a Magen Bearer."

"I'm not sure he's told them about Darlen, but he's kept himself very closed off from Ava and me..." Laurel would have said more, but an unexpected glimpse inside Marcel's mind stopped her in her tracks. "Marcel!" she demanded, "What did you do? Is he asleep?"

"I punched him in the face."

"What! Marcel, he's an old man!"

Marcel looked at his fist. "Yes," he said, suddenly

shamefaced. "I guess I acted on instinct, but he's supposed to be a telepath, and he didn't even know I was behind him. I didn't want to take a chance. After I knocked him out, I put him in stasis in the station's med bay. I've recalibrated that communications port, and it looks like I got to him before he sent the message."

Harry sighed. "I'd better go and check him out." He shot Marcel a look of disbelief as he headed towards the stations spartan medical bay. Harry disagreed with decking the old man, although he had to admit stasis was a great idea to stop him from spying; he wished he'd thought of it. Marcel was of the type to hit first and ask questions later. Laurel once said that Gabriel, Marcel's father, was a gentle person, so Harry made a mental note to ask her about that because Gabriel's son seemed to have a bit of the gladiator in him. For that matter, so did Ava, and Marcel and Ava were both Gabriel's offspring.

"Seems we were right about Sedar," Ava said, hoisting up Marcel's hand to show to her mother. Sedar was slightly built, and it wouldn't take much to knock him down. Laurel glanced at Marcel's undamaged hand and dismissed him with a wave. She took no pleasure in having their suspicions confirmed. "It's odd," she said. "I don't get the impression Sedar is a bad person. I'd like to know what it is the masters have over him."

Darlen didn't care about the whys and wherefores. "I'd have shot him," he said. "I don't like the idea of this war being on the station. I accept you feel we need to be here, Laurel, but we also need to protect Scarlett."

Ava nodded. "Darlen's right, Mom. Olyo has

suggested Scarlett go to Faris. She won't like it, and we can't spare Mer to go with her, not if we're planning to take on the masters."

Darlen agreed, he had nothing better to offer, and it seemed likely a fight was coming. He didn't know how secure the station would be. "It's a good idea," he said. "I'll talk to her."

A few minutes later, Harry returned from the med bay. "He isn't hurt, just a bit of bruising. His jaw is pretty robust for an old man, but I think the stasis was a good idea under the circumstances. He can stay there until we decide what to do with him. I hope he doesn't wake up to find he's sharing a bed with a master."

"I was a bit surprised to see him there," Marcel grinned. "Who did that?"

All eyes turned to Laurel, drawing a slight nod of respect from Marcel. He fought the Gale alongside her and knew the damage she could inflict. Laurel considered the episode closed. "Did the post-mortem on the female produce anything, Harry?"

"I wasn't too thorough. I wanted to assist Darlen and Mer with the weapons and the data from the masters' ship, and Beril already had stacks of data. I think she fulfilled her purpose. What was left was just a pile of old fractures and extensive soft tissue damage. I couldn't extract any cells I could properly examine."

"Poor creature," Laurel said, but she had no time to ponder nor feel compassion for the fate of the master's females. "Okay, perhaps we've learned as much as we need about the masters' physiology. The boy is preserved, and we can come back to him if we need to; our most immediate threat—Sedar—has been adequately taken care of. What did you find out about the masters' ship?"

"We analysed the data gleaned from the three planets," Harry said. "The lead ship has no weapons, but it does have a forcefield that covers the entire vessel. Around half the single ships that form the tail have pulse weapons strong enough to completely fry a power grid. According to the Edensai, Legion use short-range hand weapons. They don't really need much firepower if they're up against passive prey."

Darlen showed Laurel a formation of the tail ships. "The small ships targeted specific areas in unison," he told her. "They appear to have enough yield that a detonation in the lower atmosphere would take out a city or a town, and that's what they did, causing a mass migration of the population south to safer areas before they targeted the remaining population. Those that didn't or couldn't go were massacred."

Laurel expected Harry to comment. He'd been her commander when she first met him, but now, he waited for her to decide what they would do next. This was a different type of war, unconventional and not to be fought with guns and cannons alone but by natural or even unnatural forces; hers and Ava's, against an enemy who believed it was divine. And neither she nor Harry had answers.

CHAPTER SIXTEEN _

Later that night, Laurel lay on her back, staring into the dark, long after Harry fell to snoring softly at her side. She could scarcely believe she was back again amongst killing and cruelty. As a nurse and later a physician, she had saved and nurtured people, but today, as she had done so often since Darlen took her from Earth, she had taken a life without even a smidgeon of guilt. So entitled, so superior in her sense of outrage, then she had the nerve to scold Marcel for taking a swing at an old man, even though she knew that particular old man might sabotage them.

And it was for a good cause, wasn't it? Laurel tried to tell herself she knew what she was doing, that the Hebre entity brought her here to deliver the Edensai. But then she questioned. Did it? Did it really? Across Time? A nebula entity brought an emergency room nurse from Maine to save a civilisation? That's what all this was about? Her abduction? Giving birth to Ava? The doubts piled up, and Laurel groaned under their weight. The future of humankind was at stake, and Laurel was undecided if some of it was even worth saving, but she couldn't make that determination. She'd gladly see the Gale wiped out and anyone cruel to either animals or children. Murderers, torturers, slavers. The list was endless, but wasn't this for the fates to decide? Laurel realised she almost said it was for God to judge, but she didn't believe in God. Perhaps being surrounded by so many religious people was having an effect. She sighed softly and closed her eyes. She could doubt, but the decision of who ultimately would live or die in the coming conflict would rest on her shoulders. The choices were clear; try to save as many as she could by stopping the masters or retreat now and leave these people to their fate. She tried to still her breathing, listen to her heartbeat to lull her to sleep, but…

Laurel's eyes snapped open. Harry was still sleeping beside her, but there was someone else here too. A familiar figure was seated on a chair in the corner, the corridor light shining directly on his face.

"Xavier."

"Laurel."

"Have you come to judge me?"

"For stopping a monster?"

"I was just debating whether or not that was for me to decide?"

"That boy's nature was decided long before you even existed."

Laurel sighed. "I know that, but I felt no guilt as he lay dead at my feet. Sometimes I think all this war has dehumanised me, yet here I am, having doubts about my part in it."

"You have a purpose, Laurel. You know that. Now is not the time to doubt. Do you remember saying to Harry during the war with Gartrya that right is a point of view?"

"I do remember."

Xavier nodded. "And you also said that genocide is never a miscalculation."

Laurel grinned. "Why are you bringing up my rather outdated quotes?"

"Because they contain *wisdom*." Xavier emphasised the word, stressing for her its importance. "Is your position on genocide more virtuous than that of the masters?"

"Their plan is of total annihilation of every human!" Laurel burst out, waving her arms, then hushed herself, fearful of waking Harry. "Their cruelty has no bounds. They are evil, without empathy, and they won't stop until they've wiped out every man, woman and child from the face of the universe!"

Xavier tilted his head on one side, smiling at her impassioned outburst, his kind eyes twinkling.

"That's not what I asked."

Laurel hesitated, humbled. No, he didn't ask her what the masters were planning. He'd asked if her right to live as a human was greater than the masters' right to destroy her and all humankind, to take away every person's right to exist. "Oh, then, yes," she admitted, "I do believe my position is more right."

"And to stop them, you must obliterate their race?"

"What else?" Again, Laurel shook her arms to show the frustration she felt. "We can't allow them to exterminate all human life."

Xavier nodded wisely. "So it boils down to this fact; you are right, and they are wrong."

She could offer only one word in reply, only one word

that would satisfy, but that word was the final commitment to whatever would come. Laurel gave Xavier her answer.

"Yes."

"Then that is what you must act upon," Xavier said. "But remember, you cannot show them mercy or compassion. And sentiment? There will be no place for it."

"Sentiment?"

But Xavier didn't respond.

Laurel took a deep breath and dropped her face into her hands. "I don't know what to do next."

Xavier waited.

"I mean," Laurel said after a moment, shaking her head to clear her mind. "I don't understand why the masters use this slow form of killing; destroying the planet, creating a kind of nuclear winter that will ultimately poison everything—it's even having a forward effect in places it hasn't reached. There will be nothing left. The population on Riynea and Kalmed is greatly reduced; there are some survivors from those worlds on Eden, but even there, it's like…it's like a holocaust, the people are suffering malnutrition and disease." Laurel wiped away tears. "Outside the settlements, the disabled and frail lie in the streets, waiting for death. Xavier, some of these people have survived for years in these appalling circumstances. These masters take pleasure in their victims' suffering, and the people just sit and wait for it to happen. They won't fight."

"Think back to your own history, Laurel," Xavier said gently. "Not so many years before you were born, in your grandparent's time, an evil force marched across Europe. I fought in that war. I saw it first-hand. Do you think those who knew that force was coming didn't experience terror, didn't see the magnitude of what overshadowed them and knew it was too big to fight? So many wished to flee even though they believed there was nowhere they could hide from such evil."

Laurel understood. "My uncle's parents were French Jews who escaped to the States in 1943," she said. "Xavier, people did resist the Nazis, but these people simply place their misery in the lap of their gods and wait for whatever the masters dish out next. On the one hand, I want to shake them and tell them that maybe God helps those who help themselves; on the other, I empathise with the strength of their convictions." She sniffed. "I can't bear to think of them being wiped out."

"Don't judge them, Laurel. They do not understand the nature of violence."

Laurel gave a grim snort. "They're receiving a pretty harsh lesson right now."

"And you wish for them to fight, then live with their consciences for generations to follow? It may be that for them to sit and wait for death is the right way."

"It's not wrong to fight for your home and family. If they don't fight, there won't *be* any following generations for them to worry about."

Xavier shook his head. "They are lost regardless if they take that path, Laurel. This enemy is greater than a few guns."

"What do you suggest?"

"I said look to history, Laurel. So often on this quest, while you have sought answers, you have been reminded of passages from scripture. Perhaps there you will find the solution."

Laurel woke with a start. Ava was in her head.

"Coffee, Mom?"

Laurel rubbed her eyes and peered at Harry. He was still asleep, and he groaned as she gently nudged him awake. "Must I?" he mumbled.

"Yes," she nudged him again. "You must."

Harry turned then and gave her a drowsy smile. On impulse, Laurel reached down to kiss him.

"Wha…?" he returned sleepily but recovered himself enough to return her embrace, nuzzling her neck and ear. Laurel was seldom spontaneous with affection—he'd make the most of it—but that feeling gave way to suspicion. "Are you okay, sweetheart?" he said, letting her go.

Laurel slid off the bed and knelt beside him. "I'm fine, Harry. I…had a good think about our options. We need to talk to the others."

After her conversation with Xavier, Laurel had slept soundly, the formulation of a plan only coming to her in that twilight world between sleeping and waking. She had no idea if it would work, it was just a hunch, but if she were descended from this Judith, she and Ava together might just be a force to reckon with. She waited until after breakfast, and the others were seated in the common lounge.

"I've mentioned the bible before," Laurel began.

They all nodded. "Yes, the book of scripture, the basis of Earth's religions?" Marcel said.

"Yes," Laurel smiled, feeling her excitement build,

"but it may also give us a clue as to how to deal with the masters."

"How so?" Harry asked.

"We've seen parallels to scripture in many things we've discovered on our journey," Laurel said. "Serpents, Eden, casting out from paradise, even woman being made from the rib of a man, although the bible is a little less graphic in that regard. Bible text speaks of God who created the Earth and mankind," she explained. "This god gave the people laws and demanded strict obedience to his word. When the people faltered, challenged his laws or turned away from him to worship other gods, he punished them."

"What form did this punishment take?" Marcel asked.

Laurel gave him a wry grin. "Plagues of flies, pestilence; some pretty hard-core stuff to get them to turn their hearts back to him."

"Sounds like my old man," Darlen chuckled. "Are you going to tell us why you're bringing this up?"

"I'm getting to that," Laurel said with a note of triumph in her voice; the more she thought about it, the more this seemed so *right*. "God decided mankind wasn't turning out the way he planned, so he sent a flood that covered the entire planet."

"He drowned them all?" Harry cried. "You're joking!"

"Every last one of them?" Marcel had already developed a dislike for power-hungry gods; this one fit right into his criteria.

"He saved a few righteous people and some animals so they could start again when the flood subsided," Laurel added, wanting to be sure they got the picture. "Abel mentioned Hebre commanded the elements, and the elements obeyed. If that's the case, then my point is this; if we could bring the masters' ship down, Ava and I could create a deluge, one that covers the entire planet, swells the oceans and drowns the masters."

A complete silence settled in the common lounge as they considered Laurel's words. Harry was the first to venture a question. "A deluge?"

"Yes, a deluge," Laurel affirmed, sensing his scepticism, but she would not be deterred. "I'm not going to second guess my abilities. I didn't think I could cloak a ship, but I can, and if Hebre can bring rain to make crops grow, then Ava and I can bring enough rain to flood Eden and drown the masters."

"You said there are parallels to that book," Marcel mused. "How did a flood get reported if it hasn't happened yet?"

Laurel paused for thought. "Do you know, Marcel? I have absolutely no idea," then quickly decided not to worry about that particular gem. "There are three arks still on Eden. We can get as many people off the surface as we can."

"Mom," Ava said, "are you sure you've thought this through? The entire population of Eden isn't going to fit on three arks."

Laurel took a deep breath. She *had* thought it through, and she knew there would be some who would not make it to the arks. They could save many, but the aim would be to stop the masters. This was the only way.

"There's another thing you haven't thought through," Harry pointed out. "Are you sure you're going to be able to *un*-harness the elements? You'll have to stop it raining at some point, and it's likely the face of Eden will be completely altered by long-term immersion."

"That can't be helped," Laurel said. "We'll let it rain for as long as it takes for the oceans to rise; they'll do the rest. We'll stop it when we need to." She smiled. "Don't worry."

"I won't," Harry shrugged, but the grin he sent her didn't quite show complete conviction.

"What we need is an evacuation plan," she said, "and a plan to bring down the masters' ship. If we don't achieve that, a flood will only affect the masters and their Legion on the surface. We're not going to ask the Edensai to take up arms because those that survive must live with the consequences of their actions. If taking a life, no matter how evil, is so repulsive, it may destabilise their society as they rebuild. We'll arm the Sons of David if they're willing and any Kalmeddi who wants to join us."

"And how would you bring the flood, Laurel?" Darlen asked. "As you say, you've only just learned how to hide a ship."

Laurel shook her head. "I only know we have to try. I believe Ava and I have only tapped into a part of what we're capable of. I'm asking you to trust me."

"We do trust you," Harry said quickly, but he was worried. This plan seemed vague, principally based upon a few words uttered by Abel, a man they'd only just met. He could see Laurel was confident and determined but felt it only right to point out a flaw in her proposal. "There were thousands of Hebre here before, Laurel. They weren't able to overthrow the masters."

"Then why haven't we left?" Laurel said as she sat beside him, clasping his arm. "Why haven't we already given up?" She looked around. "It's because the masters haven't beaten Hebre. This is our fight. We're here for a reason."

Again, the silence descended as each member of the crew mulled over Laurel's words.

"Maybe a flood never occurred to the other Hebre," Darlen suggested after a moment. "Maybe they'd never heard of the bible. Harry, we need to find out more about the structure of that ship, see if any of the Sons of David were engineers or knew about the force field. We might be able to blow it up. Laurel, how will you evacuate the people? There are three arks and only two of you, and you have to get to the arks first."

"We need to identify their exact location," Laurel said. "Also, scan for Legion in the area; the arks are probably under guard. Legion is known to use cloaking technology, and they might if we attack, but we could synthesise some of Helen's gas to expose them; that is if we can get the Sons of David to come with us. Ava and I will make sure it's raining before we get the arks."

"Let's hope they do join because it's a bold plan for just a handful of us," Harry said, hoping he sounded like the voice of reason and not a doom merchant, but in the end, he couldn't help it. "And the first thing is to establish if you and Ava can actually manifest this weather event. Manifesting coffee and hot tubs are one thing…."

"It'll work," Laurel said brightly.

Ava sprang to her mother's defence. "It won't be a

manifestation," she said, placing her arm around Laurel's shoulders. "It will be real. And it will be deadly."

*CHAPTER SEVENTEEN_*

Beril and Jadren arrived as they were debating their plans. The two men received the news of the young master with some surprise but couldn't hide their guilty relief they no longer had to play nursemaid to a demon. Their response to the boy's death starkly contrasted with their reaction to the news about Sedar. Shocked to his core, Jadren suggested they immediately notify Olyo, currently enroute to the station from Eden. Jadren reported her concern over this development and urged them to meet with her to examine further options.

When she arrived, Olyo was not persuaded by Marcel's account, asking him question after question until Laurel thought what an excellent prosecution attorney she would make. Only when she knew that he was telling the truth did she turn to Laurel.

"I am at a loss to understand such treachery. Sedar is a good man and a friend to Faris, as he is to both the Edensai and Kalmeddi." She kept a level gaze on Laurel before adding, "And to Hebre."

"We are also at a loss, Olyo," Laurel said, saddened that their arrival had been a catalyst for the loss of faith in a trusted friend. "We believe the masters have some kind of leverage over him."

Olyo thought on Laurel's words. "His granddaughter is unaccounted for."

"He has a granddaughter?" Sedar had not mentioned any surviving family.

"Yes," Olyo said, "taken during the Legion registrations. Sedar ignored the directive to remain on Eden and managed to return to Riynea, but he paid a heavy price for his disobedience. Sedar's son, a technician and his wife were killed. Sedar also had daughters and a granddaughter, but he seldom speaks of them. They were either killed or transferred to the masters' settlements for Legion breeding. He believes his granddaughter survived."

"If he's trying to protect his family," Harry said, softening a little towards Sedar, "It would make sense he'd do whatever necessary to keep them safe."

"What sense?" Marcel disagreed. "Does he know that by selling us out, he's placing his grandchild over the safety of the whole of humanity?"

Laurel looked at Ava. Would she do the same thing in Sedar's place? How would it be if such a sacrifice were asked of her? Once again, as they had so often, Gabriel's words echoed in her mind:

"It is far better that one single soul perishes; than entire worlds continue in fear."

"Abel says you have estimated how many people remain on Eden," Laurel asked Olyo.

"Many are hiding in the mountains, others in the ruined cities," Olyo replied, "but I would estimate less than two million, mostly Edensai but with a few Riynean and Kalmeddi scattered throughout the settlements. The southern continent only holds these survivors; the rest of Eden is laid waste apart from areas where the masters and Legion dwell, and we do not approach."

"We understand each ark can carry twenty thousand?" Laurel asked.

Olyo looked to Beril and Jadren before answering. "To where do you plan on evacuating the people?" She did not need to ask Laurel her intentions; they were abundantly clear. Another exodus.

"Riynea." Laurel showed Olyo the data she'd been compiling for the campaign, more specifically, the evacuation. "It's the closest world to Eden, and we would not need stasis."

"Riynea?" Olyo's reply reflected her disappointment that this was all Hebre could come up with. "Even if you can access the arks," she said coolly, "you could theoretically only move seven hundred thousand people. Thousands more would be left to the masters, and Legion will intercept you before you make orbit, before you even leave the surface." Olyo folded her arms, her long fingers twitching in irritation.

"Judith did it," Laurel reminded her, ignoring her pessimism. "We can, too; besides, we have a plan to keep the masters busy. The difficulty is, it involves flooding Eden, and if we can only get seven hundred thousand people off the surface…"

Jadren cut in at that point. Hebre had briefed him on their plan, and he knew it would be difficult for his Farisee friend to accept. "If we do nothing, Olyo, all will die, and the masters will shift their attention to other kingdoms to cause suffering as we suffer."

Olyo had considered the inevitability, and she knew they would all live with this decision for the rest of their days. "The people are already preparing for death," she said, turning her wise gaze towards Laurel. "By your hand would be kinder than by the hand of the masters."

"Show me the components of this gas you say can uncover Legion," Beril said later as they discussed the plan for the masters' downfall. Harry showed him the formula, describing each element's relevance to the other. Beril nodded, confident such equivalents could be found. "I will have a sample ready for you this morning. Hopefully, it will be as effective as your late colleague's gas."

"She hated calling it Helen's gas," Harry grinned to Darlen as Beril left, "but she'd be glad it still has its uses."

Darlen grinned back. "That she would."

Olyo though, had remained silent since the discussion about the arks and the flood. She was profoundly against taking life. In the unlikely event it went to plan, this flood would destroy thousands of innocents, even as it destroyed the evil of the masters and Legion. She could reconcile herself to the fact it was not her war, and only Hebre could bring it to a conclusion, but she also knew she would not abandon the Edensai in their hour of need. Laurel heard Olyo's thoughts and understood her conflict, knowing the Farisee believed worse would come if they were complicit in any way in taking a life, even a life such as a masters.

Laurel would need Olyo to access the arks, so telepathically, she bade her listen. Olyo didn't react; just turned her head slightly.

"If the masters prevail, Olyo, your people will be alone in your galaxy. Every time the sun rises, you will see the destruction of Eden, the desolation of Riynea and the wastage of Kalmed. We need your help; we need your ships if we're going to make this work, but we will not ask you to take up arms."

Ava listened in and waited for Olyo's response. It took a moment before she inclined her head. "I will help you. You may use our ships," she declared before sweeping from the room.

"What was that about?" Marcel said, watching her leave.

"Just Mom giving Olyo's conscience a bit of a nudge," Ava smiled.

"Gentle people in harsh times," Jadren said wearily. "The Farisee will recover."

That night, Darlen and Mer worked with the Kalmeddi engineers, intending to duplicate weapons using the materials they found on the station. They had a stroke of luck in dismantling a small, wrecked Kalmeddi ship stored in one of the bays. Designing a firing mechanism was easy enough for Mer, and Darlen educated the two engineers sufficiently in developing pressure projectiles. The prototype was unsophisticated and a little clumsier than the old League wrist licks but workable. By morning, the two engineers had set up a system of manufacture, drafting in a handful of station personnel who had little else to do these days but stop the station from falling apart as they listened to the rumbling of each other's stomachs.

Darlen stayed on the station to oversee the work, but he was eager to learn whatever Harry and Laurel could bring back from the Sons of David about the design of the masters' ship. He hoped to discover an area that would be vulnerable to attack or even a well-placed explosive.

Harry, Ava, Marcel and Laurel returned with Mer to the surface along with Olyo, Beril and Jadren. Upon their arrival, several smaller children backed away from Mer, who tried to communicate with a few see-sawing sounds and by lighting up his red eyes. The children fled and clamoured around Olyo instead, begging for food. Ava smilingly pointed out to Mer he'd missed his cue to make friends, so perhaps he should just help the Farisee unload their supplies; there might be time to redeem himself later at the clinic they hoped to set up.

Olyo's normally sour expression broke into a broad smile at the sight of the children. She patted their heads affectionately, bent down to speak with the younger, shyer children and ended up with a child in the crook of each arm. It was a beautiful sight, and clear the compassionate Farisee were much loved and welcomed. Two Farisee attendants accepted Mer's help as they unloaded several cases, which the children helped to open with impatience, each child making sure they steered clear of the black robot. Several adults joined them to speak with Olyo and her people. The Farisee was a light amidst the darkness, although Laurel hoped that in time, that darkness would be dispelled altogether. Abel saw the ship arrive and went in search of

Laurel.

"Welcome back," he called to her when he found her helping the Farisee.

Laurel greeted him with a smile. He looked as though he'd tried to clean himself up. His hair was neater, tied back, and his beard trimmed. He nodded towards Olyo. "The Farisee Ascendant is always a welcome sight," he grinned. "It is good to see the little ones happy."

Like Santa, Laurel thought. Olyo was like Santa. It brought a sudden memory of Aunt Lucy trying to convince her on her first Christmas with them that Santa Claus existed, even though she'd already learned at an early age with her abusive mother, Santa was just a fairy tale. But watching Olyo, the spirit of giving and love did exist. Olyo's genuine respect for life was evident, and it touched Laurel in a way that brought Ava into her mind.

"Mom, are you okay?"

"A memory, honey. That's all."

Ava spent a moment searching her mother's thoughts for that particular memory; sometimes, her mom would let her in, other times, she was accused affectionately of being a busybody. This time, it was the latter, and she retreated with a smile. The kindness showed to the people by the Farisee also brought a glow to her heart.

Harry sat with a few of the community's older members, checking them with the palm pandroscope.

"You are fortunate in your choice of friends," Abel said, watching him.

"Yes," Laurel agreed. "Harry is my..." Laurel was about to say "partner", as there had been no kind of formal arrangement between them, but instead, she found herself saying, "husband". From the little she knew of the Edensai, they appeared to observe certain rites and rituals.

Married. Of course, she was. Abel felt his insides twist into a knot. He knew this woman could not be the Judith he'd loved, but she was so like her in face and form. If these people had truly travelled through time, then his Judith was many centuries dead, but this woman? Her spirit was the same. He *felt* it. And surely that spirit would have a memory of him? And Laurel—what a strange name, a name that didn't sit comfortably on his tongue. He could say "Judith", and it felt familiar and beautiful. When he looked at Laurel, he wished he could say "Judith", and it be true, that she had come back. But it was only a dream, so instead of giving in to his sadness, he forced himself to say the unfamiliar name.

"Laurel, Yosser and I sent word to the Sons of David on four other settlements to tell them you have visited us. There are others, but they are unreachable using the limited transports we have, but the Farisee can reach them. Do you have any words for us? We are eager to assist in bringing about the end of the masters' reign."

"We do have a plan," Laurel said, "but it's very…" she looked for the right word, "…grand. It will have devastating consequences for many here on the planet."

"For many?" Abel raised an eyebrow. "That is less than everyone. The masters' plan is devastating for all."

"I understand that…"

Laurel saw that Abel was studying her, waiting for her to divulge even part of the suddenly very real and overwhelming proposal to drown an entire world. She saw

Harry jogging towards them. She would give Abel a full explanation later.

"We have a crew member on the station who has designed weapons for those who wish to fight," she said. "Harry is also an expert in explosives, and once we identify a way of penetrating the forcefield on the masters' ship, he'll construct a suitable device."

"A physician and a knowledge of weaponry," Abel said as Harry reached them. "Quite diverse, but both with practical applications we may utilise fully in the coming conflict."

"I was in the League police before I became a physician," Harry told him. "I became a soldier when the League was attacked."

Abel raised his eyebrows. Yes, Harry was diverse and remarkable in his way. And deserving of Hebre as a wife.

"We need to stay here a while, Harry," Laurel said. "Abel would like the Farisee pilot to see if she can gather up a few more Sons of David from the furthermost settlements. It might take her a few hours."

"You need that time anyway, Laurel," Harry said brightly, seeing an opportunity to set up a clinic and help the people. "Have you told Abel the plan?"

Laurel shook her head. "I only got as far as mentioning the weaponry. Perhaps we all need to be together to discuss it."

"I think you should tell him." He turned to Abel. "Laurel's plan will have far-reaching consequences for everyone on this planet," he said. "I can design an explosive to bring down the masters' ship, but it will be untested.

Laurel and Ava will deliver the decisive blow." Harry looked from Abel to Laurel. "You don't need me to explain your part of the plan, and Abel may give us the answers we need to take back to Darlen."

Laurel had considered that, but Abel had said before he wasn't an engineer, so it was unlikely he'd know the specific schematics of the masters' ship.

"And while Laurel demonstrates her proposal," Harry continued, "we brought diagnostic equipment to help your people."

Harry had plans to rig up a makeshift clinic just outside the compound, but Abel wisely cautioned them about doing anything that might change the appearance of the settlement and draw the attention of a passing Legion patrol, so he set up the equipment inside the shelter. Within minutes, it became busier than any emergency room Laurel had ever seen. Marcel was reasonably competent in using the pandroscope, so Laurel felt comfortable leaving them both with Mer to attend to the patients while she, Ava and Abel discussed destroying the masters' ship and securing the arks. Laurel had been correct in her assumption; Abel had no knowledge of the structure of the ship. He had been a lowly Legion soldier, but he knew of others wise in such things, and he would ask the Farisee pilot to make sure she brought them to meet with Hebre.

"If you are successful in destroying the masters and Legion on the ship," Abel said, "what of the thousands of masters and Legion already here on the surface? The winter progresses, and Legion is placed to wipe out those the cold and hunger does not kill. We are in the end times. Even if the evacuation takes place, Legion will hunt down the arks." He shook his head. "I pray you bring to us a plan that goes beyond the destruction of the masters' ship."

"We do." Laurel looked at Ava. She hoped Abel had not been overly fanciful when he told her Hebre commanded the elements. Right now, a lot was riding on it. "You told me Hebre brought rain to make crops grow."

Abel nodded and pointed to the sky. "They made entreaty to the clouds." Abel hadn't been the only one to witness Esther and Judith command the elements. "The clouds parted to allow the sun to warm and incubate the seeds and plants in the earth. They also brought rain, and for the first few years of our exile, we were able to grow food." He collected a handful of sand and let it filter through his fingers. "Until the poisoned earth spread here."

"Abel," Laurel said, "We will once more 'command the elements'." Laurel had to admit, it felt both strange and defiant to say it, but every fibre of her being told her this was the only way to beat the masters. Abel dusted the sand from his hands and waited for her to continue.

"We will bring a flood to cover the world," Laurel told him, expecting him to shake his head at any moment, to point out how many deaths would result, say such a venture would be futile, or terrifyingly, refute their ability to create a catastrophe of such proportions, but Abel simply listened. Encouraged by his silence, Laurel pressed on. "The seas and oceans will rise, and Eden will become a water planet. Legion and the masters left here will perish."

Abel hadn't at first known what to expect, but the

potential lit a flame, thrilling him and filling him with hope. He took a deep calming breath. There would be much to consider with such a bold plan. "And we would save many on the arks?" he asked.

"As many as we can."

Abel nodded slowly, there would be losses, but there wasn't a soul in this community who wouldn't gladly give their own life to save another.

"We need to know as far as possible the positioning of the Legion relative to the arks," Laurel said, "And while all my instincts tell me this is how we will defeat the masters, Ava and I have never actually commanded the weather."

Abel had no doubts, no concerns they would bring about this miracle. "With my own eyes have I seen the elements obey the will of Judith and Esther," he said, not seeking to conceal the reverence he felt towards the two Hebre. "We will go somewhere quiet, somewhere peaceful, where your powers will be remembered and where the evil that creeps upon this world can be momentarily forgotten."

CHAPTER EIGHTEEN _

The Farisee had provided four of the communities with land transport to help ease the isolation. The carrier was a small bug-shaped car designed to attach to the Farisee ships' underside and also served as secondary landing gear and escape pod. Only meant for two people of similar build to the Farisee, it was a tight fit. Abel was a large man, and as he knew the area, he acted as pilot, with Ava and Laurel perching on the back. They certainly weren't in any danger of falling off due to speed because the transport spluttered like an old barge with a bad engine, but the terrain would have been precarious to negotiate on foot for the uninitiated. Laurel looked down at the craggy rocks that skirted many of the foothills, and while she didn't have a lot of confidence in the transport, she knew walking would have been an impossibility.

The little car slugged its course upward almost vertically, with Ava and Laurel hanging on for dear life, one hand on the vehicle and one hand on Abel's large shoulder to keep balance as they pitched and rocked up the steep incline. They breathed a sigh of relief when the ground opened onto a plateau, with a spectacular view of the mountain ranges reaching out to the horizon.

Jumping down onto the frosty, gritty ground, Laurel shivered. It was far colder up here, and the hazy sunshine gave no warmth to the day. Ava walked to the edge of the plateau.

"Look at this," she cried out, smiling, her arms held wide.

Across the canyon, clouds streamed across the mountain plateaus and cascaded like waterfalls down the rock faces, pooling in the gorges far below in seas of mist. Hard against the deep wintery blue of the sky, the effect was breathtaking; an untouched part of Eden that soon, if all went to plan, would be no more. Laurel wondered at the contrast of all the ruin she'd seen up to now because this was glorious. Unspoilt.

"It's beautiful!" she breathed, quite overcome.

"If we're successful," Ava pointed out a little sadly, "this will be gone, and it will be a long time before the planet is ready to be inhabited again."

Abel joined them. He knew the road ahead would be long and complicated, but it would not be filled with the utter despair that those who would survive, felt up to now.

"My people took the beauty of this world and crushed it," he said, not hiding the shocking regret in his voice. He looked out to the cloudfalls. "This is all that's left, but there is beauty in even the most barren world if kindness and mercy dwell in the hearts of its people. The masters and Legion have not yet crushed all that is good here, and now you have returned…" He smiled. "You have brought hope."

"You know a good deal about Hebre, far more than

we do," Laurel said.

"Only what my eyes and my heart tell me," Abel replied with complete sincerity.

"Do you know what Hebre did to control the weather?" Ava asked, drawing a short, sudden laugh from Abel.

"I said I know Hebre. I never said I *am* Hebre." And with that, he strode off toward the transport to await them.

Laurel and Ava watched him for a moment, then Ava turned to Laurel. "Perhaps we should have tried this from the station, Mom. I kind of feel pressured with Abel waiting for us."

"I think he's happy, grateful even that we are trying. I don't feel pressured; besides, the station isn't Eden, and I believe we need to use our empathy with the planet to do this."

"Okay," Ava agreed as she inhaled deeply. Then she let go of her breath to add, "Do we close our eyes?"

Laurel didn't know if there was some kind of ritual or incantation or even if the process called for two, but each other was all they had for support. Ava squeezed her eyes shut. A moment later, she opened them again.

"Your eyes are open," she said to Laurel.

"Does it matter?"

"I don't know," Ava frowned. "Do we close our eyes when we hide the ship?"

"I don't," Laurel answered, "and to be honest, with that view—" Laurel gestured at the cloudfalls, "I don't want to miss a moment of it. It makes me feel powerful."

Ava looked out towards the mountain range. "You're

right; it is inspiring. Perhaps this is exactly how it's meant to be."

Icy and bracing in Laurel's lungs, the air tasted pure, unlike the contaminated air in the compound. How wonderful it would be, she thought, if she could bag it up and cart it back to the settlement, let the people breathe in fresh air again. The cold blushed her cheeks and the tips of her nose and ears, and instinctively she reached up to loosen her hair, enjoying the sudden spread of warmth as it fell across her neck and shoulders. Her eyes blinked slowly as if preparing for sleep, and she watched the amber vapour rise from her fingertips, curling upwards, brushing her face. She turned heavy eyes to Ava. It's all so simple. *"Just surrender,"* she sent to her daughter, but Ava had already discovered that same surrender.

Holding out her hands, the smoky violet vapours mingled with those of her mother, and they stepped into each other's light.

Abel watched them from a distance. He'd seen a scene such as this before, Judith and Esther, the blending of amber and violet, their physical bodies enraptured in gentle light. He felt the air around the plateau warming and becoming damp. Taking a deep breath, he forced the polluted air from his lungs, the iciness no longer stinging his throat. Dark clouds skimmed across the sun, and a low rumble was heard from the east. A single, large drop of rain pinged noisily on the front of the transport, then another, and he felt water on his face. Within moments, he was drenched by cleansing rain. He laughed softly and closed his eyes, lifting his arms in silent praise to Hebre. Laurel and

Ava kept the spell for several minutes until the darkness receded and the sun returned. A rainbow appeared in the sky as a validating covenant to what they had brought to pass.

"Wow, as Auntie Helen would have said," Ava laughed jubilantly, looking down at her rain-soaked flight suit and twisting the water from her long hair. "I hope the masters didn't register an unusual weather event."

Abel, soaking wet and smiling, walked towards them. "We did it!" Ava exclaimed. Abel nodded calmly, droplets of rain sparkling in his beard. He beamed at them both.

"Never doubt yourselves."

Laurel didn't doubt. She knew all along she could do it; it was just the human side of her that needed reassurance.

"Maybe the hardest thing we have to face," she said, although she didn't wish to cast a pall on today's success, "is getting to the arks and bringing down that ship."

CHAPTER NINETEEN _

The new pandroscope constructed by the Chaese was hard-wired into the Canaa, therefore, not portable. The palm pandroscopes didn't have sufficient scope for extensive diagnostics, and realising this, Harry lugged the retired and archived, grossly limited pandroscope from Darlen's previous ship along to diagnose and deliver medication. Each person received much needed, long-lasting relief for their brittle bones, and medicine to support their cellular regeneration and ease for their pain. Laurel had prudently disabled the pandroscope's noisy prognostication tool as it would have loudly proclaimed most patients to be at the point of death and not worthy of their time. Most diseases they treated resulted from vitamin deficiencies, overcrowding and poor hygiene; easy enough to manage in normal circumstances, but without water and the proper nourishment, which didn't seem likely at this stage, any treatment was a temporary measure. There were a few cancers, likely because of exposure to the toxic cloud, and cold was a problem. Still, the adults did a fair job of sheltering the younger ones from the elements until the meagre warmth from the Farisee's evaporative heating tube kicked in at night.

The Farisee supplies were little more than a soft cake with a porridge-like filling, which upon testing, provided a hit of carbohydrates and little else. The fungi from the lake had better nutrition through proteins and amino acids, but it also had a high level of a chemical composition reminiscent of cyanide. The fungus, which Laurel learned had only been growing since the water pollution, was probably responsible for as many deaths as the malnutrition and disease. She recognised the Farisee were not experts on human dietary needs, and with only a single physician available to advise and no way to synthesise proper nutritional supplements, she saw how Yosser's comment on having a full belly while starving made complete sense. She took her findings to Harry. He agreed they could supply some supplements to the Farisee, then privately wondered if there were any point. From what he'd seen, there would be a few deaths in this compound alone before Laurel and Ava could put their plan into action. He even had a few concerns about toxins in the air and had scanned the pandroscope's conclusions. Too late now, he thought, he'd already breathed it, but they'd had far less exposure than all those who had survived this long. Harry gave himself a mental slap in the face. Letting the current hopelessness of the community's situation get to him served no purpose. Laurel had returned triumphantly from her rainmaking expedition, and Abel had sent for the other Sons of David to hear the plan. The faint rumble of thunder had even reached the compound, so Harry knew if anyone could deliver these people or defeat the masters, it would be Laurel. Just her presence had given the people a reason to smile again. Perhaps it was not hopeless, and those in the community who died, would at least die in peace.

The next thing was to determine how many people could be mustered to enter the arks. Olyo estimated the smaller communities held up to eight hundred people, the larger as many as two thousand. Abel relied on Farisee ship sensory data, but with the scattering of people in the mountains, it would likely be unreliable. He believed there might be other settlements across a polluted watercourse to the southwest, but it was impossible to be sure without adequate transport. After registering Legion activity, the Farisee had elected not to fly in that direction, so there could be no confirmation. Harry showed Abel the data the Canaa had compiled on the current population of Eden. There appeared to be a concentrated populace in a remote region in the West. The Canaa's scanners had reported technology present; therefore, Harry assumed Legion and masters probably occupied that area. The remnant of another civilisation was concentrated around the southern continent. As far as life signs went, there were no settlements other than those previously reported.

Abel took the news without emotion and confirmed the masters had occupied a city in the west when they invaded. The masters breeding practices were never undertaken on the ship; a woman's presence would be a violation there, so the city would be where the masters reproduced. He reported cannibalism was practised within that city also, with the harvesting of whatever poor unfortunates remained of the Kalmeddi.

Yosser listened in on the conversation, asking to see the data. He still grieved for the people he'd lost, but now, even though there were no tears left to cry, he still felt an overwhelming sadness. Drawn by his strong emotions, Ava followed him as he walked away from the group.

"We'll do our best to give you back some of what you have lost," she said, sitting beside him, hoping she wasn't making a promise she couldn't keep.

Yosser looked at her, his eyes heavy with sadness. "I am but twenty-four years old," he said. "Yet I feel more ancient than the Trah."

"You're only a few years older than me,"

Fifteen years had passed. Esther would be in her early thirties now. "You are so like someone I knew," he said, studying her face.

"I sensed that," Ava smiled. "Hebre? From when they were here before? You would have only been very young."

Yosser inclined his head in acknowledgement. "After Legion orphaned me, I was taken in by a young Hebre woman, Esther."

"I've heard her name. Did she leave on the arks?"

Yosser nodded. "Two of the ships made it to Sheerguhd. The third, our ship, was intercepted by Enoch, one of the two Magen Bearers who remained loyal to the masters. He was returning from Kalmed and so was not on the masters' ship when Judith was there. Hebre cannot hide from Magen Bearers, just as they, and Legion, cannot cloak themselves from Hebre. We were boarded by no more than a dozen Legion. They took many children during the battle, and Esther fell, trying to protect me." The memory was still evidently painful to him, and he took a moment before continuing, "The masters nor other Legion came to the aid of their Magen Bearer. Hebre repelled him along with his forces, but the children had already been spirited away. I was in their number, and they returned me to the surface. I lost my real parents and the woman I called sister before I was nine years old," he added with such profound sadness, Ava's heart broke for him.

"I'm so sorry, Yosser," she said. "I can honestly say I feel your pain. As an empath, quite often those senses are more acute than my telepathic abilities. My father died before I was born. I wish I'd known him."

"Was he Hebre? Or did your mother have violet eyes?"

"My mother?" The question stunned Ava. Didn't they realise that Laurel was her mother? "I inherited my eye colour from my father," she said. "Did many Hebre receive violet eyes?"

"Esther was changed before she reached the age of chaos," Yosser said. "As far as I'm aware, she was the only Hebre with violet eyes." He returned Ava's gaze. To see her like this, the fairness of her skin, her gentle expression, the sunlight on her hair, all brought searing memories of his adopted sister. Yosser shook his head and turned away. "She looked exactly like you, same colour hair, the same face. Looking at you hurts." Unable to hide his pain, the young man looked down. "She was good to me."

Ava mulled over this information. If Esther was the only Hebre with violet eyes, she couldn't have died on the ark. "Yosser," she said, placing her hands on his shoulders and turning him to face her. "I don't think Esther died at the hands of the Magen Bearer."

Yosser shook his head in confusion. "I saw her fall as the Magen Bearer snatched me up," he said. "When a Hebre body dies, the entity returns to the nebula."

"Well," Ava shrugged, "we're still learning about the entities, and I can't say I know how Esther managed to survive, but a bunch of Hebre would be a pretty formidable fighting force; it's beyond me why this Magen Bearer took them on in the first place. What I do know is that a violet-eyed Hebre woman performed impressive deeds on a world called Isilia. She looked like me. I've seen a recording of the event, and I trust the source."

Yosser took a moment to digest this news, scarcely able to believe what he heard, but this was Hebre telling him Esther had survived. "You are certain?"

Ava nodded. Yosser held his head in his hands as he fell to his knees, taking a few deep breaths to calm himself. When he finally looked up, his face was streaked with tears of joy. He truly believed he had forgotten how to cry. "Do you know?" he said, gripping Ava's hands in his own, "When my eyes first beheld you. I thought you were Esther returned."

"I knew you recognised me," Ava grinned and squeezed Yosser's hands. "I hope you are not too disappointed I'm not her."

"At first," he admitted, "but now, to know she did not perish at the hands of Legion…" Yosser's voice was filled with happiness, and he wanted to shout the news from the rooftops, had there been any left, or at least run to tell Abel. Instead, he forced himself to remain calm and thank his benefactor for this wonderful news. "I am grateful for this knowledge," he said humbly.

"Yosser," Ava said gently. "Everything will be alright. Life won't be the same, but I believe you have a future. I trust my mother's judgement."

"Your mother?"

"Yes, Laurel is my mother. Does that surprise you?"

Yosser looked over to where Harry, Abel and Laurel were speaking together. Abel and Judith didn't have children, and Laurel didn't look old enough to have a child of Ava's age.

"To be the child of two Hebre?" he said, although no surprise would diminish his joy at this moment. "Perhaps, but I think I am entitled to a little surprise today."

Ava hesitated. Yes, that is a puzzle. Her parents, both Hebre. Beril said it was impossible.

"We should join them," she said, taking Yosser's hand. "We have a war to discuss."

The Farisee pilot arrived back early in the evening. Abel was keen to begin the discussion immediately and took Laurel, Harry and Marcel to an area away from the settlement where several of Abel's friends from the compound had already gathered, along with a few Kalmeddi men and women. The pilot had crammed quite a few Sons of David from the outlying communities onto Olyo's ship, and together with those from this compound, the gathering numbered at least one hundred and fifty souls. Olyo also attended, and in her arms, a scrawny, slumbering infant wrapped in a threadbare blanket. Jadren sat wheezing beside her, his body looking more wasted and cachexic with each passing day. The trip to Eden from the station had taken a toll, but he'd politely declined any help from Harry and Laurel, saving his angrier rebuttals for Beril, who was accustomed to his friend's resistance to medical care, or even a temporary alleviation of his suffering. Beril understood Jadren's reasons for seeing no point in prolonging his life. For Jadren, the release of death couldn't come quickly enough. He often wondered how the cosmos could play such a cruel trick in keeping a weary and defective heart beating in such a sad, emaciated, and starving body. For what purpose? Having no god of his own, Jadren sometimes blamed the Farisee gods for his suffering, and at other times, the god of the Edensai. But mostly, he blamed the masters.

A further thirty or so filthy, weary-looking males sat with the others in muted conversation, broad shoulders hunched, wondering why their brother Abel had been so insistent they come. Hope sparked in their breasts when they learned Hebre had returned, only for that hope to be dashed when the Farisee pilot told them there were only two. What could two Hebre accomplish that thousands could not? Abel knew it was a question many would ask. Besides the men, two other ancient females were in the group; Holy Trahs from other settlements. From a distance, the community's inhabitants watched the assembly with curiosity, wondering why the Sons of David and the Holy Trahs joined with the Hebre women in conversation.

"We are here to find a way to help these people," Laurel said to Abel, nodding towards the compound. "Should they be excluded from this discussion?"

"You plan to flood this world, Laurel," Abel said gently. "Such a statement, even coming from Hebre, will not ease their hearts. Their Holy Trah will tell them only of the evacuation and of the need for some to be left behind."

Abel was right; Laurel saw that. Jadren, as Kalmeddi leader, would also be burdened with informing the few Kalmeddi not among those entering the arks of their fate. Laurel could not make those choices; better this heartbreaking task falls to the leaders.

As Laurel and Ava approached the gathering, both women were engulfed in a wave of intense emotion. Two of the broad-shouldered men rose.

"My eyes trick me," said the first, pushing forward, his delighted gaze directed at Ava. The second man shoved past him. "Do you not remember us, Esther?" he cried, placing his hand on his chest. "I am Lemet." He then pointed to his companion. "This is Mazier. Are we so changed? We are your friends."

It took a moment for Laurel to sift through the crowding emotions of all the men present to isolate the two men's thoughts. They sincerely believed they knew Ava. To tell them they were mistaken seemed unfair, not when their tired faces lit up with hope.

"We are from the future," Ava came back quickly, her words sending a stunned murmur through her audience. "Descendants of Esther and Judith."

The two men stopped where they stood, questioning their eyes and their ears. Another voice called out. "They are Hebre. Time does not hold them."

Lemet turned at the voice and nodded, although his

face still showed his confusion. Mazier grasped his arm and drew him back to the rubble they were using as seats.

'They were unprepared for us," Laurel sent to Abel, not troubling herself that she was thrusting a thought into his mind uninvited. She copied Ava in, and to her surprise, Abel sent a thought back, *'Did they need a warning? Even the memory of Judith and Esther inspires us."*

"Are you a telepath? Are the Sons of David telepaths?"

Abel smiled. *'I had a good teacher,"* he sent, *"but I can only reply, not initiate."*

Laurel nodded. She understood because Harry could do that too. Abel was right; even though they weren't the beloved Judith and Esther, their likeness to them and the knowledge they were Hebre brought a surge of hope and confidence. These men, these Sons of David, once bent on destroying humankind, would now do all in their power to defend it.

Harry was the first to speak; for him, it was imperative they learn as much about the masters' ship as possible so they could work on a plan to bring it down. There was little point in flooding the planet and killing thousands if the masters could simply fly out of here and back to Sheerguhd. He brought out a datacache and produced a schematic for all to view.

"We compiled this from data recorded by Edensai sensors when the masters first arrived," he said. "Our ship's sensors also gave us some useful, additional information." Harry chose his words carefully; he didn't want to insult the Edensai by saying their sensor technology was almost useless. "We can penetrate the hulls of the tailing ships," he continued, "but the lead ship seems to have a different configuration. We know each Legion ship draws power from that location, but so far, we can't find a way to penetrate the surrounding forcefield. We need your expertise."

Several men conferred, examined the data, and there followed a few moments of discussion.

"The only defence is the forcefield around the head of the serpent; the tailing ships have no protection," one man said, "but the head is not vulnerable. I have personally seen this fired upon, and it is impervious to attack. The defence is a fortification manufactured into the ship's structure and considered by its designers in the first kingdom as indestructible. The masters seized this ship when we invaded the designer's planet."

"What kind of weapons were used in the attack?" Harry asked.

"The first kingdom civilisations were more advanced in space travel than this system," the man said, "but not all were passive, and there were far more inhabited planets. Most acquiesced and accepted their fates, while other warring peoples resisted us with advanced weaponry. The serpent's head was made by one such world to withstand their enemy's weapons. If I may?" The man took the datacache from Harry and provided a different schematic.

Harry looked at Abel and Laurel. "That's a modified repulsor," he said. "The basic structure has similarities to those found in the League. It looks cumbersome, so I'm not surprised it didn't do much damage."

"The missiles were not integrated into the attacking

ship's systems," the man continued, "but mounted on separate platforms that flew in close formation with the host and operated remotely. They had no effect, so if you propose the use of such a weapon, I will say don't waste your time." He looked about him at his comrades. "Accept your fate."

"Majo is right," said another. "Any attempt to breach that forcefield would have to emanate from inside the ship itself; only then would it be vulnerable to an attack. If you can crush the serpent's head, what is left of the tail will be rendered ineffective. You are correct. Legion ships draw their power by relay from the head."

"Can we breach the forcefield from anywhere inside the lead ship," Harry asked, "or do we need to find a weak area?"

"The forcefield surrounding the lead ship comprises several tiers of particle energy from the bulkhead out," the man called Majo continued. "The field generates singly through all those sub-tiers before it is externalised. Even though those tiers are individual, they harmonise one with the other. If you take down one tier, those remaining will make up the deficit, so even if you destroy all except one, the ship will be protected. Only a devastating blast from within the centre of the serpent's head, the area from where the field is generated, would destroy the ship, but it would be impossible to get to that area without the masters' knowing. Only Hebre—" he dipped his head towards Laurel and Ava, "or a Magen Bearer could accomplish such a deed."

Laurel still hadn't confirmed Abel's suspicions that a

Magen Bearer was among them, and she didn't do so openly now, just gave a slight nod to the man.

"What would happen if the masters on the surface were alerted to a blast on the ship?" she asked.

"I do not know if such a contingency is in place," Majo replied, "but theoretically, they would mobilise Legion and take to the skies to determine what transpired. If the ship is crippled and unable to be saved, both Master and Legion will turn on the remnant of the Edensai. As it is…" he gave a resigned lift of his shoulders, "we do not understand why they have not finished us off and gone back to Sheerguhd. They have no reason to be on the surface now their work nears completion."

"We're planning another exodus," Laurel informed the gathering, knowing her words would fall on unsuspecting ears, so she was not surprised by the rumble of disbelief that went up. Laurel heard thoughts and words that questioned Hebre's wisdom to mount another evacuation when people were too weakened, and the masters and Legion still so strong.

"Is that your intention?" Majo asked Laurel, "to follow Judith's path? Some say she caused a deep sleep to come upon them. The masters' do not suffer a female to come into their presence in such a way."

Laurel shook her head. "I have no idea how she did that. No, we believe we have another way of planting the device. We need to move the arks, but first, we need to know how well they're guarded—or even if they're guarded at all. And what would happen if we were able to plant a device on the ship as we began evacuating the settlements?"

Majo stroked his chin in thought, then drew their attention to an image of the serpent he'd brought up on the datacache, a device he seemed to have no difficulty operating. "The remainder of the tailing ships are docked prow to stern," he said. "They draw power from the lead ship for life support and propulsion. Legion destroyed some of the ships the defecting Sons of David took with them, but we disabled the others ourselves to stop them from falling back into the hands of the masters. If you destroy the serpent's head, there will be fewer ships to disengage and fight back."

"And our ship, the Canaa, could easily deal with the rest," Harry said.

"Your ship may be powerful," Majo cautioned, "and perhaps the Legion ships will not match your firepower individually, but one against three hundred? You will be outgunned and outnumbered unless you bring them all down."

Laurel showed Majo a schematic of an axispod. "We've got three axispods as well, each with weapons arrays, so that gives us four ships, and we could rig up an external cannon array on Sedar's ship, but it's slow and not manoeuvrable. And we may need volunteer pilots."

Abel looked around. "Sedar? Did he not accompany you?"

"He met with a bit of an accident," Harry said, then seeing Abel's alarm, added, "Nothing serious." He didn't elaborate, and fortunately, Abel didn't question further.

Another voice called out, "What of those Edensai, Riynean and Kalmeddi that do not board the arks?" The man stood, and Laurel locked eyes with him. She could see he was not convinced.

"We will save as many as possible," she called back. "The masters' reign needs to end here and now. It may be that some will perish, but we cannot surrender all of humankind to the masters." And here she was again paraphrasing Gabriel's last words to her. Part of her believed those words to be wise; another part despised their finality.

The men fell to speaking amongst themselves, debating the implications of the evacuation and the prospect of becoming armed against their former masters. The man who asked about the arks was against the proposal, insisting the death blow the masters would deal as a result of an insurgency would be more terrible than anything they currently faced. She knew the people needed more; she needed to tell them about the flood.

"They're not buying it, Laurel," Harry said, speaking the words she had in her mind. "Tell them the rest of the plan."

"I get a sense some are coming over to our way of thinking, Harry, but it's a fragile unification. I didn't want to just blurt out about the flood. It seems so…final."

"It is the most essential part," Abel countered swiftly, and Laurel sensed from his tone she must now lay her anxieties to rest. This was not the time to lose courage.

"If you bring down the serpent's head," a Kalmeddi woman spoke up, "how would you deal with Legion and the masters scattered across Eden?"

Laurel held up her hands. "Bringing down the ship is

only part of the plan. Please listen."

And the crowd received the words of Hebre in stunned silence as Laurel told them of her plan for the destruction of the masters and Legion, a strategy that would destine many people on the surface to perish alongside their oppressors. After she finished, the silence continued for several moments. Then all eyes turned to a man who stood and approached.

Abel whispered to Laurel this man was Plio, the eldest of the Sons of David. Like Abel, he was in the last generation of the war against the first kingdom and a man who found peace and solace in his old age amongst the Edensai. If that peace was matched with death, then so be it, but such an attitude encumbered the man with negativity.

"There are two of you," he said levelly, directing his mistrust towards Laurel. "What can you accomplish that a hundred thousand of you could not?"

"Plio, my old friend," Abel said, placing his hand on the man's shoulder. "We speak of a way to defeat the Sons of Benjamin. A chance to rebuild. Is this not what you turned your heart towards?"

"I turned my heart to find peace," Plio responded coldly, shrugging away Abel's hand. "Our people are weary of war. I beg you, do not ally yourself with Hebre." Plio regarded Laurel with steely blue eyes. "Let the end come, I say."

"You find peace in hunger, Plio?" Abel said, once more taking the older man by the shoulder, determined to make him see this was the only way. "Can you tell us you find peace in the cold? And what of the young people? Of those not yet born. Do they not deserve this chance to be free?"

"We cannot bring down the masters," Plio hissed and pulled away, swinging towards the crowd. "Hebre fled before in the face of the masters," he bellowed. "I ask you; will they once more flee and leave us to our fate? Is Eden better for the presence of Hebre? I say we do not listen. Return to your homes and wait for the release of death. Do not fight, or you will watch the masters butcher your wives and children before your eyes."

Hagar suddenly wobbled to her feet, waving away the collection of hands that reached out to help. Her eyes shone brightly as she lifted her hands in a gesture to quieten, to calm, and Plio respectfully fell to silence. Hagar's soft mouth moved, but as always, her voice became lost in the folds of her gums and lips. No matter, she didn't need words to command a hush to come over these big men. Abel bent his head, and Hagar repeated herself.

"Our mother bids us not to question," he told the quietened crowd. "Hebre will deliver us. It is written."

"Where is it written, Abel?" Plio said triumphantly. He had studied Edensai scripture, and nowhere was mention made of a flood.

Abel looked down at the diminutive Trah so that she may answer. Hagar's hands were still raised to uphold the silence, but she had turned her face away from him and the crowd. Radiating calm and focus, her gaze settled on the two Hebre women, the expression in her eyes sending shivers right down to Laurel's toes. Before she knew it, words burst forth from Laurel's throat, "It is written in the future," she proclaimed to the stunned gathering. "Your descendants have made a record of these events."

Laurel was unsure such a mysterious response would be accepted after Plio's outburst, but they were already faced with two women who had travelled through time to lead them into battle. Again, the murmuring began, but now it was to choose between Plio's words and those of Hebre. Laurel and Ava listened to many thoughts as they wavered between one choice and another until, one by one, they rejected Plio's words.

"We can make sure the people are ready," Abel said, "but only those in the compounds. How will we spread the word to those in the ruins?"

"We will bring word to them," Olyo offered, still holding the sleeping infant. She stood and spoke to the gathering in a powerful voice that caused the baby to squirm. "The Farisee cannot take up arms, but we will supply ships to Hebre and aid as many as we can to achieve the mustering points that they may enter the arks."

"Those who fled to the mountains will not make it in time," one man said, and Olyo looked to Laurel for an answer.

"I—we can't save everyone." Laurel had no choice but to acknowledge the flaws in their plan. "But with the Farisee's help, we hope to get the people off Eden as the masters' ship is brought down."

Jadren waved a trembling hand towards a group of men and women. "There are Kalmeddi here who will fight with you, present now to hear your words."

"There are Legion close to where the arks are docked," Majo said. "They have technology which hides them and their ships in battle. If Kalmeddi fight beside us, they will not be able to see them. Only Hebre have the sight. Even we, as former comrades who fought with them, have spurned all vestige of our servitude to the masters and destroyed all ocular aids. Now we will also be blind to their presence."

"If you can give us specifics of this technology, we can counter the effects," Harry said. "We know of a vapour we can drop onto the troops; it is already being developed and will highlight those hidden."

"And if the masters are present?" A lone voice shouted from the crowd, "Do you have powers enough to protect the Kalmeddi from their stench?"

"We can't," Laurel admitted. "We've tried to find ways of filtering it out but with no success. We'll assess the situation again from our ship before we return with the weapons, but we need to know how many are going to stand with us."

Laurel now felt a greater sense of unification from most of the former Legion present; others were hesitant, but she believed they would follow Hebre. They trusted their words, and even though they had adapted to the ways of the Edensai, they had not sworn never to follow a leader into battle. Thus, did the Sons of David reconcile their consciences; this they would take to their pacifist Edensai wives as justification. The meeting dispersed, but Laurel felt there was still so much to be said.

"I wish there were another way," she told Abel sadly.

"I can't believe we've just talked about drowning innocent people simply because there isn't any room on the arks."

"The fate of those left behind will not have changed, Laurel," Abel reminded her. "The voice of death whispers in their ears every moment of every day."

CHAPTER TWENTY _

Hours later, not one of the Sons of David had returned to their settlements; even Plio had undergone a cautious conversion to the cause under the weight of his brothers' determination. However, he was still unsure he would take up arms. Fewer than a hundred Kalmeddi within the compound rallied for Jadren, who hailed them his "weakling warriors" in jest, only because of their physical debilitation, but as they told him, their hearts were willing.

Abel asked Laurel if she would like to tour the area around the settlement and visit the Place of Peace while they waited for the ship to be made ready. There was little for Laurel to do; Harry had the clinic's dismantling under control, and she was curious about the surroundings, so she agreed. They walked first toward the ruined city.

"Your Magen Bearer will be the one to bring down the ship?" Abel said.

Laurel grinned. "I knew you guessed, but I didn't want to identify that we had him with us."

"How would you be in Sheerguhd's eye otherwise?"

"I have so many questions," Laurel sighed. "About Sheerguhd, Magen Bearers, even about Hebre."

Abel nodded. "I too have questions. Perhaps there will

be a more peaceful time when we can discuss these things."

"I hope so." And Laurel truly meant what she said.

The city was a ruin, but Laurel had a sense of what it once had been, neat, tended, a place of honest industry, inward-looking towards the people's needs and spiritual growth. Even amongst its rubble, Laurel still sensed the city's heart, how it housed its people, sheltered them, provided a happy place to live, and made them content with their lives. Technology, development, acquisition of power; none of these had been as crucial as devotion to faith. Laurel couldn't help wondering if that faith had been shattered for so many living amongst these ruins, because now, large groups of people clustered together on the filthy streets amongst vehicles, ruined buildings and household items which were left where Legion blasted them years before. Sad eyes regarded them without interest, too immersed in their despair to care who or what came now. These people waited for death, or at least the end of someone in the compound whose release to that blessed state might allow one of them into where at least there was warmth at night and some meagre sustenance.

"This would have been a beautiful place," Laurel said, steeling her heart against the misery of the peoples' thoughts. Even their memories brought them no joy now. "When we passed over it the first time, I could see that once it was so neat, so ordered, and even though none of the buildings are intact, it's easy to see how it would have looked before Legion destroyed it." Laurel had meant no reproach, but Abel wasn't quick enough to disguise a rush of guilt at her words. "Abel, I'm sorry," she said hastily, "I wasn't laying blame."

"I will suffer remorse and shame every day for the rest of my life," Abel confessed, sharing with Laurel his profound sorrow. "It is worse for Legion of my age and those older, like Plio. We visited destruction in the first kingdom, the death, the persecution. We were seized then of the same mindless evil as the masters, born to serve them and their will without challenge. There is no penance great enough to atone for what we did, no sacrifice I can make to give my conscience ease."

"Perhaps you need to forgive yourself," Laurel said gently. "The people in the settlement forgive you. I would say they even look to you for leadership."

"The masters and their loyal Legion see that as a weakness," Abel said. "The people didn't elect us as leaders, but without Hebre, they needed someone strong at their head. I…we, have led them nowhere, only been part of the instrument of their sorrow, yet we are absolved, loved even."

They continued through the streets, the smell of human waste and decay so overpowering, Laurel tucked the lapel of her jacket over her face. Abel seemed immune, but for him, it was part of his every day.

"Sometimes, the Edensai will leave a body where it falls," he told her, "rather than lay it to rest in polluted ground. They feel that would be surrendering the remains to the masters." He stopped to point to several small, pitifully thin children lying on the ground beside their mothers. "They wait here because the Farisee has occasionally dropped bread in this location, but not for a while it seems, as these poor wretches look as though they will not survive much longer. Those mothers look as if they are too weak to forage in the forests. The bread quells hunger, but Yosser is right, perhaps it merely prolongs the suffering. Maybe it is kinder to let them die."

"All the people we examined today were malnourished," Laurel said as she watched the heartbreaking scene. "The fungi you forage from the lake contains toxins, but for those of you who can tolerate them, it has slowed the starvation process. The Sons of David appear to have an entirely different metabolism; none of you are suffering the effects of malnutrition in the way the others are."

"We can go longer without food," Abel nodded, "and we are not affected by the fungi, but the supply is not unlimited. I fear we will be left standing when no other human is left, and then the masters will exact their punishment upon us."

"What form will that take?"

Abel seemed about to answer, but he stopped himself.

"It is for the future if we fail," he said instead. "Come, we tried to rebuild one of the Edensai Places of Peace…I'll show you. We don't share their devotions, but we greatly respect them."

The Place of Peace was nestled in amongst the ruins of the A-framed buildings at the city's heart. All around was desolation and debris, but several small sections of rubble were cleared and set up to give shelter from the elements. The faces of several children peered at them from behind the ruins.

"Fertility has declined now," Abel said, nodding towards the children. "Perhaps that is a good thing, as any child born lives on borrowed time, and mercifully, most perish before they even take their first breath. The ones you saw in the streets were born while we still had a few crops to sustain us. Now, the winter that will never thaw makes its way to finish off what starvation couldn't." Abel pushed aside several stones and showed Laurel into an alleyway. "How many will survive even this natural winter season we are presently facing remains to be seen."

Laurel followed him into the dingy walkway. "It sounds like it's the masters who are prolonging death."

"In the first kingdom, it took the people seventeen generations to die out," Abel told her.

That didn't make sense; Abel couldn't be more than fifty. "But you said you were there."

"I was," he replied, "for part of it. My people are long-lived, up to one hundred and thirty years. I was born during that war and raised to be a warrior. We are not like the Sons of Benjamin, who reach maturity much earlier and endure only until their fortieth year. Their kind lived and died as they oversaw the extermination."

"Their fortieth year? That's pretty specific," Laurel said as Abel pulled open a wooden door and invited her inside a dusty building. Abel told her the people seldom visited the Place of Peace but that he'd regularly brought the Holy Trah before she became too frail.

The considerable amount of choking dust in the air that floated in from the dusty ruins outside showed the building had not been visited in a long time. Still, a lot of thought had gone into its construction. Several squat arches supported on pillars were arranged between the entrance and the large main room, which had an altar-like display at one end. The room was bare of any furniture. As the building didn't share the other buildings' A-framed roofs, the ceiling was comparatively low. Crude supporting beams stretched from one side to the other, and Laurel saw how much of the roof had been wrecked, but the rebuilding work was neat, and if you didn't look up, any other damage around was minimal. Two windows at each side of the altar appeared to be like any stained-glass window from any cathedral on Earth; only the representations were not of biblical scenes or even of people, but of native flora and fauna, their species long-since destroyed by Legion and the masters.

The hazy late afternoon sun lent pale light to the interior, and Laurel felt it was indeed a place of peace. Outside was turmoil and anguish, where birds no longer sang; children had no spirit to run and play, where hope and enthusiasm and success had been snatched away by evil. In here, amongst the dilapidated surrounds, Laurel sensed the potential for restoration, for survival, a place where the people's faith in good could be renewed. She wondered how often people had visited in the past to hear the words of the Holy Trahs, to be uplifted and energised by the teachings of their god. She looked at the layer of undisturbed dust on the floor that told the story no-one had been here in a long time to seek their creator's solace. Given the decay of spirit she sensed in the ruins, she saw how the people might believe their god had abandoned them. To a devout people, that was just as cruel a fate as death by starvation.

Stepping up onto the altar, Laurel found a cloth scroll draped across a handmade lectern. The manuscript was of a simple, wrinkled fabric of immense proportions, quite unlike the delicate silk embroidered scroll Gabriel had sent her so long ago. She touched the cloth and looked up.

"You may open it if you wish," Abel said, his form a silhouette in the fading light. "It is seldom seen now."

Laurel reached into her pocket, pulled out a torch, and then gently unrolled just a few inches of the scroll. The cloth was not old, but the writings were an historical account of an ancient civilisation. She recognised the language as Edensai, in form so like the most ancient Hebrew.

"An Edensai word keeper, Joshua, wrote the scroll," Abel told her. "He was apprenticed to Hagar, and he memorised the culture and laws of the Edensai. It is the duty of all Edensai to commit their family history to memory, but it is the obligation of the Trah and their apprentices to recite the laws of the Edensai God and record the oral traditions and tenets." Abel gave a ragged sigh, once again remembering bitterly his part in the devastation. "When Legion arrived, Edensai archives were destroyed, so Joshua secretly transcribed the ancient records onto this scroll and kept it hidden. The Holy Trah recovered it when Joshua left on the arks. He also recorded the history onto the stone."

It all sounded familiar somehow, the scroll, this place. Abel saw Laurel's brow furrow as she touched her lips with the tip of her finger, as if searching for something in her distant memory. She felt his gaze on her.

"It's just that it seems like I've been here before." She angled a glance in his direction. "Somehow, I don't think that seems strange to you."

"Hebre is tethered to this place in ways I cannot explain nor fathom," Abel said. "Do you still have the stone on which you found the story of the people who fled the planet in League space?"

"The stone was the property of the League," she confessed guiltily. "I borrowed it without permission."

"You stole it?" He almost laughed. Judith advocated total honesty in all dealings with her fellow man, although he knew there were some things she omitted to tell him.

"Borrowed," Laurel corrected, although she felt the whisper of Judith's name. "Harry tried to open it, but it only worked for me."

"What did you learn from the stone?"

"Enough to know at least one ark made it to League space," she said, "although it was before the League was formed. I believe the masters did find the Hebre and the other survivors. The story goes cold there. Darlen, whom we call a Soul Monger and quite possibly a descendant of the Sons of David, told us of the myths his people handed down." Laurel shook her head. "I don't know how much of them are embedded in fact, but the children born to Hebre and humans, were sold throughout the systems as slaves, seemingly by Legion. Some of the Hebre and the humans managed to escape Canaa—the planet on which they made a home—and fled into the Transcender, the portal... the Eye of Sheerguhd—sorry." Laurel tapped her forehead. "It's not easy to find my way around the different titles.

From the information on the stone, the masters followed and perished. The information must have been sealed into the stone by a whole soul—a Hebre who was left behind."

"Then the Magen Bearer was not among the masters," Abel said. "If the masters followed unprotected by the star, Sheerguhd would swallow them. Canaa?" he smiled, "The land of hope. It makes me sad to know their exile did not bring them peace and that only one ark survived."

"I said at least one of the arks survived," Laurel corrected him, "perhaps all three did." She didn't know how many arks made it through. "I know three arks were present when Esther and the Riyneans arrived on Isilia. They left there because they knew the masters were following. According to the Riyneans who remained on Isilia, the arks went into the nebula. I believe the masters pursued them for years."

"Years?" Abel seemed surprised.

"I don't know how many," Laurel shrugged. "It could have been generations. I encountered an immortal being, a wraith, on a League planet close to the nebula. The wraith told of a ship that emerged from the nebula, and from the wraith's description, it was an ark. A few children aged around ten, left the ark and came to the planet, becoming the first human inhabitants. These children were born on the ship, but I didn't learn why the children left."

"Humans are controlled by the intellectual threshold of time," Abel said. "Hebre only by its practical utilisation. The children may well have been born on the ship. If Hebre removes a man to their dwelling place, however long he is there, it is but a moment. Hebre would not have remained within Sheerguhd; they would have moved into the nebula where Time follows their will."

Laurel was dumbstruck. She'd declared that the part of the nebula in which they'd travelled somehow registered speed and distance but not time. But even with that realisation, she failed to see those intellectual thresholds had inhibited their movement. It made sense. Intellect hindered her psychic abilities on more than one occasion, but if she'd known then what she knew now about that part of her that was the entity, she would have had a far greater understanding. Humans programmed the ship, so it registered human intellectual thresholds, and as a human, at least in part, she observed those thresholds and believed what she was seeing. She knew that Time was at play; she just didn't understand how it connected to her. Had she known, she could have prevented the destruction of Darlen's ship, but then they wouldn't have met Baii and Ilivi. Perhaps there was a reason…

Laurel looked down at the scroll, the delicate edges a little tatty from the loving touch of the Holy Trah, sensing that Hagar stood here to instil into her people, they must continue in faith that their god had not forsaken them. Abel stood below the altar, looking up at her as she traced her fingers over the symbols on the scroll. "On my world," Laurel told him, "the world to which I believe the Hebre and Edensai and the others escaped; this language, or a language very much like it, is called Hebrew." It was almost unbelievable to Laurel that the two worlds were so linked across the vast expanse of the universe. "They became a great civilisation with a rich history, but I think there is more to their story. A book on Earth has an entry regarding a woman being made from the rib of a man. It tells of a serpent and even mentions a paradise called Eden."

"And is the flood that you are to deliver written in this book?"

"Yes." Laurel frowned, "And it is a mystery because it hasn't happened yet, but Hagar…she seemed to have some foresight. But don't ask me how it's recorded. I don't know." She stepped back from the scroll. "Would you read some of this to me?" she asked, "At least the first part?"

Abel climbed the altar and stood at the lectern while Laurel propped herself against a wall to listen. Although he was willing, Abel found it wasn't easy. He rarely came here now, not since Judith left. They would sit here for long hours, happy just to be together, in peace. The first time he approached the scroll after she left, he felt unworthy, as if his very presence defiled the virtue of the Edensai. He alone felt responsible for their destruction, although he was one among thousands, but somehow Judith had made him whole again, given him back his humanity, soothed his broken soul, and redeemed him. Reverently, he ran his fingers across the words that told the story of the Edensai, the very people he had come to destroy, and he knew that until the end of his days, his heart would weep at the destruction his people wrought.

Slowly, he recited from the scroll. Laurel had settled cross-legged on the dusty floor, watching her little torch bob about in Abel's hand, listening to his deep voice gently split the quiet of the hall. And as she listened, she began to shake her head. There was nothing recognisable in this text. She had expected to hear words from the Torah or other scriptural writings, but this was like none she'd ever heard at college, apart from the initial sentence about the creation of the first man and the first woman. However, this account had them created separate and equal. There followed no violence, no casting out, no sibling murder, no shame at nakedness, no fig leaves, no tempting apples or beguiling serpent. The account was that of an altruistic and generous creator who loved his people, endowed the land so crops would grow, gave them the most magnificent world upon which to flourish and demanded nothing in return. No ritual, no adoration, no sacrifices. This was not the god of the Old Testament.

Laurel fidgeted. Even in the gloom, Abel saw the movement and shone the torch at her.

"It's not what I expected," she said.

"You had an expectation? From a text you can't possibly know?"

"I thought it would tell a different story."

Abel covered the scroll and descended from the lectern. "What did you think it would tell you?"

"Not what I heard," Laurel said honestly. "I presumed it would be like the scriptures on my world, but..." she shook her head, "it's not. I'm convinced now that the masters' culture and Edensai scriptures somehow became interwoven into the religious texts of Earth."

"The masters' truth was mine for many years," Abel said as he turned the torchlight towards the door. "But I ask, if this supreme being the Edensai worships exists and is all-powerful, why does he tolerate such suffering? Could he not have stopped us? Stopped the Sons of Benjamin?"

"Perhaps the Edensai God knows something we don't," Laurel suggested.

"The Edensai do not hold their creator directly responsible for this evil. They only lament it found its way to them and wonder why he has forsaken them."

"I have heard it said there are those who believe it a judgement," Laurel said. "Then there are those like the Farisee, who will help even if they risk retribution from their multiple gods."

Abel smiled at her in the gloom, but she was sure she caught a twinkle in his eye. "It is a mass of confusion," he said, holding the door for her.

Laurel glanced up as she stepped back out into the rubble and desolation. She didn't need to tell him. It confused the hell out of her as well.

They walked back via a hill overlooking the compound. Night had drawn in, and the light from the moon cast eerie shadows in the dark. From the hilltop, Laurel could see Olyo's ship almost ready to leave. She sat on the hard ground, and Abel slid down beside her.

"You surround yourself with good people," Abel said. "Your husband, a clever man to be trained in both the healing arts and in weaponry. Does not one cancel out the other?"

Laurel saw his point. "It might seem that way, to not cause harm and then to fight, but I suppose it is from the perspective of the common good."

"You have both helped the people," Abel said,

"brought them hope, comfort, and eased their suffering."

Laurel looked back towards the city. "I wish we could take it to those out there."

Abel fell to silence. It had been so long since the compound had been free of the wails of starving children or the mourning over a loved one just passed. Laurel listened quietly to his thoughts; it was hard to believe this man, so compassionate and kind, was once an instrument of death and destruction.

Abel turned and placed his mouth against hers, his lips soft and warm. Laurel felt the tip of his tongue against her lip, and the brush of his beard as he pressed her against the grass. He pulled her close, and her arms encircled his neck. Again, that strange scent filled her head, the warmth of spice and musk. He gently wound his fingers through her hair, and she sighed as his lips moved to her neck...

Laurel blinked. Abel still sat beside her in quiet reflection. It was a memory, and not one to which she was entitled. "Abel," she said. "What was Judith to you?"

Abel looked up. He knew this time would come; Laurel wasn't so removed from Judith as she believed. "Judith was every star in the night sky," he told her, turning his face to the heavens. "She was the moon, the sun, and she was eternity. Before she turned my heart, I killed people she cared for, I attacked and destroyed homes and villages, yet—" he bowed his head, "she saw something in me worthy of her love, worth saving. Judith was my wife."

After the memory vision, Laurel knew this would be his answer.

"Why didn't you leave with her?"

Abel shook his head. "Mercy was one thing, but to take

the place of an Edensai, a Riynean or a Kalmeddi, we could not allow ourselves to be saved over them. The only Sons of David to enter the arks were the fathers of infants. Otherwise, we would not take the place of the innocents we wronged."

Laurel understood. "Did Judith have eyes like mine?"

Abel smiled and nodded. "Unique among Hebre, as were the violet hue of Esther's eyes. Esther and Judith were the strongest of all Hebre."

"In what way?"

But before Abel could answer, Harry distracted them by waving wildly and pointing towards the Farisee ship.

"It looks like you're needed," Abel said.

Laurel stood and brushed the dust from her slacks. "They're ready to leave. Thank you for showing me the Place of Peace." She glanced at the city in the distance, its ruins rising like ghostly memorials in the moonlight. "I'm sure all of this was a place of peace at one time." She looked down at Abel, still seated on the ground. "I know that Eden is stable in time," Laurel said, "but I wish I could turn it back as Esther did on Isilia."

Abel blinked slowly. "I wish it also," he murmured as Laurel started down the hill.

How he loved her, even now. He knew Laurel had seen the memory, the last sweet time he and Judith were together, before the ark bore his love away. Love, so unexpected after his years of blind hate. He'd fathered so many children on unwilling girls, destroying many female infants at the command of the masters, allowing another's hate and anger to fill his soul. Then he met Judith. The woman who offered him humanity. And whatever part of her remained within the woman, Laurel, didn't remember him.

He watched Laurel as she ran towards Harry, her husband, who waited for her. Abel was incapable of jealousy; nevertheless, his heart ached. But his longing was short-lived. A strong sense of impending danger hit him squarely in the chest. Leaping to his feet, he ran towards Laurel, shouting a warning. She turned, but as she did, it was not to see Abel nor Harry. It was to look into the cold eyes of a Magen Bearer as he plucked her brutally from their sight.

CHAPTER TWENTY-ONE _

"Enoch!" Abel bolted down the hill towards the stricken Harry who'd seen the whole incident. Several other Sons of David rushed from the shelter, alerted to the presence of a Magen Bearer. "It was Enoch!" Abel twisted his hands through his hair in anguish.

"Enoch?" Harry echoed. "A Magen Bearer?"

Abel grabbed Harry's arm. "The masters. They must know Hebre have returned."

Ava raced back from the ship, her senses telling her something terrible had taken place.

"A Magen Bearer took Laurel," a distraught Harry called to her as she reached them. Ava ran into his arms. Stumbling over his words, Harry turned to Abel. "Where? To their ship?"

Ava clung to Harry, her heart pounding. She'd had no warning, no sense of danger. "We think Sedar told them about us," she said to Abel. "We didn't realise they'd come looking."

"Then you were foolish," Abel snapped, softening immediately as he saw her stricken face. "What do you mean, Sedar told them?"

"When we first arrived, I had a sharp sense of it," Ava

told him. "We were on the Farisee scout. Sedar was with us, and my mother sensed he had closed himself off mentally. Later, Marcel caught Sedar sending a message to the masters."

Marcel and Olyo joined them, and Marcel confirmed what he'd witnessed and how he had placed Sedar in stasis, not bringing up the punch to the jaw.

"This is out of character for Sedar," Abel said, looking to Olyo, who nodded in agreement. "It is possible the masters believe Laurel is Judith…"

Plio joined in. "The woman has Judith's likeness; the masters may be deceived by her eyes and will fear her. If so, they will not dare to cause her harm."

"What do we do?" Marcel said. "We can't just wait around. We have a Magen Bearer…". The sudden murmuring from the Sons of David stopped him mid-sentence. He realised too late that it wasn't common knowledge, but he couldn't take it back. "Could he not go in and get her?"

The Sons of David gathered closer. The man had made a curious statement. A Magen Bearer? Abel had them stay their curiosity; now was not the time. Marcel had spoken out of turn, and they didn't need loose words that might lead to the masters discovering the Magen Bearer also. Abel told Harry there was little they could do but wait.

Harry was not so easily placated. "Marcel's right," he said, helplessness and anguish overwhelming him. He felt as he did when Laurel was taken prisoner at the fortress on Semevale 7. "We can't just leave her!"

"I could place a mantle on the Canaa," Ava suggested.

"Darlen could slip in and pick her up."

Abel held up his hands to stop the debate. "Why would Sedar tell the masters about Laurel, but not of the Magen Bearer?" He frowned as he looked at Ava. "And why did they send only Enoch and not a squadron to apprehend you both or to attack the station? I do not understand why Sedar would only tell them part of the truth. It makes no sense to me."

"You cannot go to the masters' ship, child," Olyo told Ava firmly. "We must conceal your presence and that of the Magen Bearer from the masters. I understand this burden, but if you are also captured…"

"We have always believed the Magen Bearer executed Esther," Abel said. "We now know that not to be true. It is likely Enoch announced his victory to the masters, and they would not expect Esther to return."

"So why would Sedar not tell them there had been a mistake and Esther lives?" Harry asked. "We know she's not Esther, but Ava has violet eyes, and like we say, she and Laurel may be descendants."

"I see your pain, Harry," Jadren said, "but Sedar is a good person. I have known him for many years. The masters or at least their ruler might know of Judith's vow to return. If so, then I suspect they charged Sedar with scanning for that return. When he believed she had, he informed them. The masters took his family; he believes one alone survives."

"A granddaughter. We know," Harry said, "but this is not about Sedar. This is about Laurel. I think we should go back to the station and work out a way to rescue her, follow through on Ava's plan." Harry started towards the Farisee ship, but Abel checked him, barring his way and planting his large hands firmly on Harry's shoulders. He knew Harry's anguish only too well. He shared it now, but his concern was tempered with greater knowledge of the masters. If they concluded Laurel was not Judith returned, they would not keep her on the ship. Judith would have known the approach of a Magen Bearer and not allowed herself to be taken. This was in Laurel's favour. The masters would have doubt she was anything but a likeness of Judith, perhaps Hebre, but one alone was no threat. Abel believed they would let Laurel go.

"Harry, my friend. We cannot. What we must do is proceed with the plan to destroy the masters."

Harry glared at him and shrugged himself from Abel's grasp. "I can't. I can't just leave her. Ava's right: Darlen can get her."

Ava laid her hand on Harry's arm. "Dad," she closed her eyes and took a deep breath, centring herself, allowing the emotion surrounding her to drift away. "Abel's right, and at this moment, nothing has happened. Mom's okay."

Harry stared down at her and swallowed hard. "Are you sure?"

Ava nodded.

"Let us be calm and think. The masters would be curious," Plio said. "Years have passed. If they feared Judith had returned with an army of Hebre, they would have come themselves to do battle."

There was silence throughout the compound, waiting for Harry's reply. He knew enough about warfare that to take on a more powerful enemy when they had not yet raised a fighting force themselves might prove futile at best and at worst, end in Laurel's death.

"A day then," he agreed. "If she isn't returned to us. We go and get her. Okay?"

Ava hugged him, wishing she felt more sure. "Okay."

Laurel didn't recall being taken from Earth by Darlen. Not until now. Just before the Magen Bearer picked her up, she had become aware of an unfamiliar presence at the same time she heard Abel calling her name. At that moment, when the rough grip of the Magen Bearer around her middle drove the air from her lungs, and she looked into those intense eyes, she remembered the moment Darlen took her from a Chicago street. She'd caught a glimpse of her apartment block, the yellow cab and its startled driver, a cat in a trash can; it all seemed so long ago. And she had not defended herself. Not then, not now. Last time, she woke in Darlen's ship. Now, she sprawled across the cold floor of a large chamber. Her ribs hurt, but she pushed herself to her knees, then got to her feet. She sensed two figures behind her, motionless, just observing. One, the Magen Bearer who bore her here, the other, a master.

She didn't turn. Eden was visible through the viewport, its deathly cloud creeping upon its surface. The sun was gone, and much of the planet lay in darkness. She was alone. Here, on the masters' ship, like Judith before her. What did Judith say then? What did she do? Was Judith brought here by a Magen Bearer? Abel didn't say so. Laurel felt a shift deep within her, a stretching. A power. She turned.

The Magen Bearer was a large, hairy man with deep scars crisscrossing his face. He breathed deeply and audibly, each inhalation expanding his already enormous, armoured chest, with each exhalation whistling past an obstruction in his deformed nose. He carried a pulse weapon at his side, and Laurel didn't doubt he'd use it against her if he deemed it necessary.

The Magen Bearer's presence, impressive as it was ugly, was eclipsed by the beauty of the being who stood beside him, legs planted slightly apart, powerful arms folded over his muscular chest, the sheen of his smooth copper skin reflecting the soft lights of the chamber. His golden hair curled in the same way as the young master on the station, but this man's hair tumbled to his shoulders. Heavy chains hung around his neck, and circlets passed around each mighty bicep. A narrow band circled his head, with the form of a swaying serpent above his eyes. The man was naked, besides his adornments and cloth slippers.

To behold him was like staring into the face of a god. Perfect. Exquisite. And he was at least seven feet tall. He didn't blink as he appraised her, exuding feigned majesty and imagined superiority. Laurel expected his voice to be like thunder, but when he spoke, it was articulate, mellow, almost intimate.

"Judith?" he said softly. "Or an imposter who stands before me?"

Laurel didn't move, nor did she speak. The master approached, circling gracefully, studying. She didn't raise her eyes to his until he stood before her, not even responding when he reached down and rubbed a lock of her hair between his fingers.

"Hmm," he murmured, then ran a smooth finger around her jawline, bringing her gaze up to meet his.

"The traitor Abel would be glad to see you after all these years. Enoch?" the master addressed the Magen Bearer, who reached him in three full strides. "Are you certain this is Judith? Perhaps Sedar has deceived us." The master didn't take his eyes from Laurel. "This woman seems…diminished."

"My Lord, how can this not be Judith?" Enoch said with a bow. "See her eyes? They are of the deepest amber."

"Then how were you able to take her?" the master barked, suddenly nasty. Then he softened. "Judith would have sensed you." The master inspected Laurel's face, then turned aside briefly to address Enoch with a sneer. "Perhaps your powers become weak? Perhaps the light of your star fades?"

Enoch lifted his chin but didn't reply, and the master returned to his study of Laurel. "It could be trickery. Judith has deceived us in the past," he said, frowning. Then he stepped back. "If you are Judith, you will recall the last time you stood in my presence, when you urged me to let your people go. I was obliging that day, despite all the trouble you created. And to repay our generosity, you put us all to sleep." He twisted his magnificent body toward Enoch and laughed. "Perhaps we needed the rest!"

Laurel felt the entity stilling her tongue. She yearned to rebut, tell the smug bastard he wouldn't win, but the entity knew better. It would direct her, and now Laurel knew how Hebre escaped. She just wished she knew how to put the masters to sleep.

"Enoch tells me you are raising a battalion," the master said. "Fascinating. I wonder from where this army will be drawn. The Kalmeddi?" He sneered again, and the sneer transformed the beauty of his face to a brief, monstrous ugliness, only returning to its perfection as his expression relaxed. "Perhaps the traitorous Sons of David will join them. What do you think, Magen Bearer?" Enoch didn't move. He was his master's servant. Others might betray the masters, but he would not. He would defend them to the death.

"It matters not," the master said to Laurel. "You come too late to save the humans; what is done cannot be undone. You appear to us as Judith, even making fools of Sedar and Enoch with your sorcery. I see now you are but a single Hebre, come to wage war against the Defenders of Heaven; to pit yourself and the pathetic mortals against the might of the Sons of Benjamin and David." The master laughed, then made the same soft hissing noise Laurel had heard from the young master. "It will be a lively diversion. One hundred and forty-four thousand Hebre fled in the face of the masters." He tilted his head, daring her to defend them. When she didn't reply, he lowered his voice and leaned close to her ear. "Judith promised to return," he whispered, his mouth brushing her cheek, "and I see now what has returned is nought but a weak copy! We have nothing to fear." His eyes became dark and menacing. "You will *fail!*"

Enoch reached out, and seconds later, Laurel was flung across the Edensai compound into Harry's embrace.

"Laurel," he sighed as he held her close. "What

happened? What did they do?" He stepped back to inspect her for injury.

She shook her head. "Nothing. He just wanted to see me for himself. He knows I'm not Judith, and he's not concerned. He seemed to find me laughable." Laurel put her arm around Ava, her relief to be back reaching every person in the compound. "He thinks I'm alone. Sedar only told him about me. I'm certain he doesn't know about Ava and Darlen yet."

"Was it the ship? Did you meet the masters?" Marcel said, joining in the group hug with Harry and Ava.

"Yes, only one."

Seeing Laurel unharmed, Abel struggled to keep the emotion from his voice. "Did he wear a band on his forehead?"

Laurel nodded.

"That is Cephus," Abel said, "Lord of the Sons of Benjamin and David."

"He knows we're raising an army," Laurel told them. "He's not taking it seriously."

Plio stood in front of Laurel, and she sensed his now solid but as yet unspoken allegiance to Hebre. "That you are returned safely," he said, "tells us Cephus believes you are not Judith. He does not fear one Hebre alone. He has made a grave error."

"He confirmed that Judith caused a sleep to come over the masters—" Laurel sought out Majo's face among the crowd, "just as Majo said. That's how the arks managed to escape fifteen years ago. And there's something else…" she grinned and took Harry's datacache. "I didn't just stand around chatting…" Laurel quickly drew an accurate diagram of the inside of the chamber. In the upper bulkhead, she sensed the exact location of the forcefield emitter. She handed it to Harry.

"Are you sure?" he smiled, wide-eyed.

"Positive," Laurel nodded. "And surprising because technology is usually Ava's thing. You would have to plant the explosive in the centre of that chamber, under the emitter, to have the desired effect. It's the only weak spot. There is other technology within the walls for use as a flight deck or a control room, although the chamber itself looks empty. I don't know how many masters would likely be in there at one time."

Harry felt like cheering. Laurel safe and with extra intelligence about the masters' ship. He didn't care who stared. He gave her a noisy kiss on the mouth. "You are awesome; do you know that?!"

Laurel laughed, startled, and felt Abel's eyes on her, but she could do nothing about his feelings. They were part of his memories, not hers. His was a love for a woman long dead.

CHAPTER TWENTY-TWO _

Laurel sat next to Harry on the trip back to the station, quietly reflecting on the events of the day. She'd allowed him to check her with the pandroscope despite her assurances she had not been harmed. Thinking back to Plio's comment about Cephus making a grave error in believing she wasn't Judith, she remembered the masters had underestimated Hebre before. Perhaps they were about to do it again, and Laurel was grateful the entity made sure she didn't say or do anything in her ignorance that would sabotage their plans.

"Seven feet tall. I can't believe it," Harry whistled out a breath, jarring her from her thoughts. "How are we going to take on an army like that? Like Majo said, outgunned and outnumbered."

Laurel shoved him. "Don't be so gloomy. We have to take advantage of their arrogance and their confidence in their invincibility. Cephus thinks a single Hebre, without Judith's powers, is powerless against them."

"So they don't presume you've got any new tricks up your sleeve?"

"No, he was clueless," Laurel grinned, but still, what if she *had* been Judith? Cephus couldn't have been sure when he brought her on board. That was why there was no-one else in the chamber. Laurel had an instinct Cephus wanted to be the one to capture Judith, to present her to the other masters, but when he saw Laurel, it was just her eyes that confused him. Otherwise, he found no prize, no glory. The other masters would be of the same view as Cephus, that a single Hebre had returned and posed no threat. That knowledge alone was almost worth being abducted by Enoch because it meant the masters would not come looking again, hopefully until it was too late.

"I had an interesting conversation with Yosser," Ava said. "After his parents were killed, he was taken in by a Hebre woman, Esther. She had violet eyes, like me. Yosser believed she was dead, executed by the Magen Bearer, but I told him I thought Esther was the woman who brought the Riyneans to Isilia. That's why at the gathering I said Mom and I were descendants of Judith and Esther."

"Abel mentioned her just after Laurel was taken," Harry said, remembering Abel's comment from earlier. "Supposedly you resemble her. Yosser must have told Abel what you told him, but I don't think anyone is absolutely certain you're not the real Esther and Judith."

Ava had been glad to deliver good news to Yosser, but... "He was over the moon and couldn't wait to tell Abel. At first, he thought I was her because he didn't know any other Hebre with violet eyes. I guess I didn't convince him."

"It seems too that Judith was the only amber-eyed Hebre," Laurel said. "No wonder people think we're either the originals or reincarnations."

"Could you be?" Darlen remarked when they later

related the events of the day back on the Canaa.

"No," Laurel said, remembering the intimate vision with Abel and knowing that it was not from her own memory. "I don't believe in reincarnation. Descendants, probably, although I don't know how. I'm not Judith. I only look like her." But even as she spoke those words, a movement deep within her, the same as the one she had on the masters' ship, gave her the sense they fell far short of the truth.

"Can you estimate how many Hebre children were born here and who left on the arks during the exodus?"

"I can give you exact numbers, Laurel," Beril said. "Why?"

"I'm curious as to how a Hebre/human infant acquires the entity." Among a myriad of others that had no hope of being answered just yet, this question had kept Laurel up half the night. "If the original Hebre or their descendants made it to my world," she continued, not expecting Beril to have an answer, "and they had children, where did the entity come from in each succeeding generation? Did it pass from parent to child?" Laurel made a face as she pondered the conundrum. "I can't see how that would work. The parent would have to die before the birth of the child unless the entity could somehow share itself or separate."

Beril's blank expression reflected his lack of knowledge. "We knew so little about Hebre. The only information they ever provided is that each entity is 'of itself'. When the physical body dies, it returns to the nebula. I wondered as you do, but in the end, concluded a new entity from the nebula inhabited the infant."

"But the nebula doesn't cross into the dimension that holds Earth." Laurel had considered the possibilities. "How would it get from here to there when a new baby is born?"

Beril gave a non-committal shrug. "That would be where any theory falls down. Our only other observation was that no child could result from the union between two Hebre; I know only of three such unions, all childless."

"Are you sure about that?" Laurel probed further. "About two Hebre not reproducing?"

Beril tilted his head from side to side. "The evidence points to a barren union. Besides, a child could not inherit two eye colours!" He laughed, weighing up the impossibility by executing a juggling motion with his hands. "Hebre infants had the same eye colour as the Hebre parent."

"I have amber eyes," Laurel said, recognising her following statement would rock Beril's carefully organised opinions "And Ava's father had violet eyes. Beril, this will come as a surprise. Ava is my child."

The physician was indeed stunned, and the grin on his face shifted to puzzled disbelief. He gave a shaky laugh. "I— It is not possible."

Laurel smiled at his confusion and repeated her statement, though he heard her well enough. "Ava is my child. The child of two Hebre."

Beril put his hand to his head in confusion. "And this conception took place…where? It was not here, not before you left…"

"I'll just remind you, Beril," Laurel said. "I am not Judith." With both of Gabriel's children present, it seemed too public to debate such intimacy, but she would confine herself to facts. "I was a prisoner-of-war," she continued. "Gabriel, my captor, was Hebre. He is Ava's father. He already had a son, Marcel."

"You became pregnant to your captor?" Beril was horrified. He glanced across at Marcel; he'd already noted Marcel's grey eyes, so not Hebre.

Harry looked on. He could see Laurel was trying to be delicate for Marcel and Ava's sake, but Laurel was in complete control. "There was no coercion," she said after a moment, not looking at her daughter as she recognised the implication of Beril's statement. "But Gabriel was Hebre, the son of a violet eyed Hebre woman brought to League space by Darlen when he was a Soul Monger. Gabriel was conceived on Earth."

Beril looked at Darlen and took a deep breath. "One day, my friend, I wish to discuss this Soul Mongering with you."

Darlen grinned. "Any time."

Beril turned back to Laurel, ignoring the ever so slightly embarrassed expressions on both Ava and Marcel's faces. "During conception," Beril asked clinically, "are you able to report any extraordinary phenomena? I ask because of the lights that appeared above Eden before the imps were changed. Did you experience anything unexpected?"

Darlen coughed to hide his inappropriate laugh, and Harry had to hide a smile behind his hand. They should all have got up and left, but Beril's indelicate questioning was rather distracting. Laurel had opened a can of worms. It would be interesting, not to mention entertaining, to see how she handled it. Laurel was aware of their amusement and stole a glance at Marcel and Ava, who were not sure they wanted to hear her answer.

"As a matter of fact," Laurel said, matching Beril's objective approach, even though she wished she'd kept this topic for another time, "I was aware of an intense violet-coloured light. Neither Gabriel nor I knew what it meant."

Beril's face creased into a frown. "Do you have more details?"

"Yes, but you can't have them," Laurel declared, but suddenly, the violet light she saw the night Ava was conceived took on a whole new meaning. Semevale 7 was close to the nebula. And where was Esther's entity at that point in time? Clearly, Gabriel's entity did not inhabit Ava, nor did his mothers. Ava's entity came from somewhere else entirely.

Beril stopped. His interest was purely scientific, but this was personal, intensely so, and he was insensitive. "Oh, yes, of course. Umm. Interesting. What became of this Gabriel? Does he live?"

"No, he was killed at the end of the war."

Beril was fascinated. For sure, Ava and Laurel were Hebre; it was just… "If this took place in some other time or some other galaxy," he wondered aloud, "perhaps natural laws are different from here."

"I only told you because I was trying to understand how Hebre managed to survive so long in human bodies for so many centuries," Laurel said. "I just can't work it out."

"Maybe you will understand when you are at the end of your life and Hebre returns to the nebula," Beril suggested.

"She won't wait that long," Darlen swung himself out of his chair, the afternoon's entertainment ended. "Laurel likes her answers quicker than that. Beril, we need to get the gas condensed." He flicked a glance at Harry. "Coming?" Harry got out of his seat and headed towards the Canaa's cargo bay with Beril and Darlen, throwing a cheeky grin at Laurel as he went.

Helen's gas model was untested, so they just had to believe it would work. Beril was confident. He understood such things, working as a skilled chemist alongside his work as a physician. Olyo insisted that she pilot the ship and release the gas on Legion so her attendants would only be involved in the evacuation and not have direct contact with the battle operations.

The Kalmeddi engineers worked hard at weapons production but seeing the components spread out on the Canaa's cargo bay floor made Laurel realise just how dismal a resistance they would make, particularly if the masters realised they planned to take the arks. They'd located a Legion battalion positioned near the holding area, and Laurel assumed the size of that unit would be proportionate to the ships' vastness. The Canaa's sensors located three city-sized, solid objects hovering above a valley. Olyo told them the arks were of basic design, usually landed and that she was unaware of any technology that would keep them hovering, or even why. The valley was hemmed in by tablelands containing mineral-dense rocks that effectively caused shadows on the Canaa's sensors, resulting in a "now you see them, now you don't" scenario that took Mer several hours to define accurately. In time, the precise position and scope of each craft emerged. The only thing they were unable to work out was how close the arks were hovering relative to the tops of the bluffs. The proposal was for Olyo to drop Laurel, Ava and Marcel as close to the ships as possible under Hebre cloak. At that point, Laurel and Ava would start the rain and gain entry to the arks. Then as Harry and Abel began their attack on Legion, Olyo would disperse Helen's gas over the Legion battalion, and any cloaked Legion, to ensure their attention was taken up by the resistance, hopefully preventing them from doing anything to stop the arks from leaving.

Ava had suggested bringing the rain sooner, but both Abel and Harry believed it would turn the dusty terrain into treacherous, slippery mud, giving them a disadvantage when their soldiers attacked the Legion guards. Meanwhile, Harry and Darlen had built a device with the potential to blast the masters' ship out of orbit. It would have the unfortunate effect of adding to the toxic cloud already encroaching upon Eden, but that couldn't be helped. If everything went according to plan, most of the planet would be underwater by the time the resulting toxins settled, and many of the people safely resettled on Riynea. Darlen would deliver the device in a single hop from the station, applying a magnetised forcefield he hoped the masters didn't have the technology to remove before it exploded. Everything was in place; all that was left was to fit Olyo's ship with the gas reservoirs.

"I pray the Farisee will escape the wrath of Lilith for

the slaughter of her children," Olyo said as she and Laurel worked together. Laurel faced her. She liked Olyo, but she also saw through her. Olyo seemed untroubled that the words she spoke often didn't fit her true thoughts. As Farisee Ascendant, Olyo was compelled to live by her people's customs, but she also had opinions, private opinions she couldn't hide from a telepath. Laurel raised an eyebrow at her Farisee friend.

"You only found out about Lilith from the story told by Legion, Olyo," she said with a smile, "then drew on that as an explanation for the imps. We've pretty much proved the imps were caused by a virus that altered the Edensai's genetic coding."

Olyo pursed her lips and flicked a glance at Laurel. "Where do you believe the justification for any belief in a god comes from?"

Laurel took a deep breath and gave the question a moment's thought. "I guess I always believed it came from faith or tradition. Are you telling me your personal belief system isn't grounded?"

"Oh, I *believe*," Olyo said, a little defensively, "but I am not a fool. My people's traditions are ancient, timeless; for them, life can have no meaning without the gods. The Farisee discover new gods to worship in private devotion every day, and some of those are presented to the Ascendancy in response to some 'miracle' or other. Mainly, they are invented." Olyo smiled sagely. "For me, Laurel, gods are as grains of sand. There are so many; I am sure that if I did not look where my foot fell, I would grind them under my heels!"

Laurel grinned at her analogy. "At least you know Lilith isn't going to come after the Farisee."

"I know it," Olyo nodded. "Unfortunately, my people think otherwise. That is why it is I who works beside you and not them."

"But they trust you?"

"Only very few will ever know what I have done," Olyo replied. "If I had the courage, I would fight alongside your friends."

Laurel couldn't allow such a comment. "You are courageous, Olyo, taking food to the Edensai, helping them."

Olyo snorted. "It isn't courageous to prolong death, but it is in such things I have to lead my people in the way their gods teach them, and that is to respect and preserve all life."

"I suspect you don't include the masters in that statement?"

Olyo snorted again. "I do not, but my people believe Lilith to be a goddess, and you cannot hide these deeds from her."

Laurel sighed. Some convictions can't be argued against. "Okay, but you and I know there isn't any Lilith to hold you responsible."

Again, Olyo gave Laurel that sage grin and left her to finish up just as Harry arrived to overhear the last part of the discussion.

"They take a very unsophisticated view of their gods' personalities," he said. "If there really is an all-seeing Lilith, the chances are she'd see through the Hebre cloak."

"Olyo is honouring their beliefs, that's all," Laurel said, shifting her shoulders as they tensed, and she rubbed the back of her neck. From the moment she arrived in the League, she had been at war. The Gartrya, the Gale, the Ferle, and now her family followed her on this expedition to find answers, and here they were again, amid yet another conflict.

"Are you okay?"

"Just a headache, Harry."

"Ava's complaining of one as well. I'll check you both out. It won't help your concentration if you're both in pain."

Laurel followed Harry to the Canaa's med bay. The pain had become severe enough for Laurel to need to lie still, close her eyes and wait for Harry's conclusions, even though she was entirely capable of diagnosing herself. It felt nice to have Harry fussing over her even though it was just a headache, but Harry was silent for just a second too long. Laurel had shut off her senses to rest her mind, and it took a moment for her to register his bewilderment, then his alarm.

"Show me," she said, pushing herself up into a sitting position to check the pandroscope. It indicated an area in Laurel's central brain had become indistinct, brain activity had increased, and a bizarre pattern developed that had the pandroscope battling. Laurel's entire brain registered heightened stimulation.

Baffled, the two of them examined the pandroscope.

"I wonder why the brain has been stimulated in this way," Laurel said. "I have an elevated heart rate, raised adrenaline; reasonable under the circumstances, but I wouldn't have expected these changes." Laurel looked at Harry; she understood. "The entity. It's preparing for war."

"You are the deliverance."

"What did you say?" she said sharply.

"I didn't say anything," Harry replied, puzzled. "I don't know what to say."

Those words had not come from Harry; Laurel heard them as an echo. There was no time to ponder the mystery. She directed the pandroscope to administer a painkiller and hopped from the table. "I'd say this is what's happening to Ava as well."

"Possibly," Harry said. He wasn't at all sure about these changes or the damage they could do. "Do you feel any heightened cognition, greater strength than before? How would you be if I gave you a complicated math problem?"

"Probably useless, maths isn't my strong point. There's only one word to describe how I feel. Fearless."

"Despite your physical body showing signs of anxiety?"

"Despite that."

"That's interesting on its own."

Laurel stopped and grinned, just to reassure him. "Yes, it is, isn't it? Shows I'm human."

"At least we agree on that. How's the pain now?"

"Easing. Let's check on Ava."

CHAPTER TWENTY-THREE _

Marcel and Ava spent several hours each day with the exercise holoenemies in the cargo bay as they prepared to return to the surface. During Marcel's slumber in variance, Scarlett practised her reprogramming skills on the holoenemies and changed them to interactive characters from the fairy stories told her by Laurel. By the time Marcel began his exercise routine, there was little opportunity to reset their appearance. Ava loved the kick-ass Pinocchio and Cinderella, but Marcel had trouble taking a winged fairy-princess seriously, at least one that used a wand as a weapon. He swore he would get Mer to add a subroutine when all this was over to block them from ever being changed again.

Laurel, Ava and Marcel went over their part of the strategy many times while recognising they knew too little about the arks' location and the troops' capabilities for defending them. There simply wasn't time to return to the surface to pump Majo and Abel and the others for more information to take away and analyse. Harry and Darlen were confident with the explosive device they'd designed, although they realised some variables could result in its failure, such as the magnetic field failing or the masters somehow destroying it before it got the chance to detonate. The "what if's" got firmly dismissed by Darlen, and satisfied there was little else they could do, Laurel and the others prepared to return to Eden to arm the Sons of David and Jadren's "weakling warriors" with weapons and a strategy.

Olyo transported them to Eden in her ship, along with several attendants to pilot the evacuating arks. The Farisee had already taken word to every Edensai congregation they could find, and three scouts went to the mustering point in anticipation of the arrival of the arks. Ava took the tandem axispods just in case an orbital battle ensued or as a possible means of escape.

The pitiful assortment of troops assembled, primarily housed in surrounding caves, hidden away from any aerial observance, but there were not more than four hundred Sons of David and about as many from Jadren's weakling warriors. Eight hundred against thousands, aided by two hopeful Hebre, a Soul Monger and Harry and Marcel. Laurel resisted the urge to let her spirits fall as the weapons were circulated and tested. The Kalmeddi's uneasiness in the use of armaments got the better of them over and over until Laurel wondered if the Kalmeddi might be more of a hindrance. Abel watched with her.

"You've provided basic weapons, simple to use and capable of causing damage to the Legion battalion," he said. "Remember, the focus for you is to bring the arks and to cause the waters to rise."

"According to the sensors," Laurel said with a sigh that showed her concern, "the arks are gigantic. A few days ago, I felt fearless. Now I think I'm more jittery about flying one of them than I am about bringing the rain, which Ava and I seem to have mastered now. I've only ever seen an ark in a vision and a diorama, Abel; they're like small cities."

"They are at that," he agreed. His last view of Judith was when she boarded the ark. "But they are also silent. The Farisee find noise vulgar and intrusive upon their devotions, and the arks are used as portable homes as they shelter from the extremes of weather on their homeworld. Laurel, you must not lose courage now."

"I have a human side that doesn't have the wisdom of the first Hebre."

"It is Hebre's task to free the oppressed."

Laurel smiled thinly. "I expected at this stage in my life, I would be living a peaceful existence, not taking part in yet another war."

Abel understood how she felt. Peace was something he and Judith longed for. "We will prevail against the masters," he said. "The time is right." He looked around. "The Magen Bearer is not with you?"

"He's on the station," Laurel told him. "He'll deploy the explosive that will bring down the masters' ship. If he's successful, and he's required here, he'll join us."

"Is he of the covenant?"

"Covenant?" Laurel frowned. "What covenant?"

"The covenant whereby the Magen Bearers return Hebre to the nebula," Abel explained. "It was their oath to Hebre they would not be forever estranged from their home."

"Hebre entered Sheerguhd from League space," Laurel told him. "When they got to Earth, they were effectively scattered through time. The Soul Mongers, as we call them, took them back to League space, not to return them to their home, but to sell into slavery."

Abel shook his head. "Then the covenant has become lost. Corrupt. You must remind your Magen Bearer of his promise."

"I will," Laurel said. "I absolutely will." And Laurel knew Darlen would be glad to receive that news.

"There is something else you must know, Laurel," Abel said. "While Hebre is resistant to the masters' stench, the bane can paralyse even Hebre. If they spit, your body might be vulnerable."

Laurel groaned. Another thing to consider. "If the masters only had their scent and bane as weapons," she sighed, "how the hell did they destroy an entire kingdom and other star systems?"

"Creation is spread across many kingdoms," Abel explained, "but there are few systems populated by humankind. The first kingdom only had fourteen planets inhabited by humans, but many others with intelligent, non-human species that the masters spared."

"Then the masters would have had a problem in League space," Laurel told him. "They have thousands of inhabited planets. And with a lot of different species who would rise up to resist them, human and non-human."

"It was so in the first kingdom," Abel said, his voice low, filled with regret. "Yet no human life exists there now, and the planets are cold."

Laurel squeezed his arm gently. "And we are going to stop it happening here. I think you've just told me humans are not the dominant species throughout the universe, throughout Sheerguhd. Scientists on Earth wouldn't like to hear that."

"The masters say there are six kingdoms within Sheerguhd that support human life," Abel said. "Their creator rests in the seventh kingdom. It is his realm."

"What do the other kingdoms contain? The ones that don't support human life?"

"I don't know," Abel answered, "alternative life, new creations? The masters say those, as all non-human species, were created by Lilith. I know Judith knew the truth, but I know she kept some things from me. To protect me."

"I didn't know Judith, but I like her very much."

Abel grinned. "So did I."

Laurel, Ava, Marcel and Harry were introduced to each group. Laurel was happy to see Majo again, accompanied by Plio, who had arrived wearing parts of his old armour. He didn't speak, only inclined his head towards her, another silent declaration he would stand beside Hebre in the coming conflict.

Laurel handed Abel a communicator. "The signal is designed for Darlen to understand and carries only a Farisee signature. The signal travels as far as the station. If things go bad," she warned, "it's between you and him."

Abel took the communicator, but his look showed his resolve that absolutely nothing would go wrong.

Harry outlined the plan to the Kalmeddi volunteers and the Sons of David. It was simple. There was only one stronghold to attack, and even though they would be outnumbered, Helen's gas would doubtless even the score by exposing any stealthed troops. Harry told them that as the fighting commenced, then so would the masters' ship be destroyed. There followed a ripple of subdued cheering, although both Laurel and Ava saw not all present were persuaded the plan would work, but the overall sense was at least they were doing *something.*

Laurel also spoke, mainly because the presence of Hebre seemed to bring consolation to the people. Aided by the Farisee, Abel reached out to as many settlements and Holy Trahs as possible, revealing the probable serious impacts and limited capacity on the arks. Wearied by a lifetime of hardship and despair, many were unconcerned if they were not chosen to be part of the exodus; still others hoped they would make it off Eden alive. However, the Trahs did not reveal the flood to their congregations, knowing that to live with the prospect of drowning was nearly as terrifying as facing the wrath of the masters.

"Whatever happens now, Laurel," Abel said, "it will be the end. The Sons of David, at least those without children, will remain on Eden, but I mourn for the other families and young people who will not find a place on the arks."

"As do I," Laurel said, "but there is a toxic cloud headed this way, and if we do nothing, all of you will die, but if we are successful, some will survive, and mankind throughout all the other kingdoms will be preserved."

"And those yet to come."

"What do you mean?"

"Within the folds of Sheerguhd, other galaxies, new kingdoms are formed, and Sheerguhd breathes life into humankind."

"Do you believe humankind was created, Abel?"

He shrugged slightly. He'd pondered the question before, but even Judith, with all her insight, could not give him a clear answer. "As Sheerguhd came into being, so did we. Pure light, childlike, eager to learn, waiting as the galaxies and stars set themselves in the heavens."

What an odd response, Laurel thought; she hadn't picked Abel as religious. "Not the answer I expected."

Abel smiled. "*You* told me that."

"Me, or Judith?"

But Abel didn't answer.

"And what do the masters believe?" Laurel asked.

"That the creator was brighter than any star in the heavens, and so commanded the lesser stars."

"And is this where Lilith comes in?"

Abel nodded. "His consort. Lilith brought forth all variety of fantastic and exotic creatures, animals, non-human…"

"The masters consider Lilith their mother, and they hate humans, yet they're human for the most part."

"Perhaps," Abel said cryptically. "Or perhaps we are all creations of Eve."

It all seemed to Laurel much like religion on Earth, whatever serves your belief system.

"God never featured much in my life, Abel," she said in all honesty. "I have to say that if this creator brought forth humankind, his blueprint for them was pretty random. There is a lot to love and just as much not to." And here she was calling this creator "him", awarding it gender and a personality. To Laurel, the god so worshipped on Earth didn't exist as an entity. Did every individual who ever lived begin as an arbitrary point of energy until something more powerful harnessed them and made them human? Was a physical body so much easier to control? Did he, this creator make them subject to mortality and so bend them to his will? Or was it an act of love borne out of his union with Eve? If the masters' creator did exist, Laurel wanted to go no further than destroying the masters; she would choose not to seek out their deity. If he slept now in the seventh kingdom, let him slumber.

The rebellion woke to a bitterly cold, diamond-hard morning. Laurel and Ava stayed up the entire night, neither of them feeling any fatigue, only a vitality they could not define. Hagar discovered them before the first fingers of dawn streaked Eden's sky. She held their hands and sat between them, rocking gently as she hummed a low mournful tune. Laurel and Ava listened, the mesmerising throaty keen allowing the story of the song to seep into their bones, a narrative of a time before the masters, a time when the sun shone, the breezes warmed, and the people were filled with the joy of living. Hagar kept up the song until the army gathered and many Sons of David bowed at her feet to ask for a blessing.

Harry sought out Laurel. He was doing a splendid job of disguising his fear for her and attempted a bright smile, but he knew she saw right through him, and his pretence fell rapidly away. "I can't help it," he groaned, pulling her close. "I seem to be too often in a position where I might lose you."

Laurel slid her arms around his waist and held him tight. She feared for him too. "But you haven't lost me," she murmured against his chest, "and you're not going to lose me now either. This is the critical strike—" She looked up, desperate to reassure him so that he would not be distracted by his fears when he went into battle. "It will be over soon, I promise."

Many people in the compound were wrapped in similar embraces, knowing that when the ark eventually arrived, their loved one might have already perished at the hands of Legion.

Harry held her tight. "I love you, Laurel. I would follow you to hell; you know that?"

Laurel once more rested her head against his chest as the thought came to her, silent and unbidden, *Perhaps this time, my love, you have.*

CHAPTER TWENTY-FOUR _

Late that night, Olyo flew the cloaked ship as close to the arks as possible, but the narrow gulley proved a precarious passage even for her small ship, and barred her from flying underneath. A tethering field encompassed each massive vessel.

"The arks are too high to access from the ground," Olyo said, "and there are no entryways on the upper or lower hull; all access has to be through these ports here and here." Olyo showed them half a dozen sealed entrances, three forward and three aft; too few for such a large ship, and Laurel knew this lack of access would slow down the evacuation.

Ava examined the field of the closest ark, her eyes narrowed in thought. "Those fields..." she murmured, mostly to herself, "are generated—" She pointed out the forward viewport, before adding, more loudly, "—from a single power generator at the location of the Legion unit. They're not to keep anyone out of the ark; they're to stop it moving. So even if we get onto the arks, they're fixed in place."

Marcel double-checked Ava's findings and nodded his agreement. "Then we have no alternative but to disable the tethers at their source."

"And get back here," Laurel added. "But that will delay Harry and Abel starting their strike on Legion."

"It can't be helped, Mom. We predicted a few obstacles."

Olyo dropped down behind one of the arks while the others deliberated on what to do about this unexpected barrier. "How close do you need to be to disable the generator?" she asked.

"Pretty close," Ava said. "It might be better for you to drop me at a distance from the Legion camp. I'll knock out the power, and you can pick me up. The problem is, I don't know at what distance I can reasonably keep up the power disruption. It might kick in again before we get back here."

"What if you drop the three of us, Olyo. We can conceal ourselves no problem to enter the compound," Laurel suggested, "then you send a message to Harry that he needs to destroy the power generator. We'll make it to the arks on foot. Ava will be able to keep the generator down for a fair distance."

Olyo nodded. She knew that she would become visible as soon as Hebre were off the ship, so she wouldn't be able to put down too close for fear of detection and raising suspicion. She dropped them behind a ridge that consisted of the same minerals that obscured the Canaa's sensors. The location placed the Legion guard squarely between the group and the arks, but Laurel didn't see this as an issue as they could circumvent the area on the ground under cloak, then Ava could bring down the power, which in turn was likely to create a diversion, working in Harry's favour. If it all went to plan, Laurel, Marcel and Ava would reach the arks in a reasonable time. The only shortfall was Marcel was not equipped with Hebre speed and so would likely slow them. There would be nothing for it but for him to be carried. He wouldn't take kindly to the proposition, so Laurel decided not to mention it until the power was out and they were on their way to the arks. This entire operation was put together with heavy reliance on luck and innovation. Marcel's dignity had to be the least of their worries.

The Legion battalion had made themselves at home on an abandoned plantation, perhaps more detached from the arks' mountain storage than wise, but it was clear they didn't count on the Farisee coming back to recover their property.

"They look like they've been here for a while," Ava whispered as they viewed the goings-on in the compound. "They seem quite at home."

"I would have thought it made more sense to establish a stronghold *under* the arks rather than at a distance of miles," Marcel whispered back.

"Maybe they're not being overseen," Laurel suggested. "The gulley floor was pretty rocky; it would be far less comfortable. These troops are assuming victory. I learned in the Gartryan war that once the soldiers believed themselves victorious, they slacked off."

Within Laurel's Hebre shroud, an act that for Laurel always carried powerful reminders of Helen, the group encircled the enemy compound unseen. Marcel commented that none of the soldiers were handling weapons nor guarding the few small un-uniform ships. Ava and Laurel identified perhaps a dozen pairs of stealthed soldiers patrolling the perimeter, but their presence was mainly token, a loose nod to protocol, their interests dedicated to conversation with their comrade. Although they were armed, they were decidedly not at the ready—another advantage for Harry.

They moved closer. The soldiers in the compound were filthy. Planetwide, the water was contaminated and unsafe even for washing, although, unlike the Edensai, the soldiers here showed no visible signs of dehydration. It was possible Legion was provided with water rationing by the masters. Thanks to the more robust constitution of their particular variant of human, they didn't look undernourished. Ava picked up Laurel's observation as to the shabby living circumstances.

"Won't be long now, Mom, we'll give them a good drenching," she smirked, referring to the flood to come. "That'll make them smell sweeter!"

Several laughing Riynean females emerged from one of the huts, moving freely amongst the hovels and Legion soldiers. These women were probably captives of Legion from years before and who had since become resigned to captivity. At least four of the women were heavily pregnant. Several youngsters, all boys, accompanied the women and proceeded to run amok amidst laughter and encouragement from the men. A fire blazed centrally, and a dozen or so Legion were arranged lazily to get the benefit of the warmth. One woman, perhaps in her late twenties, slid to the ground next to a soldier who cupped her against him as he kissed her ear affectionately while continuing his discourse with his fellow troops.

"Hostages?" Ava suggested.

"There's an easy familiarity between those women and the soldiers," Laurel pointed out. "These women were likely taken from Riynea years ago, maybe as children, probably to supply the next generation of Legion."

"The girl in that man's arms, near the fire, looks quite relaxed," Ava said.

Laurel nodded, "Yes, and these women looked to have fared better as Legion hostages than the Edensai; they would need to if they're producing sons to reinforce the ranks of Legion. Some prisoners do become fond of their captors," she said without thinking. Ava looked across sharply, sensing an absent-minded reference to her mother's imprisonment in the fortress on Semevale 7. But Laurel hadn't paid attention to the thought that surfaced unbidden as matters of war threw a mantle over other considerations. "Abel told me they kill most of the female newborns," she added.

"Why?" Marcel's disgust for these monsters had more layers than he cared to consider.

"They don't fight," Laurel said. "And they wouldn't be able to procreate for at least twelve or so years, so what use would they be? Look, there's the generator beside that ship."

Ava moved away. "I'll do it when we get to the entrance of the valley. It looks like the generator also powers those perimeter lights, so they'll be in darkness as well. That anchoring field has an extensive range, Mom. If Harry and the others get beaten back or don't destroy it, Legion could theoretically spark it up again and stop us mid-flight."

Laurel waved away the comment. Harry wouldn't get beaten back, and she wouldn't let Ava even think it. "It's not going to happen," she said firmly. "Let's get across."

Going straight through the compound would have taken them less time to reach the mouth of the valley, but Laurel was afraid any inadvertent contact with either a person or object might reveal them to Legion or the women. They were cloaked, but they were still solid, and they needed to be on the arks and out of here before Harry and Abel's company arrived.

With little more than a brief moment of intense concentration from Ava, Legion was plunged into darkness. The ensuing chaos after the generator went down would have been amusing had they had time to observe. Shouting, arguing, issuing orders and even torches lit from the fire added to the commotion.

That done, the trio headed into the valley towards the distant, silent, sleeping monoliths silhouetted in the moonlight. As Laurel decided earlier, and to his consternation and alarm, Marcel was hoisted unceremoniously onto her back. She carried him at a speed he would never have matched. At the first ark, she pushed him off. He didn't say a word, just puffed out his breath as if his lungs had simply suspended their function for a few miles. There was no sign of the tethering field, but the ark was too high even for Laurel's impressive leaping abilities.

Marcel looked up. "They're practically in orbit," he said with a sinking heart. His faith in Ava and Laurel was supreme, but to have Ava use her power over local technologies and for them both to bring the rain, to hope Abel and Harry's troops were successful, then cloak and steal the arks and attempt the evacuation suddenly seemed like a lot of "ifs". Just for a moment, he paused, mentally listing the events that would need to come to pass. Ava poked him in the arm.

"Don't say that."

"My lady sister, I said nothing."

"Well, don't even think it."

"We need to figure out a way to get onto those ships," Laurel said.

"Rain first, Mom. I know a way we can get onto the arks."

Laurel was going to ask how but instead suddenly found herself on the plateau where she and Ava first brought rain. She looked out across the mountains. The cloudfalls were every bit as spectacular in the moonlight. "Why are we here?" she asked.

"Marcel," Ava smiled. "He's trying not to be negative, but he is. And it just felt right to be here; besides, none of this will matter if we don't get the flood happening."

At their first attempt when Abel took them to the plateau, a few scattered rainclouds gathered, producing just a brief, sharp but saturating downpour, enough to reinforce their conviction they could deliver a flood. This time, the moon sank behind black, brooding thunderheads that clashed in the heavens. Jagged lightning streaked across the sky, and the first drops of rain fell on Laurel's face. The change from the whimsy of a moonlit night to that of a violent storm was sudden and terrifying, but the power of the elements coursing through Laurel's body was as electrifying as the storm above. She opened her eyes. She was now underneath the second ark, rain dripping from her chin and nose and her clothes drenched. Already the ground underfoot was changing to mud, and Marcel was nowhere to be seen. Laurel knew precisely what had taken place.

"You put Marcel on the second ark, didn't you?" she smiled at Ava through the rain.

"Yes," Ava nodded, "it made sense seeing as we were cloaking it anyway. After transporting us back to the plateau—just by thinking it—I tried it out on Marcel, but I had to tell him to shut up because he started whining about dissolving. The look on his face as he disappeared was priceless." Ava took a moment to grin. "Mine was probably the same. I don't know where all this is coming from, Mom, but I'm glad of it. Are you ready? I'll put you on the last ark, and I'll take the lead." She paused. "Or can you do this yourself?"

Laurel shook her head; somehow, she didn't feel teleportation was in her repertoire, or if it was, it hadn't occurred to her to explore it. She opened her mouth,

"I…"

Laurel materialised alone on the ark's vast flight deck, surrounded by Farisee religious emblems and icons, before she even finished what she was about to say, which was that she preferred Ava to do it. The bridge was a simple configuration but looked as though part of the array was disassembled, possibly for spare parts. It explained why the arks hadn't been destroyed. They might have been a resource for Legion. She sent a thought to Ava.

"I can fly this ship, but it's damaged. I'm not going to have much manoeuvrability."

"Don't worry. Just keep me on visual."

"Okay. Can you make sense of the controls?"

"Yes, not unlike manual on the axispods. Marcel will have no problem."

Between them, Laurel and Ava hid all three arks. The operation was like raising three cities from their foundations, an operation that had to be accomplished in complete silence, at least not above the roar of the thunder and lightning exploding all around them. As the ships lifted higher, scenes of an intense battle filled her senses. She reached out for Harry. He was safe, for now. Abel was also safe. Abel? Laurel hadn't reached out to him, but… Laurel bit her lip, no time to puzzle over it. Legion was diverted, their power still down, and hopefully, their transmissions and sensors deactivated, so there was no way the soldiers could contact the masters or other Legion. She wondered briefly about the safety of the women and children in the compound, but that had to be Harry and Abel's concern.

Marcel, Laurel, and Ava had all considered the prospect of the Magen Bearer, Enoch, intercepting them, but Darlen appeared to have some kind of ace up his sleeve, which he didn't convey to the others. He told them if he didn't make it through a "showdown" with the Magen Bearer, Mer would have to be sacrificed to set the explosive. Darlen had made the weapon's modification to Sedar's ship and planned to join the battle as soon as the explosive was in place. The Canaa was to remain safely at the station for whoever made it through the coming battles.

The ark rattled nervously as it came to life, then answered Laurel's commands. It glided from its mooring as its immense hull delivered just a few ear-splitting clangs and internal shudders that left Laurel activating all her senses, even though she was positive the din could not be heard by anyone on the ground. Accustomed to lighter and more manoeuvrable ships, Laurel was impatient as the purpose-built arks plodded slowly towards the darkened sky. Their sluggishness also frustrated Ava.

"When this is all over," she sent to her mother, *"we need to teach the Farisee about widespeed. I feel like getting out and pushing."*

"Our paths will deviate soon. Take care, honey. I'll see you back on the station."

"Okay, Mom. Love you."

"Love you too."

Laurel sent a farewell and "love you" to Marcel, who received it and grinned. In a moment, he would be on his own, uncloaked and vulnerable.

CHAPTER TWENTY-FIVE _

Laurel landed the ark as near to the compound as practicable, but because of its size, it still meant the people had to tramp a fair distance through drenching rain and mud. Personal possessions were to be left behind to free up as much room as possible. Children and older people were carried on parents and relative's backs in a steady stream of hopefuls leaving the compound and heading towards the ark. The Farisee had transported evacuees from the outlying areas to the mustering point, seemingly without detection by either the masters or Legion. The Farisee attendants were busy ushering the people onto the arks; it was chaotic, but there was a need to hurry. Laurel was glad to see the people make way for Yosser to enter the ark with Hagar hoisted onto his back, the enormous Place of Peace scroll tied to his chest. His frail body was weighed down, but his expression was one of pure joy. The presence of the Holy Trah, the mother, would bring much peace to the people during this time, and knowing she and the laws of their god were safe, would comfort the poor unfortunates left behind to perish in the coming flood. The frailer community members with a place on the ark would suffer trying to navigate the torrential rain and ankle-deep mud, which would slow the whole process. Laurel knew it couldn't be helped. They'd held off on the rain as long as they could, but they needed the floodwaters to be rising as the arks left to stop any ground forces mobilising. The majority of the Sons of David were fighting alongside Harry and Abel, so it was left to the community's stronger members to assist those that needed help. Many others who had declined a place on the ark, declaring their condition did not warrant them being preserved, or feeling they had nothing left to lose, helped as best as their weakened state allowed.

Laurel pitched in to help with a growing sense of urgency. The operation wasn't proceeding as quickly as she'd hoped. There was no place for luxury on the ark; it was simply a matter of herding the people on and packing them in like cattle, for those chosen to go, infinitely better than being left behind to the masters.

That is if all went to plan. Families elected to remain together whether they got onto the ark or not, and many of the older members of the community stood aside to make way for younger Edensai, refusing to board until they were sure they were not replacing another more worthy or more likely to survive. Laurel looked out at the sea of wet, hopeful faces and her heart ached with the knowledge there wouldn't be room for everyone. Even cramming people into the control area, the ark would hold only two hundred and fifty thousand, perhaps a few more. The journey to Riynea was likely to see many deaths.

The Farisee had proved remarkably efficient in reporting the possibility of evacuation to the mountain and city dwellers, and despite the pouring rain and uncertainty, thousands assembled in anticipation. Not one person jostled for a place; not one voice raised to claim worthiness above another.

Marcel and Ava were further south, in regions neither had visited before, although the Farisee assured them they would make sure the arks were filled. Ava's destination would have a problem with the Southern Ocean, which would almost certainly have risen, but so far, all was progressing as best it could. Laurel had considered the implications of wet bodies crowded together with little room to move or even properly lie down, resulting in exhaustion, possibly pneumonia and, in some cases, hypothermia. She felt their sodden garments as she helped them clamber onto the ark and knew there was little else she could do.

Laurel did not automatically support the idea that when things look too good to be true, they often are, but now…something was not right. The people were entering the ark through the several entries, the Farisee attendants keeping up their urgency. Farisee engineers inspected the damage to the control panel, declaring the removed components to be no barrier to the ships flight capability to Riynea. It was just…so easy. Too easy. Laurel looked around. She wished she could shroud the ark, but then no-one would be able to see it, and she couldn't help the people board alone.

Laurel should have been encouraged by the ease, but a tiny worm of suspicion churned in her stomach. Everything was progressing, the deluge, the arks… She handed over the small child she carried to a Farisee attendant and moved away from the mustering point. Above her, the dark storm clouds lowered underneath the blackness of the night. The only illumination came from the open hatches of the ark. The stinking lake had already overflowed and flooded, even though its stench had been somewhat cleansed. Laurel's boots made sucking, squelching sounds as she waded through the mud, her senses urging her to distance herself from the people. Even though she only trudged a few metres from the ark, she was on such high alert, there was no room for the noise and clamour of the people boarding the arks. The voices faded, and she looked up. Even the thunder and rain seemed…

The first weapons fire blasted against the ark, deflecting towards the ground and sending a group of waiting Edensai into the air. Others were devoured by fire as they exploded upward, many more dying as they impacted the ground. Those on the fringe of the blast drowned as their unconscious bodies sank face down into the mud. Laurel was knocked by the explosion but scrambled to her feet intact. The attacking Legion ship banked to send another volley but was intercepted by the Canaa's axispod, piloted by one of Abel's men. Two visible Legion fighters then swooped low over the crowd, creating overwhelming fear and confusion; the only blessing being the Legion ships had inferior weapons alignment, constructed originally for large targets such as plant and machinery, not fleeing humans, even those who could scarcely run. Two Legion ships landed while a third kept up its assault. The ark appeared to be untouched by the weapons fire, and Laurel saw the hatches close. Only then did the terrified crowd set up a wail of anguish with the realisation any chance of rescue was barred to them and that they were to be sacrificed to the attacking Legion. Laurel pulled out a sidearm and checked her wrist lick. If the masters knew about this ark, they probably knew about the others, and if they attacked Ava, they would see Laurel was not the only Hebre. And the masters would come for them.

Plio ran towards her. "Judith," he yelled as he drew close, either forgetting her real name or never having believed Laurel was not the woman who saved him. "You need to get away. A Farisee scout is waiting. The masters know you are here."

But Plio's warning came too late. Ten armour-clad giants walked coolly out of the rainy gloom amidst the deluge, the mud, the blasts and the shrieking. They stopped to assess the scene as weapons fire and lightning lit up the sky. They were here for Laurel, and upon sighting her and Plio—now a traitorous Son of David, their eyes blackened, and their exquisite mouths twisted into terrifying smiles. Laurel threw her sidearm into the mud. There would be no point. It would just be an encumbrance.

Those men and women capable of running did so, fleeing in terror and confusion towards the dead timber forest beyond. Sobbing mothers held their children close, clinging to the ark and crying out to their god. Others summoned the last of their energy to make a human barrier between the ark and the masters, only to fall into the mud as the masters' paralysing scent reached their nostrils. Those out of range of the stench were hit by a narrow beam fired from a weapon on the back of the masters' hand, resulting in an agonising flame that quickly consumed the victim's body. Around two dozen Legion dropped from a ship to join the fight and advance on the ark. Plio, his men and Jadren's weakling warriors struggled to hold them at bay, only creating a diversion for Legion as Laurel dealt with the masters. Laurel sensed the Farisee pilot preparing to pull away, even though less than half the anticipated number of evacuees had boarded the ark.

These masters were not here to take prisoners and would exterminate anyone who got in the way of securing the prize. Laurel knew they didn't plan on killing her, at least not yet, but there would be no mercy for the others, not for any man, woman or child. The sickly smell of scorching flesh stung Laurel's eyes and nostrils as she circled her enemies, trying to divert them away from the chaos around the ark.

Laurel flew at the master closest to her. She struck him, just missing that sweet spot near his ear, but he was like a mountain, harder and taller than any other enemy she had met in battle. He tried to flip at her as though she were a bug, but he missed. He might be bigger, Laurel realised, but he was slower. Several Sons of David engaged the masters, but they were no longer the warriors they once were, and they too fell, writhing in agony as fire consumed their flesh. Laurel didn't miss with her next three kicks to the masters' heads, crushing one's neck and cutting down the other two. Only a single giant staggered back to his feet, his perfect teeth knocked from his head and missing an eye. He backed off, damaged. Using the mud as a slide, Laurel skidded into the shadow of the rising ark, watching for her advantage, but there were seven of them now and only one of her.

Plio, remarkably agile and fit for a man of his age, along with those left of his men, pressed forward to protect Laurel. One master retaliated by firing a lethal beam which sent Plio hurtling into the mud; his leg severed from his body. He lay still, face down, and the master who fired the shot raised his large boot-clad foot and ground Plio's head into the sodden earth. The other masters advanced. Laurel leapt and kicked the master who killed Plio, firing her wrist lick to disable and distract. Lifting the same weapon he used to sever Plio's leg, the master deliberately aimed at the ark to deflect fire towards her, ensuring she would only be disabled rather than killed. They had been charged with not directly firing at the woman, and not one among them wished to be the one to present a dead Hebre to their Lord Cephus. The beam ricocheted, just as he anticipated, and it sent Laurel spiralling through the air, crashing to the ground in a spray of mud, a jolt of fire searing her shoulder. Stunned, she rolled several times, but agonising pain prevented her springing to her feet before the masters descended upon her. Despite her physical strength, even Laurel could not overpower the combined weight of the five towering men who now had the advantage, each leaning a single boot against her chest, forcing her down into the mud. Standing over her, the pressure from their boots crushing the air from her lungs, she looked through the thick haze of rain and hissing weapons fire, up into their faces. Once perfect in beauty, those faces were now utterly evil, cheeks contorted outwards, eyes wide and dark, their lips thin and peeled back as salivating beasts anticipating a meal, slime dripping from their gaping mouths. An extra row of teeth lifted from under the swollen tongues as a torrent of their paralysing fluid burst towards her. It stung her eyes, and she gagged as the hot, foul-tasting bane flowed into her nose and throat. Her last vision was of a master dropping to one knee to fasten a cruel fist around her neck.

Laurel had to will the tumbling and rolling to slow. Steadying herself, she felt removed from her mortal self, and with that strangeness, she was oddly comforted as fingers entwined with hers, a warmth, an embrace she recognised. Gabriel? The churning slowed, ribbons of colour bore Gabriel away, and Helen reached for her, smiling, her image dividing into millions of Helens that stretched into infinity. Loving arms buoyed Laurel for the briefest of moments, then she was freed, the nebula sending her forth with its blessing she should leave. It was not yet her time. Her purpose was not yet fulfilled.

CHAPTER TWENTY-SIX _

Laurel's return to her body was like the gradual awakening from variance, but here there was no desperate gulping for air, no instrumentation dragged from her barely conscious body, no sucking of fluid from around her back and thighs. Her eyes were closed, and the blood throbbed in the wound on her shoulder, a reminder she still lived. The entity's comforting presence flowed within, but she felt the nebula kept part of her when she left.

The ground was hard beneath her feet, and she sensed the presence of the masters. The remnants of the viscous, foul-smelling liquid the masters issued from their mouths oozed down her back, reacting to the warmth of her body and creating tiny tendrils of steam that rose to invade her nostrils with its stench. Her hair clung to her face and head, and her already close-fitting one-piece flight suit was stiff and plastered to her body with a mixture of mud and sticky bane.

Laurel blinked a few times. Mercifully, the light was soft, and her eyes quickly became accustomed. The shapes took on the distinct forms of the masters, this time many more than the last, several of whom looked as if they'd gone a few rounds with Hebre. Laurel recognised one master, minus one eye and all his teeth. The others had fared better. Even in her recovering state, Laurel was glad to see she had exacted some damage. From where she stood, in the same place as before, Laurel saw Eden far below, shrouded in thunder and lightning. She smiled. The storms raged, and Laurel knew that even now, although the masters believed they had thwarted the plans to evacuate the Edensai, they had no idea of the devastation still to come.

The masters stood in a semicircle, not communicating, not moving, just waiting as her awareness grew. Soon she would return to her natural strength, and many masters would join to crush or kill her if their ruler so directed.

Cephus joined the assembly. This time, he wore a cloak of human skin and hair that smelled as bad as the stench of the drying bane rising from Laurel's body. His eyes were narrow and dark with anger. He'd initially rejected the notion Judith had returned, confident that even she of the same blood as the Sons of Benjamin could not live forever. He had concealed from the other masters' knowledge of Hebre's return until he satisfied himself this woman was not Judith. He saw now he may have erred, at least in part, and that made him angry. He had little dominion over Judith's mortal body; a body granted to her and changed by Lilith, and one which had endured through aeons. When Sedar reported Judith's return, Cephus knew it would be for only one reason; to destroy the Sons of Benjamin. But Judith had not made contact with him on her return, had not made an appeal, and he had become curious, so he'd sent Enoch to see if this was indeed Judith. Had Judith not wished it, no Magen Bearer in creation could have taken her, but this woman came easily into his presence. When he, Lord Cephus beheld her, he saw only a solitary Hebre with an extraordinary resemblance to Judith but unpossessed of her power and presence. Cephus had dismissed the woman as unworthy of his attention. She was just a foolish Hebre, perhaps one from the nebula with aspirations to protect the Edensai against the might of the Sons of Benjamin. He told his brethren only of a lone Hebre who had come back to raise a dissident Legion army. It would provide little more than a diversion, at least for the masters, but now, he'd seen the results of her fighting abilities, heard reports of her speed and strength and her successful removal of the arks. She was not acting alone, and he was no longer sure this woman, at least in some part, by some trickery or magic, was not Judith, returned.

Laurel held Cephus's gaze. He was standing only a little off-centre of the shield emitter, almost precisely where Darlen would need to drop the explosive. Laurel didn't dare reach out to Darlen. If she did, she knew he wouldn't deliver the device because it would mean certain death for her unless he could snatch her as he left, but he told her that each hop was single purpose; either to release or to take. And she scrambled to close her mind to Ava, hoping she had not yet sensed her mother had been taken captive and decide to teleport onto the ship to attempt a rescue.

"Very clever," Cephus said, his voice as smooth and level as when she first heard him speak, but now tinged with anger. He had initially scoffed when he learned of Judith's pledge to return. Even so, he had commanded Sedar to watch for that day. When Enoch brought her to the ship,

Cephus had allowed himself to be deceived, and now, after the battle on the surface and movement of the arks, he'd had no choice but to declare his lapse in judgement to his brethren. But he could blame the woman. "You did indeed deceive me into believing you were not Judith, although I should have seen through your magic. The likeness is pronounced." He blew out a stinking breath into Laurel's face. "So, you would have me believe our sister has returned? What is it Hebre say? Under the heavens, there is a time and a purpose to all things? This is not your time, Judith. It is ours. Have you forgotten your words? I recall them, even if you do not. 'If you free the people, brother, I will take Hebre back to the nebula'."

Laurel stood unmoving, but her mind was sifting through this new information. *Sister? Brother? Judith had promised to let the masters continue their killing if she could take Hebre to the nebula?*

"I let Hebre go," Cephus continued evenly. "I am not without honour. The dishonour was yours, my sister. You lay down your truth. After your betrayal, after the departure from Eden, and how you deceived us, I learned of your pledge to return, to deliver the Edensai from their destiny."

The entity within her reacted only mildly to Cephus's words. A memory flashed into Laurel's mind, clear and concise. "You didn't free my people, Cephus," Laurel said. "And I do not need you to remind me of my words. I did not promise to take Hebre back to the nebula. I said only, 'Let my people go'."

Cephus sneered, but inwardly, his doubts about the identity of this woman grew. Only he and Judith shared that conversation, and he had only spoken of it now to test her.

"Who would I let go, Judith? These are not your people. Not Hebre. Not Edensai. *We*, the Sons of Benjamin, *are your people*."

Laurel quelled the disgust rising in her and willed herself not to react. Laurel knew she and Judith were somehow linked, either as a descendant or by some ancient bond with Hebre. Laurel had come to Eden to learn her origins. It never occurred to her that knowledge would come from the foul mouth of a master. Laurel closed her mind to the implications of Cephus's words. Abel would return to the station with Harry, where he would fill in the gaps, she was sure, provided Judith had told him her shocking history.

She turned her thoughts to speculating on how Judith would have acted when she stood here. Did she become passive? Pleading? From what Laurel knew of her, she doubted it. It was more likely she was calm, in control, perhaps defiant and determined. Laurel believed the masters feared Judith, but she only had the scant knowledge of the former Legion to go by, and by their own admission, they had witnessed no interaction between the masters and Judith. Laurel got the impression that Cephus viewed her as an equal, even though he was still undecided about her identity. She searched for some clue as to how she should respond, but beyond being a calming presence, the entity did not try to control her actions nor still her tongue. Laurel lifted her chin in defiance, a gesture that irked Cephus. "Hebre, in mortal form, *are* Edensai," she declared.

Cephus frowned for a moment, then threw back his

head in laughter. "Has your love of the pathetic Edensai caused you to forget who you are? Is it *I* who needs to remind you that you are Judith, not a Hebre imp, and that you did not issue forth from the filthy loins of an Edensai female?"

The other masters murmured between them. Cephus had never informed them of Judith's pledge to return; this was news to them, as was the fact that Enoch had lately brought this woman into Cephus's presence. In turn, Laurel had to deal with her own confusion. Abel had not mentioned Judith being anything other than Hebre.

"When I learned the arks were taken," Cephus said, "I saw that I might have been incorrect in assuming you were a lone Hebre, mewing threats in the face of our might." He snorted in derision. "Judith was also strong, agile, emboldened, but you are different, you attack, you kill, you do not save, so I sent the brethren to test you. And I discover our bane can paralyse." He smiled triumphantly, looking around at his comrades. "It would not affect Judith." He leaned close to Laurel's face and spat the words *"because she was born from the bane of our father."*

It took every ounce of Laurel's determination not to react, but she couldn't stop her heart from quickening, nor from taking in a sharp breath at the impact of Cephus's words. Cephus saw and raked her body with a disdainful sweep of his eyes. He'd reached his judgement.

"Judith has returned," he announced to the masters, "but not in the body given to her by Lilith. It is weakened." Cephus sniggered suddenly and gripped Laurel's chin hard in his broad grasp, sure now that as she didn't possess

Judith's body, she would still be under the influence of the bane and could not resist. "Judith was servile to the word of our father," he scoffed, "every rule, every word must be obeyed. And yet here you stand in other, lesser mortal form, helpless before us, where once you caused us to languish while you fled with your Hebre friends and the wretched humans." Cephus released her and narrowed his eyes. "Are you truly powerless, Judith? Is this further mockery of your brothers? Or does the creator now mock Judith?"

"My Lord Cephus." One master came forward to stand beside his ruler. "If this is Judith," he lowered his voice, "in whatever form, do not provoke her. We believe Hebre have other powers; the power to lift themselves from one place to another. My Lord," he said urgently, "tales have been told…"

Cephus barely glanced at his subordinate. "See? She stands before us now as weak and pitiful as any Hebre. If she commanded such a skill, why does she stand here? Why does she simply not remove herself?"

Cephus viewed Laurel as if expecting her to accept the challenge, but she did not, could not. And Cephus continued in his belief she was now a watered-down, weaker, lesser version of Judith.

"My Lord," the other master urged, glancing at Laurel, but avoiding her eyes that she might not see his nervousness. "It may yet be a trick, a conjuring by Judith or the Riynea, but she may…"

Cephus raised his hand sharply to end any further argument. "Judith stood with the Menworan council when they cast out the Sons of Benjamin." He stared down at

Laurel. "Do you remember the words of our father? *'Get out of my house?'* Judith condemned us and defied our mother, Lilith."

"My Lord," the man would not be silenced, for he spoke for all masters present. "Your brethren beg you to destroy her while our bane yet thralls her body. If she is weak, as you say, it would be but one stroke."

Cephus considered the man beside him. "I testify to you—" he looked around the chamber, making eye contact with every master present, "The Sons of Benjamin are in righteous pursuit of justice in Sheerguhd. When we have purged humankind, when we have avenged our mother Lilith and crushed the creations of the whore Eve, who took our mother's place at our father's side, only then will we return to the bosom of our creator." He placed a consoling hand on his comrade's arm. "What now lives will once again pass into paradise. The creator will remove the curse and punishment of mortality from us, and we will dwell with him in the seventh kingdom, but he will not forgive us for killing his daughter."

But the master was not to be so easily mollified. "My Lord, I have seen her in battle. See her eyes? We believe she is the true Judith, come back, against all laws, even her own."

Cephus smiled an evil smile. "But this time, she is like other Hebre, weak, compassionate, human, easily subdued."

Laurel soaked up their words. She'd learned Judith was not born an imp, and if she'd heard Cephus rightly, he couldn't kill her. She also knew now Judith was not born of an Edensai woman either, intimating she was of the same race as the masters. But she would be ancient, so just how did she come into being?

The other masters appeared not to care who Laurel ultimately would turn out to be. They wanted her gone. They didn't want to take the chance she was Judith returned and might cause a sleep to come upon them as she did before, not now, when they were so close to victory, and they didn't understand Cephus's reluctance. He had never made mention before that it would be sinful to kill Judith.

The ship made a slight heave. Not enough to make Laurel lose balance but enough for the masters to exchange puzzled glances. Except for Cephus, who was fixated on Laurel.

"Only Judith would carry out such a bold plan," he said. "Only Judith would place herself above a sacred law." Cephus leaned down and thrust his face into Laurel's, the sickliness of his breath turning her gut, bane dripping like venom from the corner of his mouth. She would have loved to vomit in his face, but this time, her body didn't give in to her wishes.

"Humans." His face contorted. "Weak, pathetic, and they fear us." He drew away from her. "Far from delivering the Edensai, you have quickened their end. Enoch has disabled the arks and removed the people." Cephus glanced through the viewport. "Ironic," he smiled, his darkness and hatred reaching in to clutch her heart. "The heavens are open. It is a token from the creator, a symbol of cleansing. Soon all humankind will be cleansed from this kingdom. Even the mighty Judith will not turn us from our sacred crusade."

The ship lurched again, and Laurel stumbled backwards, recovering herself as it stabilised. She felt now was not the time to reveal she was completely restored from the bane's effects. A resolute strength surged through every fibre, every sinew that made up her body. Cephus looked to the other masters, a mute query as to what was happening. The ship's lurching didn't feel accidental to Laurel; this was Ava's doing. She also had a clear sense that somehow Ava knew Laurel had been captured and that she needed her to buy time, that a new plan to bring the ship down had been made. Laurel followed her intuition.

"You are human too," she said, drawing Cephus's attention back to her. "I've examined one of your kind—" she made an exaggerated, almost mocking movement of her head. "Yup, definitely human, but in a more 'failed experiment' kind of way."

"What language is this?" One of the other masters strode forward, aggressive, some of that anger directed towards his ruler. "We must destroy her. Lord Cephus, you waste time."

Cephus ignored him. He alone would decide about Judith. He'd never needed to make judgments in the past. His title was symbolic, hearkening to the days when his people were ruled over. He was a mere figurehead, but the other Sons of Benjamin would not move against him, even though this would be the second time Judith had made a fool of him. Judith knew their history. As Benjamin's twin sister, she was part of that history, the first woman to be born and not made, beloved child of the Menworan king, and she had also been the first to return from death. The restored Benjamin had forbidden all rulers who came after him to put Judith to death; Lilith had other plans for her in the destruction of mankind.

And that was why she had overcome him and all the masters that first time because she revealed her true self to him, and only to him. He believed if she ever returned, she would again overcome his reason, turn him back to a state of remembrance that saw him and the other masters curled in a slumber of terrifying dreams. But this Judith was not the Judith of old, unless…

"Perhaps you have commanded Time? Ordered it to return you here, yet you are possessed of the flesh of an ordinary mortal…" He reached out and plucked at the exposed skin on her arm.

Laurel was coming to realise Judith possessed elements that were either eternal, like the wraiths on Diriarden, or at least long-lived, long enough for her to have witnessed the events on Menwora and the casting out of the Sons of Benjamin and the exile of the Sons of David. But Laurel was human, born of human parents, and where her destiny had collided with Judith's remained a mystery. Laurel chattered on about the failure of the masters to prevent the conversion to peace of so many of their troops, losing all their Magen Bearers, how the masters tried to deny their humanness, all to buy time, even though she had no idea why it was necessary. Just a feeling. A powerful feeling, but Cephus had a sickening trick of his own. Leverage.

As the ship lurched again, this time more violently, two of the masters left the chamber, and it was at that moment, Laurel became aware of Harry. She slipped into silence as she checked her feelings. A vision of Harry's body, crushed and tortured, his heartbeat erratic and dangerously close to death, came to her. Laurel knew he was nearby but made no outward show of emotion. Seemingly, Cephus appeared to have some awareness of their relationship and grinned evilly as two Legion, followed by a dozen or more masters, dragged Harry's mangled form into the chamber and threw him to the floor in front of Laurel. He moaned a little before blessed unconsciousness delivered him from his pain.

"Restore him," Cephus ordered, "that she sees his suffering…" He turned again to Laurel. "You attack the serpents head, it shakes in the heavens, yet we see no ships. What secret powers do you yet conjure?"

There seemed to be no part of Harry's naked body not covered in blood and bruising, and she had to brace herself at his shocking condition. Still, she did not give away her emotions,

"Perhaps what's happening to the ship is a manifestation," she shrugged, deliberately and painfully paying no regard to the quivering mound of flesh that was Harry. "The Riyneans are pretty good at that."

The master spat at the ground and delivered a resounding blow to her face, sending her staggering backward against the bulkhead. The masters who stood behind her parted to allow her to make hard contact with the metal. Cephus strode forward and stood over her.

"I believed you espoused to Abel. Yet this man, not Hebre, not Edensai, nor is he Kalmeddi, commands your affections. So where is he from, Judith? Did you bring him from another Time to fight in your war?" Abruptly, he exploded once more into laughter, but this time, Laurel saw he was not so sure of himself. "You have such faith in one human? "he said finally. "Why not bring an army?"

You have no idea, Laurel thought. She made a show of struggling to her feet. She could have leapt and downed Cephus, but now was not the time. The reckoning was coming.

The other masters didn't join Cephus in laughter; instead, the ship's repeated instability led to a flurry of movement as the masters ran to mobilise various consoles and instruments that unfolded from the walls. The only one who didn't move was Cephus.

"What have you done? Tell me!" he roared, his eyes blackened with fury. As his anger swelled, the shape of his face transformed; his forehead bulged, his eyes slipped back into their sockets, and his jaw widened. Laurel's revulsion at his metamorphosis came from an awareness deep within as a memory flashed into her mind, an ancient remembrance of a heinous violation, a father so grieved by the loss of his son he would challenge death. The masters descended from this unnatural line. Their humanity was lost to them, and now they knew only evil.

Cephus's face continued to change. Before, the features so beauteous to behold, exposed the monstrous horror of a shocking pedigree. As she observed the metamorphosis, Laurel remembered Ava telling her, so many years ago when she was just a little child, when they visited the planet Canaa, she didn't like the men with mean faces and was scared to step onto the planet. It made sense now, and as she watched; she felt the faintest of instincts. It started as a germ of a notion that had no real foundation, but tugged somewhere in her remembrance, suddenly turning into a massive leap in reasoning which had no basis other than the fact it *felt* right. Benjamin's father believed he could restore his cherished son to life because *he had successfully performed this deed before. With Judith!*

As Laurel stared into Cephus's hate-filled eyes, she came to yet another massive revelation; the sure knowledge that Judith was indeed the sister of Benjamin! Did that mean Judith was made from a rib or was she simply another step in an evolutionary process? She hoped Judith had discussed these things with Abel.

Harry regained consciousness under the hands of the masters. His agonised groans reached Laurel, and she tried to send him comfort, to reassure him all would be well, even as the four masters awaited Cephus's order to deliver the torturing beams from their weapons.

Cephus delayed for what he supposed was Judith's natural empathy to influence her, still convinced that the woman who stood before him was a disappointing facsimile and that she would bow to him to save the human male. Cephus wanted her to beg. Even Judith, the sister of Benjamin, the sister who cheated death and whose soul dwelt amongst the stars until Lilith once more clothed her in mortal flesh, had begged him to let her people go. He saw it now. Judith was no longer immortal. She was an aberration to the Sons of Benjamin. And still, Cephus erred. Laurel did not see herself as Judith, and she did not beg.

"Torture, cruelty, that's your thing, isn't it?" she yelled as the ship pitched again and again, tossing the masters to the floor of the chamber and drawing agonised groans from Harry. As the ship levelled, Laurel squared up to Cephus. Whatever happened now to her and Harry, she knew the masters would soon be destroyed. "The first kingdom," she spat. "This kingdom, the next? I know your history. You are inconsequential." She sneered at him as his rage built, his transformation to devil growing more pronounced. "Small men made big by their power," she snickered, looking him up and down disparagingly. "So, do to him what you must. It will make little difference." Laurel poked Cephus hard in the chest. "Your reign is *finished!*"

Convinced she was still weakened from the masters' bane, Cephus grabbed her face, roughly massaging her jaw before twisting her head and shoving her hard. Pain from the shattered jaw exploded in her head, but she did not fall. At that moment, Darlen snatched Harry from the floor, and Abel appeared in his place. The shock and outrage at the unexpected arrival of an unfamiliar Magen Bearer caused the masters to step back. Whispers of Enoch's whereabouts came to Laurel's ears as she and Cephus faced off. When Cephus realised what had taken place, he issued orders to contact Enoch, but Enoch didn't respond, and there came speculation as to how any Magen Bearer could deliver and extract in one hop. Laurel heard the masters agree that a Magen Bearer had returned with Judith and now worked with Hebre.

Cephus's chest heaved with anger and confusion. Still, he brought himself under control, relaxing his countenance as he turned from Laurel to stare down at Abel, his devilish transformation retreating, but his face didn't return to its previous beauty.

Abel had bent at the knee and bowed his head, as if in submission.

"A prodigal?" Cephus prodded Abel with his foot. "Do you suppose a welcome, Abel? I am more prompted to learn how you appear on this ship. Do you work with another Magen Bearer? One who is in league with Judith?"

"My Lord," Abel said in a loud, imploring voice, "the woman, do not be deceived. She is not Judith." Abel was compelling as a prodigal son, but his mind was open, and she saw with horror and numbing sadness what was about to transpire and what she needed to do. As her bruised jaw fell open in silent anguish, she felt Abel's composure at his impending fate.

"If she is not Judith," Cephus said, "then tell me, is she sorcery? Perhaps of the Riynea or of Hebre?"

"My Lord Cephus, the woman is from the future. A physician. A mere human. She possesses the skill and swiftness of Hebre, but she is not Judith. Judith imparted to us the true history of the Sons of Benjamin."

Cephus's expression made it clear he had not expected Judith to be so free with such information.

"Yes, my Lord, these are the truths which she used to turn our hearts from you."

"Truths, Abel?" Cephus said, wanting to see just how much Abel knew. "What truths?"

"That we, the Sons of David, are Menworan; equal to the Sons of Benjamin."

Cephus angled his body so he might observe both Laurel and Abel. The other masters watched in silence. The traditions and stories of the Sons of David had been destroyed. Menwora was not spoken of to the Sons of David. Benjamin had allowed the truth to fall away and brought about a new history, one that would keep the Sons of David in servitude and further his quest, at the behest of Lilith, to destroy all that was created by Eve. Generations of his heirs upheld the lies until they became the truths of the masters, and the ancient ways were forgotten. Their crusade was now only to fulfil the evil ambitions of the resurrected Benjamin, who had looked into the face of Lilith and seen the deception of Eve. Lilith had shown him the glory of heaven and welcomed him as her son before his father, who in his selfishness, snatched him from paradise and reclothed him in mortal flesh. Flesh upon which he would take righteous vengeance as the goddess Lilith commanded.

Cephus stood over Abel's bowed form. "Sedar the Riynean told me Judith arrived from the nebula, but he lied. I see now she has a Magen Bearer with her, only one such as he can open Sheerguhd's eye without us knowing. And perhaps there are more Hebre? The removal of the arks, hiding them can only be accomplished by Hebre. And now you say my first instinct was correct; that this woman resembles Judith, but is not? Am I to believe my eyes, Abel? Or the words of a traitor?"

"You are deceived, my Lord." Abel looked up, his pleading reflecting in his eyes; his acting was buying the time they needed. "It is Esther who has returned, not Judith. It is Esther who deceives you on Eden. There is an army of Hebre. The battalion which defended the arks sought comfort and shelter and turned away their gaze. My Lord, I do not know how Hebre gained access; the ships were high above the ground. Legion was distracted by the attacking force and did not see. Their eyes were not upon their duty." Abel bowed his head. "As mine were not."

Cephus signalled to one master to raise his weapon at Abel. "Esther perished at the hands of Enoch. He swore it. She has returned to the nebula."

"No, my Lord," Abel said, making a sideways glance at his would-be executioner. "Esther lives."

Cephus went to speak, but his words failed as the ship heaved so violently, they were all once more thrown to the floor. Abel was too isolated from Laurel for her to reach him as the ship began a slow, spinning descent, but he raised his eyes and sent her a smile filled with sadness and triumph. This would be his sacrifice for the wrong his people brought to Eden, and the form of his beloved would be the last thing his eyes beheld.

Laurel felt the sense of fear from the many Legion in the tail of the ship. The explosion was coming; Laurel knew it, just as she knew that for the explosion to affect the tailing ships, the force of the blast also had to be extended towards the collar of the lead ship. She got to her feet in one fluid movement and tensed her body, waiting. From where the power came, she couldn't tell, it was just...*there*, and Laurel witnessed the sudden slowing of Time.

The masters sought to rise but barely moved. Cephus comically staggered and half rose, reaching his hands towards her. Laurel could even see microscopic flecks of skin and hair rising from Cephus's cloak, slowly diffusing into the surrounding air. Cephus never reached her.

The sound from the explosion came from far away, little more than a distant peel of thunder. In normal time, the light would have blinded her. Instead, it grew slowly from its beginning as a tiny flicker inside Abel's body. The anguish of watching him slowly torn apart as the device Darlen buried inside him detonated threatened to distract her, but she would not give in to sentiment; she would not waste Abel's sacrifice. Laurel steeled herself and raised her arms, clenching her fists to radiate some of the blast towards the ship's collar. The rest of the explosion continued its movement towards the bulkhead. As the fire began a slow burn against the walls, Laurel closed her eyes, and Time waited for her command. Willing the explosion to move forward, she heard the tearing of the bulkhead as it came apart, the cries of the masters and Legion, then she sent what was left of Abel's mutilated body containing the spark of the ignition into the tailing ships. In a flash, Time moved on, and the full blinding light and rush of the explosion blasted into normal time. For a moment, Laurel rolled and tumbled, then gathered her wits about her as fragments of the bulkhead, Legion, masters, and various pieces of the tailing ships rushed past her into space. Moments later, she found herself in Ava's arms. Around her, what remained of the serpent from Sheerguhd uncoiled poetically as it sank towards Eden.

"The Canaa's here, Mom," Ava sent to her. *"Marcel's waiting. I'm going to let you go."*

The Canaa appeared underneath them, and Marcel dragged Laurel through an access port. Ava pulled herself in and secured the port behind her. Laurel was deafened by the blast and unable to speak; she also didn't register that a moment before, she had survived open space without a support suit. Marcel caught both women in a hug. "I wouldn't have believed it if I hadn't seen it with my own eyes!"

Laurel's relief at seeing Ava and Marcel unharmed was quickly taken over by renewed fear for Harry.

"He's in the med bay, Mom," Ava said. Laurel's ears were ringing, so she shook her head. Ava repeated her words telepathically, adding, *"He is badly hurt. Beril is trying to stabilise him."*

Laurel turned to run toward the med bay, but Ava grabbed her arm. *"Mom, you're covered in that stuff the masters spit out. It stinks, and we don't know what type of bacteria it contains. Clean yourself up and decontaminate before you see him. Beril's doing a good job. Mer's helping."*

Laurel hesitated, torn between good sense and terror Harry would die before she got to say goodbye. But Ava's words were wise, and she would not give up on him. Within minutes, Laurel had scrubbed all traces of the masters' vileness from her body, dressed in clean clothes and decontaminated herself as she entered the med bay. Beril looked up.

"I am not trained in the pandroscope's use. Mer—" he gestured to the black robot, "has been very helpful. The pandroscope first pronounced Harry in organ failure, but I have stabilised him." He stood back. "I know you have suffered an ordeal yourself, but I believe your ministrations will be more effective than mine."

CHAPTER TWENTY-SEVEN _

The tell-tale glow from the pandroscope gave an ominous warning of the extent of Harry's condition. He'd suffered crush injuries to many bones, and as Beril said, he was in kidney and liver failure. His skin was deathly pale, and the pandroscope battled to warm him. It complained vociferously when Laurel tried to take his hand in hers, reminding her to "not touch the patient". The pandroscope had initiated full life support as healbots tackled the vital issues within his body. Beril had no choice but to free up a few healbots to repair lung damage. He then employed his own medical skills to treat further injuries when it became vital for him to assign healbots to other equally critical tasks. Throughout Harry's body, healbots and painbots worked at repairing his nervous system and extracting fragments of skull lodged perilously close to his spinal cord, but with only a limited amount of the miniature devices, Beril knew that to save his patient, they were against the clock.

Laurel cast a practised eye over Harry, identifying a trauma that compromised blood flow to his leg, an injury that would doubtless cause loss of the limb if left untreated. But there were just not enough healbots to go around. She could do nothing elsewhere; the healbots dealt with the deeper and more immediate issues, but she could do something with this.

Laurel quickly examined her jaw with a palm pandroscope, identifying several small loose pieces of bone. It needed a healbot, but she wouldn't take any from Harry, so it would have to wait. Pushing a painkiller into her arm, she thanked Beril for his help and told him she would remain with Harry.

Harry's leg was blackened and cold, and Laurel decided on some good old-fashioned surgery to repair the crush injuries. She extracted a lone healbot from Harry's kidney that had just completed its work and was checking function. The pandroscope would signal if any organs became compromised. Together, Laurel and the healbot put the bones of Harry's lower leg back together piecemeal and removed compromising fragments to restore blood flow to the limb. They worked tirelessly for several hours, with Laurel and the healbot locating and restoring the pieces like a jigsaw puzzle. When the healbot was recalled to a problem in Harry's kidney, Laurel made a makeshift repair of the remaining fragments so she could reoperate when Harry was stronger. At least now, the limb was perfusing as well as could be expected under the circumstances.

Laurel stepped back and rubbed the weariness from her eyes, flinching when she absent-mindedly knocked her jaw, remembering for the first time in hours it was still broken. The healbot remained in Harry's kidney, but it had communicated to the pandroscope the kidney was stable, so Laurel extracted it once again and introduced it subcutaneously into her jaw. Sinking to the ground beside

Harry, she allowed it to do its work on her shattered bone.

Ava checked in on Laurel telepathically, each time finding her mother's mind occupied only with working on Harry. She elected not to disturb her. Beril told her Laurel wanted to stay with Harry and assured her she would be alright. When Ava checked in telepathically later, she decided to go to the med bay, where she found her mother still slumped on the floor, arm reaching up onto the bed, Harry's limp hand in hers.

Ava looked at the pandroscope. It had everything under control and had even dismissed a few of the healbots. Harry was breathing with only token assistance from the pandroscope, and he looked peaceful and out of pain, unlike when Darlen brought him back to the Canaa almost twenty-four hours before, nearly dead from the torture the masters had wrought on his body. She knew her mother saw Harry on the ship and wondered how she endured the horror of seeing him like that, and then to witness Abel's sacrifice. Ava sat on the floor beside her and gently wrapped her in her arms. Laurel opened her eyes and tried to smile. The healbot had long since found its way back to the pandroscope and Laurel's jaw was neat and tidy, if a little swollen.

"Hi, honey," she mumbled with a lopsided smile.

"We're back at the station." Ava lifted up a beaker of coffee, then eyed Laurel's swollen jaw and fat lip and frowned. "I should have brought a straw."

But Laurel wasn't interested in coffee; she shifted her body so she could rest her weary head in her daughter's lap.

Ava stroked Laurel's hair, allowing all her mother's emotions and thoughts about the past days to flow through her mind.

"It must have been awful," Ava said softly as Laurel telepathically shared her despair at seeing a broken Harry on the masters' ship, the sadness of Abel's sacrifice and the remorse she felt about placing the people she loved in this situation. "We didn't have a choice, Mom," she said, "Judith made a promise which we fulfilled in her place. We were meant to do this. We had a purpose."

Purpose? Laurel heard that so many times before. Had she fulfilled her purpose? She was still alive, so clearly, death didn't automatically follow. Was there another purpose? She groaned, hoping that whatever it was didn't mean another war. Ava heard her but didn't quite follow the inference.

"I keep fighting, finding wars…" Laurel tried to speak, but her jaw hurt, far more than it should have after treatment, but perhaps all the emotional anguish she felt demanded a focus, so she reached into Ava's mind. *"I just want to be peaceful, but I keep finding people to fight."*

"War," Ava sent back, *"is invariably followed by peace. Peace is what people fight for."*

CHAPTER TWENTY-EIGHT _

"We've taken out all Legion ships on the surface," Darlen said, tracking the last remnants of the masters' rule on Eden. "Most of the ships that tailed the serpent's head broke up in the atmosphere. The Canaa took care of the rest. There are no life signs on the planet. It's nothing but a giant puddle now."

They were on the flight deck, five days after the battle for Eden. The arks were well on their way to Riynea. Unfortunately, there had already been a death, and despite the Edensai's surprise and distress about the temporary destruction of their homeworld and the discomfort of being herded together with barely room to lay down, the knowledge they were free of the masters and headed towards freedom, carried their spirits.

"After all this," Marcel said drily, "apart from the boy, I never got to see a master in the flesh."

Laurel was thankful that was his only complaint. "You were lucky they didn't attack you. Believe me, you would have had your hands full."

Marcel had gained hardly a scratch, a blackened eye, a cut here and there, but that was the scope of his injuries. His had been the last ark to be identified. "Legion attacked me," he said with pride, "and I managed to beat them all back."

Ava rolled her eyes. "There were only three of them, Marcel."

Marcel grinned and showed them his grazed knuckles. "At least I did it with my bare hands."

Laurel shook her head and grinned. Three Legion against a riled-up Marcel? Probably not a fair fight. "You never told me," she said to Ava, "how many masters intercepted you at the landing site?"

"Only two," Ava replied with a dismissive wave of her hand, the dread of running into them now fading since they were safe. "I don't know how they managed to see my eyes, but they recognised me as Hebre. That second of distraction was all I needed."

Marcel's eyes widened. "Did you teleport them someplace?" He still hadn't got over his sister's impressive new ability.

Ava burst into laughter. "No! I shot them. Darlen left his sidearm with me when he turned up in the axispod after I told him I thought Mom had been captured." She looked at Darlen. "I don't know what you did to it, but the damn thing breathes fire. The masters got charred to a crisp."

Darlen grinned. Yes, with that particular firearm, he had made a few extra modifications.

Laurel had scarcely left the medbay over the last few days, reluctant to leave Harry, even though his condition improved, so there had been scant time for a debrief. But Laurel hadn't overlooked a few noteworthy events, and so far, no-one had explained.

"How is it we can survive in space without environmental suits?" she asked bluntly, looking from Ava to Darlen. Somewhere between them was the answer. Ava nodded towards Darlen, inviting a response from him.

"You did it once before, Laurel," Darlen said. "Remember when we were hurled from the nebula, just before we got tractioned to Isilia, Harry smacked his head on the bulkhead, and you went to the galley to collect a medkit?"

Laurel remembered; the old ship was extensively damaged, and the medkit kept in the galley.

"I didn't see you go," Darlen continued, "I was too busy trying to stabilise the ship, but I saw you come back. Laurel, most of the hull on the way to the galley was missing; only the auto forcefield between the common room and the exit had ignited. There was one in the corridor, but it didn't ignite, yet you ran to the galley. When you came back, you were surrounded by amber light."

Laurel certainly didn't recall seeing a hull breach. "I was in open space?"

"You must have been," Darlen said. "I've never spoken of it. I thought I must have taken a bump to the head too, but you whole souls, it seems you can do all kinds of stuff I never realised."

Laurel frowned. "You'd think I would have noticed part of the hull was missing."

"Your mind too fixated on the medkit, perhaps?" Darlen suggested. "I don't know."

"Hebre are space-dwelling, Mom," Ava said thoughtfully. "Perhaps that's the explanation. I teleported directly to you on the masters' ship; the amber glow was evident there too."

Laurel thought back to that moment. She'd been controlling the explosion by using Time—she hadn't even dared to explore how that happened yet—and when she had accomplished the diffusion of the device into the tailing ship, Time reverted to normal. She didn't remember getting blown into space.

"Did you teleport Abel onto the ship, Ava?" Laurel asked. "It threw the masters into confusion. I knew it couldn't have been Darlen after he took Harry, and the masters realised it was another Magen Bearer. They went frantic trying to contact Enoch but couldn't."

"Ah, Enoch." They all turned to Darlen, a slow, mischievous grin tugging at his mouth. "I baited him, and he hopped onto the Canaa. Each Magen star has a signature," he explained, "and whoever bears that star is identified by the 'bleat'; the sound it emits. It's only discernible to a Soul Monger…Magen Bearer, whatever. I had to institute a hop, then not follow through, and it alerted this Enoch. It was easy enough for him to trace, and he turned up seconds later. God, he was a big bloke!" Darlen laughed. "He recognised me as a Magen Bearer, but not one previously known to him, and even though I had the advantage of surprise, he almost took me down with one punch."

"If he recognised a Magen Bearer," Laurel said, "then he would have expected someone who left on the arks fifteen years ago. Any born since would have been too young."

Darlen held up an object between his fingers, a tiny five-pointed star. Laurel's mouth dropped open in amazement. "You took Enoch's Magen?"

Darlen gestured to Mer, whose eyes lit red. "Mer took it. I don't think Enoch expected a robot in this part of the universe, and by the time he realised what was happening, he was dead. Mer broke his neck." He held up the shiny object. "I can give it to Scarlett, then there'll be two Soul Mongers, not that I plan on going Soul Mongering again unless it's to fulfil this covenant you told me about."

"I teleported Abel onto the ship," Ava said, her eyes wide at the thought of her own unexpected awesomeness and the awfulness of what she had to do. "Darlen was just about to deliver the explosive when I alerted him to you being on the ship, but Mer had already found a problem."

Darlen nodded. "It was going to plan," he said. "The arks were at their landing coordinates, the Farisee were ready, I was about to do the hop and deliver the device. Mer was monitoring activity on the masters' ship when he picked up a field at the neck of the serpent's head. It wasn't there before, and I thought it could be some kind of periodic reinforcement or maintenance or…. Anyway, we couldn't establish what was going on. We only knew the force of the blast, and any damage to the head and tailing ships would be minimised."

"Abel used the link you gave him to notify Darlen that Harry had been taken prisoner," Ava added, "so Darlen brought an axispod to my location. By then, I knew you were on the masters' ship."

"And in between the station and Ava's location,"

Darlen continued, "Mer found something else. The device Harry devised was unstable. We had few components to work with, but the Kalmeddi engineers came up with a kind of—I don't know, an organic timer that kept the device in a state of inertia. On the face of it, it looked great, and at least we were sure the bomb wouldn't go off and blow this station into oblivion."

Darlen's mind was ahead of his words, and Laurel saw why she had to buy time with the masters and why Abel had to provide his ultimate and Oscar-winning performance as the prodigal son. "The organic timer reprogrammed the device?"

"Exactly, a ninety-second delay once activated, but we had to get you and Harry off the ship before the detonation, and as I can only go in once…"

"Darlen brought Abel to my location," Ava cut in. "I told him I was going to the ship to rescue you. He was surprised about the teleportation thing, but he said not to go, that the entity would protect you."

"And it was Abel who came up with the idea to implant the device in him?"

Ava nodded sadly. "He claimed that Hebre, some Hebre anyway, can manipulate Time. Abel's strategy was for Darlen to embed the explosive in Abel's stomach, Darlen would rescue Harry, and I would teleport Abel to the coordinates. I was prepared to take the explosive myself, seeing as Abel was sure the entity would protect us, but Abel believed the masters would paralyse me on sight. Apparently, the paralysis does something to the entity, so I might have got blown up. He said if the masters spat on you when they took you, you would have recovered by the time the explosion happened."

"And manipulating Time?" Laurel prompted.

"Abel said he would keep his mind open." Ava thought of her last meeting with Abel, his determination to see this through, to make things right. "He said you would know what to do. In the meantime, as Darlen was introducing the device with a trigger for Abel to initiate the detonation sequence, I was to shake the masters up a bit, make them lose composure."

Laurel thought about those awful moments. "It worked, and I did know what to do; at least part of me did. When the blast happened, I made sure the entire chamber was affected, then I drove what was still radiating from Abel towards the ship's neck, that reinforced area you identified. After that, Time went back to normal, and I was in your arms."

"There's more, Mom," Ava said. "While Darlen was putting the explosive inside Abel, he told us no-one recalled an amber-eyed imp, that Judith seemed to spring into existence sometime after the imps changing by Hebre."

"The masters were very forthcoming about Judith," Laurel said. "According to them, she played a part in their history."

"What? How?" Marcel shook his head. He'd been amazed and inspired by what happened between Darlen, Ava and Abel, but this… "The story Abel told about Benjamin was ancient. How could she have played a part?"

Laurel sighed. "I plan on making sense of it, one way or another. I'm pretty sure Judith was not what she seemed.

Despite what Abel thought, I'm not her, and I was just getting comfortable with being Hebre. Now I'm not sure where I fit in."

"Abel was certain something of Judith lives in you," Ava said. "But we still don't know how that worked through successive lifetimes, or for that matter, how I'm descended from Esther."

Laurel stood and went to the viewport. "It seems the more our questions are answered, the more the mystery deepens."

Eden, shrouded in grey, its toxic cloud obscured by intense global storms, hung desolate in the heavens. Laurel thought about the men, women and children who didn't make it to the arks but instead fled into the petrified forest to escape the masters and Legion. She thought of those who elected to stay, to give the younger people the best chance of restoring their civilisation. They were all gone now.

"We look the same as the originals," Laurel said. The others had observed her in silence. "Ava, me, each succeeding generation who lives on Earth must be identical to the previous. I wonder how they do it?"

Darlen shrugged. "Beril seems sure it's the entity that gives the offspring the eye colour."

"But what happens when the host body dies? It is human, after all."

"Maybe the entity creates another body for it to inhabit," Ava suggested, "then enters the body and awaits its birth."

"Hopping from body to body sounds like a parasite," Marcel said, not keen on Ava's explanation.

Laurel disagreed. Ava's theory made sense. "No, it makes it sound like a survivor. It's biding its time until a Soul Monger finds it and returns it within proximity of the nebula, where, when the physical body it currently inhabits dies, the entity goes back to its home."

"I wonder why it has to have a physical body when it's not in sight of the nebula," Marcel said.

Ava scrunched up her face. "I wish I could ask it questions." She had become accustomed to her increased abilities; she was even aware now of the presence of the Hebre entity within her, but never once had it communicated, other than manifesting her wishes and strengthening her body. Yet, she knew it had a separate consciousness.

Laurel had several conversations with Beril about Hebre and their survival, each being circular, and neither of them coming up with an explanation. It was clear to Laurel the answers lay elsewhere, maybe not even with the Edensai.

"Tell me," she said, changing the subject. "Were many of the Sons of David left behind?"

"Quite a few," Marcel replied. "The unmarried ones declined to board my ark until everyone else was safe. They feared more Legion might turn up."

"And there was no room once the Edensai were on board?"

Marcel cast down his eyes and shook his head.

Laurel knew the men would sacrifice themselves to save the Edensai, just as so many of their brothers did when Judith took the first arks. It was their way of atoning for the catastrophic events they'd brought to a peaceful race. It was as they would have wanted.

Laurel turned to Ava. "And your newfound ability. Teleportation? It ties you further to Esther."

"I know." Ava tried to smile, but it was hard to feel happy whenever she thought about the people left on Eden, but she hadn't really discussed her new ability so far. "When we needed to get on the arks, it just came to the forefront of my mind, urging me on. I knew it would work. The plateau—that was just a test run." She smiled a little, "but back at the arks when Marcel disappeared—" Ava turned to Marcel and laughed. "The look on your face was priceless—I was surprised but glad it worked." Ava tossed her head from side to side in wonder, she knew she could do it, but it still seemed fantastic. "When it came time to put Abel onto the masters' ship, I didn't hesitate."

Three weeks later, Laurel called out happily from the med bay, "Harry's awake!" Harry had opened his eyes and smiled at her, relatively strongly considering it had taken a significant amount of time for the brain swelling to reduce and the neck fracture to heal. When he was injured in the incident in the nebula where they lost Xavier, Harry was left with a slight weakness that allowed some minor spinal cord damage which challenged the few healbots capable of treating such an injury, even with the aid of the pandroscope, which now reported no neurological deficits. Harry sat up as the fussy pandroscope corrected his blood pressure and checked for blood supply to pressure areas before advising on bowel and bladder patency, avoidance of dehydration and exertion, with an insistent reminder he should be lying flat. Harry waved it away.

He laughed a little as Laurel went into his arms. "Oh, sweetheart," he sighed against her hair, "it seems like we sleep away our lives in one way or another, what with stasis, variance…" He held her away from him so he could see her face and grinned at the single tear that rolled down her cheek, despite her beaming smile. "When we leave here," he said, in mock seriousness, "We're retiring."

At that moment, relieved to see him recovered, Laurel would have agreed to anything, but it would still be another week before Harry won the debate with the pandroscope— and Laurel—about getting out of the med bay.

On that day, he needed a steady arm to support him as he walked the short distance to the common lounge, and Marcel was happy to oblige. Harry felt liberated by just the short burst of movement and grinned as Marcel lowered him into one of the soft chairs. Laurel sat beside him and held his hand. He still looked pale and tired, but she knew she was like the pandroscope, just being fussy.

"I don't remember anything," Harry said, launching into a brief account of the event that put him on the masters' ship, "Only a bunch of giants appearing from nowhere." He blew out a hard breath. "We all know how I reacted to that stench. Even the pouring rain did nothing to drown it. I thought I was dead for sure, but they must have only wanted to injure me. They obviously had some way of moderating it. I suppose if they paralysed me with the bane, I wouldn't have felt the pain, but…" He frowned. He thought he recalled…no, it was gone.

Harry's injuries were consistent with being run over by

a herd of stampeding cattle, so it gladdened Laurel he was shielded from the memory. How he survived was beyond her. Cephus ordered his torture as leverage, to make her admit she was Judith or prove that she wasn't. Then what? What was Cephus's plan of coercion after that?

Harry squeezed her hand. "You're not listening," he said gently. "Am I repeating myself?"

"You have told me all this once or twice," she smiled, "but before, you were rambling. You're more cohesive now. I was thinking about what you said about retiring." It wasn't a direct lie, but she couldn't help feeling responsible for what happened to Harry, about placing them all in danger.

Harry grinned. "I was kidding. I'm not sure you can stay still long enough."

"You know, it does have a certain appeal," Laurel conceded. And it did, but she wanted to find Eli and Chloe before she settled down. Eli seemed happy in the message he left in the beacon they found as they travelled the nebula all those years ago; perhaps this cloaked planet could be a place for them also, somewhere to spend time if they were welcomed. Even so, she didn't want to be the one directing any of them where they should go.

As Harry recovered, details of the campaign on Eden following his capture by the masters were slowly revealed to him. Abel's sacrifice grieved him, even while seeing sense in his judgment. "We had a few moments before we attacked the Legion battalion," he said to Laurel. "He admired Judith and Esther. He said they had remarkable powers, so I asked him why they hadn't thought of flooding the planet or perhaps bringing down the ship, using their abilities. I was surprised by his answer."

"What did he say?" Laurel asked.

"He didn't know why they didn't. He knew Esther could influence mechanical equipment, even though he admitted the masters' ship would have challenged even her. He also said that Judith appeared not to be bound by time, but he couldn't explain how." Clearly, Abel's vague response still puzzled Harry. "Apparently, Judith often said, 'there is a time to every purpose' when asked about the masters. I don't know what she meant by that. Perhaps Hebre plays by a set of rules."

Under the heavens, there is a time and a purpose to all things? Laurel heard that on the masters' ship. Was Judith's purpose to save as many Edensai as was within her power, then return to destroy the masters?

Harry broke into her thoughts. "I've been thinking. Remember the diorama Ilivi showed us? The one that depicted the dark-haired woman who looks like Ava?"

Laurel nodded; Harry was talking about the woman who teleported the Riyneans from the ark to the surface of Isilia.

"Judith must have been there too. I think it was Judith who reset time, not Esther."

Harry's theory made sense. Esther and Judith appeared to work together, just as she and Ava did. And in this one thing at least, Cephus might have been right, even though he had misquoted the famous words from the bible.

"To every thing, there is a season and a time to every purpose under the heavens."

CHAPTER TWENTY-NINE _

A few weeks later, a shuffling and humbled Sedar, his head bowed and escorted by Olyo and Beril, stood before the crew of the Canaa. Laurel asked Beril to bring him out of stasis and, once revived, return him to the Canaa to meet with them. They knew he kept his knowledge of Ava and Darlen from the masters, but still, he needed to explain himself.

"I didn't recognise the configuration of your ship," he said simply. "Apart from the Farisee fleet, only my old ship remained. It was tolerated by the masters, but since Hebre left, they warned me that my granddaughter would suffer if I did not report Judith's return. She is with Legion..." he glanced sadly out the viewport at the water planet, "*was* with Legion. I sensed Hebre quickly, and the Magen Bearer. That is why I implored you to hide your ship. The masters do not routinely use scanning technology, so they didn't realise a ship had emerged." He raised his eyes to Laurel. "I told the masters a woman who resembled Judith had returned."

"And you did this to protect your grandchild?" Marcel asked accusingly. "The masters had already signed the death warrant of every individual on Eden. How would informing the masters save her?"

Sedar shifted his miserable gaze to Marcel. "It wouldn't save her," he conceded, "not in the long term, but they said she would be with me in the last days. They took my eldest daughter, Amiri, who was to become a mother for the first time in the spring following the invasion. The masters forced us to watch as they tore her body and that of her unborn child and feasted...." He didn't finish, just took a deep breath to steady his emotions. "My two other daughters suffered the same fate, but Legion took my granddaughter."

Laurel felt his outrage and his heartbreak. Sedar's could not have been an isolated case, and he must have felt powerless, desperate to do anything to protect what was left of his family.

"I'm sorry I punched you, old man," Marcel said, his natural compassion returning now he knew the awful extent of Sedar's personal tragedy. He cuffed Sedar gently on the arm, and Sedar accepted the gesture with a sad smile.

"You are very gracious, all of you, but I deserved it, even though at the time, I wasn't trying to send a message to the masters; I was contacting a Legion soldier who had sympathy for the Edensai. It's how I found out before that my granddaughter was still alive. She was only five when they took her, and all I knew was that she was at the camp near the three Farisee arks."

"There were Riynean women at that compound," Harry said. "Was she there?"

Sedar nodded. "A year ago, she was. She would not remember me; she has been at the mercy of Legion for almost two decades. I cannot imagine what she has endured."

"We saw the women, Sedar," Laurel told him. "They didn't have their freedom, but they didn't give the appearance of being badly treated."

Sedar smiled thinly; they were just being kind, a kindness he didn't deserve, and he wasn't comforted.

"Well, I don't know about individual women," Harry said, "but we killed all the Legion soldiers in that encampment, presumably including your informant friend if he was there, but all the women were saved. Olyo and another Farisee pilot rescued them during the exchange and took them to Marcel's ark…" he paused. "There were children," he said to Olyo. "What happened to the children?"

"Two babes in arms," Olyo replied, her heart shredded by the horror she witnessed at the encampment, not just the barbarism of Legion but the savagery in battle of people she liked and respected; good people like Abel and Harry, both men of conscience. This, she supposed, was the price of deliverance. "The older children perished by Legion's hand," she continued, "lest the father's sins in defeat are visited upon the child." Olyo turned to Sedar. "If your granddaughter was at the encampment, then she is safe and among those heading to Riynea."

Sedar put his hand against his throat, trying to speak of his joy, but the words would not come easily. "It is more than I dared hope for," he whispered at last, his eyes shining with unshed tears. A moment later, Marcel caught the frail old man as his legs crumpled. Overwhelmed with regret for his actions and relief at the possibility his granddaughter might still be alive, Sedar gave way to sobbing in Marcel's arms. Marcel held him until he ceased his weeping, then Olyo gently eased her old friend into her embrace before helping him to a chair.

"We will take you to Riynea to see if your grandchild is among the saved," Olyo soothed gently. Sedar had been a good friend all these years, and she prayed now that he would find his kin among the women they rescued.

"Thank you, Olyo," Sedar smiled weakly. "I pray it will be so. To hear that she may be alive—that I can hope…" The tears threatened again, but he took a deep breath and swallowed hard. "It is more than I deserve." His voice trembled with emotion, but he made steady eye contact with every person in the room. "I humbly beg your forgiveness."

Laurel and the others watched quietly and respectfully all this time, and Sedar closed his eyes as an affirming murmur he was forgiven rippled into his mind. Laurel was surprised to find Sedar's mind suddenly opened to her.

"You believed me to be a good man, and I let you down."

"I'm not sure I would have done anything differently to you," Laurel sent back. It was an honest reply.

"Thank you…" Sedar then opened his eyes, filled with such deep gratitude. *"For everything."*

Laurel looked out the viewport. Dawn was breaking over Eden. She and Ava had stopped the rain after forty days, and now, the blueness of the water shone like a sapphire in the blackness of space. A tranquil resting place for good and evil alike.

Perhaps now, Laurel thought, we can all rest in peace.

A little over eight weeks after the first rains fell on Eden, sensors showed evidence of the waters receding. The sight of Eden's transformation to a water planet had been spectacular, its blueness shining in the heavens, cleansed and purified of the presence of evil. Yet, Laurel could not feel thankful for the destruction of the masters and their ship without feeling a huge burden at the loss of so many Edensai and those Riyneans, Kalmeddi and Sons of David who gave their lives so others may board the arks. Olyo tried to comfort her, assuring her that on Riynea, the people immediately started to rebuild, their culture and holy scripture were intact, and their gratitude to Hebre was eternal.

Laurel decided the best way to get her emotions under control was to go with Marcel and Beril to Riynea to offer what help she could. Darlen and Ava would be on the station with Harry to make sure he didn't overexert himself. Sedar and Jadren had already left with Olyo, and Sedar had been reunited with his now-grown granddaughter who, as Laurel had promised, had not been ill-treated and was among the healthier young people now rebuilding a society. Olyo was thrilled to report that one infant she saved was Sedar's great-grandchild, but an older brother had perished by his father's hand. Laurel sent a lengthy communication to Harry upon her arrival, detailing the deficiencies in accommodation for the people. It also seemed that too few Riyneans with manifesting skills had survived, but she also reported the Edensai, despite having lost their homeworld for now, indeed for many generations to come, took a pragmatic and cheerful view, and as their strength returned, organised themselves into teams tirelessly cutting wood, building shelters, gathering food and spending time in re-establishing their religion and culture.

Riynea's human population had been devastated, with few surviving the Legion onslaught, but the masters had not detonated any poisonous devices in the atmosphere, so vegetation and small animals not taken for food by the masters and Legion, had survived. Untended, much of Riynea's formerly inhabited sections had turned to forest.

Laurel and Olyo went on to Kalmed to check on the situation and advise the end of the occupation. The small world held fewer than fourteen thousand souls concentrated into one area, and word of the liberation spread quickly. The cities on Kalmed had been reduced to rubble, but food was available, and the people were in reasonable condition. There were a few of middle-age and above, but most did not make it out of their twenties before the masters harvested them. Some younger men and women eked out a living in the mountains, trying not to become the masters' next meal. There were no small children, a choice made by the Kalmeddi not to produce a generation of food for the masters. Most of the older people refused to leave their homes for resettlement on Riynea, and many of the younger ones wanted to rebuild Kalmed, but others were happy to leave. Laurel left with a promise to the people she would return with technicians to repair power hubs and establish medical facilities.

On Riynea, Marcel worked with the Farisee, erecting neat huts for the people to help them move from the cramped and unhygienic conditions of the ark they used for shelter. Fortunately, the weather was mild, and annoying insects notwithstanding, living and sleeping outside would not be an issue until winter. By that time, they would have constructed enough homes for most, with the arks as a backup.

Another concern Laurel found on her arrival on Riynea was sterility. To effectively rebuild, there needed to be more children. Many survivors of the initial invasion had retreated from Eden's north after the toxic cloud began its journey. Its deathly grip on all life undoubtedly took its toll on the fertility of any individual who had even minimal exposure. An established analysis of Eden's evacuees showed a mere ninety-two Kalmeddi survived the exodus, and among the men, only five were fertile. With those Laurel and Olyo brought from Kalmed, the Kalmeddi population on Riynea swelled to three thousand. Amongst the Kalmeddi evacuees from Eden, there were nine girls of childbearing age, the youngest only sixteen, but none strong enough at this stage to face the potential perils of childbirth. The women brought directly from Kalmed were a better prospect as they had received better nutrition and were mostly fertile, even though there were not many of them. Jadren sent Laurel a gloomy message predicting the demise of the Kalmeddi, telling Laurel that even she could not halt this inevitable march to extinction and that they would need a miracle. Laurel gave him the figures and informed him they had enough of a gene pool to rebuild and that he would soon see his people flourish, but he refused to be comforted. Laurel felt saddened he could find no optimism now, after he had been a staunch supporter of Hebre. She resolved to seek him out when the opportunity presented itself.

It had been decided that Laurel and Marcel would take Mer to aid the rebuilding programme on Riynea to give Harry time to recover from his injuries before taking up duties as a physician in the fledgeling communities. He would also serve in any other capacity where he might be needed. On the station, Darlen monitored the watery surface of Eden carefully. The sensors showed no human life, but just to be sure, he elected to take the axispods down to check on the progress of the receding waters and look for himself.

Harry, bored but not fit enough to pilot, stopped Darlen on his way to the axispods. "The water might still be too deep," he said, "but I would be interested in examining one of the masters. I'd like to compare the young one with the adult." He dropped his voice even though Laurel wasn't there to hear him. "Laurel won't let me do anything physical. She asked me to review the data on the fertility issue on Riynea." He shook his head. "It took five minutes. Interbreeding is the only answer if they're all going to survive; there doesn't seem to be much in the way of genetic stock. That's all I came up with, and Darlen, I'm bored."

Darlen grinned. "Perhaps Marcel can spread himself about a bit. He's young, and he would father some good-looking kids. For that matter, you and I aren't…"

"No!" Harry stopped him in horror, whispering fiercely. "I'm not impregnating random women, not even to save a race. I'll advise and treat infertility if I can, but anything else…"

Darlen grinned at Harry's mortification. "I was thinking of sperm donation, Harry. You know…" he raised an eyebrow, "imagination and a little cup? What were *you* thinking?"

"Oh," Harry's jaw dropped. "I—I thought you meant…you know."

"Well," Darlen slapped him on the arm, "that would work as well. Maybe Laurel and Ava can do the same and carry a few babies."

Darlen grinned at the stunned Harry as he headed for the cargo bay. "I'll find a corpse for you to play with," he flung over his shoulder as he went.

The tops of Eden's mountains shone in the morning sun, the water sparkled, and the world was at peace. Ava and Darlen spent several hours performing underwater sensor sweeps, but Darlen was eventually satisfied there were no survivors of the flood. The northern hemisphere still suffered the effects of the cold, where several ice floes had formed. The sensors showed significant toxicity to the planet's surface that penetrated several metres into the muddy earth. Darlen wondered whether the masters had done too much damage there for the planet to recover for centuries. He scanned for corpses; there were many thousands in just this area alone. Darlen guessed these were masters; the cold would have preserved a body far better than the south's warmer waters, so he decided this might be the place to pick up Harry's specimen. Darlen landed his axispod on one of the plateaus and climbed. He had only set foot once before on Eden, as the battle for survival raged. Then he was knee-deep in mud and trying to see through pouring rain and darkness. Now, despite it still being winter, the sun was warming. Looking up towards the chilly blue sky, he watched as a few clouds scuttled about, a balm to the lightning that scarred the sky for almost forty days. At this height, the air felt thin and icy, and in the silence, he thought of Helen and her peaceful resting place among the flowers on Isilia. He would lie beside her one day.

An axispod comm alert disturbed his peaceful meanderings. It was Ava.

"Ava? Are you okay?"

"I'm fine, Uncle Darlen. Dad wanted a master to examine? Well, I got one."

"Dead, I hope?"

"No, alive and singing nursery rhymes," came the caustic reply. Then Ava's voice took on a sombre tone. "Uncle Darlen, there's something else. I need you to see it. Meet me at my coordinates."

"Sure." Darlen climbed into the axispod. "On my way."

Darlen had no idea what awaited him when he reached Ava or what could be so urgent. He landed next to her axispod on a muddy plateau, where she stood with a macerated but preserved body of a master. It looked unremarkable to Darlen, blue and mushy, but that was to be expected after more than a month in the water. But Ava wasn't looking at the master. Her attention was captured by what lay beyond. Bobbing on the surface of the subsiding waters, was a large, perfectly ovoid, translucent, tense-walled and fluid-filled membrane encompassing the body of a child of around seven.

"One of their unborn offspring?" Darlen squinted through the sunlight and took several steps forward.

Ava nodded. "There's another over there, but it's dead. The sac was open. I thought this one was too but look…" Darlen obeyed and was stunned to see the child move its head. "The sac is airtight and watertight," Ava reported, "so it's preserved. It registered on my local sensors."

Darlen looked around. "I made a thorough check for any kind of life in the north and found nothing. Carry on scanning. If there are any others, we can destroy them from the axispods." Darlen removed his sidearm and aimed at the sac, but Ava moved too quickly and knocked the weapon from his hand. He flexed his fingers in surprise.

"That hurt!"

"You can't destroy it," Ava hissed fiercely, dismayed he could even consider such a thing. "You know how the masters used these women. It hasn't done anything wrong."

Darlen picked up the weapon. He was not inclined to take on Ava, but sometimes, she was altogether too merciful.

"Ava," he said in a reasoning voice, "it's the product of a race that was planning on annihilating mankind. Be sensible. Now, step back and let me do what needs to be done. If I don't, the job of defeating the masters is not finished. Not until every last relic of them is gone."

"I can't let you!" Ava stood defiantly between him and the bobbing sac. "I think we need to take it back to the station and see what happens. It's not for just us to decide.

We're a team."

They faced off for a tense minute, both unwilling to back down. In the end, it was Darlen. With a sigh, he placed his sidearm back in its strap. "Okay, Ava, you win. We can kill it after Harry's checked it out."

Ava loaded the master onto her axispod, cloaking the entire ship so the body wouldn't deteriorate on the flight back to the station. Darlen took the sac and deposited it in the well of his axispod after Ava extracted from him a vow not to harm it. They both followed through with the sensor sweep. Not a single sac was located, leading them to assume the one they had on board was the sole survivor.

An eager Harry met them in the cargo bay. "Did you find any?"

"We got one," Ava said, unceremoniously dumping the master's corpse onto the cargo bay floor, "but we also have this…" She pointed to Darlen as he lifted the sac from the axispod, a little too roughly for Ava's liking. Harry's eyes widened, and he stepped closer. He touched the sac.

"It's alive!" he whispered.

"It was cold when we lifted it from the water," Ava said. "It must have been drifting around since the flood started. I can't believe it hasn't died of hypothermia."

Harry checked out the sac from all angles, ignoring Darlen's unspoken complaint about holding it. "We don't know if the masters used any kind of incubation or heat for these," he said. "Perhaps there's some kind of thermal inertia; I don't know." He looked up at Ava. "What are we supposed to do with it?"

"I was going to shoot it," Darlen said, depositing the sac on a hover trolley. "Ava didn't think it deserved to die."

"I wonder if the fluid is capable of paralysing," Harry said. "We should be careful." Ava and Darlen both realised they'd been somewhat careless in carting the sac, forgetting the fluid from the masters had a paralysing effect. They were lucky it hadn't burst as a result of Darlen's rough handling.

In the med bay, Harry gave the sac a thorough examination. The sac was surprisingly heavy, considering the thin and petite creature contained within. The sac membrane was thick, robust and flexible, returning promptly to its ovoid shape after moulding by pressure from a palm pandroscope. A fair amount of fluid surrounded the foetus, but rather than the opaque "bane" reported by Laurel, the liquid was clear, resembling amniotic fluid. Harry shook his head in disbelief. "It is fascinating," he granted, "but it might be wiser to destroy it."

Ava gave him a look of horror. "Don't you dare! It's a child. You can't possibly know that it has the temperament or objective of the males."

Darlen scratched his head in irritation. Bringing a dead master on board was one thing, but something a master created? Something alive? That was another.

"It's motivated by instinct, Ava," he said, trying to make her see that being idealistic about anything belonging to the masters had inherent dangers. "It's going to be born into a world where it does not belong, where it does not fulfil its potential. You've seen the graphics—you may be condemning it to a course that goes against its nature." He saw she wasn't responding to reasoned irritation, so he took it down a couple of notches. "We know far too little of this species."

Ava folded her arms. "You don't know that it's solely driven by instincts. If Mom were here, she would say the same thing. It's defenceless. We don't know what it's capable of achieving if we give it a chance. You can't kill it. I won't let you."

They didn't tell Laurel about the offspring. Communications between the station and Riynea weren't reliable, and Ava felt it would be better for her to learn of the find in person. When Laurel returned, she immediately involved herself in debriefing the others on the conditions on Riynea. When she finished, she waited to see if any of them had questions, but none were forthcoming; instead, she saw that at least two members of her audience looked guilty. She gave them a suspicious grin. "I might be a bit preoccupied," she said, "but I'm still a telepath, and if I need to, I'll go in and find out what it is you're not telling me!"

For reasons best known to himself, Harry suddenly lost courage and looked at Ava, who also felt less sure of Laurel's reaction to the secret in the pail in the medbay. Laurel hadn't sensed its presence, not yet anyway.

"We heard Marcel's going to be a sperm donor for the genetic programme," Harry said, not sure why he was stalling.

"That's right," Laurel confirmed, allowing them the distraction. They'd tell her in their own time. "I asked Beril to contact you. You're still young enough."

"Yes, well," Harry mumbled, "he did. They'll use me if

they can't complete a suitable gene pool."

"Suitable?" That surprised Laurel. Harry was a fit and healthy man, notwithstanding his recent injuries, but that would have no bearing. "Beril considered you unsuitable? He didn't say."

"Umm, yes, they don't want people with red hair."

Laurel's eyes opened wide, then she erupted into peals of laughter.

"What's so funny?" Harry demanded, his guilt over the offspring momentarily giving way to indignation.

"Because these are a people desperately trying to establish a new society, enough to eventually populate three worlds, but only if none of them has red hair?"

Harry grinned. "I didn't think they'd be so prejudiced!"

"I suppose they're trying to preserve their characteristics," Laurel said. Harry certainly had none of the characteristics of any of the races. "Marcel has dark hair and grey eyes; there are quite a few Kalmeddi with those attributes."

Ava agreed with a knowing grin. "Beril told me a few of the Kalmeddi and Riynean women, now they are better nourished and feeling more 'normal', who would prefer his donation to be a little more direct!"

Laurel groaned. "Truly? I bet he's flattered, but he speaks so often of Ilivi. I believe she is where his heart is."

"They're not interested in where he puts his heart," Darlen laughed.

"Uncle Darlen, you are so crass!"

Darlen snorted a laugh at Ava, then he turned to Harry. "Shall we stop prevaricating and tell Laurel about our little discovery?"

Laurel blinked. "Discovery?" She looked at each in turn, inviting any of them to explain.

"We found an offspring," Ava blurted out, no point in trying to hide it now. Laurel stared at her. "An offspring? An offspring of what?" And in a moment, Ava telepathically made the "what" crystal clear.

Laurel didn't hide her dismay. "You should have told me first thing; the briefing could have waited. I can't believe you brought something like this on board." She levelled an accusing stare at Harry; unfairly, he thought, as he wasn't the only one in on the decision.

"Where is it?"

"In the med bay," Harry said. "In a sealed bucket."

Laurel couldn't believe her ears. What were they thinking? "You put a living being in a bucket?"

Darlen stepped in to defend Harry and Ava. "It's a part of the masters. We don't know what could happen even in this state, and we know bane can paralyse, although we've all touched the sac and we're all okay," he added.

Laurel headed off towards the med bay. "I want to see it."

The sac fitted snugly in the bucket, which was flexible enough to contain its growing proportions. Laurel had to acknowledge it certainly provided a barrier and also kept it hidden, which she would have done in their place. Darlen carefully tipped the contents of the bucket under the pandroscope. The sac spread out like a soft water-filled balloon.

Laurel followed the child's movement within, its fists

clenched against being disturbed, its body uncurling to expose thin legs and tiny feet, the sac stretching easily to accommodate its contents. Monsters created this female. Who knows how much was passed into this child to contribute to that species' ongoing brutal nature. Part of Laurel believed destroying it made sense; its origins were questionable, its nature unknown, but watching it now, her initial horror dissipated, and she saw it was also possessed of something so innocent, so *guiltless*. She didn't even need to wrest with her conscience. She couldn't kill it. Not yet.

Laurel touched the sac, and the child turned its blind, still unseeing eyes towards where it sensed pressure on its cocoon.

"I know what you're thinking," Harry said, "that it's just a baby, but if you back engineer what little we know, Benjamin somehow managed to procreate after he was restored to life, however briefly. He was never reborn as an infant; he was resurrected vile and corrupt. Don't tell me that's not unnatural. Their offspring, this…" Harry gestured at the sac, "is an aberration."

"I don't believe the original Menworans mistreated their women, Harry," Laurel said, "but I do think this process forms part of their reproduction. Somehow, I sense the resulting female was revered and honoured. The brutality bestowed on the mother by the infants only came, as you say, when these girls were born from the resurrected Benjamin. He established his dynasty alone. And it raises another point."

"Which is?"

"We're calling this 'offspring' and 'child', but she isn't.

She has been created as a mate. She is not a child," Laurel said firmly. "She will be born a woman, fully capable of conceiving and giving birth."

Harry agreed that assessment was sound. "I accept that what she actually bears is the true offspring," he said, "but you can't refute that this is a foetus, granted, a remarkably advanced foetus, but with a particular and defined purpose."

"We can't kill her, Harry," Laurel said, "regardless of what she was bred for. She would have an innate expectation of life, something from somewhere before the masters."

Darlen, though, had seen nothing to persuade him the female should be allowed to live.

"You can't be sure the original Menworans weren't barbarians as well. You might just be taking a romantic view of them."

"Yes, I can, Darlen," Laurel retorted sharply, "because Judith was—is not barbaric." She looked down at the sac, lying under the probing eye of the pandroscope. This life, its survival, or death was in their hands. To coin a phrase, they were playing God, and Laurel didn't like the feelings it brought up in her. She had killed so many times in the past, and besides losing the people on Eden, she felt no guilt, but this time…

"It's tragic," Laurel said sadly. "The first contact this girl would have after emerging from the comfort of this womb would have been a savage attack by a master."

Harry had thought of that, and it *was* tragic, but facts were facts. It was a creation of the masters and, therefore, unknown, and possibly, dangerous.

"What do you propose?" he said to Laurel.

"Let her emerge from the sac," Laurel said. "Treat her as we would any newborn, with kindness and patience, perhaps part of the Menworan still lives within her, we may be able to nurture that. We at least need to try."

"We will be taking on an extraordinary responsibility, Laurel," Harry pointed out. "The rib forms a rudimentary spine, and she has a spinal cord which runs along the inner side, protected only by a membrane. Her nervous system is—well, it defies description, and she appears to have no immune system or at least one I can identify. Like the masters, she doesn't even make sense at a cellular level. This child is a feeble version of a human being, designed to fulfil only one purpose; reproduction. Her reproductive organs are perfectly formed, although the bifurcated uterus seems like overkill. I think your response is emotional." Harry folded his arms. "And I knew you would take this view. I do not think she is viable."

"You knew?" Laurel tilted her head. "I think we need to give her a chance. If it doesn't work…well, we'll cross that bridge when we come to it." She could tell both Darlen and Harry were not in agreement with her, although she realised support was coming from an equally stubborn Ava.

"If it doesn't work," Darlen said as he carefully inserted the sac back into its pail, "and she creates chaos; which one of you kind, compassionate souls here present is going to terminate her?"

CHAPTER THIRTY _

"I worked on the male first," Harry told Laurel later as the group discussed the master's autopsy. "Anatomically, he was unremarkable, except his bones were unnaturally dense. I went over him several times with the pandroscope and used some of Beril's equipment. He would have found it interesting."

"He would," Laurel agreed, "but he's doing an amazing job on Riynea, even training a few people in the practice of medicine."

"I know," Harry nodded, "I regard him as the authority, so I'll hand over everything I've learned." He went back to his report. "This male had a rib missing, suggesting he'd fashioned a female. Where the rib had been removed, the thoracic spine had hairline cracks and contained an accumulation of cells I could only partially analyse. I couldn't believe what I found there." He smiled at the expectant faces, but he knew only Laurel would understand. "The master had an xxy chromosomal profile. Same as the boy you killed." He nodded to Laurel, his voice raised a little in excitement, then added, "It might explain why he was so tall, but I also found, not infiltrating the juncture of the removed rib, a remnant of xx chromosomal material, independent of the master's structure."

"A mutation?" Laurel suggested. "At a single site?"

Harry raised his eyebrows and opened his hands. "I don't know! Fascinating, isn't it? And if the master is resurrected, how did he have intact cells? And is he human? Well, that's still to be determined, but a sack of female chromosomes? I couldn't believe it!"

"This may be normal for Menworans," Laurel said. "Or do you think this is something he brought back from the afterlife?"

Ava picked up Laurel's thoughts and saw where she was going, but Darlen didn't see it. "I think all this religion is getting to you," he declared.

"We know the masters originated from the Menworans, that your people—" Laurel looked at Darlen, "the Sons of David and the Sons of Benjamin most likely share an ancestor, but this is a major difference between you and them. I don't know where those ancestors came from or how. Perhaps they were made by someone; someone who designed them to procreate in that way."

"You mean like a god?"

"No, Harry," Laurel said impatiently. "Not a god. Why does it always have to be a god that creates? Is that the only explanation? We create stuff. We invent and bring into being. Perhaps there are advanced species capable of creating life in the same way as we follow a recipe." Laurel shook her head. "I believe the Menworans reproduced using this rib method, but their view of womanhood was vastly different to the view the restored Benjamin took. I think the Eve story developed from their folklore, perhaps an Adam and Eve-type story that the sons of Benjamin used to back up their justification for wiping out humanity."

Harry sat down. They had so little time together before she went to Riynea. There'd been little opportunity to discuss the events; he'd just been glad to see her safe. "Did you discover all this while you were on the masters' ship?"

"No," Laurel confessed, "some of it is guesswork, but Cephus, the ruler, told the other masters that Judith was part of the council that cast out the resurrected Benjamin from Menwora. That suggests to me that women played an equal role in society."

"Maybe, centuries ago."

"I know that, but what I am sure of is this; Benjamin wasn't the first to be brought back from the dead. His father did it before, successfully."

"Who with?" Harry and Ava chorused.

"Judith, his daughter," Laurel announced. "She returned from the grave as good and as merciful as when she went to her death."

"So, where did Judith spring from in the first place?" Darlen asked. "Did they create daughters the same way they created mates? What would be the point?"

Laurel was at a loss. "I couldn't read Cephus's mind, but things he said—he called Judith 'sister'. I just kind of gleaned the information, but I might be imagining it all." Laurel sighed. "It just feels right."

"There is part of you that many believe is Judith," Harry said slowly. "Abel believed it."

Laurel nodded. "I know, but what I don't know is where Judith's path and mine crossed."

"When I look at you," Darlen said, unconvinced, "I see a whole soul, not a phantom."

"I can't explain it, Darlen," Laurel said. "I wish Judith would reveal herself to me, explain why I behave as a whole soul, as Hebre, unless as an immortal, she also exists in the nebula. Perhaps the power comes from there."

"It might explain how you and my father were able to have a child where normally, two Hebre can't," Ava said. "Perhaps you are different from Hebre."

Laurel had considered that, but it didn't go far enough. "Harry," she said, "after all your investigating, would you positively conclude, in a scientific sense, forgetting all the supernatural stuff, the masters are human?"

Harry was unsure and took a moment. "To classify a species as human, we have to look at different factors." He shook his head. "I'm not an expert in interspecies medicine. I would have to go by the chromosomal profile, there are heaps of variations, and none of those variations makes someone less human. Still, having the chromosomes co-existing, one set in a single bone in a host body containing xxy chromosomes would make me wonder if this was a human or some kind of copy. It brings the resurrection story into question, as in resurrected or genetically manipulated."

"But you found no evidence of cloning."

Harry shrugged. He couldn't answer. "What would make me hesitate to confirm they are human are the sacs at the back of the mouth that produced the bane and the extra row of teeth. That's not a human feature; it has more in common with the Ferle. The females don't have them, and if, as you say, Darlen's species and the masters have a distant, common ancestor before either this genetic manipulation or resurrection, then why doesn't he have them, or at least some sign they were there at one time? Darlen?" Darlen looked up. "I need to check your genetic profile."

"Sure," Darlen agreed. He'd never heard of these extra teeth in Soul Monger lore.

"If the fluid they spit out at procreation is the same fluid they used to paralyse me," Laurel said, "we will have to make sure that we aren't too close to the sac when it ruptures."

Harry agreed. "The pandroscope says it's a protein as I would expect, full of a hormone that appears to act like progesterone, but it does possess a paralysing agent. In the simulation graphic, the masters sprayed the bone with bane, and it formed the sac. I wonder if that was what happened to you when they took you, perhaps wrapped you in a neurolysing caul of some kind to subdue you. The foetus is obviously immune."

"According to Cephus, it didn't work on Judith fifteen years ago because she was born from the bane of her father," Laurel said. "I would say at some point, his doubt that I was her got the better of him, and he decided to test his theory. And because I'm not Judith, not physically anyway, it worked. Did you get to look at the master's brain?"

"Well, I would have liked a better examination of one living," Harry said. "The dead master's brain was covered in nodules, mainly attached to the hypothalamus. At a guess, I would say the masters' brain, if this one was typical, would cause them to be highly excitable and aggressive. Other parts showed far less stimulation. They would have been very focused." He chuckled. "It's the brain of a bad person."

"Very scientific," Laurel responded drily.

"He was made that way!" Harry declared. "So I would say, yes, very scientific."

"I guess it's all irrelevant now," Laurel said.

Darlen disagreed. "Is it? Not if you and I are related to them."

Harry shrugged. "I've never met a species like it, neither human nor non-human."

Laurel thought back to her words on the ship. "I told them they were a failed experiment."

"Or a successful one that believed they were superior," Harry said, "or divine even because at their foundation was one who cheated death, even though the first Benjamin did eventually return to the grave. The two masters I've examined were mortal in every way; I'm just reserving judgement on the human part."

Laurel pulled out the pandroscopic data of the child in the bucket. "It's interesting there are no signs of xy chromosomes in the girl's spine."

"It is interesting," Harry agreed. "And it makes the story of Judith all the more fascinating because whatever part of you is affected by her, your spine is essentially normal, except..."

"...for the extra vertebrae," Laurel finished his sentence. "Yes, Harry, I know. I'm beginning to wonder if the spaceborne virus, Lilith, perhaps originated on Menwora. Maybe all life originated there."

A shriek of delight and Scarlett's excited arrival stopped any further discussion as she threw herself into her father's arms, spreading her hands over his bald head and kissing his face over and over. The girl treated everyone to as much fuss as she told them about her visit to Faris, the caverns, the animals, the yucky food, and the other children. They listened, happy to hear her young voice full of enthusiasm for the experiences of the last few months, even though, at first, she had not wanted to go. On Faris, Scarlett had been protected from the war and its aftermath, but they had missed her—Scarlett was so like Helen—impossible to overlook, and she seemed to have grown since she'd been away. Listening to her excited chatter was a welcome distraction from the sombre conversation.

Olyo had detoured to deliver Scarlett back to them herself on the way to Riynea, where she took a very hands-on approach to rebuilding, providing labour and materials to keep the work going, so she didn't stay long, which was a good thing, as the master's mate chose that night to emerge from her sac.

Except for Scarlett, who was asleep in her bed, they all attended the emergence. The container was large enough to stop any fluid from spilling all over the med bay, but Harry hadn't been able to determine how much of the paralysing components remained.

The "birth" was intense. The girl clawed and bit frantically at the sac, tearing a massive gash in the membrane. It took less than two minutes, and as the fluid gushed and drained, the girl relaxed back into the container and drew her first breath.

Harry had called her a baby, and seeing her naked and panting, it was easy to believe she was, at least for the first few moments. She opened her eyes, trying to focus as she took in her surroundings. Laurel wondered if it would have been the cruel hands of a master that guided her through these waking moments. Laurel hoped she wouldn't witness some kind of fundamental, supernatural power that would come into play, but the girl simply looked at the people in the room, her chest and throat shuddering as she tried to suck in air.

Darlen moved quickly, covering his arms with a cloth to shield himself from the dregs of the bane just in case it still had the power to paralyse. Ignoring the girl's alarm, he tipped her onto the floor, forcing her to move.

It was so obvious; this was like variance. Just as Darlen had made Laurel move when she first emerged, so this girl needed to purge the bane to allow her body to function.

Darlen tried to give the girl antidote, but this was a child who'd never eaten, and none of them had any idea of what other process was required in these moments after birth.

"Perhaps we need to contact one of the Legion on Riynea. Maybe they'll know what we need to do next," Laurel suggested.

Harry shook his head. "It's not likely. Remember Beril said no-one had witnessed this stage of the masters' lifecycle. If you think about it, she has no memories of ever being touched, wearing clothes, eating. We're going to have to teach her all that, make those things familiar and comfortable."

"According to your findings, the female's diet is mainly meat protein."

"That's right, Ava," Harry said, "but I'm reluctant to offer her a slab of meat at this stage. She might choke. Let's just observe."

Darlen tried to cover the naked girl with a gown, but his attempts resulted in a primitive howling, with the girl squatting down and covering her head, peering up at him with frightened eyes. She seemed fine if she wasn't touched.

"The palm pandroscope registered pain when Darlen tried to put on the gown," Laurel said. "She has heightened sensory neurons. Touching her hurts. We might need to administer a pain suppressant." Laurel edged slowly towards the full pandroscope, trying not to alarm the girl. She got as far as programming a suitable dose of a neurolytic agent, counting on the girl's metabolism not to suffer any adverse reaction, but when Darlen tried to encourage her to the pandroscope, the girl careened around the room like a wild animal, only coming to a stop when Ava threw a mantle around herself as protection, grabbing the girl's arms and holding her close. Ava sat down under the pandroscope, and the medication was delivered without a murmur from the girl. A moment later, she curled into a ball on Ava's lap, her face angled away as Laurel read the pandroscope from a safe distance. All the while, the girl made soft yelps and growls, like an anxious puppy.

"You still think this was a good idea?" Harry said, his face grim.

"She's frightened," Laurel whispered. "We need to

gain her trust. She'll come to see we won't hurt her."

"But what if that is her purpose? To suffer, to serve the masters?"

Laurel turned to him. "Harry, I don't believe she is capable only of serving as the vessel for the masters' and her children's bestial proclivities. There must be more to her than that."

"And are you hoping to see something of what Judith's people were in this child?"

Harry's words shook her, but she couldn't deny there was at least some truth in them.

The pandroscope verified that while the girl was defective in many areas, the systems she possessed were functioning within accepted parameters. In the few days before her birth, Laurel and Harry had observed her breasts had swelled, but there had been no other sign of sexual maturity until the birth. All this in readiness for the brutal onslaught of the master's abuse and the ongoing torture of bearing his children. If the girl had an instinct to follow this course of action, it would likely manifest in a day or two. Laurel had no idea how many days after the emergence of the female, mating took place but recognised that in many societies, both on Earth and in the League, it was traditional for girls to begin childbearing at a young age. So many accepted it as part of the rites and rituals of their peoples. The pandroscope confirmed that physiologically the girl was around fourteen years, but the idea of such a young female mating horrified Laurel. And she had seen a naked master— no wonder the young women suffered so.

Ava volunteered to remain with the girl that night, but Darlen instructed Mer to keep watch. Ava wasn't such a big person herself, and who knew what kind of metamorphosis might take over. In the morning, the girl was still sleeping in Ava's arms, the pandroscope keeping her nervous system in check. She appeared to be suffering no pain when Ava woke her and covered her in a gown. The pandroscope had also revised its findings regarding her youth, drawing a sigh of relief from both Harry and Laurel.

"Growth hormones," Harry said with a sigh. "Overnight, she's gone from the hormone profile of a girl of fourteen to a girl of around seventeen. I expect there'll be a growth spurt to match soon."

"She just seems like a little kid," Laurel said. "This reading makes me feel a little better."

"There's also a layer of subcutaneous fat that wasn't there yesterday," Harry said. "The other thing is, she can't mate yet, or not conceive anyway. She's not ovulating."

"It would seem the masters have to wait a few days, that it's not immediate."

Harry nodded. "I suppose so, unless she's like the Carpadi females who ovulate at copulation."

"Fortunately, we won't get the opportunity to find out."

They brought the girl to the common lounge and instructed her on how to sit down in a chair. She resisted and instead slid to the floor, where she lay on her back until Ava took up a sitting position beside her and encouraged her to sit up. Darlen went to get Scarlett, determining he may as well introduce his daughter to the newest member of their group. She'd had a dose of aliens on Faris; chances are she'd accept this one too, although he wasn't sure he did.

"We need to give her a name," Ava said. "We can't keep referring to her as offspring or the child."

"We could call her Nika," Scarlett suggested, peering curiously at the girl before giving her a beaming smile. "Like in daddy's stories about his planet." Scarlett took Nika's hand and looked her in the eye. "Hello Nika," she said brightly, "you're very pretty. Would you like to wear some of my mummy's clothes? She wasn't much bigger than you."

Nika returned Scarlett's gaze and then looked down at their joined fingers. To everyone's astonishment, she allowed Scarlett to draw her to her feet and take her over to the antidote that sat discarded on a bench. Scarlett took a sip, smiled, and offered it to Nika.

"It's very nice," she lied. Scarlett hated it but knew its value for when people came out of variance. It was even more disgusting when left on a bench for a night.

Nika allowed Scarlett to place the beaker in her hand but seemed uncertain about how much pressure she should exert to keep it from falling, so Scarlett helped, sharing the grip on the cup and guiding it to Nika's mouth. Harry and Laurel were gladdened to see the swallowing reflex looked fully developed. Nika took a few more sips, then let the beaker fall to the ground when Scarlett took her hand away.

"She is a child in many ways," Laurel said. "Perhaps Scarlett could be the one to guide her."

"I don't know about the pretty bit," Darlen remarked. "She's pretty ugly, in my opinion. If you look like Judith," he grinned at Laurel, "the original Menworans must have had better looking ribs!"

Darlen was right. Where the masters were exquisite in feature, Nika's heavy brows and deep-set eyes gave her a Neanderthal appearance, not helped by a small skull, flattened at the back. Nika's poorly formed jaw contained normal upper and lower rows of perfect teeth. A quick examination by Laurel while Nika slept revealed the girl was not possessed of the bane glands.

Nika paid no mind to anyone else. Scarlett took her hand and led her out to the corridor and to her quarters, chattering all the while at the bewildered girl. The others followed at a safe distance. There was a strong sense Scarlett was in no danger; Nika's mind showed confusion, but there was also curiosity. Laurel noted that Darlen was wearing a wrist lick at the ready; if necessary, he would sacrifice the girl to protect his daughter.

But it turned out to be unwarranted. Nika allowed Scarlett to scrub the neutralised, sticky fluid from her in the shower, accepting the ministrations and obediently lifting her arms when Scarlett demonstrated. Clean now, Nika's head was covered in a cap of tight curls, the only trait she shared with the masters, although the colour more closely resembled Laurel's hair. As Scarlett and Ava dried and dressed her, the girl hissed softly, then shifted her dark, life-empty gaze towards Laurel.

Darlen drew the line at allowing Nika to remain with Scarlett unsupervised that night. Any attempt to remove her from Scarlett's side caused the girl to wail and make defensive actions. Mer and Darlen took babysitting in turns, and when Laurel rose the following day, Scarlett was showing Nika how to dress up Mer.

"She had the antidote again," Darlen said. "I offered bapth, but she seemed clueless as to the idea of chewing. It just kept falling out of her mouth; even Scarlett couldn't help her make sense of it."

"It's odd," Laurel said, "because she has adult teeth, so one would have thought chewing would be natural. Harry found only evidence of a protein diet in the remains of the mother. We might not be offering something that stimulates that sense."

"She needs a Big Mac," Darlen grinned, smacking his lips. "That'd get anyone stimulated."

Laurel looked sideways at him. "You still miss those, don't you?"

"Best food in the universe," he said in all seriousness, "any universe; that manifested rubbish tastes nothing like them."

"Well, as a vegetarian, Darlen, I've never had a Big Mac, so it's a bit difficult for me to manifest a taste I've never encountered." Laurel tapped him on the chest, "but you give me an idea."

Laurel remembered the smell of raw meat, so she manifested a cube of what looked like beef. She held it up to Darlen's nose, and he nodded his approval. Laurel gave the morsel to Scarlett, all the while watched by Nika.

"See what she makes of this, honey," Laurel said. Scarlett nodded and took the little piece of manifested meat back to Nika. She didn't offer it, just made Mer open his claw and placed the food on it. Nika leaned forward and sniffed, but she would not touch the food, only glanced fearfully at Darlen.

"Darlen," Laurel said, "pick it up and take a bite. She may be deferring to the male. Go on, it's not a Big Mac, but it won't hurt you."

Darlen reached out, picked up the food, pretended to nibble, and then placed it back in Mer's claw. Immediately, Nika grabbed it, chomped briefly and gulped, as a puppy would eat, no time to taste, just swallow. Then she turned her attention back to Mer.

"Servile and submissive," Darlen observed. "It has to be instinct; she hasn't had any example."

Laurel agreed with his assessment. "Well, let's see what transpires at breakfast," she said. "We'll sit together, offer her food with us and see what happens."

As breakfast progressed, Nika appeared afraid of eating before Harry and Darlen had finished and would take food only from them or Scarlett. She refused food from Ava and Laurel, and their attempts resulted in Nika raising the high-pitched keen she adopted when anxious. But it was only her second day of life, and each day for the next few days, they learned better about how not to terrify her. Despite Scarlett's constant chatter, she didn't pick up any speech, and Laurel and Harry made a few furtive runs with the pandroscope.

"She has normal vocal cords," Laurel said, "she should be able to speak, but she seems limited in intellect. Perhaps it's beyond her. Scarlett is interested in her now, but while I thought she might be an influence on Nika, it's too much responsibility for a nine-year-old."

"I agree," Harry said. "We need to make her more comfortable with us adults."

By the ninth day, Nika's body had lost its childlike appearance. She had grown, now measuring only a centimetre shorter than Laurel, and the pandroscope announced Nika was ovulating.

"Then conception would be around nine days after birth," Laurel said. "She has to mature outside the sac. I couldn't see how she would have coped mating with a master as a newborn."

"It makes sense," Harry agreed. "Although she is still developing."

Only a few hours later, they found Nika sitting in the corridor in a pool of blood, curiously smearing the red jelly-like substance on her legs and rubbing it into her clothes, and licking it off her fingers, her mouth bloodied as she looked up, startled at the rush of attention and Scarlett's screams. Nika began her wailing to add to the din, but she surprisingly allowed Laurel to help her to her feet and comfort her.

"She's menstruating," Laurel said. "I'll clean her up. Nika? Shall we go and wash? You like being washed." Nika seemed to recognise the word and ceased her wailing.

"Is she dying?" Scarlett sobbed in Ava's arms.

Ava quickly soothed the frightened child. "She's not dying, Scarlett; of course, she's not. We all expected this, don't worry."

"There must be a very narrow window of opportunity to conceive," Harry said, following Laurel and Nika to their quarters. "Like everything with this girl, nothing is delayed, and if there's no conception, nature is obviously going to take its course. I just can't believe it was this rapid."

"We can't place the attributes of ordinary humans on her," Laurel said as she stripped Nika of her blood-soaked clothing and waved on the shower. "We're learning too."

Harry knew they blindly overlooked what would have been an obvious outcome given the girl's metabolic speed. On his return to the common lounge, he passed Darlen and a distressed Scarlett, her arms wrapped around her father's neck. Looking at Darlen's face, he expected a reproach, but besides a thunderous look, Darlen didn't say a word.

Two days later, the bloody event forgotten by Scarlett, although not by Darlen, Nika still would only eat if the males offered her food, although she was comfortable with Mer. Besides the single contact with Laurel for a wash, and Ava on the first day, she remained wary of the two adult women. Also, despite the occasional wail, she never spoke.

Within two weeks of her "birth", Nika washed and dressed with no help nor encouragement, but she took no other initiative apart from squatting in front of Mer and awaiting directions to draw on him or dress him up. It was as if that pastime was her total expectation of what life offered. She even seemed content to sit like that for hours until Scarlett came to play. Laurel wondered if this was how it was to be from now on. They had dealt effectively with Nika's pain responses, and the menstruation was easy enough to sort, but unless there was a breakthrough, Nika would require almost constant supervision for however long she lived and would likely never be independent. Harry reminded her it was early days, and while Laurel stopped short of regretting saving Nika's life, she did wonder what path that life would take. From what she could see, Nika had severely limited capacity for intellectual growth.

The turning point came when Nika was a month old. One morning, at breakfast, instead of waiting until after Darlen and Harry ate before accepting food from them; a ritual Darlen and Harry found tiresome, Nika took an initiative which they all at first thought was progress until they realised this was again a primitive response. She removed food from Darlen's plate and sought to feed him. Darlen refused, roughly shoving her hand away from his mouth. She moved to Harry, who tried to rebuff her kindly, but she was insistent, bordering on violence in her second attempt and making throaty sounds when he refused.

"Perhaps just take one bite," Laurel suggested. Harry wasn't keen, but he allowed Nika to push a piece of food into his mouth, which led to an eerie, gentle purring from the girl. Laurel suddenly started. This was not progress. She grabbed a palm pandroscope, which gave her unwelcome news. Nika was ovulating again. "Harry…" she began, intending to warn him, but Nika had leapt into his lap, her body curling around his in a blatantly seductive manner. Darlen tried to unlatch the girl from him, but she was not letting go, so he turned his attention to his daughter, who was far more interested in her breakfast than the goings-on with Harry. Darlen took her hand and ignored her protests. She hadn't finished eating. He strode out of the galley, leaving Ava and Laurel to sort the mess that, in his mind, they'd created.

Laurel tried to prise Nika from Harry. She wasn't as strong as Laurel but forcibly removing her was likely to injure either the girl or the unwilling object of her desire. Nika clung to Harry like a limpet, and realising Laurel was trying to separate them, she snarled, then set up her keening, but this time, she cried real tears.

"Failure," Ava said. "Mom, she's failed to get the man to mate with her. I thought the male just, well, did it. It seems like there's a whole ritual."

Laurel could only speculate. "Maybe that is how it works under normal conditions, but I don't know if any of these females have been rejected before or not conceived the first time and had to wait until another ovulation. And maybe this has never happened, and her instincts have kicked in."

Harry, shaken and angry, snapped at them. "I don't care, just get her off me!" The girl had bitten his ear, and blood dripped down his neck.

Unable to remove Nika from Harry without causing further distress, Laurel and Harry went together to the med bay with the still weeping girl wrapped around him. Fortunately, with her face buried in Harry's neck, Nika could not see Laurel programming the pandroscope to deliver the necessary stimulant to halt the responses. In moments, the girl loosened her hold on Harry and allowed him to lay her down under the pandroscope where a holographic comparison was projected, detailing Nika's condition before delivery of the stimulation to the moments immediately after. Laurel and Harry focused on the girl's brain.

"The shot we gave her last time should have lasted for months," Harry said. "She must have some kind of immunity to anything that overrides her natural responses. Look at the hypothalamus. It's hyperstimulated." He pointed to the pandroscope hologram. "The nucleus accumbens looks like it's about to detonate."

Nika looked up at them with innocent eyes as Laurel changed the picture to the moments after the pandroscope delivered its stimulation. "She would have no control over this, none at all, but the brain appears to have returned to a normal pattern," Laurel said. "We'll have to keep these responses under control, at least until she can communicate with us."

Harry was silent as Laurel led Nika from the med bay. He didn't follow, just watched them leave. This morning's incident had rattled him, and he wondered why Laurel was so blindly taking this path. He was trying to be patient, but this— Harry rubbed his ear and pushed a heal bot into the wound. This had to stop. He valued life, all life, but he wasn't sure that what had just left the med bay holding Laurel's hand qualified. It was animated, sure, it had a brain, a heart, but it didn't seem to have…he couldn't find a word. He supposed the Edensai would say she didn't have a soul. He didn't know that already Laurel had come to the same conclusion.

Laurel took Nika back to the common lounge, followed soon after by a still unsettled Harry. Darlen had taken Scarlett out in the axispods to divert her. Nika looked around wildly for her young friend, and when her eyes lit on Mer, who was a second choice to Scarlett, she sat at his feet while he worked on synthesising vitamin and mineral supplements for their next visit to Riynea.

"Darlen's not happy," Ava said, seeing that Harry was also not in a good mood. "He thinks Scarlett's too young to be exposed to this kind of disturbing behaviour."

"She is!" Harry exploded, uncharacteristic annoyance mounting inside him. He heartily agreed with Darlen's judgment. "And Nika's not acting like a child. She's not a suitable companion for Scarlett. So far, we've had to suppress pain response and ovulation, and now we have this most recent behaviour..." He flashed an angry look at Laurel. "When is it going to end? When will you accept this is a mistake?"

Laurel didn't answer. She had to admit, Nika showed no signs of ever being anything other than a procreation tool for the masters. There was no real flicker of life, little intellect and no concept of happiness. She just *existed*. Was that enough? Ava heard everything Laurel thought. "What do we do? We're alienating Darlen," she said aloud, not wanting to exclude Harry from their thoughts. The trio stood in silence for a moment, both women unable to shield their senses from the unfamiliar onslaught of Harry's anger. They watched as Nika patted Mer's foot, then leaned down to suck his metallic claw. She was so innocent, so primitive.

"You're right, Harry," Laurel said miserably, "I've made a huge mistake."

But Harry was too fired up to be appeased by the acknowledgement, and Laurel's regret came far too late. "I'd like to know what you plan on doing with her when we return to Riynea?" he thundered. "We can't take her, that's for sure, and I'm not staying behind."

Laurel honestly hadn't thought that far. She shook her head and blew out her breath in a deep sigh. "I don't know. If she isn't displaying this hypersexuality, perhaps they would accept her." Even before the words passed her lips, Laurel knew it would only inflame the situation. In any case, introducing Nika to the Riyneans would never become a reality.

"You're kidding!" Harry snarled. "They won't want her anywhere near them! After everything they suffered at the hands of the masters?" Harry took a few deep breaths, his face crimson with anger. "And we absolutely could never leave her there. We're stuck with her!" Harry's emotions started to get away from him. "Laurel, you're a telepath. Think! You said you wanted peace. Is this peace?" he yelled.

Laurel stared at him, bewildered. Never once had Harry raised his voice to her, and Ava shifted uncomfortably. This was new to her as well. She should never have insisted on bringing the sac to the ship. Harry's thoughts were a jumble of fury, dismay, fear, disappointment, and her mother's simply of pain and hurt as Harry turned and stormed from the room.

CHAPTER THIRTY-ONE _

When he and Scarlett returned from their flight, Darlen angrily announced to Laurel and Ava that Nika would need to get used to the others as companions and that they must try to keep her away from his daughter. Harry was present, but the atmosphere was thick enough to cut with a knife. Darlen felt it, but it didn't stop him from adding to the bad feeling. He told them Nika was not a little child despite her simplicity, and he felt her sexual precociousness was an unnecessary component in any friendship for Scarlett. He rejected Laurel's assurances Nika had been appropriately treated now, arguing this whole venture was nothing more than an exercise in futility and an experiment designed only for her to learn more about her origins. He chided her uncharacteristic inconsideration of what was best for the group. Laurel pointed out it wasn't she who brought Nika on board, so he must also share blame, but her argument fell on deaf ears. Harry's lack of input to the conversation didn't go unnoticed by Darlen, but he didn't know his statement had come so hard on the heels of Harry's outburst. When he finished speaking, Laurel quietly excused herself to go to her quarters. Mer kept Nika with him, Harry went to the medbay, Ava went to the cargo bay to train with the holoenemies, and Darlen and Scarlett went for a long walk around the station. Laurel felt the division, and despite pointing out to Darlen that he'd brought Nika on board, she knew he'd bowed to Ava's insistence. And Laurel herself had to take some responsibility it had gone so far. She should never have been so forceful. In everything else they had done, the others had encouraged and supported her, even when it had seemed reckless and culminated in a war that could have killed any one of them. Only Ava had been on her side about Nika, and now it was clear they couldn't move forward until this was resolved. They were due to return to Riynea in a few days, so Laurel thought stasis for Nika might be an idea, just until they returned, but there was a chance, however slim, someone on the station might discover her. Once or twice, the engineers had come on board without announcement, usually searching for a healbot or painbot to borrow. Leaving Nika on the Canaa was too much of a risk.

Alone with her thoughts, Laurel wondered if Nika ever experienced moments of happiness or was her expectation of life too integrated into fulfilling her purpose of becoming a vessel of procreation for the masters. Nika would never achieve this purpose. To have any chance, they would need to get rid of her current reasons for existing.

Much later, Laurel was startled awake by Ava's thoughts in her mind.

"Mom! Quickly!"

Laurel leapt from the bed and sprinted to the common lounge. For the second time that day, a furious Darlen strode from the room with a tearful Scarlett in his arms. Ava was on the floor with two kittens, Nika beside her, head flipped back, a look of terrifying ecstasy on her face. Her clothing was torn away, and blood trickled from a scratch on her breast, not deep but provoking enough discomfort to fill a masochistic need in the girl.

"What happened?" Laurel said, kneeling to examine the wound. She got the furious, spoken version from Harry and the telepathic version from Ava simultaneously.

Ava had manifested the kittens to amuse Nika. Scarlett, hearing their mewing, had come from her room, despite Darlen's caution she must play there today, and joined Ava and Nika on the floor. Darlen saw and relented, knowing how much Scarlett loved playing with the kittens. Ava sent Laurel an impression of what developed. Nika was gentle and affectionate to the animals, and Laurel saw a mothering instinct. In Ava's imagery, Nika rubbed the kitten on her cheek, making the little cat purr. Without warning, Nika tore the front of her top and put the kitten to her breast, trying to encourage it to suckle. Being purely a manifestation, the kitten had neither need nor instinct for food, but as it was a memory extrapolated from Ava's knowledge of cats, it did have claws and teeth. It bit and scratched Nika, resulting in the state of euphoria Laurel now observed.

Clearly, Harry was still mad. "Happy?" he said fiercely. "This is what you think we need after all we've been through? Laurel, I have supported you all these years, never questioned your judgement, but now—" he gestured to Nika, keening as she recovered from her blissful state, deprived of her comfort, "you go too far. You ask too much. From all of us!" He glowered at her for a moment, then pushed past her roughly, leaving her and Ava alone with Nika. Mer stood silently in the corner.

"Twice in one day," Laurel said softly. "What's more, he's right."

Ava nodded. "Nika is all instinct and little humanity, Mom. We got it wrong, me as much as you. I refused to allow Darlen to destroy the sac when we found her on Eden."

Laurel didn't know that. "Why didn't you let him?"

"Because she's a life. An innocent. It seemed...wrong."

"Is she a life?" Laurel was uncertain now of what she believed. "Or is she just a postscript to the masters?"

Ava's shoulders sagged. "You know, Darlen tried to tell me that."

"In her current state," Laurel said, sliding down beside Ava, "Nika can't function independently of the masters' purpose for her. Her destiny is too linked to theirs."

"But we can't destroy her." Ava looked from Laurel to Nika, engaged in tapping the floor around her in search of the kittens she'd seen disappear when Ava ended the manifestation. When she couldn't find them, she lay flat on her back and stared at the ceiling. It was then Laurel saw liquid soaking through the torn remains of Nika's shirt.

"She's lactating," Laurel groaned. "Contact with the kitten has obviously prompted the milk. What a mess."

"What are we going to do, Mom?"

"Maybe we need to put her into stasis," Laurel said. "When Harry and Darlen have calmed down, we'll discuss what happens next."

"Marcel is expecting us on Riynea," Ava reminded her. "They need us. We need to make a decision soon."

Laurel nodded and rubbed her forehead. She'd made a colossal error in judgement, but after all the killing, it just seemed right to preserve at least one life.

Ava heard her thoughts. "We saved thousands of lives," she said aloud. "If we find we can't preserve this one, it doesn't make us failures."

Laurel realised that, but she wished Nika was a link, however tenuous to Judith, and Laurel desperately needed to understand Judith's origins. She'd pieced much of it together, but a more in-depth study of Nika might have produced some answers. Laurel looked at the girl, flat on her back, staring at the lights above her, her arms raised above her head, mindlessly tracing some imagined shape, and she knew Nika had no answers. Even though she told herself she couldn't take an innocent life, Laurel knew she had been wrong to preserve one for her own selfish reasons.

Harry was in the med bay, making a noisy show of tidying the desks. He glanced up as Laurel entered but didn't speak, just carried on stomping about, moving everything around with an angry clatter.

"Nika's lactating," Laurel stated simply.

The news made Harry slam things down even harder. "Great!" he muttered.

Laurel's heart sank. The bad feeling between her and Harry was all so new and raw and painful. She waited miserably while he pointedly ignored her. He truly believed

Laurel had gone too far and felt justified in his anger, but he wasn't seeking an apology. He wanted Laurel to come up with a solution, even though he'd conveniently forgotten his lack of resistance at the decision to allow the girl to continue to birth. Right now, though, he didn't feel as though he was thinking clearly; he just wanted to make a noise.

"Harry," Laurel kept her distance. "I need your help. We can't kill her."

Harry glared but didn't face her. "Ask Darlen," he snapped. "He'd do it gladly."

"I was thinking if all else fails, we could place her in stasis," Laurel said quietly, hoping anything she said didn't inflame the situation further. "But before we resort to that, why don't we attempt a Belling procedure, like the one they do on Katmos R14 to control the population?"

Harry's glare relaxed into a sober appraisal of what Laurel proposed. Somewhere amidst all his anger, the stasis idea had occurred to him too, but a Bellings? "I've never performed one," he declared, "and I know you haven't either."

"No, but I know the principle, and we can do it together. Harry," Laurel ventured a few steps forward, scarcely able to believe her next words. "If she dies, what will she have lost?"

"And if she survives, then what?" Harry made exaggerated gestures with his hands. "Put her on an uninhabited planet somewhere and leave her to die?"

"There wouldn't be much point in doing the procedure if we were going to do that," Laurel said. "I believe if we give her a different reason for living, she could be happy."

"Where? On Riynea?" Harry responded with sarcasm. Despite her contrition and good ideas, he still wasn't ready to let Laurel off the hook. "She sure as hell won't be welcome on the Canaa no matter how much we fix her up. You'll end up choosing between her and Darlen."

"I know, I know," Laurel said. That was a possibility, and not one she was prepared to chance. "But it might work on Faris."

Harry couldn't believe his ears. "Faris?"

Laurel nodded. "They are highly structured and live an ordered, devotional life. It might bring a new purpose to Nika. My instincts are telling me this is what we need to do."

Harry snorted, but he was no longer shouting. "Your instincts? They didn't serve you so well this time, did they? Why didn't the entity whisper in your ear at the start of all this? Besides, good luck with Olyo."

Laurel ignored his cynicism, even agreed with it in part. "She should be on her way back from Riynea," she said. "I'm going to contact her and ask her to detour."

Harry held Laurel's gaze for a moment before stepping forward and sweeping her into his arms. He held her close. "I'm sorry, sweetheart. I don't mean to be harsh. This situation, it's...." He chuckled. "I don't think we've ever argued."

Laurel rested her cheek against his chest and felt his anger draining away. "I've argued," she said, grateful the rift between them was mended. "Remember one hundred moons? You just never argued back!"

<hr>

Olyo answered the communication that intercepted her

return to Faris and arrived within two days. She was surprised to have been diverted and immediately demanded to know why, as she had given much of her time to the rebuilding on Riynea. She now needed to attend to matters on her homeworld and wished not to be delayed, explaining she would not return to Riynea for a while now that so many of her people were engaged in rehabilitating the people there. She felt she must now turn her attention to home.

Olyo followed Harry and Laurel to the med bay where Nika lay, sedated. Olyo stared wordlessly at the sleeping girl.

"Ava and Darlen found her in her sac on Eden," Laurel told Olyo, feeling an unexpected rush of guilt as Olyo turned disbelieving eyes on her. "We…Ava and I felt it wrong to destroy her or leave her to die, so we allowed her to complete her gestation and tried to help her."

"Help her become something she is not?" Olyo asked. She respected Laurel, but at this moment, her humanity had not served her well. Laurel felt guilty all over again under Olyo's intense gaze.

"We've already determined her function is intrinsically fused with the desires of the masters," she explained. Laurel was getting nothing from Olyo, other than perhaps a mild accusatory standpoint, but she pressed on regardless. "Yesterday, Harry and I performed a procedure that severed the link that no amount of devoted behavioural therapy would accomplish."

"And what did you do that can intercede with nature, with what the gods intend?"

Laurel gave Olyo a "come on, Olyo, we know your views are not set-in-stone" face, but she didn't want to expose the truth of the Farisee Ascendant's personal feelings. Instead, she said simply, "We took away what made her a mate to the masters."

Olyo returned her gaze to the girl. "And now she is nothing?"

"She can learn," Harry assured her. "We have permanently suppressed her pain responses, which of course presents difficulties on its own, and she has no 'needs', sexual or otherwise, so you would have to hold her hand for the remainder of her life, which isn't likely to be very long."

"And when you say 'you', Harry—" Olyo allowed herself a thin smile, "I assume you mean me, or at least the Farisee?"

"You claim reverence for all life," Laurel said, reminding Olyo of several of their conversations. "Even killing the masters was against your beliefs." Laurel sensed many emotions churning within Olyo, but the one she was relying on eventually took centre stage. Compassion. Now was the time for Laurel to make her case. "Olyo, I have seen you with children. They respond to you. I know it looks as though we created a problem, and now, we're asking you to clean it up, but it's not like that."

"And if we fail to bring contentment to her?"

"I sense strongly you will," Laurel replied. "I feel wholly at peace with this decision. Otherwise, she will be placed in permanent stasis."

Olyo fluttered her eyelids as she looked from Harry to Laurel, then back to Nika.

"Wake her when you are ready."

CHAPTER THIRTY-TWO _

In removing the focus of sexual impulses from Nika's brain, they'd allowed new pathways to stir into existence, barely registering in many instances, but they gave Laurel hope. Nika had undergone the equivalent of a sexual lobotomy. With Nika's already rudimentary brain, Laurel had no idea if it would just turn her into a breathing mass of skin and sinew that would have no quality of life, but what she had been before the surgery didn't represent quality either.

Olyo returned to her ship to await Nika's arrival. Laurel stayed alone in the med bay to watch Nika's progress. She drew up her knees and rested her chin. The pandroscope charted Nika's new pathways and brain activity; there was potential for a personality now she was no longer a monster making machine. In her relaxed state, Nika's heavy brow was softened, and her thin mouth seemed fuller. She still wasn't beautiful, but she looked at peace, untroubled.

Somewhere through the quiet, Laurel became aware she was no longer alone. It wasn't a presence she recognised, and she couldn't form a telepathic or empathic connection. She felt no fear but still called out, "Who's there?"

A movement distracted her, and she looked toward the

disturbance. No-one revealed themselves, but in the airtight confines of the med bay, a strange soft breeze lifted Laurel's hair and caressed the skin on her cheek. A woman's voice sighed in her ear, sending shivers down her spine. *"I am here,"* was all Laurel heard before she found herself standing on a lofty, narrow mountain ledge where the soft breeze changed to a hard, icy wind that whistled all around her. A man of regal splendour and clad in furs, faced an upright scaffold that held a skull and torso suspended on a frame. Laurel could see the skeleton partly covered in sinew and skin, but even the ice and snow freezing her bones and the fact she knew she couldn't possibly be here did little to hide the stink of a decaying carcass. Four men circled the corpse, tall men, giants, perhaps seven feet tall. They were not as regal as the other man but no less commanding as they worked over the corpse, casting powders, calling lights from the heavens, chanting incantations and supplication to what sounded like gods and demons. The figure began to form, its ragged muscles becoming robust once more, doubtless as they had been in life. New skin stretched to cover the chest and chin, radiant with the colour of burnished copper, and the patches of hair regrew into a cap of golden curls. Laurel watched in disgust as the regal man lifted the corpse's head in his hands and laid his mouth against its cold lips to breathe in life.

The resurrected Benjamin opened his dark, soulless eyes and pulled himself free from the frame. He focused first on the four men around him, who fell to their knees quivering in fear, then he rounded to the regal man who likewise dropped to the ground, slithering on his belly to kiss his son's feet. Laurel heard the man cry out in joy, repeating Benjamin's name over and over, but Benjamin was fixated on Laurel, her presence unnoticed until now.

"For what purpose do you bring my sister here? To my restoration?" Benjamin spat, but he didn't move towards her. Each man returned to their feet and composure slowly, but it was apparent none could see Laurel.

"My son," the regal man chided gently, "Judith is not here; she is not part of your second coming."

Benjamin pointed to where Laurel stood. "She stands there."

The old man looked around in confusion at the holy men. "We do not see her, my son. Perhaps a reminder of the grave? Perhaps your dear sister left a shadow in the netherworld, and it is this you see?" The old man reached out to embrace his restored son, but Benjamin stepped back, dismissing his father, who dropped his arms to his sides and bowed his head. "Benjamin, my son, my heir, you are restored!"

Benjamin did not take his cold eyes from Laurel. Instead, he reached out and picked his father up by the neck." You are a fool," he said, taking only a moment to survey the shocked eyes of his saviour, then he wrung from him the life he had so lately shared, and flung the body over the ledge into the chasm below. The four men cowered against the cliff face, but Laurel was not given to see their fate; she was swiftly transported to a pavilion that looked out over a verdant hillside. Outside, Laurel saw sloping fields and pastureland, animals being herded, and people busy with their daily industry. Technology didn't seem too advanced from this vantage point, but the few vehicles visible were off-ground and silent. A distant city displayed buildings that rose several storeys towards the sky.

And this is where Laurel came face to face with that part of her origins that confounded her. Judith sat on a stone seat, her hands working skilfully and quickly at embroidery or some form of needlework. Her hair, a mass of fair curls which looked never to have been cut, was secured with a narrow scarf that passed around her forehead and settled in folds down her back. Her modest gown was long and flowing; bracelets that glittered like gold filigree adorned her arms and ankle. In face and form, she was identical to Laurel save for one vital detail, for when she looked up and smiled, Judith's eyes were green, not amber.

Judith put her handiwork aside and stood. "Be at peace," she said mildly, "for each purpose has its own time."

Laurel shook her head. "I don't understand. What is my purpose?"

Laurel fell forward with a start. She looked at Nika's sleeping form. "Do you know something I don't?" Laurel whispered. It was all so frustrating. Where her origins were concerned, Laurel felt as lost as Nika. Harry had tacitly accused her of using this innocent girl to find answers. Even after having seen Judith and the vision of the forming of Benjamin, she was no closer to understanding. Laurel leaned back into the chair and covered her face with her hands. Be at peace, Judith said. Well, Laurel wanted peace, but she always seemed to get into very unpeaceful situations, dragging the people she loved with her. Laurel took a deep breath. She would go to Riynea and do what must be done there, and once she'd fulfilled her purpose…Laurel frowned. Fulfilled her purpose? She heard that phrase, that word, so often. Perhaps there would be no answers while she lived.

Nika recovered enough to travel to Faris. Laurel had wanted a gradual introduction, but with the need to be back on Riynea, that was a luxury they couldn't afford. The surgery, which isolated so many pathways of arousal, including fear and anger, had rendered Nika docile. Scarlett was inconsolable at losing her playmate, having forgotten all the angst Nika's precociousness had caused, but seeing Nika accepting Olyo's hand in welcome, gave Scarlett some comfort.

"You'll be her friend, won't you?" a tearful Scarlett begged of Olyo.

"I am not just going to be her friend, Scarlett. I am going to be her mother," Olyo said, patting Scarlett's head. "Remember all the children you had to play with on Faris? You had a lovely time, didn't you?"

Scarlett nodded. "I don't like this, though." She pointed to the language pin lodged in her neck. "You'll hurt Nika if you put one in her. She might not understand."

"Nika will learn our language," Olyo reassured Scarlett. "We will not put the pin in her, but you were only visiting and needed help to understand us. I promise she is going to be happy."

Nika stood beside Olyo, listening, and although Laurel saw no real understanding, she sensed there was a processing of information. She glanced at Ava.

"I think you're right," Ava sent back. *"Without the previous focus, there is an opportunity for her to grow."*

"A side effect of the procedure we performed on Nika is memory loss," Harry told Olyo. "It means that while she won't fear sensory input as she did when she first emerged—" he looked at Nika, returned to babyhood, "She's like a newborn again."

Olyo smiled at the girl. "The masters were the only enemies my people ever encountered. Even though they did not attack us directly, their assault on the Edensai, the Kalmeddi and Riynea brought us considerable pain and challenged many of our beliefs. Nika will remind us that even in our enemies, there is a part that love can reach."

Laurel saw Harry flick his eyebrows, and Darlen bite his lip against a grin. The Farisee would be the only race anywhere in Sheerguhd that believed the masters possessed any lovable qualities.

Laurel handed Olyo a box. "Nika has a protein diet. She can chew but prefers that food is offered to her, although that is likely to be different now. It's just that so far, she hasn't taken the initiative in feeding, except for once, and that won't be an issue. These are just synthesised nuggets of meat. She will accept them as she gets used to you. Up to now, she has only accepted food from Harry or Darlen, sometimes Scarlett. I don't know what the Farisee eat."

Laurel had previously noted the Farisee had small, even teeth not designed for eating the flesh of animals.

"If she is more comfortable accepting food from a male, that can be arranged," Olyo said. "Most of our nourishment comes from the consumption of liquid nutrients, absorbed through our hands, but we also consume nettles and other plants by mouth. If the nourishment is to Nika's taste, there is no reason why she cannot eat, and we can prepare the bread meal we used on Eden." She smiled at Scarlett. "We do not have 'nice' flavours, do we, Scarlett?"

"They're okay," Scarlett said. "They taste like Mer when I lick him."

Harry grinned. He'd seen Nika licking Mer. "Why do you lick Mer?"

"I don't lick him like this." Scarlett made two large licking motions with her tongue. "I spit on him, then wash off my colouring with my finger and then when I put my finger back in my mouth, it tastes like Mer."

Scarlett's description caused a ripple of humour and elicited a cackle from Mer.

Laurel stroked Nika's curly hair. "Well, Olyo, we know you will do the right thing for Nika. I'll walk with you to your ship."

Scarlett and Ava hugged the passive Nika, who seemed bewildered at the gesture, but she did raise a hand, copying Scarlett as Olyo and Laurel led her away. Olyo's attendants were delighted to take over the girl, her origins unimportant. All they saw before them was a bewildered child needing love and care.

"You have guilt," Olyo said as she prepared to board her ship. "It is better this way. It would not have been wise to take her with you."

"You're very perceptive," Laurel replied. "I've told

myself over and over that I couldn't let her die because she was an innocent, a life. I've tried to justify it, but I think I was hoping there would be at least something in her behaviour that would give me a clue as to her origins; my origins."

"Was there?"

Laurel shook her head. "No, nothing." She paused. "Olyo, if you know something, please tell me."

"I loved Judith," Olyo said, opening her heart for Laurel to see the sense of loss she felt. "She was dear to me. An Ascendant does not have friends nor confidantes, nor do we take lifelong mates, not in the way humans do. Judith's goodness, her tenacity, which I see in you, is why we all loved her."

"I can see she was important to you, to many people. Did she ever tell you where she came from? According to Abel, she just appeared around the time of the changing."

"I believe she was on Eden for centuries; that she did not exist in physical form. You are not Judith," Olyo smiled, "but you are of her. And you are of Hebre."

"During life, Judith had green eyes," Laurel said.

Olyo inclined her head; she didn't know that. "Perhaps before her gods clothed her once more in flesh," she said, "before she became Hebre."

Laurel couldn't help it, she dived straight into Olyo's mind, but she found only the remnants of what they had just spoken about. There was no more. Judith had obviously told her friend nothing else. Olyo embraced her briefly before boarding the ship, waving away Laurel's thanks for her kindness in taking Nika.

CHAPTER THIRTY-THREE _

Over the few short months since the evacuation, the Edensai had established a friendly segregation, in contrast to the Kalmeddi and the Riynea, who looked to have combined into one large happy family. The Edensai had always accepted both races on Eden, and Marcel told Laurel the Edensai was presently using the one ark left behind as a central homestead in their settlement, mainly so they might recover their faith and traditions so brutally disrupted during the masters' occupation. Marcel told them he had witnessed no exclusion or rebuffing of Riynean or Kalmeddi visitors to the Edensai settlement. Hence, while they were not unfriendly, they concentrated on purifying themselves of the masters.

As the Edensai looked to re-establish observation of their religious laws, the merging Kalmeddi and Riynean had settled a few other areas, seemingly rejecting the Edensai's spiritual practises, which many observed on Eden, now believing they were unnecessary to form a peaceful, co-operative society. Harry pointed out several Riynean and Kalmeddi couples cohabiting, and Laurel found with delight two resulting pregnancies. Beril's genetic programme was available to all, with only the Edensai insisting on a couple being married as a condition for the insemination, but the fertile Kalmeddi females all became pregnant as soon as the programme was up and running. No doubt, many little Marcel lookalikes would be born in the coming months.

Laurel approached the possibility this would be her last trip, and as she expected, Harry met the news with a mixture of surprise and dismay. "These people need our help, Laurel. We can't just walk away."

"We got them off Eden," Laurel said, "provided medical aid, equipment for sanitation and equipment schematics for replication. The people are rebuilding their societies as well as their homes. We don't fit in here. What else must we do?"

Harry stared at her in disbelief; she knew what he was thinking because she thought it too. Laurel twisted her hands through her hair and scrunched her face. Stooping down, she made an "aargh!" exclamation before standing upright and taking a deep breath.

"I sound so bloody self-righteous!"

Harry nodded, unmoved by the display. "Yes, you do. Look, if this is because of Nika, your guilt, we all got it wrong, but what she has now is far better than what she was born to. It's not like you to walk away from people who need you."

"It's not just Nika," Laurel sighed. "I…I'm tired. I think I'm facing an identity crisis, Harry. I don't know who I am! According to Olyo, I'm not Judith, but I am 'of her', and I am also Hebre. Where is Laurel in all this? Me?"

Harry grabbed her hand and led her away to the outskirts of the settlement. The people had cleared the forest, and while it wasn't exactly parkland, the area was fragrant with the sweet-spicy aroma of cut grass and plants. Harry drew her down to sit beside him, giving Laurel a flashback to one hundred moons when they sat together before she went to the fortress. It was there she guessed he had feelings for her, feelings she knew she'd tested over and over.

"There's no point in using energy trying to work out things there appears to be no answer to, Laurel," he said gently. "Why not focus on what you *can* do. Does it matter if you are a mixture of Judith, Hebre and human? They've all been there since you were born. Perhaps they even made certain you were born looking like Judith, I don't know. But you at least know you came from somewhere good."

Laurel leaned against his shoulder and sighed. "Judith was Menworan. She was human even after she was resurrected, although we can't even know that for sure. It's just a feeling I had, and don't forget, she was related to the masters."

"She may have been once," Harry said, "but we know the masters came from something unnatural, what they were before that may have been good, if Judith is anything to go by, but I don't think you can classify the masters as anything but evil incarnations."

"What about the Sons of David?" Laurel had never thought to ask Harry his opinion.

He shrugged. "A tribe of individuals who lost their way and got caught up with their forefathers' mistakes. In many ways, they were victims too."

"I had a vision," Laurel said, "it was brief, but I saw

the restoration of Benjamin and his cruelty. Then I saw Judith." She swivelled her head around to look up at him. "Judith had green eyes."

"Why didn't you say?" Harry pointed to his own vivid green eyes. "Perhaps Judith's related to me!"

It made Laurel laugh. "Olyo told me Judith existed in a different form on Eden. Somehow her mortal body was brought back and possessed by Hebre. That's how her eyes became amber, like mine."

Harry grinned and hugged her. "Overthinking is making you crazy."

"Sometimes," Laurel agreed. "And it's easy to forget we're in the past. Right now, on Mentelci, the concept of the League is only just being debated. It won't be instituted for years. Harry, can we be sure we'll find our way back to Baii and Ilivi's time? To our time?"

Harry nodded and took her hand, bringing her fingers to his lips. "I believe, and I'm not sure I did before, that you and Ava have more control over things than you previously knew. So I do not believe you need to hurry away from here. Either the other things haven't happened yet, or they are parallel to us. We'll find our way."

"You might be right. Like I say, I'm having an identity crisis."

"Well, don't. I'm not a psychiatrist!"

Laurel twisted her body so she could wrap her arms around his waist and enjoy these few unexpected moments of peace and quiet. She gazed at the sky with its varying shades of blue, and the fluffy, pearly-white clouds that scuttled on the breeze. A bird swooped overhead and landed on a branch, its bright red feathers twitching as it looked around, then took off with a dive in their direction before flying away.

"Did you see that?" Harry exclaimed.

"The bird?" Laurel said. "Yes, I did. The Farisee brought birds to control the insect population, which has run pretty rampant. They'll take some to Kalmed in time as well. Look—" Laurel reluctantly released Harry and got to her feet, their moment of peace over. "Darlen is waving at us. We need to get back to work."

As they proceeded through the settlements, Laurel was pleased to see how much the children had benefitted from better nutrition and freedom from fear. Now, the overgrown vegetation was cut back, and each hand-built, neat one-roomed shack housed a single person or a family, with a garden already growing food. Olyo presented several hundred animals that produced the milk they used in the life-saving bread during the occupation, but as Laurel and Harry discovered before, it had little nutritional value for humans. As it was widely enjoyed and freely available, it was collected from the animals, brought to the central depot, appropriate nutrients added and distributed.

On one settlement, as she had promised herself, Laurel sought out Jadren, still the nominal leader of the Kalmeddi. She found him, breathless and sick, lying on a bed in one of the huts. Too weak to even to sit up to greet her, Laurel was surprised he'd survived this long.

"We can help you, Jadren," she told him. "Your people need you now."

Jadren tried to laugh but instead choked out an explosion of black fluid. "What they need is not to be reminded of what the masters did," he gurgled, taking Laurel's hand. "We old ones will pass, and the new generations will take our place." He gave her a weary smile. "You were right. My people will not die out. The Riyneans and the Kalmeddi are united, are they not? Forging together a new society?"

"It seems that way." Laurel tried to smile back but was too saddened by the realisation this would be the last time she saw him. "The people grow stronger. There will be a few more children soon, children who never knew the sorrow the masters caused."

Jadren squeezed her fingers. "But they will know of the deliverers. Forever, you will be in their hearts, and I can die knowing my people are safe now—" the corners of his mouth lifted slightly, "as is all mankind. The masters will not rise from the dead a second time."

These were the last words Jadren spoke. He died that night, and Olyo arranged for his remains to be repatriated to Kalmed, that he might be reunited with the spirits of his family so cruelly torn from him by the masters, that he might find peace with his forefathers.

They caught up with Marcel at the Edensai settlement. Darlen slapped him on the back. "You've done an amazing job, Marcel," he said. "A central supply depot, settlements. I see that people are moving from the ark to establish homes."

Marcel looked to where the ark was positioned, serving

as a halfway house for thousands of Edensai. "They are, and they are happy."

"Has their desire to establish themselves away from the Kalmeddi and Riynea led to any problems?" Laurel asked.

Marcel shook his head. "None at all. The others seem to understand the Edensai's need to re-establish their traditions. The Riyneans and the Kalmeddi have taken a step in a different direction."

"I hope that doesn't lead to a difference of opinion in the future," Darlen said, knowing full well that "different directions" often led to differing opinions, and sometimes, civil war, regardless of how peaceful a species. Marcel knew what he was thinking.

"These are not warring people. I can't see them taking up arms against each other," he said, "and in the past, their differences didn't matter. The Kalmeddi and Riynea worked and lived on Edensai before the occupation. I don't think much will change just because the situation is reversed." He looked out over the settlement and dusted soil from his hands. "When my lady aunt and our people settled on Danfos 4, we had to start from scratch, but we were among friends." Marcel pointed towards a group of Riyneans hauling wood into the Edensai compound, "As are these people."

"It's wonderful to hear children playing," Harry said. "Scarlett is loving having so many new friends."

"The Farisee didn't turn her into a god then?" Marcel laughed.

"No." Darlen had been surprised the Farisee had not tried to influence his daughter in any way. "She came back happy, none the wiser as to the events on Eden and not a prayer in her head."

"The Edensai have a Place of Peace set aside for worship, but only the faithful Edensai are admitted," Marcel told them. 'The food is still rationed, but with the Farisee supplements and what we were able to replicate, along with the wild vegetation, the people are recovering. We have also imported a few edible plants from Kalmed." Marcel showed them an inventory on a datacache. "We're getting a bit low on nutritional additives, but Mer can replicate enough until the power is running at capacity. After that, I think between the animals and the plants, the people will be self-sustaining. We've rigged up some solar power—" he pointed with pride to the dozen or so spires arranged around the settlement, "mainly for lighting, but at least we don't need heat at night." He led them towards the huts. "The gardens are amazing, aren't they? And I expect you've already found a change in general health."

"We've already discovered a few pregnancies amongst the Riyneans," Harry said, "and one amongst the Kalmeddi. A couple more amongst the Riynean/Kalmeddi unions. I expect you'll want to stick around to see how many look like you!"

"Not as many as you think," Marcel laughed. "The Trah has arranged marriages, and I know from Beril, some of them did not avail themselves of the insemination programme. There are quite a few women among the Kalmeddi and the Riynea who do not wish to become mothers, although they accept that children are needed to take the place of the elderly and those lost. Some of the women have decided to carry a child, and the infant will go to an infertile couple or individual to raise. Edensai women still managed to have children when they were malnourished during the occupation. Now things have improved, I expect a new generation in less than nine months!"

"We plan on setting up a circuit clinic in each settlement," Laurel told him, "but at this point, Beril is the only physician."

"Ah, not so," Marcel beamed. "There were two Edensai women who were also physicians. Legion ignored them due to their age, but they survived up until a few years ago. Before they died, they passed on their knowledge to many others. Of course, without technology, it was hands-on, but their students seem capable. Beril is schooling them, but they do need more technology. I brought them here to meet you, and I've already trained them to use the palm pandroscope. I wondered if we could build a few for when we leave, even if only for diagnostics. Heal bots would be asking too much, I suppose?"

"We can't replicate nanotechnology unless the Farisee has something we can utilise," Harry said. "They can't have any objection. It's not a weapon. We'll ask."

Marcel and Harry excused themselves as they headed towards the settlement. Laurel lingered for a moment, and Ava wandered over from where she had been watching Scarlett.

"I rather thought that we might end up staying," she said. "Leaving feels like abandonment."

"You must have read Harry's mind," Laurel grinned. "He feels the same."

Ava shrugged. "No-one has asked us to stay, although I know we would be welcome." She hesitated. "I don't want to stay either, Mom," she confessed. "I want to go back to Baii."

Laurel knew that. "I began this journey to find out if there were more like us. I know less about myself than I did before. My mother was blonde and blue-eyed, and I look nothing like her."

Laurel had never spoken about her mother to Ava, although Ava would have liked to have known. "What about your father?" she asked.

"I never knew him." Laurel shook her head, "but Mom always called me an alien because of my eye colour, she said she'd never seen eyes like mine, so I guess his eyes were normal."

"Perhaps the entity was waiting for you to be born," Ava suggested. "Maybe it was trapped on Earth."

"So why can't Hebre enter the Transcender unless they're in a physical form?" Laurel added.

"That would explain why the Soul Mongers committed to returning them to the nebula."

It just didn't go far enough for Laurel. "But it doesn't explain Judith, or me."

Harry called to them. "Come on, you two. There's work to do."

CHAPTER THIRTY-FOUR _

Laurel and Harry spent several days in the Edensai settlement. The survivors had set themselves up well, with a few older people opening a school for the younger children and adults in better health who had been too sick and sad to bother with education. Beril had found an Edensai farmer who passed on his knowledge of agricultural practice, along with an elderly botanist, identified among the Kalmeddi, who appeared to have valuable experience of Riynean edible plants and flowers. Darlen and Mer's schematics for power hubs were looked over by Farisee engineers, who agreed they were an improvement on the power centres destroyed when the masters arrived. Darlen had sent the schematics to Faris, and all vital equipment had been delivered to Riynea. Meanwhile, several small ships doubled as power and communications systems to supplement the solar power spires.

Ava discovered Yosser on the Edensai settlement. He was thrilled to see her, and she brought him to catch up with the group. He heard about his friend Abel's sacrifice but had comforted himself in the knowledge Abel went freely to his death, knowing he was helping to bring about the deliverance. And Yosser had news of his own. At Hagar's behest, he had married. His wife Miriam was newly pregnant, and he proudly announced, with a glance at Marcel, that they had not had to avail themselves of the donor programme. He had also taken over much of the leadership of the Edensai, working alongside the Holy Trah in all things. He didn't seem at all overwhelmed by the task ahead; in fact, he sounded positive as he outlined his plans first to build a town, then establish places of manufacture for all to benefit. He gestured, pointed, fidgeted, and generally found it impossible to sit still in his enthusiasm, although he was philosophical about the progress of technology.

"Our ancestors managed," he smiled. "Growth will come, and meanwhile, we are at peace. We are free. That is what is important. The Farisee will help us, although I fear my bones will be long in the grave before we are truly re-established," he concluded with a laugh.

"Perhaps we should spend some of our time educating the Farisee on widespeed," Ava suggested. "That is something Mer could do, and it would certainly speed things up a bit."

Harry and Laurel nodded their agreement. "Their ships are pretty robust," Harry said. "Sedar's would likely shake apart."

Laurel laughed. "The arks are indestructible; nothing shakes them. We might not get them moving as fast, but it's worth a try. Do you think you can rely on the primitive lifestyle of your ancestors until then, Yosser?"

Yosser nodded. "I am content to be able to feel the sun on my face, the breeze in my hair, and my belly not rumbling for want of food."

***

At the end of a particularly long day where Laurel and Harry had examined enough pregnant women to give hope of the survival of the Edensai, they sat around a fire with Marcel, Darlen and Ava, quietly mulling over the events of the day. Laurel watched the smoke from the fire curling heavenwards. On Eden, this would have brought down the wrath of Legion on their heads, but now all the people could enjoy every aspect of their deliverance. Many small fires burned cheerfully throughout the settlement, as the newly liberated Edensai cooked food and socialised. Laurel had a sudden memory of a camping trip she once took with her aunt and uncle, a pleasant memory that made her smile.

Harry draped his arm about her shoulders. "You look a bit dreamy," he murmured, trying not to be too intrusive.

Laurel sighed. "Thinking about my aunt and uncle. It all seems so long ago."

"A lot has happened."

Laurel didn't answer. That life, the one she'd just thought of, almost seemed as if it had *never* happened.

"The children all seem to have improved in leaps and bounds," Laurel said, turning her attention away from thoughts that served only to confuse.

Harry agreed, he'd been pleased to see that for himself, and the pandroscope bore out the findings. "It's unbelievable. A few months ago, I was treating them for rickets and malnutrition. Now they're tearing around and playing, just as children should."

"And the overall health of the adults has improved,"

Marcel said. "They have better living conditions, better food and hygiene, but I suspect some of the older ones still won't make it. It's a shame the Edensai won't mate with the others, make one big tribe."

"The Edensai traditions forbid them to lie with a stranger to their land," Laurel said.

That drew a snort from Marcel. "Quite a few of the women lay with the Sons of David."

"True," Laurel had to accept his point, "but perhaps they were so demoralised some of them lost their faith. Although come to think of it, I haven't seen any of the Sons of David these past few days."

Marcel pointed vaguely into the distance. "They have their own settlement with their Edensai wives," he said. "You are right, some of the women did lose their faith, and now they choose not to live the Edensai tradition. They are free to choose their path, and the path they choose is with their husbands."

"Abel told me the Sons of David lived by the word of the Edensai God but had not sworn themselves to his ways," Laurel said. "We need to check on them too."

"They'll embrace you, Laurel," Marcel replied, "but I think in time, they will have different laws. I think it will be them who eventually return to Eden."

"That's very profound," Ava observed.

Marcel nodded. "I know you know this—" he looked around "—all of you, but I do not support pacifism, and I don't just mean in war. The Edensai allowed the masters to invade; to not challenge them was to give permission for suffering and despair to come upon their heads. It was left to Hebre and then to Laurel and Ava to bring them from darkness. The Edensai didn't take up arms, but they allowed others to protect, save, deliver."

"They had no awareness of war and weapons," Ava pointed out.

"There is *instinct*." Marcel placed heavy emphasis on the words. "*Survival.* I see them now, they accept all help, but their main focus is their God and building a temple so they may continue with their devotions. Even in rebuilding their civilisation, such things come first, and with that, they are not as proactive as the Kalmeddi and Riynea. No, it will be the Sons of David and their posterity who will bring hope for Eden. They will pave the way for a new Edensai people. Successive generations of this tribe you see before you here will watch the dynamic growth of the new Edensai and join them. The old ways and traditions of this tribe will die out, I am sure of it."

They all thought it was a harsh appraisal, and Ava said so, but Marcel defended his position.

"It's what I've seen. Go to what the others call the Legion settlement. Listen to the people. You'll see what I mean."

Harry frowned. "So that law about not lying with a member of another species would only have been written after contact with the Farisee; because the Edensai didn't know anyone else existed."

There was a nod of agreement from the group.

"Who wrote that law?" Harry continued. "They say all their laws come from their god and are ancient truths. Do they claim some sort of direct connection to him?"

But Darlen was in no mood for a metaphysical discussion. "I think labelling the Sons of David with a name that invoked terror is a bad sign."

Ava wasn't too keen on the negativity of that term either. "As long as they continue to rebuild in a spirit of co-operation, that's all that matters." She nodded towards the settlement. "I see Mer is working through the night."

"He'll go round the clock," Darlen said. "The Farisee engineers have a roster system. It'll get done. I'll need him on Faris to work on widespeed and see if we can do anything about healbots and painbots, but…" he shook his head, "they were even beyond Chaese engineers. The Farisee are good, but not that good."

"I would like to see Faris," Laurel said. "Olyo never speaks of it."

"It's not so beautiful." Sedar appeared from the shadows and sat beside them, accepting their warm welcome. "Eden was considered the most beautiful planet of all four, but now, I can say with pride, I think Riynea eclipses it."

"It is beautiful, Sedar," Laurel smiled in agreement. "As we flew in, we crossed stunning wilderness and forests. It truly is an Eden itself. And the people are doing a wonderful job of making it their home."

Sedar nodded in satisfaction. "Yes, the power hub and communications will make life easier for us. Your kindness, I don't mean just in ending the occupation, but your skills since the evacuation have also been lifesaving."

"You are very welcome," Laurel said. "How is your granddaughter?"

"She is well. The infant, a boy," he looked at Darlen, "is Legion, and we do not live within the Edensai settlement. An older son perished in the fighting. We have settled with the Sons of David and their Edensai wives. I heard you were here and came to see if you would be visiting us."

"We will, and we're sorry about your other grandson," Harry said. "I know Olyo did all she could."

Sedar bowed his head. "I am grateful at least my granddaughter survived, and her child. I have a family now."

"I am grateful you did not bring the masters female here."

Laurel turned her head as Sedar's voice reached into her mind. *"Did Olyo tell you?"*

"Yes, the people are doing well, but their hearts are broken at the loss of their world, and their feelings of anger towards the masters and the loss of so many loved ones run deep. Each time they see Eden rise in the afternoon sky, they pray, mourning what they have lost. Some even blame the gods."

"We felt it would be wrong to kill her. She was innocent of any wrongdoing."

"Laurel, there are some who believe the gods have sent you. Some of the old ones remember that you, yourself came not from the imps. They see you as a religious icon, and some even pray to you."

Laurel suppressed a gasp. *"Stop them, Sedar. You must tell them I'm not divine, that I'm mortal."*

"They would not listen. The faith of some of the Edensai has faltered, particularly among the wives of the Sons of David. Even the Trah cannot comfort them. Laurel, you need to leave us."

"Harry says we can't right now; we still have work to do."

Sedar dipped his head in acknowledgement. *"Go to*

Faris with Darlen. Take Ava with you and allow your menfolk to finish the work."

Laurel was shocked at this turn of events. She looked at the others, caught up in their conversations. They hadn't noticed the telepathic exchange between Sedar and Laurel, although Ava had listened in with half an ear. Later, after Sedar had left and the others filtered away to their beds, Harry and Laurel sat alone under the stars.

"This is a beautiful world as well," Harry said.

"Yes, it is. I'm glad the masters didn't get around to wrecking it like they did Eden."

"I think they were less interested in the planet than they were the people. I can't believe it; three civilisations almost wiped out."

"And in less than twenty years," Laurel said.

"I know. I don't understand how there are so few inhabited worlds in this system."

Laurel looked up at the star-filled sky. Other galaxies, other kingdoms were safe now. "The masters spoke of seven kingdoms, but we don't know how accurate that is. They were also accomplished liars. They could have just made it up." Laurel lay back on the grass. She had a mind to stay here all night. "I guess we'll never know for sure."

Harry lay beside her, checking the direction of her gaze to see if she was watching anything in particular.

"Sedar wants me to leave," Laurel said suddenly. "He says a few of the Edensai are deifying me."

"Really?" Harry propped himself on his elbow and turned to look at her. "Then he's right. You should leave. That's an unhealthy development. I suggest you go to Faris with Darlen and Mer; Marcel and I will finish up here and meet you back at the station. It might be a few weeks, though."

"I'll take Ava," Laurel said. "Scarlett can come too if she likes, but us leaving will slow down the work here a little."

"We'll manage," Harry assured her, but this was all rather worrying. "If Mer needs to come back," he cautioned, "you stay away. Perhaps not seeing you will let you fade in their consciousness."

In the end, Laurel did not go to Faris. All the pieces that made up Laurel, the immortal Judith, the powerful Hebre, and the frail human side sank into weariness. Ava wanted to contact Harry, but Laurel protested, allowing Ava only to leave her and the Canaa at the station and continue to Faris in an axispod without her. Scarlett stayed with the Farisee as they returned to their homeworld to meet up with Ava when she got there. It meant Laurel could rest with no interruptions. She cleared her mind, not allowing in stray thoughts, deliberately not using telepathy, nor manifestations to help her when she cleaned up the Canaa. It was cathartic, but she had to ignore the little worm of guilt that while the others were hard at work on Riynea and Faris, she was doing a tidy up at her leisure. Laurel knew enough about psychology to realise she was worn out, a condition that mercifully had escaped the others. Fortunately, no visions plagued her at night, and over a few days, her mind calmed. Harry contacted her to make sure she was okay and to see if she needed him, but she assured him she didn't. Otherwise, he kept his conversation light and made only encouraging reports on the situation on Riynea. Laurel improved, and in time found the only thing that dragged down her mood was the sight of Eden. So, she stopped looking.

Olyo made one visit, her inaugural at widespeed. It had taken her only a day to arrive at the station, and her delight was palpable. She didn't enquire as to why Laurel was on the station, and Laurel didn't offer an explanation. Olyo was enroute to Riynea with provisions for the engineers; she reported on the remarkable progress with widespeed, adding it was less than Mer and Darlen hoped for, but still far beyond anything the Farisee had ever experienced. She told Laurel the arks presented difficulties because of their size, but she was confident Mer would quickly find the solution. Laurel learned that Nika had settled, but still did not speak, although the girl regarded her new world with wonderment and eagerly embraced religious devotions. Nika and Scarlett renewed their friendship under Darlen's watchful eye, and Darlen planned to return to the station within weeks.

Laurel had little to say, and really, she just listened. When it was time for Olyo to leave, Laurel was stunned to be caught in an embrace.

"I am to lose you a second time?" Olyo said, although there was no sorrow in her voice, just understanding.

Laurel had thought about it so much these past weeks. Her head told her there were many reasons why she should stay, but her heart urged her to leave. "We—I, don't belong here," she said.

Olyo smiled, then she stepped into the accessway and

was gone. It came to Laurel this wasn't the first time she had made this sad farewell.

Ava and Scarlett were the first to return from Faris, while Darlen continued to Riynea to complete his work. Marcel turned up a few days later in a widespeed-modified Faris scout. Harry had despatched him from Riynea due to a fever and a rash he developed, which Harry wanted identified and treated in the Canaa's med bay. Harry and Darlen arrived back the day Laurel declared Marcel clear of all infection. Harry swept Laurel into a hug, then looked around. "Looks like you cleaned up?"

Laurel nodded. She breathed in the smell of fresh grass and wood smoke from his clothes. "You smell like Riynea," she said, kissing him and wrapping her arms around his neck. She waved at Darlen over Harry's shoulder. "Scarlett hoped you would be back sooner."

"I better go and find her," he said and headed towards Scarlett's quarters. Seconds later, Scarlett could be heard chattering wildly about Faris, about Nika and how she and Ava had seen flowers on Faris ten feet tall and could talk.

"Talk?" Harry raised an eyebrow and looked at Ava.

"Their lips rub together when they catch an insect," she explained with a shrug. "It sounds like loud whispering, but I think they're munching, a bit like the noises Mer makes."

Mer responded with a characteristic munching sound. "Like that," Ava said.

Scarlett rushed into the common room, followed by Darlen, who looked around at the crew.

"All together in one place, again," he grinned. "Good to see you recovered, Marcel."

Marcel had been protesting ever since he arrived. "I think Harry was overcautious. He could have treated me with the old pandroscope we left on Riynea."

Harry disagreed. "It has a few limitations; it is a field pandroscope after all." He turned to Laurel. "You'll be glad to know we permanently deactivated its vocal processor. I agree it was a bit gloomy."

"And the Faris have been educated in widespeed, even though precipitation is less than in League space," Darlen said. "The engineers were surprised at how simple it was and wondered why they'd never detected it before."

"Ten babies born in the two weeks before we came back," Harry reported. "Two premature, but they're fine. The other eight were full-term, so the women were obviously pregnant just before the evacuation. The mothers comprised eight Edensai women, one Kalmeddi female and a Riynean woman rescued from the garrison near the arks. She's staying with Sedar and his granddaughter on the Legion settlement." Laurel saw he was concerned as he added, "That seems to be the place the outcasts go."

It also bothered Laurel there was any segregation, and she echoed Darlen's earlier concerns. "I hope there won't be problems in the future."

"They're too busy just trying to make sure there *is* a future," Marcel said. "There's no animosity."

"Did you know some of the Edensai think you're a god, Laurel?" Darlen grinned.

"Yes," Laurel rolled her eyes. "That's why I left. I hope

that's not the case now."

"Secretly, perhaps," Darlen was clearly amused at the notion, "but they abandoned their plans to build a temple in your honour."

Laurel's eyes widened in horror. "What!"

"Only joking," Darlen laughed. "It was a passing phase; it's all settled down now."

For a while, they sat in silence. Laurel loved having her family around her again, and for her, there was no need for words. Harry lounged in a chair; his eyes closed. Marcel watched as Scarlett and Mer talked together in some secret language, and Ava fidgeted with sensors. Darlen was the first to speak.

"So, what now," he said. "Do we stay, or do we go?"

All eyes turned to Laurel, but she shook her head firmly and held up her hands. "No! not me. We take a vote." There followed a moment's awkward silence before Darlen looked around, then hoisted himself from his seat.

"So, we're leaving," he announced and headed off toward the flight deck, followed by Mer. Harry and Ava immediately went to set the Canaa ready for flight, and Laurel checked on ship's systems. They all returned to their old jobs automatically and without another word.

CHAPTER THIRTY-FIVE

The Canaa and its crew had been in the Eden system for four hundred and twenty-one days. They'd stopped an invasion, drowned a planet, saved three civilisations and ended another.

Days after leaving the station, Marcel joined Ava and Laurel on the observation deck, where they viewed the strands of the Miran Forin nebula curling towards the ship. "Does that feel like a welcome home?" he asked.

"It feels familiar, that's for sure," Laurel said. "Strange that this part of the nebula doesn't seem to have a core, though. It's just rainbow colours."

Marcel peered through the viewport. "I can only see blue and red and a kind of aurora or brilliance. I don't think I see what you see."

"The Hebre allowed their colours to show when they were above Eden," Laurel reminded him. "I can see the blues and reds that you see in any nebula. In the Miran Forin, we see other colours too."

"Was it like this inside the Transcender?" Marcel asked Ava.

"No, it was like I was viewing it from a distance, but there, the core was evident; it would have been an infinity away, I guess."

"I'm not looking forward to variance." Laurel shuddered as if she could feel the sticky fluid already, " and as you travelled through once, it might be safer if you go in as well, Ava."

"Darlen doesn't think so."

"I wonder how they got all those masters and Legion who weren't Magen Bearers into variance?" Marcel stated matter-of-factly. "They must have required thousands upon thousands of variance chambers."

Ava and Laurel stared at him. "Good question," Laurel said. "Perhaps the Sons of Benjamin might have been immune to the Transcender; they were unnatural after all, but the others..."

The trio took the question to Darlen, who also found the subject intriguing. "Well, they ate, they slept, had sex, and were breathing before we drowned them, sounds pretty human to me. That said, if Legion comes from the same stock as Magen Bearers, they might have been okay, and possibly the bane protected the masters. That stuff has all the hallmarks of variance fluid." He grinned. "Perhaps not as sweet as mine!"

"Ugh," Laurel responded. "I don't want to go into variance even more now. Thanks for reminding me."

Darlen shrugged. "And it begs the question of how the Farisee knew of stasis pods? You said in your vision from the Diri wraiths, there were people in stasis. Is that right?"

Laurel nodded. "Thousands of them, but the Farisee would never have needed to develop stasis pods. They only moved between the four planets and the station. There weren't any on the arks we took."

"Maybe the converted Magen Bearers told them," Ava said, "but the Diri wraith vision showed only whole souls in the pods, and they were no longer in the nebula. Why would that be?"

"Well, they were physical beings," Harry offered logically, "it may have just been a way to conserve supplies. They would have had no trouble surviving physically in the nebula."

That made sense. "But Abel said they had a unique bond with time, yet the boy the wraiths discovered said he was born on the ark, and he was about ten years old."

"When we were in the nebula core," Darlen said, "we were all carrying on normally while our chronometer was registering millions of years passing. You said yourself the nebula core didn't register time, only movement. I can't do those maths, but what I am sure of, Isilia is in our past as we remember it, but because we have just taken part in an ancient event, Isilia is now in the future. When we get back to the nebula core, if you want to return there, and if you want somehow to avoid variance, we've got to figure out this 'Time' thing."

Marcel suggested going back to Riynea to ask a Son of David about variance, see if they used that method, or if there was a way it could be avoided, but there was a general accord that returning to Riynea was premature.

"I don't want to go back," Laurel said, "but I don't want to go into variance, either. Darlen, how can you be sure Ava doesn't need variance? She's been through a Transcender once. I thought she couldn't go through again."

"Yes, but the issue was with the trip back from Earth," Darlen said. "We knew from experience we couldn't bring humans from Earth into League space without variance, they always died, and that was bad for business. Ava has never been to Earth, and I know she'll be fine in this Transcender."

"How do you know?"

"I just know."

"And variance fluid, how did you find out about that in the first place?"

"I'm not telling you."

"Don't be precious."

"I'm not. I simply don't need you to know details just before you go and bathe in it."

"You let it slip once, you know." Laurel pulled a face at him.

"I know, but not the whole recipe. The fluid serves a purpose. It preserves human flesh."

"At what point in the journey back from Earth did those first whole souls die? Was it in the Transcender?" Harry asked.

"No," Darlen said. "It happened when they arrived back into League space. History tells us there were ten on the ship, they were all in normal stasis, but none could be revived."

"I told you that when the masters paralysed me with the bane," Laurel said, "I found myself in the nebula but came back as I recovered. I *wanted* to come back, even though I didn't feel the same afterwards."

"We're second-guessing," Harry cut in. "We can't know, not unless the Hebre entity tells you, and so far, it hasn't had much to say."

Laurel agreed. "It does prompt my instincts, though, mostly. Ava's too. But I think it has a method."

Scarlett wandered casually into the common lounge. "Daddy, the Transcender's back," she said as if reintroducing an old friend, her first terrifying vision of it forgotten. "It doesn't look so big now."

Darlen jumped out of his seat, and the group rushed to the flight deck to see the Transcender's stormy petals swirling in space. "How come I didn't sense it," Darlen said.

"I did, Daddy," Scarlett smiled. "It made my tummy flutter, but I wasn't scared."

"There's nothing to be scared of, sweetheart." Darlen patted Scarlett's head. "The Transcender is part of our heritage."

Laurel ushered Marcel and Harry from the flight deck. "We don't have time to deliberate," she urged. "Let's get into variance. Darlen, just leave Mer in charge…"

Suddenly, Laurel's head felt as if it were being sucked into a whirlwind. Harry slammed against her, his head dropping against her shoulder and turning into a dead weight on her arm. An amber glow permeated the area around them. Laurel's arm was still extended from where she was pushing Marcel out to the corridor, and he was attached to her hand, his eyes closed, and his head slumped forward. Both men were shrouded in the glow. Laurel pulled her wits back together and spun slowly, just in time to see Ava reach to take Marcel into her shimmering violet aura. As Laurel and Ava moved, their colours swathed through slices in their lines of vision, each slice representing a moment in time. Laurel saw Darlen watching the spectacle, his eyelids flicking up and down in slow motion. Scarlett barely moved, her fingers in her mouth, not understanding what could possibly be going on. Laurel could see the viewport, but the Transcender petals had wrapped around them as they moved deep into the curlew. Sheerguhd had sucked them into its depths, and all Laurel could see outside was darkness. Darlen stood, his movements matching Laurel's, slow and deliberate. It was just as it had been on the masters' ship when Laurel slowed time. She had no real sense of initiating it then, just as she didn't now. It was a mystery to her that she made no conscious effort. It could only be the entity. Confident that Marcel was safe in Ava's embrace, Laurel lifted her arm to fully envelop Harry. She felt no respiratory movements, heard no heartbeat, but he was neither dead nor dying. His heart had not stopped, but his body was poised for its next inhalation, suspended in that space where the heart prepares for its next beat and between one breath and the next.

Darlen came to a halt mid-step. Laurel's aura spread its amber threads towards him and Scarlett; they were in no danger from the Transcender, but Laurel instinctively needed them to move to the same beat as the others. To Laurel, the scene was like a tableau. Beyond the viewport, Time sparked into life, coming into its own season, moving independently of them and dispelling the dark to create spectacular displays of birthing planets and galaxies, joining star systems and conducting a symphony of its own. The

Canaa had effectively become a Time Machine. Mer was silent and unmoving, there was no sound from the instrumentation, and Laurel closed her eyes, committing to the feelings within her, trusting Time to carry her to the right place. Surrender. She sent the thought to Ava. Just like bringing the rain on Eden. Complete surrender.

It was over as quickly as it began. The Transcender spat them out into the margin of the nebula, Laurel and Ava's auras withdrew, and Marcel and Harry were shocked to find themselves in such firm embraces. Darlen looked around and scratched his head. Something had taken place; he just couldn't remember. The sight of the receding Transcender made him turn questioning eyes to Laurel, but Harry beat him to it.

"What the hell just happened?" Harry exclaimed, modifying Laurel's embrace to something less untidy.

Laurel helped him to a chair. "We entered the Transcender. Look—" she pointed out the viewport as the Transcender gathered itself and departed.

Darlen was dumbfounded. Yes, the Transcender, *without variance?*

"Without variance," Laurel confirmed. "But we didn't do it on our own. We had help. I think it was Hebre."

"This hasn't happened in the history of whole souls," Darlen said, drawing up a seat and checking Scarlett suffered no ill effects. She was taking the event in her stride and had already shifted her attention to Mer.

"I firmly believe we need to be near the nebula for this to happen," Laurel said, then outlined a feeling that came to her during the episode, one that echoed Abel's words to her when he spoke about Hebre and time, that belief was the one thing that got in the way. Laurel, Ava, all of them didn't believe they could manipulate time, but on the masters' ship, Hebre had made a demonstration that Laurel did have that ability. Laurel's attachment to her humanity had got in the way as they journeyed to Eden; had she followed through on her thoughts about time, they wouldn't have needed variance, and she wouldn't have lost those years.

"That doesn't explain why whole souls die on the journey back to League space from Earth, or on a couple of occasions, the other way," Darlen pointed out.

"Maybe the location of the Transcender is just too distant from the nebula," Ava suggested.

"Variance suspends life, all life," Darlen said quietly. "Even life we cannot see."

"What?" Marcel frowned.

"You want to know what variance is made of?" Darlen said to Laurel. "You're right. Saliva. My saliva carries a mild paralysing agent which, if I spat on you, would have little effect, and you would just think I was disgusting, but if I remove the Magen and spit on that, then touch you with the star, you wouldn't move for a couple of days. I keep enough of my enzymes to ensure a supply of concentrated variance, its energy supplemented by the Magen's infusion. So, you see, the Sons of Benjamin and I are not so unalike."

"Why was this such a secret?" Laurel could never wrest this from Darlen, even telepathically, and now, it seemed rather a tame revelation.

"Because no-one needs to know the power of the Magen," Darlen said simply. "Moving through dimensions can change the history of worlds; the Magen is a power not to be taken lightly, nor should it fall into the wrong hands. My forefathers knew that whole souls carried a power within them, and that variance kept that power tethered to the physical, kept it anchored."

Laurel didn't understand. "But I went into the nebula when the masters spat on me."

Darlen shook his head. "No, you didn't. Something might have, but it wasn't the entity."

Laurel closed her eyes. She'd been in the nebula, saw the colours, saw Gabriel and Helen, how…and it became clear. *Judith.* But why?

"How did you discover variance?" Ava asked.

"I didn't," Darlen shrugged. "Soul Mongers have known for generations."

"And you used it to keep the whole souls alive?"

Darlen shrugged again. "Once we started to use variance, whole souls who were revived after they left the Transcender didn't know they carried the entity and didn't discover their powers until after reforming their attachment to life; by then, they were slaves. You are the first to know about Hebre. I'm certain no Soul Mongers knew the origins of the entities."

"Why tell us this now?" Ava asked.

"You obviously don't need variance," Darlen said. "At least not in that Transcender you don't. You are fully realised as Hebre. You only need a Magen Bearer to get you in."

"But I need variance?" Harry never liked these conversations; they always made him feel out of place.

Darlen nodded. "If no Hebre was present, yes. Scarlett's the same as me, so she's safe."

"I'm just glad we don't have to drink that godawful antidote," Marcel grinned, then his face changed. "Please don't tell me it's made of spit."

Darlen pulled a face; he'd given up enough secrets for one day.

Ava looked to her mother. "I think it was Mom who changed Time. I somehow drew my entity out because of what she was doing. I saw the vapour at the tips of my fingers, then next thing, Marcel slumped forward, and I grabbed him."

"It was just like what happened on the masters' ship," Laurel said, "but this time, I needed to keep Darlen where he was, Scarlett too, so they stayed in Time with us."

"The Canaa is a Time Machine?" Darlen grinned proudly. "I told you I designed the best ship in the universe…um, Sheerguhd. No, I like 'universe' better."

"I thought of the Time Machine angle, too," Laurel laughed.

"So where were we in time, Laurel?" Harry looked up at her. "Where are we now?"

"Does it affect universal time?" Darlen asked.

"I can't tell for sure," Laurel said. "I would have thought only as it relates to us, or wherever I happen to be. I saw the dawn of new ages outside the viewport. It was sublime, but Time was only influenced on the Canaa. As to where we are, we should check the sensors."

Darlen stroked his chin and peered at the instruments, busy sorting themselves from the unfamiliar to the familiar.

"We're at the edge of the nebula where we entered the Transcender after leaving Isilia. Look—" he pointed outside the viewport as the ship turned to reveal the nebula core.

Marcel could scarcely contain his excitement. "We're back where we started," he exclaimed, pushing past Darlen eagerly and snapping out the sensor data to fill the flight deck with a star chart, one they recognised. "How long until we get to Isilia?" he yelled in delight, happiness lighting up his handsome face. Moments ago, they were centuries in the past, but now, he was precisely where he needed to be, headed towards Isilia and a reunion with Ilivi. He didn't regret his decision to continue with the others, but now with Ilivi so close…

The sensors gave him an estimate of arrival on Isilia from their current location at their current speed.

"Can you get us there quicker, Laurel?" Marcel asked, hopefully.

"I'm not sure, Marcel. We were in direct contact with the nebula when it happened."

"Were you in contact with the nebula on the masters' ship?"

Laurel puzzled over the question. The ship had been a reasonable distance from the nebula, but she sensed it close, and it had been all around her while she was paralysed.

Here, although the nebula shone outside the viewport, they were outside the margin. She knew she could not influence the time it would take to get to Isilia, and her answer disappointed Marcel.

"It's new, Marcel. I need to explore it, but we will head straight to Isilia."

They didn't linger. Marcel's excitement about returning to Isilia spread to Ava, even though her response was far more measured than his. And they all agreed they'd earned some peace and quiet.

"A rest will be nice," Harry said to Laurel later after endless hashing and rehashing about Time manipulation, and a dozen failed attempts to recreate the scenario.

"A rest?" she laughed. "What happened to retirement?"

"On Isilia? I can't see you settling there. Not yet, anyway."

"I can't be where Ava and Marcel aren't, Harry. I know they're grown-up, but they're still our children."

"I know, but…well," Harry pulled a face, "Ava is still looking for her purpose…" Laurel glanced up, that word again. "…and settling isn't on her agenda." Harry grinned at Laurel's puzzled expression. "Mind reading works for fathers of daughters, even adopted fathers."

Laurel let the thought about purpose float away. Isilia was the perfect place for a rest, and she could fill in all the gaps in Riynea history. She only regretted she had not been able to salvage any historical artefacts, but the masters and Legion had left little behind. After destroying most of the civilisation, Legion also destroyed its history and ancient relics.

The traction beam brought them down in a familiar place. The portal approached, opened, and once more, they beheld the beautiful province of Meas. A beaming Onoth appeared, accompanied by Baii and Ilivi. It was too much for Marcel. For two days since exiting the nebula, he could not rest, paced the floor, then sat with his head in his hands before standing and repeating the procedure. And now, at the sight of the beautiful Ilivi, dressed in sunshine yellow silk, her lovely almond eyes shining her welcome, Marcel rushed forward and lifted his tiny sweetheart into the air, neglecting any acknowledgement of royal protocol. Ilivi had already decided to surrender her royal dignity and stepped from the portal to greet him, laughing joyously and wrapping her arms about Marcel's neck, unmindful of her stunning formal robes draping into the red dust and the surprised gaze of the onlookers. Onoth was startled at this transgression, but he knew Marcel was not just any visitor. Baii was more restrained, but his relief at seeing Ava was unmistakable, and while he acknowledged the others warmly, he drew Ava into his arms and closed his eyes. Laurel heard him sigh. "I counted each day," he said as he breathed against Ava's hair. "And each day was an eternity."

Ava rested her cheek against his and smiled, biting her lip against tears. She didn't want to cry in front of everyone, but a single teardrop escaped and spilt onto her cheek. There had been times when she wondered if she would ever see him again.

Despite the informality and rejoicing at the reunion, Ilivi, who loved rituals, had arranged a formal—what she called "family"—ceremony at the palace when the Canaa was detected at the nebula.

"My sister has been unable to settle on anything since our sensors picked up your ship," Baii laughed as he, Ava and Laurel sat together later that day. "She is not one to assign her responsibilities, but for once, I advised her it was indeed acceptable and that she should accompany us to meet you. Her councillors were amused by her excitement, and joyous to see her mood had lifted. She missed Marcel deeply."

"He missed her, too," Laurel said. "I must admit, I was a little surprised he left in the first place."

Baii gave her a knowing look. "Family. Marcel is a loyal man who lost so much, and you and Harry represent mother and father to him. If you leave us again, it may be that he will need to make a choice," he added shrewdly.

Laurel had already considered it. She looked over at Marcel, sitting with Harry and Darlen, Scarlett playing with the lizard-like creatures Baii manifested for her. Ilivi was preparing the ceremony in their honour, and Marcel kept looking up, anticipating her arrival. Being with Ilivi again, Laurel knew what Marcel's choice would be.

Ilivi led her attendants out onto the terrace. She remembered Harry hated the flying tea droids incessant buzzing about and had thoughtfully arranged a tabletop pot for him. Ilivi hummed as she had before as she began the tea ritual, and it was as beautiful as the first time they heard the ethereal melody. Ilivi, so proud of her culture, made a special fuss of Marcel, and the love they shared sent happy shivers right through Laurel. She squeezed Harry's hand, and he smiled with a shared understanding that they both knew what it was like to love someone so completely.

The ritual of honour over, the servants left and were not included in the festivities; a mark of a "family" only ceremony. Ilivi tucked her beautiful ceremonial robe under her as she knelt, the jewels on her headdress sparkling in the evening sun as she turned to smile at Marcel. She offered the cushion beside her. Marcel didn't need to be asked twice; Ilivi was disregarding protocols, even in a family affair.

Baii flicked a grin at Laurel. "There are no servants here to witness the Empress stray from custom," he grinned as he lifted Ava's hand to kiss her fingers. "It is fortunate for me that I am not bound to serve such traditions."

The tea was served by the pot droids, who gave Harry a wide berth. The succulent leaves and flowers in the centre of the table were sampled, and Baii and Ilivi had no shortage of questions about the journey. They'd begun the story on the trip from the western region, and now they continued, not leaving out even the worst parts, although sanitising and using alternative words in Scarlett's hearing.

"I am allowing the sensors to record our conversation," Ilivi said, and with a wave of her hand, brought up a compiling diorama, "so that our records may be added upon. I didn't realise until now how deficient they were without the history of the Hebre. It is all so tragic, but you did accomplish much of what you set out to do; you delivered the people from the masters. Although..." she turned her exquisite face to Laurel and smiled, "I sense you are not wholly satisfied with the answers to your origins?"

"When I proposed this journey," Laurel admitted, "it was because I believed Ava to be the last whole soul. I knew nothing of Hebre or masters or Eden. I was naive. The whole souls with me in the League, and those I read about from the past, were good, kind people, part of a subculture; I didn't expect to find out about Sheerguhd, about the

Menworan, and particularly about the strange events that brought about the Sons of Benjamin. I still don't understand why they had such hatred for humans. And of course, in seeking answers, the mystery deepened when I learned about Judith."

"I wonder how Judith," Baii mused, "in spirit form as this Farisee Ascendant told you, came to be on Eden."

"We've debated that," Laurel said. "I only know her body was restored to her, and she is identical to me. The only difference I saw was in a vision I had of her. She had green eyes. The Farisee Ascendant said the gods restored her body. Hebre must have inhabited her and changed her eye colour to reflect the entity. Before that, she must have existed in a wraith-like form for some centuries."

"It might be that you will never know," Ilivi said. "We believed we would never know the full story of the Exodus, and now we do, so there is hope. You have two Magen Bearers. You have two Hebre." She smiled at Laurel. "One with a little extra. The future may hold answers for you."

Laurel had to content herself with that, at least for now. She hadn't stopped learning; she hadn't fulfilled all her purposes, and she didn't yet know all the laws the one master said Judith violated, although she guessed gaining another physical body was likely to be one. The probability the masters were her ancestors held no appeal. In fact, she felt ashamed.

"You have many planets in the League, do you not, Harry?" Baii asked.

"There are two hundred and seventy-nine separate systems," Harry nodded. "Thousands of planets, moons, many inhabited."

Baii was impressed. "It would have been indeed ambitious of the masters to seek to overcome the League."

"They overcame the first kingdom," Marcel said. "According to the older Sons of David, some of whom related their oral history, some with first-hand knowledge, and who I got to know well on Riynea, there were several systems, and none of them ultimately withstood the masters, even though some were equipped with weapons and advanced space travel. It all came down to hand-to-hand combat, and that smell, once it got into your nostrils, you're good as dead."

Harry took up the story. "From what we know, the masters were more proactive in the first kingdom than on Eden. The Edensai were submissive, so they just needed to detonate the toxic device, poison the world, commit mass murder on Kalmed and Riynea, and they could torture those that were left at their leisure. Legion took the young women so they could reproduce. I think they had a system until Hebre rebelled, but though that was an inconvenience, it didn't scare them away. When we arrived, they realised they'd underestimated Judith and Esther." Harry lifted his hands as he realised he'd misspoke. He meant Ava and Laurel, of course, but it hadn't come out that way.

"Abel said the annihilation of the first kingdom took a long time," Laurel told them. "He called it an ancestral war as the masters who invaded the first kingdom preceded their posterity by several generations, same for Legion."

"Did Legion, the Sons of David, take wives with them?" Baii asked. "Children? Did the masters have wives?

Concubines?"

Laurel glanced at Scarlett. She was absorbed in her play, but there were signs she was listening with half an ear. She was getting too wise. "The Menworan had a unique way of procreating," Laurel said quietly. "They fashion a mate out of one of their own ribs."

Baii laughed. This must be a joke.

"The fluid I described?" Laurel went on, accepting his scepticism, "The bane that paralysed me? That is what they use to create the foundations of a mate. We can show you a graphic, but it is an extrapolation from an account by a Magen Bearer."

"And how do Legion continue their line?"

"Legion kept women in compounds on the surface. The masters would not tolerate females on their ship. They believed womanhood to be vile, and they held nothing but contempt for them."

"Except Judith," Ilivi said.

Laurel nodded. "Except Judith."

"The Sons of David," Harry said, "made up by common Legion and Magen Bearers—we have yet to learn the distinction— only reproduced with females taken from the conquered races. Any boy had to have inherited Legion genetic codes. Most female infants were destroyed, but I suppose the boys would end up back on the ship eventually." Harry looked to Laurel for confirmation, but she honestly didn't know.

"The Legion converts on Eden adhered to local laws and married their Edensai wives," she said, "but they have separated themselves now on Riynea." This action surprised

Baii.

"Do they feel mixed-race unions are less valid than pure?" he asked.

"I think it's more an indication of what went before," Laurel said after a moment. "The Edensai are good people, but even subconsciously, the Sons of David know there might be a residue of fear and suspicion."

"When we left, there was only a spirit of co-operation," Marcel said, stubbornly refusing to accept there was any kind of apartness. "I believe it will endure."

Much later, Harry and Laurel looked out from their balcony across the sparkling ocean.

"Do you remember when we were first here, and I wondered how we got two views from this balcony," she smiled. It all seemed so long ago.

Harry remembered. "And that hot tub felt so real."

"I can manifest one now if you like."

Harry grinned and rubbed his eyes. "I think I'd be too tired to enjoy it. I just want to go to bed."

"It's been just over a year," Laurel said wistfully. "I feel like I've lived a lifetime since we stood here. I never want to face another war." She turned to Harry. "What do you think is going to happen with Ilivi and Marcel? She can't leave here, and I doubt he would be able to leave her."

Harry knew this was on her mind from the moment Marcel and Ilivi reunited. She didn't need an answer, so he climbed into bed and pulled up the sheet, his tired brain making a massive error in making a too flippant and ill-thought-out response. "Just prepare yourself."

Seconds later, the cover was yanked off him. "What do you mean, prepare myself?" Laurel demanded. "How does *anyone* prepare themselves to part from someone they love? Harry, I can't *prepare* myself. I can't get myself into a countdown of emotions so that when we leave him here, it won't hurt!"

Harry should have given this more thought. Marcel was important to him too, and in many ways, he *was* like a son, but Laurel's connection to him went far deeper, and his comment hadn't given that credit. He felt like a fool, but not enough to not recognise the weight of what she had just said. "So, we're leaving?"

Laurel's temper settled, and she turned back towards the ocean. The moonlight sparkled on the water, and the distant islands rose dark and brooding. "I want to find Eli and Chloe," Laurel said softly.

Harry knew this was coming, they'd only been here a day, and Laurel was already planning their next move. He was okay with that, but the others? He wasn't so sure…

Harry was too quiet for Laurel, so she rattled into his mind like a steam train. He pulled a face at her. "I know you're in here," he said, tapping his head. "You're looking to see if I still want to go back to the League, and you want to see if we can do it after we find Chloe and Eli because you always get your way?"

Laurel withdrew and tilted her head to the side; she knew he knew she was in there. "But you aren't decided about returning to the League."

"You could have asked," Harry grunted, folding his arms. "I'd have given you an honest answer."

"Then I wouldn't have seen the rest of what you're thinking. That I'm being controlling."

"I don't need to tell you you're bossy," Harry grinned and patted the sheet beside him. "It's too soon to make decisions, and you said you don't want to be where Marcel and Ava aren't. Give yourself some time, don't be in such a hurry."

Laurel climbed onto the bed, tucked herself into her favourite spot under Harry's arm and rested her head. He was asleep in moments, and Laurel shifted her position onto her knees. In the moonlight, she watched the rhythmical rise and fall of his chest.

Woman, she whispered to herself, *made from the rib of a man*. Then she got out of bed and left the palace.

CHAPTER THIRTY-SIX

"My lady!" Laurel turned to see Marcel jogging towards her. They'd been on Isilia for almost six months, and Laurel had pushed all other thoughts save relaxing out of her head, instead enjoying all the wonders Isilia offered. Two of those wonders were the beautiful love stories of Marcel and Ilivi, Ava and Baii.

"My lady?" Laurel laughed. "You haven't called me that in years."

Marcel ran his hands through his hair. "No, Laurel, sorry, my head is all over the place." He paused, just in case she was looking into his mind. She didn't do that routinely, but he knew he was acting strangely. "I have something to tell you…"

"What is it, Marcel? You're very breathless and not from just a short jog."

"I know you wish to continue the journey, to find your friends…" Marcel shook his head, grappling to find the right words. But he didn't need to say anything. His expression was enough for Laurel. She touched his arm; switching off her telepathy was a skill she mastered long ago but reading intent had proved a little more complicated to ignore. As she predicted, Marcel had no intention of leaving with them.

"You're not coming with us?"

Marcel took a deep breath and tried not to look her in the eye. He knew this decision would be difficult for her; she'd been as a mother to him, although he suspected she knew it was coming.

"Ilivi and I, we are to have a child. A son."

Laurel's jaw dropped into a wide smile. She had no idea. With a gasp of delight, she hugged Marcel tight, and it occurred to her with a pang of regret, and despite her deep love for him, she seldom embraced him. "Marcel, that's wonderful! I don't know what to say."

Marcel's face relaxed into a proud grin. "Even before we knew," he said, "I had decided I couldn't leave Ilivi, I just didn't know how to tell you, but with the baby now, I knew you would understand. I tried to catch you and Harry together, but I just couldn't wait."

"Harry will be thrilled!" Laurel could assure him of that. "We always knew you and Ilivi share something extraordinary."

Marcel grinned and nodded happily. "I believe there will be someone travelling in my place." He turned slightly, and Laurel followed his gaze to where Ava and Baii walked hand in hand in the garden. "We already know," Laurel smiled, "They don't even need to tell us. How would Baii leaving affect Ilivi?"

Marcel took a deep breath. "In a personal sense, it will be difficult for her, but she sees how happy Ava makes him. Ilivi has spoken to me about regnant duties that need to be carried out alongside her that Baii has undertaken up to now. It seems I will not be leading a quiet life!"

"We won't leave until your baby is here," Laurel assured him, sensing that was a concern. He wanted desperately to share this with the people he loved. "I simply could not head off into the nebula without welcoming your little boy into the world."

"You and Harry will be the grandparents of the child," Marcel told her proudly, "and Darlen and Scarlett will stand alongside you both and my lady sister as treasured family."

A grandchild! When the formal announcement was made, Ava teased Laurel she scarcely looked old enough to have a child of her own, let alone a grandchild, and when Marcel and Ilivi's baby arrived a few months later, Laurel felt the familiar outpouring of love for him she had with Ava and Scarlett when they were born. From being a lonely nurse in Chicago, quite apart from all the fantastic events she'd been part of over the years, perhaps the most amazing was having a family, becoming a mother, an aunt, and now, a grandmother.

In the weeks following baby Gabriel's arrival, Marcel became the Empress's official consort in a lavish ceremony that also incorporated the new royal child's presentation to the people. Every governor of every province, every sub governor of every sub-province and all guardians attended the ceremony. Laurel and Harry were officially declared grandparents to the Empress's child. In the following days, the entire family, which now officially included Darlen and Scarlett, travelled to each region to present the baby to the people. Laurel had never had the opportunity to see the people's reactions to Ilivi. She was adored wherever she went, and although Marcel was at first met with a little envy by the young Chaese men and women, Laurel once again noted that quite a few of the young men envied Ilivi her new consort.

Onoth was a steady guide and companion to the royal party, not surprisingly taking credit for introducing the Hebre and their companions to the Empress. Still, on their return to the palace and despite her delight in her new grandchild, Laurel felt a pull to leave. Ava still had not mentioned Baii coming with them, but she knew that would be the case when the time came.

Laurel sat alone one evening on the terrace and wondered if perhaps Helen would visit her. She had thought her purpose might be fulfilled with the deliverance of Eden and destruction of the masters, but it seemed not. There was more for her to do. She turned at a soft footfall, half expecting Helen with cryptic words of wisdom, but it was Harry, trying not to blunder in and disturb her. A cushion offered itself to him, and he let himself be seated.

"Hiding yourself away?"

"Just meditating."

"I think you're edgy. I know you went out to the meadow today. Did you see Helen or Xavier?"

Laurel shook her head. "No, but it was peaceful, restful. We've had a busy few weeks."

"You've been searching for peace for a long time," Harry said, "but it's never peace that finds you, is it?"

"Honestly? I haven't got there yet. And I think that's my purpose, peace. No wars, no cartels, just peace."

"And it's not here?"

Laurel had given that much thought. "It could be," she said. "One day." She breathed deeply of the fragrant, clean air. "If I finish whatever journey it is I'm on."

"You were right, you know," Harry confessed, "I did once think we'd go back to the League, perhaps to our old life in some measure. If it's peaceful again, we are still young enough to continue our medical careers."

"We took a big detour, didn't we?"

Harry nodded. "But I wouldn't change a thing, except for losing Helen on the way."

"It's been nearly ten years since we lost Helen," Laurel said. "I still miss her. I guess I always will. Do you know, in real age—" Laurel gave a little laugh, "I'm over fifty?"

"And I'm ten years older than you." Harry didn't find it at all funny. "I would be signing up for age reversal now!"

"Well, we didn't age in stasis or variance, so we have to knock off eleven years."

"You always looked youthful, Laurel. I like to think you looked like your Aunt Lucy."

"She was blonde and very dainty, a bit like her sister, my mother." Laurel made a face, "Nothing like me."

Harry reached out and took her hand. "If we leave here, can we be sure we will be able to get back?"

"I know we will," Laurel said, leaning in and kissing him squarely on the mouth. "I got us here, didn't I?"

"Marcel's a family man at heart, Laurel," Harry smiled, catching her in an embrace. "He's not an adventurer, but it would break his heart if he thought he would never see you or Ava again. You are a link to his father. Besides, he loves grandeur, and he fits right in as the Empress's consort!"

"He certainly does!" Laurel was astounded to see how easily Marcel slotted into his new role. "Did you know," she said to Harry, "when he found out he was the son of a slave, he was horrified. Princess Shumuyi'beh already knew, she'd known for years, but the news he wasn't of noble birth shook him hard." Laurel grinned. "I expect this makes up for his shattered royal image. And I've never seen him so happy."

CHAPTER THIRTY-SEVEN _

Laurel joined Ava on the flight deck where, through the viewport, she watched Baii receive instruction from Darlen in flying an axispod.

'How are you feeling?"

"Oh, you know, Mom. I miss Marcel, and it's only been two days."

"You do know we will see him again?"

Ava nodded. "I do know, I have no doubts, and having Baii with me, I can't tell you how that makes me feel. I don't think I could have left Isilia without him."

"No-one would have asked you to. How's Scarlett? She hasn't cried for a few hours."

Ava glanced over to where Scarlett sat on Mer's lap. "She's fine. She likes Baii. It's a new world for him, space travel!"

"Let's hope he doesn't get sick. I told him he might need some intervention, but…"

That hope came too late. On his return to the Canaa, Baii, his face even more pale than usual, leaned on Darlen for support as they came up from the cargo bay.

"A fair chunk of his breakfast is on the axispod floorwell," Darlen grinned. "Here—" he handed the trembling Baii to Laurel, "I'll go and clean it up. He needs the pandroscope."

Baii was mortified, sure he was showing himself as weak, and sought their assurance that it happened to everyone.

Scarlett was watching on. "It's never happened to us," she chirped.

Laurel threw her a frown. "Scarlett, you're not helping."

"I have never felt like this in my life," Baii groaned, his shoulders sagging. "Darlen turned us upside down as we scanned the training beacons he set out. I couldn't tell what way was up in the first place. Perhaps flying axispods isn't for me."

"I don't like flying axispods either, Baii," Scarlett said.

"You can fly an axispod? You are a child!"

"Daddy taught me years ago," Scarlett said, grossly inflating the time frame. "I didn't get sick."

Baii smiled sheepishly at her as she scampered back to the flight deck, her work in making Baii feel much worse, done.

"She was born on Darlen's old ship," Laurel said. "She would have no business getting space sickness. You'll be fine in a few minutes. We'll get you to the pandroscope to disrupt some of those sensory pathways to your brain. It'll last long enough for you to acclimate to space travel. And you'll feel less movement inside the nebula heart. If I can get it right, you won't have time to get sick."

"I would be most grateful if you and Time came to a quick arrangement," Baii said, making a feeble attempt at a quip, but it got drowned as he doubled over and spilt the remainder of his breakfast all over the cargo bay floor.

Darlen had stored the sensor data from his old ship, so they could plot a reverse course through the nebula heart. The sensors recorded millions of League incil measurements of distance, an impossibility as the occupants of the ship would have been, as Harry put it, "dust." But no time had registered on the sensor clock. Darlen calculated an endpoint, something he'd overlooked when they were testing advanced widespeed. Now, he entered the endpoint at the coordinates where they found Eli's beacon.

"It's gazillions of incils, Laurel," he said, trying not to sound bleak. She reminded him of the incident in the Transcender, but to Darlen, that was a totally different matter. "Time may work differently in here, but unless you can give it some structure, this nebula might be our home for years."

Laurel looked around, they'd entered the nebula heart some hours before, and it all seemed normal, familiar. Everyone was going about their business except Laurel and Darlen, who stood on the flight deck. "Check the sensors, Darlen," she said.

Darlen gave her an odd look but did as she asked. "They're saying we're travelling at seven-plus widespeed."

"Now check the sensor clock."

Darlen compared the readings and looked up. "How the hell did you do that? No amber clouds, nothing!"

"We don't need protection in the nebula; you know that," Laurel reminded him, "and any human is safe just by the presence of Hebre…whole souls. In the Transcender, Hebre needed to protect the human bodies from the effects of the transdimensional shifts while manipulating Time. If you look, the ship is registering its speed. It isn't conscious of Time passing. It's just doing its job, what you programmed it to do."

"Are you making a point?" Darlen said as the others gathered around. As they did, the ship returned to normal readings. Laurel knew precisely what was taking place.

"We're programmed to believe that Time passes," she said, now understanding what Abel meant. "As humans, we're bound by it. Turn off the chronometers, Darlen, and the day/night sequencer, leave Mer on the flight deck, and all of you, except Ava and me, are going to sleep. We don't need your preconceived ideas about time."

An hour later, the ship was silent. Mer was in lower power mode, and nowhere on the ship was there any way the human part of Ava and Laurel could be reminded of hours or minutes.

"I get what you're trying to do," Ava said. "Eliminating the elements that are reliant on time, but we are human too."

"I've got heaps of theories, Ava, but time; be here, do this, in a minute, in an hour, kill time, make time; it all has a constricting effect. It's conceivable we could have moved along the nebula heart without stasis before. I sure as hell don't want to go there again. Ignore distance on the sensors; it won't be accurate; just sit down and let's see what happens."

Ava woke with a start; she'd dozed off with all the

waiting. Laurel was watching her.

"You were speculating how much 'Time' this would take," Laurel smiled. "You put the human perception and constraint of time on the experiment, but because I was able to clear your mind telepathically, you went to sleep and didn't disturb me. I wish I could have done that when you were teething!"

Ava leapt out of her seat to check the sensors. "Where are we?"

"Look out the viewport."

Ava did, and turned to her mother, sending her a congratulatory smile. "We've cleared the nebula heart!"

"We have. At the coordinates of Eli's beacon."

"How did you do it?" Ava plopped herself down beside her mother.

Laurel knew her explanation would sound simplistic, but the truth was, she wasn't entirely sure how it happened. "As you said, I removed the elements that embedded us in Time. I found a focus and as we did when we brought the rain, surrendered."

"How long did it take us?" Harry asked as he drifted in and caught the end of the conversation.

"No, Harry, that's not the question," Laurel chuckled. "And it's why I needed you asleep because you would measure how long it would take. It doesn't take Time. That's the secret. Taking Time suggests the use of Time. When we got sucked into the Transcender, Ava and I continued to be able to move while you and the others simply stopped. You had no heartbeat; you didn't breathe. You were in between those things, in between where life suspends and starts again, we all were. That's where I went and, once there, decided where our lives would resume. Even Ava had a problem with it."

"I did," Ava admitted. "I knew where Mom was going, but I was still being old human me and wondering about how long we'd have to sit here."

"The instruments still register millions of incils, Laurel," Darlen said when he joined them. But it didn't make any difference to Laurel.

"Well, distance is irrelevant," she stated. "Maybe we did travel that distance. We just weren't there when it was happening."

"If we do this too often, we'll have to keep on resetting the chronometer," Darlen said. "I suppose that's a small price to pay for jumping around inside Time."

Later, Darlen brought Eli's beacon from storage; they analysed and reanalysed the message, looking for clues as to where they might find him.

"This beacon," Baii said. "I assume it is attached to a ship that tracks its own course?"

"Yes," Harry nodded, "but Eli feared being followed even though he was able to travel in the nebula core. He probably disabled the tracker."

"But that was before he found refuge on the planet, was it not?" Baii asked. "He may have needed the tracker to plot a course back to the refuge planet after positioning the beacon?"

"He might have."

"In which case, he would leave a trail."

"After all these years?" Baii's comments were a fresh

perspective and worth some thought.

"Chaese scientists have identified ships from remote systems even after the ship has been supplanted by a new model," Baii told them. "It is possible they added this technology to the Canaa."

Darlen buzzed Mer on the flight deck. "Mer, see if you can find any kind of League signature track pointing to the coordinates where we found the beacon."

Mer found a trace, nothing definitive and it would require analysing, but it didn't belong out here.

"Is that a comms fragment?' Harry asked, enlarging the filter.

Darlen nodded. "Looks like it. Eli had obviously been in contact with another ship or possibly the planet where he is hiding out, but he's filtered the communication."

"What if it *was* another ship?" Harry said. "Besides, those comms fragments would be years old; they would have degraded by now. This one is probably an artefact; the nebula margin is known to have all sorts of echoes."

"I know that Harry, I'm not an idiot," Darlen retorted, "and comm trails would have degraded if we were trying to track them using League and Independent system technology, but the Canaa is more advanced. If we know what we're looking for, we might find it. I think we need to look at the next system. If they moved from the nebula, seeking sanctuary, it's probably not too far."

Once again, Laurel pondered on the simple idea of paper trails, tantalising crumbs left out to lead somewhere, but Eli had told them not to come looking. Were they heading into more danger? Did Eli say that to throw them off his trail, to discourage them? Somehow, Laurel didn't feel that was the answer.

Ava thought the same thing. *"It's possible he was urging you not to be distracted from your journey. Telling you where to find him might not have been the right thing to do at the time. It's different now."*

"I'm wondering that. Eli warned us not to return to the League, which we might have done."

The Canaa found traces of activity near the nebula and narrowed the data down to a time frame; the first was Darlen's ship, leaving an echo from when they found the beacon. They also found a single trace, dating back years prior, but as Harry suggested, had suffered degradation. However, it gave them a pointer, and with few other choices, they followed the trail of "crumbs".

Laurel found it impossible to rest. Knowing that the planet was invisible to sensors, either she or Ava had to be awake on the observation deck. Laurel felt energised, wide awake and firing on all cylinders. She described her feelings to Harry, who didn't really understand.

"Firing on all cylinders? Is that a reference to something on Earth?"

"Cars," Laurel smiled. "You know, what we used to get us about."

Harry did know. Laurel told him about them. They sounded smelly, unwieldy and entirely inadequate. "I wonder how the inhabitants of this hidden world felt when Eli and Chloe turned up," Harry said, and Laurel pointed out they had given Eli and Chloe a home, so they had to be decent people. Harry conceded that might be true but fell into a gloomy discourse about xenophobic races he'd encountered in the Independent Systems. After an hour, Laurel suggested he take his negativism somewhere else.

For the next few days, a strange compulsion in the pit of her stomach forced Laurel to keep her gaze on the surrounding space. She only slept when Ava was available to take over, but it was on Laurel's watch the moment finally came, and the tracking sensors called the end of the comms trail. The internal clocks were still turned off, and Laurel didn't know what part of the day it was, but she sensed Harry's light sleep and guessed he was close to waking, then checked the others. The only one still sleeping soundly was Darlen, but that was too bad. She'd have to wake him also.

Laurel moved to the flight deck to input coordinates. Of course, Harry and Darlen couldn't see a thing; Baii had a sense of the world even though he didn't have as clear a view as Ava and Laurel. "They are using technology to cloak the planet," he said. "If it were a manifestation, I would be able to see through it."

"It's beautiful, even from this distance," Ava said. "It's not a big planet, but it looks from here as though there are large continents and bodies of water."

Laurel suggested they cloaked the Canaa, concerned there might be other ships in the vicinity and not wanting to draw attention to their presence.

Darlen showed them a map on the star chart. "The area you outlined has several moons, and there are a lot of planets in this system, but it's uncharted, probably too far out to be recognised by League astronomers. I'm guessing some of the neighbouring planets are inhabited and have space travel. Otherwise, who, or what are they hiding from?"

"Eli said they travelled for three years in the nebula core at full widespeed," Ava said. "This planet has to be at least that far from League space."

Darlen shrugged. "Well, we all know what goes on in the nebula core. His ship might have told him three years, but it was a scout. It's not that sophisticated."

Harry suggested that could mean they were a long way from League space.

Darlen had no idea. It was certainly possible, but without knowledge of this system, there was no way of knowing for sure.

"Whoever runs that planet isn't giving anything away," he said, "no scans, no probes, no traction. If you hadn't been here, Laurel, I would have flown straight past."

Harry thought it was a definite possibility that an unsuspecting craft might crash into the planet. It was like Laurel's cloaks, invisible, but inside, you're still solid. He said so to the others.

"They wouldn't have lived to tell the tale," Darlen said. "Besides, a civilisation capable of shielding an entire world would likely have considered that."

"On Isilia, we can deflect passing ships," Baii said, "to make it difficult for them to establish orbit. I would have been one of those who flew into this planet and didn't live to tell the tale."

Darlen measured the planet's distance from the sun. "I'm guessing from your coordinates their sun is about the same distance as Earth is from your sun, Laurel. I wonder how they manage with the sun filtering through the shield; in fact, how do they manage to stop the sun's rays from highlighting it?"

"Let's hope," Laurel replied, "they welcome us and answer these questions."

For Ava and Laurel, the planet grew large in the viewport. It wasn't until landing coordinates were transmitted from the surface that Darlen and Harry saw an area of shadow with no stars.

Darlen peered out the viewport. "You have to get pretty close to see that something's there," he said. "You might be right, Baii; they must have means of keeping passing ships moving on. We seem to be welcomed."

At that moment, Laurel's face lit up. "It's Chloe! I can sense her. She knows it's us! She must have told whoever is in charge we're okay!"

Laurel happily linked her arm through Harry's and took a few deep, calming breaths. She didn't know what was in store for them on this planet with the blue oceans and vast continents, but one thing was for sure, at least for now, they were not headed into war.

CHAPTER THIRTY-EIGHT_

Ava piloted the ship on its descent. She and Laurel both sensed a civilisation spread out across the entire planet, but little in the way of buildings, which seemed strange. The sensors still offered nothing, so although Ava had a strong sense of technology, it was unfamiliar. One thing she did feel sure of was, this civilisation did not use space travel. It seemed these technologically advanced people were truly xenophobic, and although they might have the capability of going into space, they didn't have the desire. Baii cited his own planet as similar. Isilia abandoned space travel centuries before to concentrate on rebuilding the world and never again felt the need to venture back out into the cosmos.

As the Canaa cleared the shield and entered the lower atmosphere, the planet became visible to the entire group. The sensors registered a sharp drop in altitude, but the ship quickly stabilised. Moments later, controls were overridden, but Ava sensed that it was about to happen, so it came as no surprise.

As Ava and Laurel had observed on approach, the planet had several oceans and other large bodies of water, but as the Canaa took them lower, the splendour of the world was opened out to them all. The ship skimmed across soaring snow-capped mountains, swooped into deep valleys and sprayed water as they crossed a vast, blue ocean. Once again over land, they saw foothills covered in verdant green and dotted with towering forests. It seemed wild, untamed and very beautiful.

"Wow, this is spectacular," Ava exclaimed. "Look, Scarlett, come and see." Scarlett had risen from her bed, expecting breakfast, but instead found the grown-ups on the flight deck looking into space. Then moments later, she was looking at mountains and fields. She didn't know much about cloaking planets.

"We seem to be getting a grand tour," Darlen said. "I would have expected them to guide us into the nearest spaceport."

Ava pointed out this planet wouldn't need a spaceport, and Darlen conceded she had a point, but they were obviously going somewhere. And that somewhere was one of the forests. The Canaa came to rest gently in a large clearing circled by tall trees. Unlike the landscape they saw after pushing through the shield, this area seemed manicured and maintained. Darlen carried out the routine checks for toxins in the atmosphere, even though he didn't expect to find anything untoward. They stepped from the Canaa into the air, clean and tangy with the smell of grass and surrounded by copper and silver-hued trees that stretched like sentinels towards the sky. It was glorious.

"It smells nice here," Scarlett said, closing her eyes and turning her face upwards. "It's got a sun, like on Isilia."

"They must have found a way for the shield not to

interfere with photosynthesis," Baii said, crouching down and running a hand over the grass. "This growth—" he looked up, "these trees, don't appear to be compromised in any way."

A small transport, travelling at the height of a metre or so above the ground, headed in their direction. It had barely stopped when a familiar figure leapt from the vehicle and ran towards them, her arms outstretched.

"Chloe!" Laurel screamed as she and her old friend slammed together, hugging each other and shrieking with laughter. "Chloe, you're still here, thank goodness!"

Chloe set Laurel back from her, catching her hands and looking her up and down with a grin. "I most certainly am, but time hasn't been quite so kind to me as it has to you!"

When Laurel first saw Chloe jump from the transport, she recognised her instantly, but now, while Chloe was still sweet-faced and petite, she now sported a few wrinkles and a sprinkling of grey through her hair. She looked to be a woman of perhaps sixty. Laurel was suddenly lost for words, so Harry came forward and hugged Chloe tight.

"We had a bit of a stoush with Time in the nebula," he said. "I guess we weren't too accurate, and there's nothing like a few years in stasis to ward off ageing!"

Chloe laughed. "As long as Darlen didn't make you drink the antidote and bapth. I can still taste it after all these years! Hello Darlen." Chloe hugged him. "I must say you didn't get younger looking!"

"I don't get the benefit of stasis," he grinned.

Ava had only been a small child the last time she saw her, and Chloe couldn't get over how she'd grown into such a beautiful young woman. She raved about Ava's raven hair and her incredible eyes. Chloe even hugged Baii, although she wasn't too sure at that point how the group had picked him up. Turning curious eyes to Scarlett, she sensed the awful sadness at the loss of Helen. Chloe bent down and kissed the young girl. "I knew your mum," she said gently. "We were friends."

Then Chloe picked up from Laurel that Marcel was now a husband and father on a distant world. "A lot has happened," Chloe said, ushering them to the transport, insisting that Mer had to remain with the ship and ignoring the beginning of a protest from Darlen. "I can't wait to hear all about it."

"Poor Helen," she sent to Laurel. Chloe was dumbfounded that Helen and Darlen had a child together, and asked Laurel telepathically what had happened to their old friend.

"It was sudden. She didn't suffer," Laurel sent back. *"And she would be so proud of Scarlett."*

"Asde and I have a daughter," Chloe said. "She was born here. And she has a daughter too."

"You're a grandmother?"

"I am," Chloe said proudly. "Lara is seven." Chloe ensured everyone was secure before she directed the transport to turn towards the direction from which she came. "We had you land here because you probably realise this is a secluded society. The last thing they want is…" she searched for a word.

"Company?" Harry suggested.

"I was going to say contaminants," Chloe grinned,

"but that sounds so unfriendly. I work for the government, and when I alerted them about you, they agreed that I should meet you on my own. They knew you would be able to see the planet. I sent a message to Eli; he'll be here in the morning. In the meantime, I must take you to the civic hall attached to this municipality. Tavis is the local governor, and he will provide you with accommodation until you are assessed."

"Why can't we just stay on the ship?"

Chloe shook her head at Darlen. "They won't allow that. You need to be supervised, sorry. They did appreciate you cloaking the ship on your approach." She turned and tossed a camouflage device onto the Canaa before they sped away. Laurel looked back. She couldn't see the ship.

"Why can't I see it?" she sent to Chloe.

"Because it's not a cloak, it just fudges out the edges, so it blends in."

"Can't they make cloaks for ships? They can cloak an entire planet."

"Why would they need to? But they sometimes have a reason for camouflage. By the way, that's one ugly ship. It looks like a cockroach."

"Darlen designed it. It's his baby."

Chloe grinned. Of course, he did. Darlen's aesthetic tastes were always questionable.

"You'll like it here. I hope you decide to stay," Chloe smiled as they left the Canaa behind.

"Some of that depends on what's going on in the League," Harry said.

"Oh, you won't want to go back to the League." Chloe twisted around to face him. "Eli and Minet went back about thirty years ago. They were gone for years, and we thought they'd been captured. The Presidents only allowed it because Eli cloaked the scout. I didn't want him to go because I wasn't sure the scout would make it, but he insisted. He dropped the beacon at the same time."

Ava and Laurel exchanged puzzled looks. Thirty years?

"What happened in the League?" Harry asked, not having noticed the reference to time.

"The news they brought back was good and bad," Chloe told them. "Akkuh was dead, assassinated, and the Cartels driven out, but not before they managed to occupy a few planets. They thought they'd establish Akkuh again, but of course, once he was dead, they had to find another leader. Help for the League came from an unlikely source—" she nodded to Laurel, "—your friend Duchess Shumuyi'beh. She raised an army, defended Danfos 4, then gathered more troops and marched on the occupied planets. Shumuyi'beh is totally ruthless—" Chloe grinned, obviously an admirer. "She chased down the Cartels even when they were on the run. I believe it was the Duchess herself who killed Akkuh, but that might just be a rumour. Eli couldn't verify it."

"Well, she certainly had cause. And Marta?"

Chloe shook her head sadly. "I'm sorry, she's gone. That happened even before Minet got us out of League space. She was on Mentelci because it was so well defended, but you know Marta, she took it in her head to fight. She was killed but took out the prime head of the Gale with her and dozens of his clones."

Marta would have defended Mentelci with everything

she had available. And she would have defended Bela, whom Laurel knew she loved. "Was High Chancellor Bela still in power?"

"Then, she was, but not now, I would say, she'd be ancient. I wouldn't go anywhere near the League myself," Chloe warned. "It's not the place for whole souls, even without the Cartels. We can't be sure how stable it is."

"We aren't returning to the League, Chloe," Laurel said. "We've been fighting almost since we left there. We're hoping to find some peace. It's been a trepid few years."

"What if your government rejects us?"

"That won't happen, Darlen," Chloe said, "this is all a formality. They accepted us, with some apprehension at first, because Eli and I could see the planet, but after that, well, we've lived a wonderful life here. That's the municipality ahead."

They all strained their eyes to see, expecting tall buildings, industry, houses, but there was nothing save a big, blue lake surrounded by towering cliffs. As they neared, they saw transports, varying in size with no visible means of power, moving noiselessly in an orderly fashion between the cliffs and up and down their faces. The cliff faces were sectioned, and closer inspection revealed openings set out over the entire height and breadth. At the base, a skirt of single-storey stalls fashioned from the same stone as the cliff looked like shop fronts and street cafes. All very civilised. An area of tended parkland skirted one side of the lake, leading back towards the forest where they left the Canaa.

"You live in the cliffs?" Darlen said, looking up.

"Yes," Chloe grinned as the transport came to a

standstill beside the lake. "The cliffs provide natural coolness in the summer and are heated by hot underground springs in the winter." She laughed. "The winters here are worse than Earth's, but we have creative plumbers! Inside the cliffs, commerce, entertainment precincts and living suites are all set out on grids. We have no raised external structures to blemish the landscape." She nodded towards the shops and cafes at the base of the cliff. "The people here love everything to be as naturally formed as possible, but like anywhere else in the universe, they also like to dine al fresco."

Harry looked around. It didn't look like a diverse culture, but he supposed that he couldn't expect to see other species if they never had visitors. There were people with white skin and black, but he saw no one of Baii's colouring. "They're all human?" he asked Chloe. "No interspecies culture? From way back?"

"No," Chloe said. "Human as far as records go. And everyone is employed, every child educated, there is no want, no war—" She lifted her shoulder. Clearly, she believed the society had a solution. "Pockets of crime now and then, but that's my area—policing." Chloe pointed to a broad entrance in the cliffside. "That's the governor's storehouse," she said. "The title comes from a time when the people brought all their produce here to share before they became prosperous in their own right."

There was no door to the storehouse and no guards. Chloe showed them into a bare, circular hall, with nothing to distinguish it as a place of governance. Although the newcomers attracted some attention from the few individuals present, interest was fleeting, and their own business resumed. "People will stare," Chloe said. "Particularly at you, Harry. I've never seen anyone with red hair here."

"Great," Harry muttered, and Laurel sent him a thought, *"We might encounter other planets with signs that say, 'Redheads not welcome!'."* Harry ignored her.

"There are only four governors on Homeworld," Chloe informed them as they followed her along a set of corridors, "and two Presidents, who are alerted to your presence and await Tavis's evaluation." She stopped at an entrance. "Don't worry. These are good people."

"Homeworld?" Harry echoed. "Not very original."

"To its people, it's the only world that counts," Chloe said. "Now, Tavis speaks Seera, I taught him because he was interested, and we don't have any devices like Fobel nodes because there is only one language. Tavis is a musician as well as the governor, and he has a good ear. He couldn't understand how our speech was so tame! He preferred English because of the intonations, so I taught him that as well, but dull old Seera intrigued him."

Laurel and Harry instinctively felt for the language pin inserted on the station, but it was gone. Obviously, one that reabsorbed, like Fobel nodes.

A portico built into the cliff face stood on the other side of the entrance. Here, they were requested to wait as an official notified Tavis of their arrival. Building into cliffs and mountains wasn't so new; Laurel knew there were places on Earth that did it. The palace on Isilia was built into a cliff, perhaps not on this scale, but…

Laurel walked to the edge of the colonnade. It wasn't high but offered a good view of the street below. People were just getting on with their daily routines, families, children running, the slender blunt-nosed and uniform transport travelling up and down and around the cliff face; everything moved with purpose. The sun shone, making the ripples on the lake glitter like starlight. Waterbirds waded to their knees and plucked insects from the air around them, then dipped their heads under the water. It was so peaceful here, and Laurel felt no undercurrents, only openness and honesty, along with an overriding sense of self-worth and security. Chloe tuned in. She took this for granted now, had even brought up a child here.

"This is how it is, Laurel," she said. "It's a healthy society, stable, and people care about each other. Of course, there are differences in opinion, quarrels, and challenges, but the underlying base is goodwill. There is something to be said for feeling safe and not to have to lock your doors."

Laurel smiled. "Tranquil, but busy."

"The people are industrious; everything is for the good of the planet."

"But you don't have space travel?"

"Where would people who don't want to socialise go?" Chloe responded. "The only spacefaring ship we ever had was the League scout, and Eli had to nurse it back here after the trip to the League. This planet is self-sufficient. Eli and Ru are farmers, but their children preferred technology."

"How many children do they have?"

"Fourteen." She didn't wait to grin at Laurel's wide-eyed surprise. "Here's Tavis."

Tavis was no more than thirty, rather young to have the burden of a municipality. He was a stocky man with a plump face, ruddy cheeks, blond hair, and an overall manner of nervous enthusiasm. His body language suggested he was just a little overwhelmed at meeting more individuals like Chloe and Eli, who had arrived before he was even born. Chloe made the introductions.

"I hope this is not an invasion!" he chuckled with a double-take at Harry's mop of not recently trimmed red hair. "We have been most fortunate to have Chloe and Eli and their families become part of our society. We are intensely private, and you are unexpected, but I hope you will not find us unfriendly. You will meet with some wariness; since the cloak was devised thousands of years ago, we believed we hung invisibly in space." He dipped his head towards Chloe. "Not so to certain types it seems, but we will publish you; that is if you elect to stay. You will meet with some curiosity because of your appearances, but as you are human, there will be no alarm. Meanwhile, your ship is disguised in the parklands, which for now is off-limits to our citizens, and your robot is deactivated."

Harry caught Darlen as he went to protest. "Leave it, Darlen," he muttered under his breath, "they're entitled to satisfy themselves we're not a threat." Darlen was not happy losing control of his ship and Mer. Tavis saw Darlen was not comfortable but did not offer any further explanation as to why they needed to take such precautions. This was his world, and they were the visitors. "The Presidents will receive you tomorrow," Tavis continued. "I understand from Chloe that two of you are doctors?"

Harry nodded. "Laurel and I are physicians."

"And you, Darlen, isn't it?" he smiled in anticipation of a revelatory reply, hoping to appease the big man who was clearly upset.

"I'm a pilot and a bit of a drifter, really," Darlen said after a nudge from Harry. "I don't have any particular skills. I'm good at fixing things."

Darlen's self-deprecating assessment of himself took Tavis by surprise. He expected spacefarers to be accomplished in many areas and so was a little more receptive to Baii when he learned he was an authority on horticulture.

Throughout the next few hours, Tavis made a gracious and attentive host. He had cleared his official calendar for the day in a professional capacity, but personally, he could scarcely contain his excitement. Beings from another world? Such things had fired his imagination since childhood. Everybody knew about Eli and Chloe and the others who had arrived from off-Homeplanet, but for it to happen again in his lifetime… Tavis was overwhelmed, but he continued with a professional exterior. It would be expected of him. Only the telepaths present would see his thoughts that if he let down his guard, his mouth would be open in awe and his eyes wide in astonishment.

Tavis showed them around the city and asked about their travels, desperately wanting to know if there were telepaths among them like Chloe and Eli. He so admired the skill. Instead, he distracted his glee by providing several local dishes for them to try from street merchants, amused by the now calmed Darlen's enthusiasm and explanation of "fast food". Tavis, a family man himself, showed Scarlett interactive and highly realistic holograms of the animals that roamed the planet. Scarlett was captivated. She'd only seen large animals on Faris, but she hadn't been allowed near, so to touch them was magical to a child. But they weren't her favourites.

"Can you magic kittens and lizards?" she asked Tavis.

"No, I…Magic?" he said, glancing at Chloe for an explanation, but Scarlett had already turned to loudly ask Baii to "magic" some lizards. Baii felt awkward. To be recognised as a horticulturist was one thing, but manifestations might not be so welcome. Laurel sent a thought to Chloe.

"Manifest?" Chloe sent back.

"Many people of his race can do it. They're not permanent, only while he is in the vicinity. What's more, Ava and I can do it too."

"Let him do it."

Laurel nodded at Baii, and he let go of a single lizard from his hand. Scarlett immediately scooped it up to show to the somewhat wide-eyed Tavis, who was more excited about this fantastic skill than the small unfamiliar animal placed on his knee.

"Is this 'magic'?" he asked.

"Magic is a term from Laurel's world," Darlen said. "Baii's race can manifest objects."

"This is a wonder," Tavis said, beaming. "What manner of other objects do you manifest?"

"I'm afraid it only runs to small creatures," Baii said, carefully playing down his abilities. "It is not a skill I have cultivated. My ancestors were more accomplished than I."

Laurel had seen Baii manifest a facsimile of a full-sized ship on Isilia, but she understood his reasons for not promoting this skill. This could make him a curiosity, even more than telepathy.

They later met several of Tavis's acquaintances, some of whom recalled Chloe and Eli's arrival, along with the flurry of excitement and concern it caused. They recounted the uncertainty from some, the ultimate adoption, and now esteem they felt for the aliens, which was expressed in a term of endearment. Chloe did a sterling job of interpreting, but the native language, which they learned did not differ across the globe, was easy enough for them to pick up a few meanings by the end of the afternoon.

As the sun went down, they returned to the storehouse, where they found the cliff façade brightly lit. In the fading light, it looked like hundreds of burrows but also homely and welcoming.

"I have assigned a single suite," Tavis told them. "I was not sure you would wish to be separated at this point. I hope that meets with your approval?"

Laurel thanked him as Chloe herded them all back into the transport.

"He didn't ask too much about how we ended up here," Darlen said. "And what about Mer?"

"This was just him getting to know you," Chloe assured him. "And Mer will be fine."

"I don't see why we can't go back to the Canaa," Darlen grumbled.

"Relax," Chloe said firmly. "These people have been avoiding contact with other species for centuries. Is it unreasonable for them to take precautions?" Chloe turned her attention back to the matter in hand, ignoring Darlen's mutterings and glares. "The Presidents will visit soon, and they'll want to know more about you. Personally, I am dying to know everything, but I'm forcing myself to wait until Eli arrives, or you'll have to tell us all over again. He's going to be upset about Helen," she finished sadly.

"Xavier and Helen are buried in the same place," Laurel told her. "On Isilia, Baii's world."

"Really?" Chloe exclaimed. Then she frowned. "What? Xavier? *Xavier…?*" She held up her hands as the colour drained from her face. "No," she breathed, "don't tell me, or I'll never stop asking questions. In the morning, you tell us everything."

"You'll be there for days," Harry laughed.

"I expect you've all got your own stories, your own spin on what happened."

"I'm looking forward to seeing Asde again and meeting your daughter," Laurel said. "And to find out how Eli learned how to cloak the scout." She looked at Ava, "For us, it was because someone else knew we could do it!"

"Well, we all knew cloaking people was Helen's thing. Turns out…" Chloe tilted her head and smiled, "Anyway, Asde and Karen are looking forward to seeing you too, but I told them to stay away, just for now. I didn't want to overwhelm you."

The cliff's upper-level entrance was a landing bay, with transports neatly and swiftly stacked in layers by light traction. A curious non-automated addition was a parking inspector who tagged anyone leaving or taking a car. The man eyed the newcomers with interest and commented to Chloe while giving a friendly nod in their direction.

"I live here too," Chloe told them. "He knows me. He was asking about the flight suits. No-one on the planet dresses like this, and of course, no-one has…"

"We know," Harry finished the sentence, "red hair."

From the landing bay, they strolled through spacious halls within the cliffs, passing through areas obviously designed as meeting places. It was loud and friendly, and the overreaching feeling was one of companionship and ease. Its busy-ness and brightness reminded Laurel of Times Square, although she was to learn that Times Square was a dinosaur compared to what this area offered.

"It's huge," Darlen exclaimed, seldom surprised by much. "And all inside a mountain."

"See this—" Chloe held out her hand, and they were surrounded by parkland, standing next to a fountain. The sky above was blue. Tiny, brilliantly coloured birds flew above their heads, and they could see mountains in the distance. A few couples sat on the edge of the fountain, paying curious attention to the newcomers.

"Just stand still," Chloe cautioned. "You're not ready for movement in the folds yet."

"How did you do it?" Baii said. "Not a manifestation, I would have known."

"Nothing so amazing as manifestations," Chloe replied. "I'll show you another."

The scene changed to a snowy, highland region that cooled the air considerably, making them all shiver. People were gathered in groups on the slopes.

"They look like they're skiing," Laurel said.

"Not skiing," Chloe answered, "but it is a sport. One of the few that doesn't use technology. It's like potholing, challenging to do; we even have professionals who can dig at speed."

"Doesn't sound particularly interesting," Darlen said.

"Depends…" Chloe brought them back to the entertainment precinct and led them into one of the corridors. "You'll be able to move within the portals once you're established. Your presence on Homeworld needs to be announced first," she said. "Here's your suite." Chloe activated the door and stepped through, inviting them to file in. "Living spaces are all designed for maximum comfort. This is a family suite."

The door opened into a tiered area that on the face of it, seemed only marginally smaller than the landing bay. The lower tier sported a sparkling central pool. The second tier, bright and spacious, was furnished with ergometric chairs, gorgeous floor coverings and panelled walls. Laurel had no idea if this was typical or modern, but it was impressive.

"This is the living area," Chloe explained. "We all have a pool. The water comes from the springs and has remarkably soothing minerals; I promise you'll love it. All food and beverages are dispensed. Harry, do you remember when we first arrived in the League, and I asked you if the food in the Vesanecs were made up of molecules?"

Harry remembered.

"These are, but it's the real food that is deconstructed. You won't be able to tell it from the real thing."

"We hardly know what the 'real thing' tastes like yet."

"That's true, but in the cities, this is the only way to eat unless you go to street merchants or restaurants." Chloe grinned, "We have some great restaurants. If you go out to the rural sectors, they use the dispensers less. I've set up this one for Seera. It'll understand you."

"How long have you known we were coming?" Ava asked.

"Eli and I always knew we'd see you again," Chloe said. "I sensed you days ago and alerted Eli, who wanted to know as soon as you arrived. I told Tavis. He was so overwhelmed—but that was obvious—he asked me to get this place ready. I didn't know then who had left you and who you'd gained." She smiled at Scarlett, who'd had quite enough excitement for one day and was fit to fall asleep on her feet.

"Bed compartments are on the upper tier, pretty elementary. I'll show you." Chloe gave them a whirlwind tour of very spartan but private sleeping areas furnished only with enormous luxurious beds, even one for Scarlett's sole use.

"And you'll like this." Chloe extended her hand, and the roof slid open to reveal a grand view of the stars.

"You can keep it closed if you like," she said. "Each cell works separately. I'll leave you with this—" she took a device from her wrist and put it on the wall, "it works like a triconomic interface but doesn't need an implant. This one is primed for your use, so it'll understand individual commands. They'll need to be verbal until you get your own units; then, they're calibrated to any variations and desires in your body. It's very sensitive, but in here, it'll only work on the relevant technology. Out there," she grinned, "it'll confuse you with portals until you get used to it. But it's getting late, Scarlett is sleepy, and I know Asde is going to be desperate to know what happened today."

"We haven't spoken much about your life here, Chloe," Laurel said as they walked together to the door.

Chloe seemed confident they would be staying as she embraced Laurel. "Tomorrow, or the next day, or the day after that. What you found out about whole souls comes first!"

Scarlett fell asleep instantly, and they were all too tired to hash over the day's events, but they agreed the first day had been pleasant. Laurel and Harry lay side by side on a bed that had room enough for a dozen people.

"I must have miscalculated a bit," Laurel said. "I can't believe Chloe is older than me. She was only sixteen when we arrived in League space. Heaven knows how old Marcel and Ilivi are now. Isilia could be centuries in the past."

"Did you have any particular time period in mind when you moved us through the nebula?"

Laurel shook her head mutely. She hadn't even considered it, just focused on where they found Eli's beacon years before. A thought occurred to her. "Remember we were speaking about age? Maybe that's what did it. That old human side of me again. Possibly, I need an image in my mind of the person or place we are heading, exactly as we meant to find them."

Harry nodded and yawned. "This is a pretty impressive place," he murmured, looking up at the stars. "The technology here is so advanced. I can't believe they aren't spacegoing."

"It's a peaceful, prosperous society. Who knows what might be invited in if they start exploring."

"That's true." Harry rolled onto his stomach and closed his eyes, signalling he wanted to wind down the conversation. "I'm looking forward to seeing more of the planet. The scenery on the way in was magnificent. They've built quite an idyllic world for themselves." He yawned again. "In many ways," he mumbled sleepily, "Baii's people share the philosophy of keeping their planet free of visitors. Except for those in need. And Chloe seems happy."

"Chloe is very happy," Laurel agreed. "She's excited for us to be here, to be part of her world."

Harry swivelled his head around to look at her. "Are we going to be part of her world?"

"For a while, I think."

Harry buried his face into the bed, wishing Laurel's brain wasn't still churning things over. "Darlen feels out of place," she said.

"He doesn't have specific skills, but then neither did Chloe. Aren't you tired?"

"Chloe alluded to being in law enforcement still," Laurel said, ignoring him, "She was a natural leader in the League Constabulary, a well-ordered community like this wouldn't have overlooked someone with her organisational skills."

Laurel was about to say that Ava wasn't trained in anything either, but Harry had fallen asleep, so she simply lay on her back and looked at the stars until she felt her eyelids drooping. She turned towards Harry. The moonlight from the skylight above tried to find its way through the shock of red hair tousled over his sleeping face. She loved his hair, even though the rest of the galaxy appeared to find it a source of amusement. It was still thick and vibrant, even though, as he said, he would be more than sixty in real-time now. Laurel thought about working out exactly how old they were, but for the first time in so long, she felt at peace, and even the simplest mental arithmetic was the last thing on her mind.

CHAPTER THIRTY-NINE _

The following morning brought an emotional reunion with Eli, and seeing Chloe again was like meeting her again after a long absence, even though it had only been a matter of hours. Eli teared up when he learned about Helen but was thrilled to meet Scarlett, who loved being the centre of attention, and Eli was delighted to learn of Marcel's new situation as a family man and consort of an Empress. There was no official dignitary present this time, and though Darlen was more at ease, he just wasn't settled.

"I'm not too keen on these authority types," he said after the hugging and tears were done, and they were all seated comfortably in the large living area of the apartment.

"Tavis is a friend of my son," Eli said. "He's a good man, strictly by the book, though."

"Sorry," Darlen said. "No offence."

"None taken, Darlen. Now—" Eli clapped his hands together and grinned broadly, "We want to know the whole story. Beginning to end!" Laurel knew they expected her to start, and she looked into Eli's shining, hopeful brown eyes. He'd aged as well; at only a few years older than Chloe, his black curly hair had thinned and greyed, and his face more lined, but he too seemed to have found his place among this society. So, it was surprising that Laurel found herself with nothing to say. In front of her old friends, she felt inexplicably exposed and defeated. All she could think of was the day before, seeing Chloe again and sitting with her at their informal interview with Tavis, holding her hand and loving them all being back together. The other four telepaths in the room tuned in to her confusion, but Baii withdrew quickly, he was a stranger to Eli and Chloe, and his presence, even one of support to Laurel, might not be welcome.

"I'm not going to try to read your mind, Laurel," Chloe said aloud when she saw Laurel hesitate. "My telepathic skills are a bit rusty, and there's a whole lifetime stretching out in your head. But I'll summarise what we know from after you left the League, and you can tell us the rest in your own time. Is that okay?"

Laurel gave a timid nod. She just didn't know where to start. It had seemed important when she was living it, the Gale, the Ferle, Isilia, Eden, the masters, Sheerguhd, and what she knew now of the Miran Forin nebula. Looking back, she realised the stage on which she'd played out the last few years of her life was not just big; it was monumental. The others had been with her every step of the way, cast in their own roles, but somehow, it had been so...*personal* for her.

"We know you went to the abandoned prison world out near the nebula and that Minet attacked you," Chloe began. "It was really to discourage you. He knew the Gale got wind you were carrying a whole soul, and he suspected Akkuh of planning a coup."

"And Minet never told anyone?" Harry frowned. "Are we going to get to see him?"

"Sorry," Chloe shook her head. "Minet died ten years ago. He always hoped you'd come back so he could explain himself. He had a lot of time for you, Harry."

"We were friends when we were first in the Constabulary," Harry said. He'd been angry with Minet all these years, but he was still sorry to hear he'd died. "We were assigned to Semevale 8 for a couple of years."

Chloe nodded. "I knew that, but what you didn't know, while you were there, Minet siphoned a portion of the ore from the mines. He got caught, and Akkuh kept Minet's crime to himself, knowing full well he could use it to his advantage against him. The Semevalian's had strict controls over the ore, as you know. Akkuh had a lot of favours he could call in if necessary, and he threatened to send Minet's sister to the Bladon outpost on Carnap's ring. She was very frail if you recall. She wouldn't have lasted."

"Seems like leverage is alive and well everywhere," Ava smiled thinly.

"Minet told us he'd seen you at the Massiennes cluster and tried to warn you away," Chloe continued. "He was meeting with the Gale on Akkuh's behalf. He had a consignment—at the time, he didn't know what it was, but it was League signature tags for the Gale ships in readiness for the coup.

"Minet detected your ship just after you left the prison planet, but you cloaked, and if the Gale detected you also, they would have thought it was a sensor ghost or artefact. He knew you didn't have a League cloak on board, and it's not common knowledge whole souls can cloak ships. After that, he guessed you went into the nebula."

"What were you looking for on OL 3321 of all places?" Eli asked. He'd been there twice during training in the League Constabulary.

"I always had a strong sense of what direction we should take," Ava explained. "Even though I was small, I felt as though I was being led. I think Hebre…"

"Hebre?"

"We'll explain that later," Ava said. "The people in the story in the stone Mom found in the archive? I felt either they or their ancestors had been to that planet. We found wall paintings and a fragment of tapestry there. Mom was able to translate it…mostly."

"We never went to the cave area," Eli said. "We were always put up in the mountains to avoid the storms."

"The tapestry was woven from human hair," Ava continued. "It mentioned a serpent coming out of a place called Sheerguhd and people called the 'bringers of stars'. When we got to Eden, we found the serpent that came from Sheerguhd was a ship that carried beings called 'masters', bent on destroying humankind, and the bringers of stars were…" Ava looked at Darlen, "Soul Mongers, but they called them Magen Bearers, soldiers to the masters." Ava then backtracked to the loss of Darlen's ship, their arrival on Isilia, and the Transcender, stopping at the point where they met Sedar.

Chloe raised her hand, "Magen as in the Star of David?"

"Oh, how do you know?"

Chloe rolled her eyes. "Don't forget I'm from Earth," she said. "I lived near St Albans. There was a huge Jewish community there, and I had tons of Jewish friends. Hebre? Hebrew? Is there a connection?"

Ava looked across at the still silent Laurel. "Mom made some connections," she said, "but they're tenuous at best. She thinks a lot of words got mixed up across histories."

"We'd like to know about the coup in the League and your escape and settlement here," Harry said, unsure as to the reasons behind Laurel's silence. She looked close to tears. This should be joyous for her, and he couldn't understand why she'd withdrawn.

"You've just summed it up," Chloe said with a shrug. "In a nutshell, that's what happened, and it was a long time ago, but what happened to you, to all of you, has a bearing on what we are." She and Eli had got out of the League at the beginning of the coup and what Eli brought back in the aftermath was only of a society rebuilding. Neither of them knew much more.

Laurel knew her history was as much Eli and Chloe's as it was hers and Ava's, even though she still didn't have all the answers, certainly not about herself. A vision of a clear-eyed imp flashed into view, Abel at the moment of his sacrifice, the sickly smell of the paralysing bane that stuck to her hair and clothes as Cephus interrogated her, and finally, Harry tortured and close to death. The sudden starkness of the images sent Laurel to her feet.

"I can't talk about it," Laurel declared. "I'm a nobody—a nurse from Chicago. My aunt and uncle brought me up because I had a useless, no-good mother! I didn't imagine any of this…" she turned, leaving them in stunned silence as she fled to the bedroom. Once inside, she flung herself down on the bed and sobbed.

"Laurel had the most vested in this," Harry said quietly after a moment, wondering if he should follow her, but he knew he wouldn't be welcomed. "She wanted to find out the origins of the whole souls, to find out if Ava would be the last of her kind. She didn't expect to find what she did and certainly didn't expect to have to wipe out a civilisation."

"But wasn't it an evil civilisation? These masters?" Eli asked.

"Yes, but there were other people on Eden." Harry knew the destruction of evil was the part that would be remembered, but so many innocent lives were lost, and Laurel felt responsible. "In destroying the masters, many good people died."

"I remember Laurel telling us about her vision on Diriarden," Chloe said. "I'm guessing the Farisee aren't the masters?"

Ava shook her head. "The Farisee were allies. They didn't fight, but we would never have made it without them."

"I think we should wait for Laurel," Darlen said. "Things happened to her that didn't happen to the rest of us."

Harry agreed. "Give her some time. She'll be fine."

Chloe understood, she could be patient a while longer, and they would have so much time to catch up. She turned to Baii. "Meanwhile, perhaps you can tell us about your planet, your people, and the lucky lady who captivated the gorgeous Marcel!"

Baii was stunned. "You consider Marcel 'gorgeous'?"

Chloe nodded enthusiastically. "I only met him once, on Danfos 4. I could have eaten him!"

Baii barely knew how to respond. "Does your husband know you feel this way?" he said after a moment.

"Sure, I couldn't stop talking about him."

Harry grinned. He always thought of Chloe as a little girl. Even seeing her now with grey hair, wrinkles and heaps of confidence hadn't altogether wiped away the picture of the bewildered girl he met on the consular ship.

"The Empress is as fair of heart as she is of countenance," Baii said as he inclined his head, but offered no more about his sister. "As for our history..." Baii decided to employ a diorama for Eli and Chloe to see for themselves. After the initial interest that Baii did not use technology to present the images, they followed the history of Isilia up to the arrival of the ark. Chloe mentioned the striking similarities between the woman who teleported the Riyneans and Ava, but Ava told her they had a theory about that and would tell her later.

"It was on Isilia we learned the Farisee were not monsters and that Hebre were also refugees," Harry added when Baii closed the diorama. "Laurel had lots of theories after she deciphered the stone from the archives, but she needed all the pieces. I don't think she has them, even now."

"Where do you fit in, Darlen?" Eli asked.

Darlen puffed up his pride a little. "It seems I'm not so bad after all. The original Magen Bearers were part of a race called the Sons of David. I don't know who David was; we never found that out, but some of them preserved the Magen star, and it was the star that opened the Eye of Sheerguhd to them. Many of these Sons of David turned against the masters."

"That sounds ominous," Eli laughed. "The Eye of Sheerguhd?"

"Supposedly, there is only one universe," Ava told him, "and what the masters called kingdoms exist within dimensions. The Transcender, Sheerguhd, is a portal that crosses between those dimensions and can only be accessed by a Magen Bearer."

"That's right," Darlen said smugly. "Without me, humans are stuck where they are."

"I'm a Soul Monger too," Scarlett chimed in.

"That you are, sweetheart." Darlen pulled her onto his knee.

"Scarlett's a Soul Monger?" Chloe believed it was solely a male domain. "I remember you can only reproduce with a whole soul; that's why you were the only one left since the League blocked access to the Transcender."

Darlen nodded. "Helen was a whole soul, but it's not necessary to produce a Soul Monger. The child has to take the traits of the Sons of David. At least that's what we learned on Eden."

"Okay," Chloe replied, "so where is this star your supposed to be protecting?"

"It's lodged in my ribs. When I die, it will go to Scarlett."

Eli tried to work out how anyone could swallow a star.

There had to be an explanation.

"Did you swallow it?"

"Nope, I put it there."

"He's got another one," Harry said. "He took it from a Magen Bearer."

"Would it work on someone else?"

"Do you mean on a whole soul?" Darlen hadn't thought about it. "It might, although we don't know if whole souls and Soul Mongers have a shared ancestry from before Eden."

Chloe's eyes sparkled with excitement. "This just gets better and better!" The information was not complete, but it was fascinating, and she wished she'd thrown caution to the wind and gone with them.

"Ava, can you tell us how whole souls began?" she said eagerly. "We can go into the war later, perhaps when Laurel feels better."

Ava related the story of the imps, the chaos they brought and the aurora that appeared over Eden, heralding the Hebre entities' arrival. She tried to give Chloe and Eli as much information as possible, hoping to take the burden from Laurel.

"Why did the nebula entities, the Hebre, feel compelled to come and help the Edensai? What drove them?" To Eli, it seemed a remarkable act of charity.

"Hebre has never communicated with us directly," Ava responded, "so we don't know. But we do know our abilities are stronger as we get closer to the nebula. At the moment, it's only Mom who can do the Time manipulation."

"And this spaceborne virus," Eli continued, "this Lilith virus, how come it gave the imps the extra ribs and vertebrae? Do viruses add bones?"

"Again, we don't know the origin of that virus."

Eli shook his head. "I'm warming to this Lilith, the goddess theory."

"You said you studied the corpses of the masters, Harry," Chloe said, "and the remains of a female?"

"Yes. We preserved them for further study. They're on the ship. We also recovered one of their gestational sacs from the flood. The mate survived, and we have tissue samples, but we left the female with the Farisee."

"Then you should let our scientists look at them!" Chloe exclaimed. "They are experts in this field. You wouldn't believe how many microorganisms barrage the shield. They're always on the lookout, and they have remarkably advanced technology. They'd love a mystery like this!"

Harry loved the idea of further insight if it were possible and agreed enthusiastically to Chloe's suggestion. "That would be great," he said. "The female isn't complete, but the two males are intact. Laurel and I were interested from a scientific point of view as much as to discover clues as to her ancestors."

"Oh," Chloe said, puzzled. "Are they different then? Doesn't she come from the imps, like us?"

Ava couldn't really enlighten Chloe. If her mother was still trying to make sense of it, it wasn't any easier for the rest of them. "There seems to be a kind of relationship between her and the masters' origins. Whole souls began with the imps, so their ancestry as humans is from the Edensai. Mom isn't the same. Apparently, she was never born of the Edensai."

Chloe and Eli threw each other a look of bewilderment; they saw the others had come to terms with the conundrum, but as it was new to them, there had to be more to it. Naturally, they had heaps of questions, but really, it would only be Laurel who could answer. They guessed they had to be patient.

Chloe stood up. "Do you think your mum would be up for a little trip…? She hesitated, "With just Eli and me, if that's okay? We won't pester her with questions."

Ava thought it was a splendid idea and went to check on Laurel, now lying on her back wide awake, her face still blotchy from crying.

"Harry was going to come and see you, but I guess he thought better of it."

"I'm glad he didn't," Laurel sniffed, "I would have barked at him. I just needed a few minutes alone."

"Did you hear anything we said?" Ava asked.

"No, honey." Laurel sat up. "My mind was closed. I'm sorry I had to leave, I just felt overwhelmed with the enormity of it all. It was different while we were living it, but now, looking back…" She pushed her hair from her face, sticky with dried tears, and looked up at her daughter. "I just want to leave it behind, not keep explaining it. It's not just the events; it's the personal cost; talking about it is just a reminder. I made huge decisions, and so many people have died. I feel like I don't want to give any of it air."

Ava took her mother's hands in hers. "And many

people were saved. Don't forget, the people who remained on Eden volunteered to stay. They knew their death would surely come after resistance to the masters. As Abel said, better by Hebre's hand than the masters."

"I know all that, Ava, and it sounds logical and justified. I can't count how many people I've killed since I entered the Gartryan war."

"All low lifes, except for those on Eden."

Laurel nodded. "We are justified in defence of freedom, but it still makes us killers. And do you know?" Laurel wriggled to the edge of the bed and stood, "It comes so easily to me."

Ava watched her mother adjust her clothes and tidy her hair. She didn't consider her a natural killer, but she was naturally protective. It was just so many people had got in her way while she was protecting, and no decent person would casually engage in the loss of thousands of innocent lives, even if it was in sacrifice to save others. It would be a hard decision.

"Chloe suggested you go for a short trip with her and Eli. Are you up to it?"

"I'm up to it," Laurel smiled weakly. "I just had a crazy moment. I've been so desperate to see Chloe and Eli; I didn't want to relive the horror. I just wanted it all to go away."

"We've given them some information, and Chloe has promised not to bombard you with questions," Ava assured her. "We're all going out to the boardwalk area to have a look around. There's a guide coming to collect us."

Chloe sensed Laurel's fragility, and she believed she knew the ideal place for her to feel at ease, to tell or not tell her story as she pleased. They could access Eli's farm via the holographic portals, which were quite rough on the nervous systems of the uninitiated, so Chloe and Eli decided the long route would give Laurel some fresh air, sunshine, blue skies, views of the wildlife and natural beauty of the planet and perhaps soothe her soul. Chloe told Harry not to expect them back too early and that Asde would be collecting them all to go to their home for the evening.

This was indeed a beautiful world. Unspoilt, natural and unpolluted. The transport passed over steep cliffs and pinnacles, swooped into deep gorges, and crossed wide grass prairies. It all reminded Laurel of home, and she allowed herself to smile at the irony because home these days seemed to be a ship flying through space. Chloe saw the smile and decided it might be a good time to apologise.

"I didn't mean to pressure you. I was a bit too excited."

Laurel reached out and squeezed her hand. "You didn't pressure me. When we left Eden, the Transcender snapped us up like a snack—it was over in seconds, and we were churned out into Isilian space, so I guess the masters and their cruelty, the rebellion, and all the carnage is still too raw for me. Ava handles things better."

"We agreed not to ask questions," Eli said. "You've had a busy few years, and we don't expect you to condense all those experiences into a single session of explanations."

"I expected that of myself," Laurel said. "It wasn't you, but there is something I need to know. Eli, the message on the beacon, you used the word 'deliverance'. Why?"

Eli gave her a blank look. "Did I? I don't remember that. Perhaps it was a psychic link, but you know that's never been a particularly strong point of mine."

"I'd heard the word applied to us before, or sometimes just 'deliverers'. The Edensai called us that, too. I believed that tying in the stone document from the League archive with the bible, or at least the Old Testament, I was getting somewhere. The Edensai's religious records were recorded on a similar stone that could only be opened by a Hebre."

"That's interesting," Eli said, willing Laurel to expand on the subject but not wanting to push her. Then she found herself telling them anyway, in a conversational tone that just seemed to flow. "It went on the original arks, so it wasn't in the Edensai's possession, but I didn't need to read it. One of the Edensai told me it was a narrative of the history, the traditions and laws of the Edensai."

"Apart from the Farisee, were all the races human?" Chloe asked, drawing a cautioning glare from Eli. Chloe flinched; she'd already forgotten not to ask questions.

Laurel nodded. "I think the Riynea have more evolved brains. That's why most of them can manifest objects. They're lovely people, although we suspected one of them of selling us out to the masters."

Chloe and Eli were horrified. "You're kidding!" Chloe exclaimed. "You were there to help!"

"Well, they had leverage over him. Believe me, that wasn't restricted to League space, but it turns out that while he did tell them about me," Laurel said, "he didn't mention Ava or Darlen, nor Scarlett, although he recognised what she was. Ava and I were uncannily similar in appearance to two women who organised the first evacuation of Eden."

Chloe thought back to the diorama from earlier. "Hebre. Ava told us about them and the imps. Ava looks like the woman who brought people from the ark."

"Yes, we think it's probable that all whole souls are descended from Hebre."

"Harry mentioned you travelled back in time," Eli said. "How did that work if you didn't know at that point you could manipulate it?"

"I haven't mastered it, Eli," Laurel confessed. "I don't even know for sure how it works. An example of that is how you two ended up older than me!"

"A superhero who wonders how her superpowers work?" Eli laughed.

Laurel didn't think of her abilities as superpowers. "If I could have chosen superpowers," she said in all seriousness, "I would have given myself the ability to stop wars."

"The masters weren't after wars, though, were they," Chloe said. "They were just devils."

Laurel smiled drily. "Not to look at. They were exquisite, but that's where their beauty ended. Everything else about them was rotten, evil. Their faces turned demonic when they became angry."

Laurel suddenly realised what was going on. "I'm talking! You two are very clever!"

Eli chuckled. "We planned to show you the countryside, have a picnic, show you a market-town and take you to my home. That was the extent of our plan!"

"You tell us what you want in your own time," Chloe

added, even though she was amazed by what she heard and desperate to hear more.

It felt right, to be talking, and Laurel couldn't understand why earlier she felt so overwhelmed, not when she was among people who cared about her. Out here, in the fresh air, watching the passing wild landscape, the beauty of the waterfalls and the blue-hazed mountains, she felt her tension lifting. Inhaling deeply, she breathed in that same citrusy note of nature from when the Canaa first landed. It was pleasant and welcoming.

"Homeworld is a good name for this planet," she said, turning her head to take in all angles of the view. She saw a herd of something she didn't recognise in the distance, moving together, heads bent to the grass. "Do they eat animals here?"

Chloe nodded. "But there's no hunting. The government regulates meat, and there are specialised markets; we'll take you to one today. Right now though…" the transport stopped at her word, and lowered to the ground, "we're going to have the picnic we promised."

The three friends climbed down into a field covered with pink flowers that made a carpet of cherry-blossom-coloured blooms as far as the eye could see. Here, they collected soft berries and a few of the pink flowers, which had large, spongy centres, similar in taste to sugary cinnamon that contrasted sharply with their dry and bitter leaves. Chloe assured Laurel these flowers were widely consumed solely for that contrast. A nearby stream carried water down from the mountains, filtered through many layers of rocks on its journey, and tasted pure and fresh. It was magnificent. Laurel missed fresh food and water; hydroponics on the Canaa was adequate but with little variety. Eating and drinking directly from nature, out in the wilderness like this, was wonderfully freeing, filling her with energy and a desire to raise her arms and spin in a circle or run through the grass, making whooping noises. So that's what she did, without a hint of self-consciousness and to the amusement of Eli and Chloe. Laurel felt she could run for miles but stopped in panic when she startled a hairy something the size of a dog. It snarled at her, not appreciating the antics of the wild human. Laurel froze.

Eli rushed across and shooed the animal away. "Would it have bitten me?" Laurel asked, disappointed she'd gotten off on the wrong foot with the local wildlife.

"It's not likely," Eli said, "they're quite used to people, but it is wild, and any animal who feels under threat might react. Some of your moves were pretty spectacular!" he added with a grin.

Laurel watched the animal stop and sniff the air, making sure they weren't following. "I didn't mean to startle it."

Eli pointed to the foothills. "Only a few animals wander down here. There are others higher up, but most are fairly docile. The government regulates their breeding so it doesn't get out of control, and they don't have to compete for food. You'll be interested to know that animals also come under the mantle of care of a physician."

Laurel thought that would be okay; she loved animals if they didn't bite. She shielded her eyes from the sun and looked towards the mountains. "It's beautiful here, Eli, so restful."

"That's why we stay," he said. "It's not just because we don't have a space-worthy ship, not because we loved our previous lives, but because, for us, this is where the grass is greener."

Laurel realised she'd been remiss in asking about Eli's enormous family. "Do your children ever ask about your life? Do they ever wish they could explore the galaxy like their father did?"

Eli tilted his head. "Hmm, not that they've ever mentioned, but most of them were born here and all of them educated in this culture. Anyway," he shrugged, "it's all history, and I don't even think about it that much anymore."

"You've only seen a tiny part of the planet and its technology," Chloe said as they arrived back at the transport. "And seen so little of its culture. There is so much more to explore."

As Eli promised, they visited a market on the outskirts of one of the cities. Produce was sold from private hovering pallets and set up much like the farmers' markets Laurel had seen on the many planets where private industry was encouraged. The market had a variety of government-approved meats presented to suit every buyer. No-one could buy products for storage; they had to be for immediate consumption or use in the dispensers. Laurel still couldn't bring herself to eat meat, but other merchants were purveyors of exotic sweetmeats and succulent plants far more suited to Laurel's food preferences.

Eli secured a quantity for her to try and some to take home to his family. "We don't have any currency here," he explained, turning his wrist over to reveal an easily missable electronic tracker, "but purchases are recorded. These purveyors cultivate and harvest the produce, with a portion or a tithe secured by the government. The produce on my farm never goes to the markets; it is part of a government initiative that provides a quantity of basic food to every individual to ensure correct nutritional balance."

They spent a pleasant hour wandering the market. Dressed in local garb, Laurel looked like everyone else, and no-one paid her any mind. On a couple of occasions where a vendor spoke to her, Chloe quickly jumped in and answered. Laurel had quite an ear for languages and quickly knew language on Homeworld would present no difficulties.

During the last part of their trip, Chloe and Eli spoke a little about the society to which they now belonged. Laurel learned that every citizen was expected to have at least one child; that Eli had fourteen was a source of curiosity to those on Homeworld who knew him. Among those fourteen children were two sets of twins. Chloe and Asde had the requisite one child, Karen, named after Chloe's mother. There was no formal legal commitment between couples, but responsibility for a child remained squarely with the biological parents. Childcare was accessible for a parent who did not wish to avail themselves of the allowed antenatal and postnatal workfree periods before returning to their professions or trades. Children attended schools according to their age, and a child had to live at home with one or both of its parents until its majority, which was when it was deemed mature enough to live independently. Laurel supposed Scarlett would go to school if they stayed.

"Do you have rebellious teenagers?" she asked, not very seriously.

"We sure do, but not like the imps," Eli grinned. "The government has great ways of channelling energy. They come good."

"Sounds like you have personal experience."

"I do," he sighed. "All mine were rebels, but I'm very proud of them. They've done well; you'll get to know them all."

Eli explained Homeworld had villages and densely populated outlying areas within reach of the city environs. Most people who lived in these areas, even primary producers like him, often had a second home on their farm. Usually, when people wished to visit the remote areas, they would move via the portals, which he assured Laurel would get to experience later, but it required acclimatisation and could not be explored until that had taken place. Eli said he loved the journey to the farm, and he felt he missed out when he travelled via the portal.

The farm sat nestled in a wide, green valley between two low bluffs. Eli and Ru grew specific plants—Laurel could only describe them as carrots—a gangly grey root vegetable that wriggled for a few moments after harvesting. Eli demonstrated, completely freaking Laurel out, despite his assurance it was not sentient. He also ran an orchard of shady fruit trees laid out in neat rows, tended by people who all knew and obviously liked and respected him.

Eli still performed manual work on the farm, but at his age, he was expected to scale back his physical involvement and have more leisure. He confided in Laurel he had little use for recreation, his youngest twins were still school age, and they kept him and Ru busy enough.

Ru, Eli and the twins lived in the city closest to the farm. Ru had changed little, still pretty and slight, even though so many pregnancies had thickened her waistline, plumping her up around the middle. She was delighted to see Laurel and welcomed her with open arms. And she was still an excellent cook. Laurel remembered her beach barbecues fondly on Leyis, where they first met her, and Ru remembered even now that Laurel didn't eat meat and managed to accommodate. One set of twins, both boys aged fourteen, arrived home early, curious to see the "off-worlders". Eli's oldest son Jacob, who had only been a toddler when Laurel left, was a tall, good-looking man who worked in administration within the government area of civil engineering. He had a son who lived with the child's mother. Two more of Eli and Ru's sons also visited, and a daughter and her partner, along with their own small daughter, also joined the party.

Laurel didn't feel overwhelmed now, she'd purged those feelings out in the cherry-blossom field, but she felt glad no-one asked her questions and that they allowed her to satisfy some of her curiosity about Homeworld. She discovered laziness and disloyalty were considered reprehensible, that disabilities were carefully supported, and those affected were given every opportunity to contribute. Serious illness was treated, but the government advocated euthanasia as a last resort. Food waste, poor personal hygiene, littering, and poor diet was frowned upon. Exercise, productivity, availing oneself of every form of recreation possible, and community engagement was encouraged. Laurel imagined Darlen would see this society as rigid and would have trouble conforming.

"Don't worry," Chloe told Laurel, reading her thoughts. *"Reclusivity also has a place. We're not following you around to see what you're doing."*

Observing the interaction of Eli's family, the happy chatter between themselves when the focus shifted from her, Laurel felt at peace. Perhaps a society that does take an interest in the people, even if it does direct them to a certain extent while allowing for individuality, might be just what she needs. For so long, it had been her responsibility, go here, do that, and even though the others made decisions too, she invariably felt she was the spokesperson for them all.

Later, meeting up with Harry, she could see his experience had also been positive. He'd learned about the wildlife, but without the close encounter Laurel had, which made him roar with laughter. He'd explored the portals, albeit from a distance, and he also caught up with Asde. Harry beamed as he related his day, a sign Laurel knew he was being converted to the lifestyle here, even if it would only be for a while.

"I feel quite at home," he smiled, then whispered, "Darlen thinks it's a dictatorship."

"It's very structured," Laurel nodded, "and it does track its citizens, at least in purchases, so I guess whoever does the tracking knows your movements. That said, it provides for its people, and it's a mix of advanced technology and the rustic." She thought about the fantastic landscape she'd seen that day. "I saw herds of animals and heaps of edible plants; the planet has such a wild feel about it, yet the cities are neat and ordered, and no-one seems to mind that the only windows in their homes look to the sky."

"I liked the view from your apartment on Mentelci," Harry said, sighing with nostalgia. "Do you remember that great big window seat looking out over the galleria?"

How could she forget? Laurel spent a lot of time in thought on that window seat. "I loved that view, too, but for most of the last, however many years, our view from the window has been either widespeed or space. I'm used to not having a view. I can live without one."

Asde had seen Laurel arrive but gave her a moment to say "hello" to Harry. Now he approached. Laurel would have recognised him in any corner of the galaxy. Still tall, still boyishly handsome, he practically lifted her from the ground in a bear hug.

"I can't believe this day finally came," he exclaimed. "Chloe was positive you'd find us." He stepped back and appraised her. "She said you hadn't aged and she's right; you don't look much older than Ava."

"A result of stasis and variance," Laurel grinned. "But if I had known then what I know now, variance would never have happened."

Asde smiled his familiar, infectious grin. "Harry told me. You've had incredible adventures, and I'm a little envious. It took me a while to settle here because I'd always had so much freedom. Once the government offered me a job, and Karen came along, things just fell into place."

"Will we meet Karen soon?"

"Absolutely!" Asde said delightedly. "We were waiting for you to come back from your trip to Eli's farm. I took over from the guide today to show everyone around; now we're going to our home for dinner. I hope you don't mind; the Presidents made the journey to meet you."

Laurel didn't mind. She was almost surprised she and the others were allowed so much freedom after only a day. "I suppose they want to make sure that if we leave, we won't divulge your whereabouts."

"Something like that," Asde said with a tiny dip of his head, "but they also want to know about you. They seldom leave the Presidential residence, but visitors from off-world? That's quite an event! They were apprehensive about us when we arrived, so as you can see, we've smoothed the way!"

Asde and Chloe's daughter, Karen, was a copy of Chloe, small and fair with the same heart-shaped face. Karen's little girl, Lara, was yet another copy of her mother and grandmother, but neither of them bore any resemblance to Asde, something he ruefully pointed out himself. Baii manifested lizards to amuse the two children.

Chloe smiled, not hiding a note of envy. "That is one useful skill."

"Not if you want to eat what you manifest," Laurel laughed, flicking a glance towards Darlen, sitting alone and clearly not wanting to be part of the gathering. "Darlen misses Big Macs; I can manifest them because I know what they look like, and what I manifest can be chewed, but as I don't know what they taste like, they end up bland. I can't even get an approximation of taste from Darlen's thoughts. I would have to know what is in it and the taste to manifest fully. I've never had one."

"I have," Chloe said brightly. "I remember them, with gherkins and cheese, and they were delicious. I could programme something that comes close. It might be a treat for him if he's homesick for McDonald's."

"Only since we entered League space all those years ago," Laurel grinned. If Chloe could pull this off, it might wipe the glum look from Darlen's face.

"I'll see what I can do," Chloe said as she headed for the food dispenser.

The Presidents arrived in time for a meal they didn't recognise. Chloe did some to-ing and fro-ing with the dispenser and performed a few taste tests before producing a dish she believed might just satisfy Darlen's craving.

It did, and the offering amused everyone else, even the two Presidents, who turned out to be very affable and ate heartily. Darlen couldn't believe his luck, a gadget that made Big Macs. He said laughingly that he was in heaven, and his mood lifted, but Laurel doubted that when Darlen found himself alone later, that was what he really felt.

The Presidents were not related to each other but were obligated to remain together in almost everything they did apart from private ablutions and sleeping. They had to have similar mindsets, be in accord with decisions and be wholly for the people's benefit. There were four billion individuals on this planet they told the newcomers, and there was no room for indecision or favour. The Presidents served everybody's best interests; then hastened to add that the people did not pander to the Presidents' interests. Laurel took this to mean they discouraged sycophants.

"Is this a democracy?" Harry asked.

"Not for the Presidency," Buran Monk, the male half of the Presidency, advised. "On Homeworld, Presidents are bred to serve the people. From childhood, we are trained in our purpose. We have no other life. No other needs. Just to be available to those we serve," he concluded with a small bow.

Taran Monk took up where Buran left off. A lively woman in her forties, who, despite Buran saying they had no needs, appeared to be very individual in her style of clothing, the clashing colours of which reflected in her dark skin. She also seemed unable to stop eating.

"Elections are held for local government officials," she said, picking delicately at the bread while she spoke. "When that official is no longer able to serve or wishes to change profession, then the city will conduct proposals of office. Buran and I will approve those proposed, and the candidates are put forward for election. Each governor answers to us."

Darlen asked if they ever found it tedious just to be presidents and not experience what their people experienced.

Taran laughed loudly. "Our nature is controlled. It is never tedious for us."

"*Puppets*," Baii sent to Ava, first checking Laurel's

attention was engaged elsewhere.

"No, figureheads, I think, but created in such a way they don't have to follow their individual desires."

"Genetically modified?"

"I think so."

"I wonder how many other people here are genetically modified?"

"I don't get anything but sincerity. You're reading too much into it."

"I can't read that much from them at all. The others, Chloe, Asde, Eli, they don't close their minds, and I can see they're perfectly happy with the way things are."

"What are you suggesting?"

"Nothing."

"Yes, you are. You're suggesting they're brainwashed."

"Ava, I'm not, but this is a haven for people who have nowhere else they want to be. And that's because they're not allowed to make discoveries. That's not you. And that's not me either anymore."

"Mom is thinking of staying, at least for a while."

"I know. Let's not talk about it now."

The Presidents stayed until it was clear their new arrivals were too tired to continue with questions; questions the Presidents were happy to answer. They also had no idea Laurel, Ava and Baii were in their minds, checking for subterfuge or deception. Laurel guessed there was some personality modification, but that was all. Besides that, Laurel only read pride in their society.

"I loved being with Chloe and Eli today," Laurel said to Harry when they were finally alone. "Seeing Asde, meeting Karen and her child, Ru and most of Eli's children, it's been amazing." She sighed. "I feel ashamed I had that meltdown. After all we've been through, you'd think I would have had more guts. The history of the whole souls belongs to Eli and Chloe too."

"Don't beat yourself up, Laurel," Harry said. "Ava gave them the lowdown on the imps and some information on the masters. They completely understood, and those few hours out in the countryside clearly did you a world of good. Chloe said you did talk about the masters, though."

"Some, but I suppose the rest will unfold as we get reacquainted."

"Baii and Darlen were talking," Harry told her. "Baii has a few reservations about this place as well."

Laurel shrugged. "Eli and Chloe were fleeing persecution, so safety for them, and in Eli's case, his family, may have been the overarching appeal of a society like this. Baii probably doesn't want to get stuck in one place too long this early in his spacegoing career. No decisions have been made; he knows that."

"We still have the Canaa," Harry reminded her, "unless Darlen leaves while we're still making up our minds."

"He wouldn't do that. Besides, they won't let him. He can't cloak the ship."

"They might give him a cloak."

"And advertise their technology around the universe?" Laurel said. "I doubt it. I expected they've waited a long time to be forgotten by the neighbouring systems."

"Then he would need Ava." Harry waited for Laurel's response, then added quietly, "or you."

Laurel hesitated. On the face of it, it seemed like a wonderful place, but if Baii and Darlen weren't happy… did she want to be stranded here? "Darlen won't leave, Harry," she said firmly, but in her heart, she wasn't so sure.

CHAPTER FORTY _

Chloe and Laurel strolled together in one of the large parks that circled each cliff city like a moat. Shady trees formed a sweeping avenue, and the area was set to lawn and garden beds. The flowers were of the non-edible type, grown purely for their beauty and intense colours, their perfume filling the air with refreshing lemon and peppermint notes.

"Where did the entity go when Helen died," Chloe asked. She'd been very fond of Helen, and news of her death had saddened her, so Laurel had been filling Chloe in on the events that led up to the tragedy.

"Back to the nebula," Laurel answered with absolute certainty. "It's their home."

"I wonder what motivated them to go and inhabit the imps? It's quite a mystery."

"Perhaps they've got a history with the Edensai we know nothing of, but you're right," Laurel agreed. "It is a mystery."

"I've never seen anyone with clear eyes on Earth. The virus couldn't have made it that far."

"It doesn't look like it," Laurel said. "Some viruses become dormant, and some burn themselves out. Others just seem to vanish. Harry said he knew of ancient reports of clear-eyed, stillborn babies in the League."

Chloe pondered privately for a moment how Hebre procreated once they got to Earth, echoing the question Laurel had asked again and again. Laurel heard her thoughts.

"I don't know," Laurel admitted aloud. "What I do know is that the Soul Monger's purpose was to return the Hebre close to the nebula and not for the purposes of slavery."

"They must need to be close to the nebula when they die."

"That's my theory. And I think they keep on inhabiting bodies until a Soul Monger picks them up, then they honour the life they've taken over until the body dies."

"So, how come you look like Judith?"

"Fascinating, isn't it?" Laurel grinned. "And Ava is the image of Esther. At this moment, we don't know why; all we can come up with is that we are direct descendants."

"I'm not so sure I like mystery," Chloe said, linking her arm through Laurel's. "I reckon our scientists are the best bet to unravel it. Darlen and Harry are going to transport the remains of the masters and the half-eaten female to the science institute for forensics. They'll also examine the cells of the young mate you rescued and will doubtless want to check us as well. You know, make comparisons. I can't believe I don't come from my parent's family, that I'm something else."

"I know how you feel. Apparently, Judith appeared from virtually nowhere. At least the imps had families that could identify them. Judith didn't."

"It might turn out that you came from the imps too.

We don't know for sure you're from Menwora, and who knows, we might all carry some of our Earth parent's DNA. I'm wondering why the whole souls allowed themselves to become slaves. Didn't they remember their heritage?"

"Did you remember?" Laurel asked. "I didn't."

"Where does this leave all the doctrines on Earth that preach gods and souls and the bible?"

Laurel gave a cynical laugh. "The same place it always did, open to interpretation. My views haven't changed. I still don't believe in gods of any kind, but I do find myself thinking about being created by something that has the power to restore life. Judith witnessed the casting out of the resurrected Benjamin and the Sons of David who followed him. Then she popped up on Eden, centuries later, with my face."

"Harry and Ava told us about the flood," Chloe said. "We asked heaps of questions, but he couldn't tell us what happened on the masters' ship just before it exploded, but he did tell us about the man who had the device implanted inside him."

Laurel didn't want to simplify it, that would diminish Abel's sacrifice, nor did she wish to make her part sound grand or noble, but no matter what she said, it wasn't just what she witnessed, it was what she felt, and she could only communicate those feelings if she let Chloe into her mind. She didn't feel ready for that. In the end, she decided on a summary.

"I fought a few masters and even managed to knock one or two down," she said, "but they have this liquid 'bane' that they spit out…" Chloe nodded. She'd heard about it from the others, the stench and its role in the barbaric breeding practices of the masters. "It paralysed me," Laurel continued. "The masters were confused because it couldn't paralyse Judith, who they knew was one of their race. I sensed Harry on the ship, his life signs were failing, and the ship was lurching about—" She made tossing movements with her hands. "Darlen hopped in to take Harry, then Abel appeared in his place. Abel played the part of a repentant servant for a few moments; then the explosion came; Time slowed, and I found myself in space in Ava's arms with pieces of annihilated masters and their ship all around. What was left had already begun to fall to the planet and…"

"Wait," Chloe stopped her. "In space? In Ava's arms? Harry left that bit out. And how did Abel get on the ship?"

Poor Chloe was just getting snippets of confusing information. "Chloe," Laurel said, "Ava has teleporting abilities. She got Abel onto the ship."

Too stunned to interrupt, Chloe let Laurel continue without another comment.

"We can survive in space," Laurel explained. "The entity protects us by extending out from our bodies. I don't know how long the effect lasts, and I'm not keen to test it, but I suppose if the entity is space dwelling, it knows what it's capable of."

When she'd finished, Chloe stood in silence, just blinking in amazement. "I must admit," she squeaked, then cleared her throat, "that's…unbelievable! I saw a bluish colour come from my hands the first time I cloaked a ship. That was the entity? I thought it was odd, but I didn't see it again. I don't think it happened to Eli."

"I've given you a condensed version of the events, Chloe. We can talk about it at length later with Ava, and she can tell you all about her teleporting abilities."

"I haven't cultivated my skills since I've been here," Chloe confessed. "I just haven't found any need for them. I can still run fast, and I do need that in my job."

"There are compensations. You live a peaceful life."

Chloe smiled. "I do, and this place is ideal for anyone who wants that, but there is excitement to be found if you're looking. For people like Darlen…" she looked steadily at Laurel, the subject of Darlen clearly one of concern, "He has never grown roots anywhere. He might feel cloistered here."

"He'll stay while we stay," Laurel said, convincingly she hoped. "Scarlett would be devastated if they left us behind."

But Chloe didn't look convinced. "Scarlett is like him, Laurel, she would adapt if they left, and don't forget she is a Soul Monger, perhaps she will want to carry on the Soul Monger traditions, but this time for the right reasons. There are probably still whole souls on Earth waiting to return to the nebula. Laurel, I must ask, do you still see a lucency on people's shoulders or their breastbone like we did in the League?"

Laurel shook her head. "Not for ages."

"Me either," Chloe admitted. "When we arrived here, I looked for it but…nothing. It was probably why we knew the distinction between half and quarter souls was nonsense. Why did we see it do you suppose?"

"The half soul, quarter soul thing was steeped in tradition. We were new, still impressionable and our skills absolutely not honed so it was easy for us to respond to suggestion. If you remember, we all gave it the same manifestations. It was something Harry's dad had a problem with too. It seems some things we discover on our own, but with other's we need to be told, and still others, see where the entity takes us. If it takes us at all. The human side of us still exerts itself and serves to disconcert. That's my experience."

Chloe remembered Laurel's earlier comment. "You said you only found you could hide a ship when someone told you that you could."

"That's true. I might have continued in ignorance otherwise. Ava discovered her teleporting skill when it became a necessity, just like you discovered you could cloak a ship when you left the League. The entities do come to our rescue if there's a need."

"Like in manipulating time?"

"That was trickier," Laurel said. "In the nebula, to avoid being influenced by the other's expectations, I had to get them to go to sleep. There was too much energy from their ideas about Time, and it was an interference. I needed to be where Time wasn't happening, and they were all too busy measuring it."

"So, how did you manipulate Time on the masters' ship?"

"I'm sure that was the entity demonstrating the ability to me," Laurel said. "A testimony. That it is all possible. If I only allow myself to believe."

"Are you sure?"

"Yes." Laurel was convinced of it. "I'm sure."

Within a week of their arrival, the authorities assessed Laurel and Harry as suitable to work as adjunct physicians to animals. They were advised that human medicine would come as they gained knowledge of the extensive technology involved. Laurel didn't mind the work as they spent considerable time out in the glorious wilderness, but Harry found the adjustment difficult. He came to dread the outreach assignments and almost hoped there would be a human epidemic or outbreak of something or other that would allow him to flex his medical muscles among real people.

Meanwhile, Darlen had refused accommodation and insisted he remained on the Canaa. He also asked for Mer to be reactivated. Tavis patiently explained that while they would grant his wish, the ship would have to be isolated. Therefore, the Canaa was taken to an outlying part of Eli's farm, but still, Darlen wasn't happy. Homeworld engineers fitted a disruptor to the engine to ensure he didn't attempt to leave the planet without their knowledge and Mer was equipped with a proximity restraining module to stop him from leaving the immediate vicinity of the ship. In Darlen's eyes, Homeworld was a prison.

Scarlett began school and lived on the Canaa, but she missed Laurel and Harry desperately. Ava also attended school, mainly to learn the language, but Baii was asked to acquaint himself with the planet's horticulture. Baii and Ava were assigned a suite in the same domicile complex as Laurel and Harry, and even though Laurel loved being reunited with Chloe and Eli, after three months, she knew this new life wasn't working. A worrying development was when a request to untether the Canaa so they might visit Marcel had become "lost" in the system.

Exasperated by the delays, Baii finally voiced his concerns.

"What are we doing here?" He'd waited until he, Ava, Laurel and Harry were alone, a circumstance he noted was becoming increasingly rare. He felt as though they were being watched, and Chloe's constant presence was constraining. He also worried that Darlen never left the Canaa. Baii didn't want to point the finger or make accusations, but it wasn't his idea to stay, and it seemed that leaving would not be made easy.

"Scarlett hates going to school," he said, an observation made by the others as well. "She's unhappy. Truthfully, Laurel, what can she learn that you can't teach her? Is this where you expect her to live out her life?"

"Baii's right," Harry said glumly. "It's not working. At least on Isilia, we can practice our profession, and we'd be close to Marcel. The living situation as it stands on the Canaa is unhealthy for Scarlett, and Darlen won't even speak to Eli."

Laurel couldn't deny it, her family were scattered, and Darlen and Scarlett's misery weighed on her mind. They'd been happy to see Chloe and Eli again, and they loved the advanced technology with the amazing portals that led to other parts of the planet and all the wild scenery, but emotionally, none of them felt any connection to this world. It wasn't home, and Laurel knew that had Tavis not "lost" their request to visit Marcel, they would have left and never returned.

"They said we could leave anytime we like, but I don't think they'll let us, not even if we cloak the ship," Ava said.

Laurel agreed. "I don't want us to blast our way out. Perhaps we should speak to Chloe." She moved to the internal comms but found her way barred by Baii.

"No, Laurel," he said, one hand held up in an unmistakable "stop". "Not Chloe. Let's go and see Darlen."

Baii made no attempt to share why he was against telling Chloe, and Laurel was quite prepared to ignore him, but a moment later, Chloe commed through.

"Laurel," she said, "can you all meet me at the laboratories? The researchers have news."

CHAPTER FORTY-ONE _

Chloe met them at the entrance of the laboratory. "Is it good news?" Laurel asked.

"I don't know," Chloe answered. "Eli wanted to know the same thing. Darlen is coming, but he made a fuss about it; he still hasn't gotten over all the genetic profiling they did on us."

"It was for a good cause…" Laurel would have said more, but Chloe seemed preoccupied and had already turned away before Laurel finished speaking. Darlen, Eli and Scarlett arrived quickly, using a portal rather than a transport. Scarlett was irritated, catching her father's mood, but she was glad to see the others and ran into Laurel's arms. They'd last seen each other only a few days before, but Laurel noted Scarlett's hair looked unbrushed and her clothing grubby. She seemed to be moving away from her mother's fastidiousness about her appearance and becoming more like Darlen, who looked to have regressed more to his old ways every time Laurel saw him.

A technician greeted them and led the way to the science team dealing with their research. The "team" consisted of two people; Marly, a dour-faced, impatient-looking woman with one watery blue eye that appraised them all in one glance. Her other eye was hidden behind a flat eyepiece that emitted data that extended about ten centimetres from her face. She was what Laurel would have described as the picture of a mad scientist. Her colleague, younger but no less strange in his demeanour and with a burning zeal in his eyes, introduced himself as Eristal. He immediately busied himself in arranging seats in a neat semicircle for his visitors, not allowing them to sit until he had made sure the semicircle measurements were exact. He seated himself between the two last seats of the semicircle, a perfectly measured distance between.

"What we discovered was remarkable", came Eristal's opening address. His eyes bulged, and his smile, wide and forced, treated them to a view of the flaps of skin on the inside of his cheeks. He shifted a little in his seat. "Completely remarkable. We," he gestured at Marly, "have never seen specimens like these, at least specimens that told such a story." He stared at his visitors long enough for his broad smile to turn creepy, then with a twitch of his head, opened a raft of data for them to view. The detailed imaging and information on the masters' and the half-eaten female's remains were spectacular, far beyond anything offered by the most sophisticated pandroscope. Laurel and Harry realised why they weren't let loose on the technology. As physicians, they had little to offer this society. These people knew more about the human body than any other race they'd ever encountered.

Eristal swept an image of a cell into view. "Do you know what this is?" he said as if speaking to a room full of pre-schoolers.

"It's a cell," Harry said, ignoring the man's condescension, "with characteristics I've never seen before. It's very detailed. Is it human?"

Eristal nodded. "It is an ancestral cell. The first of this race would have been tall, physically strong and highly defensive. It has some peculiarities; for example, the resulting human's saliva would contain a mild neuromuscular blocking agent, possibly a feature designed to subdue prey or a mate; this characteristic does occur naturally in nature but not usually in humans." Eristal pointed at Darlen. "The cell belongs to him…"

"I have a complete genetic profile on Darlen," Harry said. "None of it as detailed as this."

Eristal was unapologetic as he acknowledged his own superiority. "That is because your knowledge and instrumentation are prehistoric. We can extract far more because we know what to look for, plus we can create an exact replica of the human it would become."

Ava's jaw dropped in dismay. "You cloned Darlen?"

Eristal saw Darlen's face turn red with anger, and he hastily denied producing any copies. "It was unnecessary," he assured them before turning back to his elaborate display. "Now, please consider the genome in this second cell."

Laurel and Harry made some sense of the genome, but there was just too much unknown information scrolling alongside it, and as Eristal pointed out smugly once more, their knowledge was too primitive. Within the cell was the familiar, tiny hourglass-shaped virus.

"Who does this belong to?" Laurel ventured. "One of us?"

"As you can see," Eristal continued, ignoring Laurel's question, "the second cell has similarities to the first, but when we stripped it down to its ancestral markers—" he glanced around, "—visible only to our superior technology, and interpretable by advanced knowledge, we found that although the two have the same foundations, this cell was drawn later from the superior original which formed the Sons of David. At first viewing of the second genome, it would seem evolution of the race had regressed, until we realised this was an attempt to create a race alongside that which arose from the original ancestral cell."

"Created by whom?"

Eristal shrugged. Why did the man with the strange hair expect him to know that?

"And it resulted in the Menworan?" Laurel asked.

"That is the name we ascribed to this inferior genome copy according to your account and the history you provided, but it would have produced a species destined not to survive. We tried to generate a facsimile—" Eristal then quickly glossed over what he perceived as a minor failure, "Unfortunately, in its pared back state, this cell could not produce a viable human for research purposes. We did learn the original template of this cell would have been male with no instinct for survival. It would probably have been preyed upon by the Sons of David depending on the availability of food on Menwora; it might even have been created *as* a source of food for the Sons of David. But of course, we cannot be certain."

Eristal stopped for a moment to enquire of Darlen, "Do all Sons of David carry jewels within their bodies? It is of a devotional significance, perhaps?"

Darlen stood and towered over Eristal, who seemed surprised by the aggressive response, and wondered why this man was so volatile. He shrank from Darlen's growling, "You are crossing too many lines."

Eristal responded swiftly, as if in fear for his life. "You told Chloe about it, and she told us. It showed when we profiled you. It is of no danger to our society. We thought perhaps a trinket or an adornment, although it is not on view. We decided because only your race can withstand its energy, you choose to wear it internally."

Darlen growled again, and Scarlett reached up to take his hand. "Daddy," she said softly, encouraging him to sit down.

Harry leaned forward. "You are suggesting the Sons of David were an established race at some point, then an unknown someone manipulated the genetic code to create another race, perhaps as an experiment?"

Marly, the female scientist, sitting in stony silence until now, stood to take over the forum. So far, Laurel resisted the temptation to gatecrash the scientists' minds, extract what they needed to know and walk out. She also knew there was no way she nor Harry could interpret the data.

Marly pushed Eristal's data aside, where it appeared to gather itself and disappear inside an opening above his ear. Her voice was a manifestation of her face, sour and impatient.

"Both tribes were an experiment," she proclaimed, "although it appears the creator of the Sons of David possessed a superior knowledge of what constitutes life."

She huffed, as if this were something they should know. "The Sons of David were fully formed humans and no doubt placed in an environment selected by their creator. Nothing more was needed to ensure their survival. The off-shoot species, however, the Menworan, are a different story. An attempt to duplicate the ancestral form of the cell was made. It has evidence of genetic tampering, and it might have been doomed to failure, but *someone* wanted them to survive, and I would say, with some certainty, that it was not the genetic meddler. That other 'someone' gave them this…"

Marly displayed the tiny hourglass-shaped virus. "This does not appear in Darlen. We first see it in the later copy of the ancestral cell, which became the Menworan." She then dismissed Baii with barely a glance and a flick of her hand. "You don't have it. There is nothing that links you to this bloodline at all."

With Baii roundly excused from the equation, Marly turned to Laurel and Harry, warming to her role as revelator.

"I will now reveal to you what you could not have possibly understood," she said triumphantly. "This is not a virus. It is a program. Of course—" she tutted and tilted her head to the side, "—it might appear as a virus to the uneducated, but it is very sophisticated, so your confusion is understandable. The program is instinct. The Menworan survived only because the first viable male, after the genome was rescued, was programmed to survive." Marly waited a moment for her words to sink in. Laurel and Harry were thinking the same thing; that someone added to the blueprint because whoever manipulated the original failed cell was somehow not up to the task.

Images of the two masters and the half-eaten female projected from Marly's eyepiece.

"After the cells yielded their information about the genetic characteristics of the Sons of David and the Menworan, we turned our attention to those you term the Sons of Benjamin. They share many features of the Menworan. The male is a gynandromorph. In his case, the female he fashions is his womb, and therefore, what emerges from the sac is not a separate life form." She gave Laurel and Harry an indulgent grin. "This would account for your further confusion in that it appears to be such a rudimentary creation," she finished smugly.

"Do gynandromorphs exist in human form?" Laurel whispered to Harry. "I thought it was just a mix of male and female characteristics in insects."

Harry shook his head. "I have no idea. Everything I believed has just been turned on its head."

Laurel spent a moment absorbing this information. "What about the pain she suffers?" she asked Marly.

"The master gives her that too," Marly said, still smug. "It appears you cannot move beyond your notion that she is somehow separate. She is nothing more than his womb. She receives from him that which she needs to give life to his children, nurture them, move her body and sustain it. She needs nothing else. Pain is not a consideration as she is fulfilling her purpose."

"Do you believe this was how it was for the original Menworans?" Laurel said. Her vision of Judith made her believe women were cherished in Menworan society.

"I dare say they procreated in the same way; it is a primitive creation after all. An experiment. Other than that, I have little more that I can add on the subject of the first Menworans." Marly sniffed. "Whoever created them planned to copy the Sons of David, as they originated from what appears to be a manipulation of the same ancestral genome. The procedure failed, and this failure was corrected by adding a program to the genome to ensure the species' survival. The result of this was additional ribs, extra vertebrae and a rather unusual method of procreation. That is all. As I said, they were an experiment and very likely a benign and submissive species, but that would be speculation."

"How do we know this isn't all speculation?" Baii said. "We don't understand the technology; we don't know what you tell us is the truth."

"Your technology, your knowledge… is primitive," Marly said, once again dismissing Baii as a mere addendum to the story. "Our science can peel back every layer of every cell until we arrive at—" she touched thumb and forefinger together, "—the quintessential spark of life. The Aile. It is exacting work but worthy of the labour. The Sons of David flourished, and after further 'programming' by a more knowledgeable and clearly altruistic benefactor, the Menworan also thrived. But the masters? I am confident they share a creation story with the Menworan, but something catastrophic came about to change their physiology and to remove from them this 'spark'. Physical examination reveals this subspecies produces a toxin and possesses additional dentition; we believe for grinding bones. You report it also has a disabling stench which it employs at will. We have been unable to ascertain the source of this, although we speculate it arises from the same glands as the toxin. The original Menworan did not have these features, except for an exceedingly mild oral neurolysing agent, which they inherited from their superior cousins, the Sons of David."

Marly tapped her lip and surveyed the images of the masters and the accompanying data before continuing.

"When we applied our knowledge, our technology, and considered Homeworld definitions of life—at every level, we concluded the Sons of Benjamin are non-living. We don't know how this being was capable of movement, of sentience. It can obviously be killed, and from what your Edensai contact advised Laurel, will cease to exist at around the age of forty. How it manages to survive at all is beyond even our technology. This—" she pointed to the image of the adult male master "—is not truly 'life'. But it is not death, either. I don't know what this is. Some kind of replication?"

"It was claimed the original Benjamin was brought back from the dead," Laurel said.

Marly rocked her head from side to side and pulled a "maybe/maybe not" face. "I've never heard of such a feat, but perhaps there is a species out there capable of such, which would explain why the master has no Aile. Perhaps his additional attributes of stench and dentition were assigned to him by whoever raised him from the grave. Then, we must question their purpose. And how can something such as a master replicate itself? I will concede it is a mystery."

The thought was of great concern to them all. "You can't reanimate him, can you?" Laurel asked. "He is evil. His kind must never again be allowed to return."

It was the first time Marly smiled without condescension. She agreed with Laurel's view. "I dare say the power that created it could make it live, but for us, it has no Aile. There is no life to bring back."

"And what of the female offspring we rescued? We found a few cells…"

Marly laughed then. "What were you looking for? That creature is a product of the master. She isn't life either."

"Well, we did debate that…"

Marly opened a shallow container containing a gestational sac, drawing horrified gasps from her audience.

"The male had a few cells which could be mistaken for life by someone with your lack of scientific understanding. We were able to grow a facsimile of his offspring." She grinned at the shocked faces.

"Oh, it's not viable," Marly assured them, her artificial eye looking them up and down as she altered her view. "It's just for research. We extracted some toxin from the mature master, so we could grow a suitable specimen. We didn't use a rib, only synthetic components."

Laurel felt something inside her; she already didn't like the outcome of this research.

"Have you turned up anything yet?" she said.

Marly nodded. "The half-eaten female is your relative, and by extension, so are all the masters spawned by the original resurrected example."

Laurel's hand went to her mouth in horror. Cephus had called her *sister.*

"The non-living, resurrected master who fashioned her, like the sac you rescued, came from the Menworan at some point in his history. As did you."

"But I'm human," Laurel protested feebly. She believed her likeness to Judith resulted from some kind of generational mutation. She didn't expect actually to *be* Judith. "I was born on Earth. Harry couldn't find that virus, that program, in me."

Marly was unimpressed by Laurel's denial. "Well, it's in the others, but unlike them, your ancestors are Menworan, who at some stage *became* human—albeit with a few peculiarities and insect-like characteristics—but human, nonetheless. The evidence is irrefutable; you, the Menworan, the masters, the sac you discovered, and by default, the Sons of David, are family, way back. Eli and Chloe are descended from the same race; Edensai, we presume. Ava is a mix of Edensai, Menworan and "other human, and the little girl results from a pairing between a Son of David and an Edensai descendant."

"Why didn't I find the program in Laurel? Show us your evidence," Harry demanded.

"Well, like we say, your knowledge in research is…" Marly thought for a moment, "archaic". Do you remember that quintessential spark of life? The Aile? It is there in the first two cells, but in the masters and its sac, it does not exist. Without it, one cannot live."

"Doesn't it go out when the body dies, and how does the Hebre entity affect it?" Ava asked.

Marly shook her head. "It leaves a shadow, a memorial that it once existed. That is why we know the masters are non-living rather than dead. They do not possess even this shadow. As for this 'Hebre' you speak of, we found no evidence of inhabitation in any of you. Another alien race, perhaps?"

"Okay." Harry stood and approached the images. "I want to see this 'Aile'."

Marly faced him. "You will not recognise it. It is everywhere."

Harry expected a less vague response and a more scientific demonstration, but Marly just kept looking at him in surprise, as if Harry should simply accept it as fact. Except he couldn't.

"And it's measurable?" He raised an eyebrow.

"No. It is not."

Harry sat down. They were hiding something. Laurel knew it too.

"I see why the Menworan needed the extra ribs if that was how they were set up by their maker," Laurel said. "But why would Chloe and Eli have extra ribs if they aren't Menworan?"

"Each imp inherited features from the parent," Marly said.

"But the Edensai don't have extra ribs."

"What infected them did. That changed things up a bit."

"I asked you this," Eli said to Harry. "Can a virus create extra bones?"

To Laurel, that brought up another question that

needed an answer. "So how did the Edensai get infected with a program created on another world?"

"The second cell Eristal showed you?" Marly said. "It is yours."

Laurel was confused. "Mine? But didn't you get information about the early Menworan males from that cell?"

That earned a shrug of indifference from Marly. "Menworans were gynandromorphs, so the cell reflected that history, although you now appear to be fully female. We stripped the cell, discovered the Menworan program, and as we replaced the layers, found a second, unique sequencer embedded in the first. You'll be glad to know that somewhere on its journey, it accumulated characteristics of its host program." She brought up the cell again for them to view. It was busy layering itself. "We did some basic recreations, matched this with other samples of your blood and tissue, and found only you possessed the sequencer. It was designed as an infection that would rewrite the genetic profile of its victims, and not in a positive way. It was deliberate sabotage aimed at humans."

"How?" Laurel couldn't see anything in the restructuring process.

Marly had no idea, but no matter; she had already established her superiority. "All I know is Eli and Chloe did not inherit Menworan genetic history. We believe they are Edensai with that little bit of historical, completely inert programming. Moreover, Laurel, you were never an imp. It was you who carried the program to the Edensai."

Eristal took advantage of the ensuing dumbfounded

silence and Laurel's horror, to speak.

"The program was far too advanced even for us to duplicate," he said. "We couldn't even see how the author, or authors, laid it down. We do know this is not a technology we can decipher."

The final, awful truth was out.

"I *was, I am* Judith?" Laurel suddenly felt her surroundings closing in. Somewhere centuries before, she had been the one to infect the Edensai and create the imps! It wasn't just a simple case of ancestry; an unnatural part of Judith had survived in her. Even knowing this was where Marly was going, and repeating it to herself, Laurel could scarcely believe it to be true. And even after Marly's rather arrogant retelling, it had to be. But *how?*

"Oh, don't worry," Marly flicked her hand, unconcerned at the effect of the revelation. "For reasons we cannot determine, the sequence program is quarantined at a cellular level and cannot be manipulated. If you die…well, who knows? We need to do further research."

Seeing her mother stricken by this news, Ava held her hand tight, offering support and comfort. "If the original Menworan procreated in the same way as the Masters," she said to Marly, "their offspring were always male. Twins. Does this mean Judith was created originally to bear the children?"

"My instinct is to say Judith was born, not made," Marly said after a moment's thought. "Perhaps she was the next step in the evolution of the Menworan, by the hand of their benefactor, bringing them into line with the Sons of David."

Harry was still trying to get his head around the revelation. "Laurel believed Judith also underwent resurrection before Benjamin. Why is Laurel not non-living?"

Marly considered it and allowed her eyepiece to click through reams of data. "Laurel shares attributes of the original Menworan, and by default, the Sons of Benjamin, who are a later, disastrous recreation. I can only say Laurel is alive," she said at length. "She has been for centuries. Chloe and Eli also. Your Ailes tell us so."

Laurel shook her head. Alive for *centuries?* "How does it tell you that?"

"The spark has not dimmed."

"Does that mean we are immortal?" Eli wondered aloud. He was grey-haired, ageing, not even aware of his whole soul abilities anymore.

"The Aile lives while you live," Marly said. "Laurel has Judith's Aile because she is of Judith. She would have been possessed of this Aile even when she was performing her nasty sowing of imps. You all have the Aile. It is a gift from the universe to acknowledge life. When your physical body no longer has need of it, it will leave. It's quite simple, really."

So, going by that, Laurel needed to know what would happen if she died. Could she be subject to manipulation by Lilith, or some other deity?

"I can't tell you that for sure," Marly answered. "In the body you inhabit, the sequencer program is quiescent, and as you say you know of no other instances of clear-eyed children, it's safe to say you haven't infected anyone else, perhaps in centuries. We—" she looked at Eristal, "theorise the so-called whole souls on the planet you call Earth are born, live and die, but the entity, this Hebre of which you speak and of which we found no evidence, achieves perpetuation by creating duplicates and characteristics of the original host, thereby providing the Hebre a vessel in which to dwell, and also, the Aile. A happy circumstance if it's true."

"Until the Soul Monger comes to claim Hebre and return it to the nebula, to its home." Laurel flicked a glance to Ava, who blinked a slow *"yes"*.

But Laurel needed more. "So, in duplicating me, the entity also duplicates the program, even though it's inactive?"

Marly bobbed her head around, making unchecked assumptions of "probably" and "yes". She wasn't convinced of any entity, but immortality troubled her.

Laurel wondered how Hebre found a way to thwart the program on Eden, and how Ava, certainly not a clear-eyed imp, was most certainly Hebre. The same for her father, Gabriel. Both born in proximity to the nebula.

"The government has asked us to prepare a report on the infection source," Eristal said, standing and indicating the meeting was over. "We will let you know the outcome."

"Didn't you scan for bacteria and infections when we arrived?" Harry asked as Eristal removed his chair almost from under him.

"We did, but not biological programming," Eristal responded, not even looking at him. "Besides, we've never seen anything like this. On the face of it, your colleagues present as normal humans."

But Laurel suddenly didn't feel quite so normal. Nor as human.

CHAPTER FORTY-TWO _

"I told you the masters were zombies," Darlen grinned, uncaring that his attempt at humour might not be welcome to those among them who had just discovered they were immortal. He'd been in a bad mood, but now, what the heck.

"This isn't funny, Darlen," Baii cautioned. "Anyway, what is a zombie?"

"Undead people. Non-living things that creep about."

"That's not Laurel. She is alive."

"I meant the masters…" Then, seeing Baii's dismissive expression, Darlen shook his head. "Forget it."

Harry didn't waste time with wisecracks. Back at the Canaa, he looked up the life spark Marly spoke of. He found a mass of information about the "Aile", and considering Tavis had not heard of magic, these people seemed quite knowledgeable about metaphysics.

"According to this entry, they claim the Aile has a scientific basis," Harry said, "although the essay here lacks details based on that claim. There are heaps of gaps in the data, but it's obviously an accepted element of life."

"Can you believe their arrogance?" Baii snorted. "One minute they're expounding their superiority, the next, admitting they don't know if it's fact or speculation. Then they throw in a universal force of nature for good measure to explain it all. And they acted like Hebre was a figment of imagination but spoke of the Aile as truth. At least with Hebre there are physical manifestations. I think they extrapolated from the limited amount of information they had, created an entire saga, and fed it to us as fact, knowing we can't challenge them. I don't believe they got all that from a couple of cells."

They saw his point. Much of it could have been bunkum.

Chloe stayed with them but kept her distance from Laurel, leaving Ava to stay by her mother's side. Eli took the news about Judith being the source of the infection well, but decided not to wonder under what circumstances the program inside Laurel might be reactivated. Instead, he thought about Ru and the children, all the while knowing full well Laurel would do nothing to compromise their safety. Meanwhile, Laurel just sat quietly.

"I've never heard of 'Aile'," Eli said. "It sounds like religion to me, and these people aren't religious. It's not something taught in schools."

Darlen gave a short laugh before turning serious. "It sounds like hocus pocus. This place, Laurel, I know you've had a shock, but what are we doing here? Don't you think it's time we left?"

Laurel didn't answer immediately. Something inside her; she wasn't sure. *Memories?* No, not memories exactly, just...*feelings.* She looked up to see Ava watching her. *"I think I know what happened,"* Laurel sent.

"Tell us," Ava said aloud, as one by one, the others fell to silence.

"Judith *was* Benjamin's twin sister," Laurel began slowly as the pieces fell into place. She couldn't rush this. "I think she was one of the first, if not *the* first, 'normal' or complete females born to a Menworan mate. If Menworan pregnancies had previously resulted in boys, and the girls were made from a male rib, boy and girl twins would be unheard of. Benjamin and Judith shared one of those bifurcated uteruses, but I think whoever fixed up that Menworan genome decided to extend the experiment and transition the Menworan to a more normal and human method of procreation. Judith and Benjamin were part of that transitional process. I know Judith looked like me, except for her green eyes, at least until possessed by Hebre."

Laurel felt a weight lift from her mind. She had no idea why these thoughts were buried, and why it took until now before they surfaced. Hebre always seemed to have a time and place for all things.

"Lilith, the first wife, created animal and insect life," she continued, now more confident in the unravelling story. "The second, or sister wife, Eve, created the Sons of David. Eve was the mother of all living, but 'all living' meant humankind. It didn't include the animals, which were an inferior creation. I believe the husband, or I suppose 'David', as the tribe was named after him, admired Eve's creations more. Lilith, who cannot create human life, took the genome Eve created to try to establish her own race of humans. It was almost as if..." Laurel's face creased as she tried to remember Abel's retelling of the event. "As if she were in competition with Eve and was trying to win back the favour of her husband. Lilith's attempts failed, so Eve, in a gesture of compassion, inserted a program that would allow the creations to live, even if they weren't according to her design."

"Perhaps Eve is a metaphor for a higher lifeform," Baii suggested.

"Eve might just be a technician, working for a higher being," Darlen added. It was a joke, but they all nodded. Anything was a possibility.

"If you are saying Lilith manipulated the genome in the first place because she could only create lower life forms," Eli said, "then what is she? The mother of everything non-living?"

Laurel believed that to be the eventual outcome. "I think that is what she became. Both Lilith and Eve's roles were to create life in all its variety, but when 'David', the father, made his preference for Eve and her abilities known, Lilith was relegated to govern the afterlife."

Suddenly, Laurel took a deep, sharp breath. It was staring her in the face. Judith didn't die! She only appeared to be dead.

"Harry," Laurel said. "Remember Abel told us the Menworan ruler's children died? What medical conditions mimic death?"

"Severe hypothermia?" he suggested, citing the obvious. "Coma? Either one of those would look like death to anyone who didn't have the ability to diagnose."

Laurel thought about the pastoral scene from her brief vision. "The Menworan, left to themselves, were not an advanced civilisation. I don't believe they would know the difference, so after whatever it was that befell Judith, it looked as if she had died. When she recovered, they would naturally believe she'd somehow cheated death. Of course, she was never actually dead. She just looked as though she was. When Benjamin died, they tried it again, but he actually *was* dead."

"Abel said there was some sort of hostility aimed at Eve by Lilith," Harry said.

"Yes, Lilith was scorned in favour of Eve, who had superior abilities." It made sense. What better way for Lilith to get revenge than to throw acid at her rival's creations by making a race of her own? She just didn't have what it took. Eve created the Sons of David, Lilith created the Menworan, got it wrong, and Eve stepped in to make them viable.

"These beings sound like a bunch of scientists conducting an experiment in a laboratory," Harry said. "So how did Lilith get the chance to make that sequencing program, or whatever it is in Judith?"

Once more, Laurel had to allow her words to fall where they would.

"By instilling it in Judith, perhaps as she hovered between life and death during the incident Abel spoke of. Clearly, Lilith knew about creating chaos, but it wasn't much of a plan, and Judith was around long enough to cast out the Sons of Benjamin. Also, there's a lot of human life out there, so a big ask for one person to wipe them out. Benjamin's death was a bonus for Lilith, another opportunity to intercept Eve's plans for her creations. I know it sounds unbelievable—" Laurel looked around at their expectant faces, "but when Benjamin died, his Aile left. He had no life essence, no conscience. A perfect candidate for Lilith's plan to annihilate mankind. She managed to manipulate Judith's program to cause chaos, but to do it, she had to get Judith's "Aile", her conscience, to move aside. Benjamin had no Aile, therefore, no conscience. His father believed he had "resurrected" his son, but it was Lilith's doing. Judith and the Menworan council recognised the evil and cast him out of their house. Lilith must have been rubbing her hands with glee. It all fell into her lap."

"And of course, the Menworan didn't know Judith had been set up by Lilith."

Laurel nodded. "That's right, Harry. I don't know why she didn't infect people in the first kingdom, and I don't know how she got to Eden. Olyo said Judith existed in a non-corporeal form on Eden for centuries and that the 'gods' restored her mortal body, but I don't think that was the case. If this 'Aile' is real, Judith never died, but I believe Lilith had the power to suspend her life until she found a suitable target."

"Eden?"

"I'd like to think it was only Eden, but there is a blank space here. The masters were a bonus to her plans to wipe out humankind, but Lilith reckoned without Hebre, who must have seen the destructive potential of the imps, not just on Eden, but if the virus went elsewhere. I think it's why Judith promised she would return, to make amends. She needed delivering as much as the Edensai."

"Why didn't Eve catch on that Lilith had put a second

program inside Judith?" Ava asked. "And why only in one person?"

"Maybe these so-called creators aren't omnipotent. Maybe they left the Menworan to themselves. Who knows?"

Darlen suddenly clapped his hands and laughed. "Laurel! Listen to yourself! I accept that you and all whole souls have this entity. I've been around you long enough to see what you're capable of. But you sound like a creationist. You don't believe in gods, Laurel. You've said that over and over. Maybe an advanced species did create life on Menwora, but there are humans throughout the entire *universe?* Come on, Laurel!"

"Perhaps it's not a 'god' who created humankind, Darlen," Laurel responded, becoming more certain her feelings were valid, despite her always being a staunch believer in evolution. "Perhaps science hasn't properly explained how life came to the universe."

"I'm going to take some convincing about the 'creation' theory, Laurel," Harry said. "It's a tall order, and if they are some kind of god, they have a lot of human attributes, including jealousy and genocide, not to mention they make a lot of bad choices."

Chloe spoke then for the first time since they'd left the laboratory. Her voice was quiet, uncharacteristically so, and there was no sign of her usual bubbliness. "I don't care what any of you think. When Eli and I die, we'll go to the nebula, like Helen and Xavier. So will Ava. The entity is home. It doesn't need to make another body now." She gazed steadily at Laurel. "It won't be the same for you. Not if you *are* Judith. Hebre may be imprisoned inside you."

Laurel sensed Chloe's sudden, heightened anxiety. Caught up with her own emotions, she hadn't noticed Chloe was pale and perspiring.

"I am the same as you," Laurel said gently, feeling an urgent need to placate, to soothe. "I'm Hebre too, the entity possessed Judith on Eden, and now I'm returned to the proximity of the nebula."

"But everything of Judith lives in you, doesn't it?" Laurel detected a dangerous undercurrent. Her eyes flicked to Baii, who had not wanted them to contact Chloe earlier. Laurel missed the signs.

"All of this came from a domestic feud between Lilith and Eve?" Eli said, not having caught the telepathic undertone.

Laurel nodded, not taking her eyes from Chloe. "We just got caught in the crossfire."

"We don't belong here," Baii declared, even though he sensed the tension. "We bring too much history, too many differences. Perhaps we need to speak to Tavis and ask him to release the Canaa."

Laurel agreed. "I don't need to go back to the apartment. I'd rather just leave. Chloe, would you contact Tavis? He got vague when we asked if we could leave to visit Marcel."

Chloe stood abruptly and drew a small neurodisruptor, levelling it directly at Laurel. Eli jumped up in shock. "Chloe, what the hell...!" Chloe held up her hand to stop him, but she couldn't hide her obvious distress.

"Laurel, I can't let you leave. The Presidents knew of the findings before Marly called for you. They have decided to place you in permanent quarantine stasis."

"Chloe!" Harry stepped forward, but Chloe shook the gun at him. "No, Harry. I didn't know it, but Homeworld was decimated by this program centuries ago, so you see, it did make its way here, before Eden. That's your blank space, Laurel. The Presidents sent for me and asked me everything I knew about you. I just thought they were interested, so I told them about the clear-eyed imps, the chaos they caused on Eden, and how you thought it was a spaceborne virus. I didn't know," Chloe cried. "I'm so sorry!"

Laurel made no move towards the distressed woman. "Did the Presidents tell you the history?"

Chloe nodded miserably, but she kept her aim carefully towards Laurel, and her mind closed. "They called it a plague. It happened aeons ago, but the story is identical to what you told me happened on Eden. Laurel, they showed me the likeness of the woman who was pregnant, the one who brought the sickness. It was you."

"Chloe, it wasn't me. It was Judith. I'm just a remnant, and I am also Hebre."

Chloe shook her head and bit back a sob, her hands shaking on the weapon. "The woman disappeared just after childbirth and was never found. The baby had no eye colour, and a childless couple adopted it. Over the next few months and years, reports of births of other clear-eyed children came in from all over the planet, along with an increased death rate among normal boys. Then the chaos started. The clear-eyed children ran amok; they were violent, dangerous; they had no empathy, no kindness. They were like wild animals. And more and more were being born."

"Chloe, that isn't going to happen now." Laurel reached out her hands, hoping to make her old friend see sense.

"Stay where you are," Chloe snapped. "The police will be here soon—" She glanced nervously towards the accessway. "Until they do, I'll tell you what I was told, so you'll know why you must be stopped. The program infects boys. If a boy is a carrier, he will live to produce male and female imps. Otherwise, the infection kills him. They tried to find a cure, and do you know what?"

Laurel shook her head.

"There wasn't one," Chloe stated simply. "It was beyond their understanding. They thought, as you did, that it was a spaceborne virus, but they were not so advanced as now. Faced with a catastrophe of global proportions, the government had no choice; they ordered parents to destroy their clear-eyed child even if it hadn't reached the age of chaos. If they couldn't do it, the children were rounded up and executed along with adult males and boys in whom the virus, as they thought then, was detected. It took decades to rid themselves of the plague because parents hid with their children in the mountains. It's why they developed the shield. I was under strict orders to not tell you until Marly gave you the results of the tests."

"Yet they still let us, and you, in. You'd think they'd be looking for the signs."

"Yes, Harry," Chloe said, "but they didn't know it was a program until they examined Laurel's cells. The host. Besides, Eli and I vouched for you."

"Does Marly know this history?" Harry asked.

"Yes, but Eristal is cybernetic; it's not in his programming."

"No wonder Marly was so smug," Darlen snorted. "I'm surprised she let us leave."

Harry took a deep, noisy breath, drawing the group's attention. "I have a problem with Lilith being any kind of creator, Chloe," he said. holding up his hands. "Hear me out. If she is, then theoretically, a being of her abilities would have no problem hoisting someone through Time and space. It seems the Hebre entity renders the program quiescent but doesn't interfere with the 'Aile'. Lilith's programming of Judith managed to move the Aile out of the way or even mask it. Hebre may have known what happened on Homeworld, then when it happened on Eden, they stepped in to stop the imps and found the source of the infection. One of them inhabited Judith's body, which was only of use to Lilith if it was alive. If she died, then the program would die with her. No Aile, no life, no program. This sequence was only found in Judith, not in the masters, so it would appear the sequencer program doesn't work in the non-living. If I was going to destroy mankind, I'd stick that program wherever I could. Lilith only had Judith. As a scientist, Lilith doesn't inspire confidence."

It was reasonable, but Chloe didn't take her finger off the trigger.

"So is Chloe right?" Laurel said. "Am I a danger?"

Harry shook his head. "No. Lilith only programmed Judith, and once Hebre got hold of her physical body, it stopped Lilith in her tracks. Judith became realised. I suspect Lilith's race had the power to keep life going, and death I suppose, in the case of the masters, but once Hebre inhabited Judith, Lilith lost her power over her. Hebre duplicated an inoperative facsimile of the program throughout the body's earthly incarnations but deeply buried. Judith's instincts needed to be awakened."

Laurel had no way of knowing how many worlds Lilith sent the unsuspecting Judith to, intending to infect the inhabitants, but Eden was the final place Lilith placed her. Olyo's explanation for her existence there probably arose from religious legend or myth. Either way, those questions may never be answered. By entering Judith's body, Hebre delivered her from the clutches of Lilith.

"Perhaps, at last, Judith fulfilled her purpose," Laurel said to Chloe. She spoke softly, reasonably. "I'm not a danger to anyone. If I die, I can't come back. Like Harry said, No life. No program."

Chloe's anxiety got the better of her, and she began to yell. "We can't be sure! Why can't you see that Hebre needs to stay within you? Marly found those cells in your body. You're Menworan. You still have Judith's Aile, and that makes you her. If you die, Hebre will return to the nebula, and Lilith can take over your body. We can't let you loose on the universe. On us."

"You are not being rational, Chloe. I'll be dead. Harry just told you the program needs me alive."

But Chloe wouldn't listen. "It doesn't matter. Lilith created masters from dead people."

Stalemate. Laurel realised there would be no reasoning, and with the police on their way, she had to bring this to a head. Dead or alive, she was already judged.

Chloe had been a capable soldier during the Gartryan war, and a few times, Laurel and she had friendly workouts together with holoenemies. This time, Laurel was deadly serious, she had no intention of going into permanent stasis, and as much as she loved Chloe, she wasn't going without a fight. She hoped Time would step in and help, but instead speed and agility came to her aid. Chloe sensed the movement but delayed just that second too long. Laurel, faster and younger, took her down and knocked her unconscious with a single blow.

Eli and Darlen were onto Chloe in a second to bind her hands. "You need to leave," Eli said urgently. "Darlen, is there any way Mer can release the clamps and flight disruptor? You're going to have police crawling everywhere soon; Chloe activated an alert when she drew the weapon."

"If he was able to do that," Darlen replied sarcastically, "do you think I'd still be here?"

Mer made a few noises. "He says if I can shut down the power," Ava said, "he can unwind the couplings. I don't know how we can disable the disruptor, though."

"I'll yank it out," Darlen made a pulling motion with his fist. "I've had a good look at it." In light of his comment from a moment earlier, they all looked at him accusingly. He pulled a defensive "just in case" face.

Ava concentrated on the power source, and they heard Mer clunking around under the ship. Eli carried the stunned Chloe outside and laid her gently on the grass.

"Darlen," he called out, as Darlen headed down the accessway to the disruptor. "Punch me, hard, otherwise, the police will think I aided your escape."

Darlen didn't even stop to debate, just swung a bone-shattering blow to Eli's jaw as he passed, an act witnessed by Chloe as she regained consciousness.

"I can't cloak the ship," Ava shouted as Laurel ran outside to help Darlen. "The area where the disruptor is located is still visible."

Darlen waved Laurel away with an "I got this" gesture as a portal opened a few hundred metres from the ship. Police poured through.

"Darlen! Mer! Hurry," Laurel shouted as she fired at the advancing force. She deliberately aimed at their weapons, knocking a few police down in the process. Darlen ordered Mer back into the ship to start the engines as the flight disruptor came loose. The first wave of police retreated, too exposed to return fire in the open field, but Ava still couldn't cloak the area of the ship surrounding the disruptor, and Darlen hadn't removed it completely. Now that the couplings were released, they only needed…

The explosion sent them all diving for the ground. Darlen was lifted several feet in the air, landing in a broken heap close to Baii.

"Daddy!!" Scarlett shrieked from the top of the accessway just as the second wave of police emerged from the portal. "Get on the ship!" Baii shouted to Laurel and Harry. "I've got him."

Laurel ran up the accessway and grabbed Scarlett. Ava stood by, ready to close the accessway. Mer was at the controls, ready to get the ship away the minute the hatch closed. The police fired, and Baii, although a tall man, was slighter in build than Darlen, so Darlen was a dead weight on his shoulder. Baii manifested a barrier at his back to deflect some of the weapons fire, but he was hit, the impact sending him sprawling forward. Laurel pushed the crying Scarlett towards Ava and ran down the accessway, extending a cloak over herself, Baii and Darlen, willing it to offer protection. Baii couldn't stand, so Laurel hoisted both men onto her shoulders and ran up the accessway. Unable to see their target, but sure they would be attempting to escape, the police kept their aim towards the ramp, and a few shots hit both Laurel and Baii. The cloak didn't give enough protection to stop them from being stung by weapons fire, but the police weren't there to kill; they were there to capture Laurel.

Laurel dropped both men on the floor and joined Harry in firing a few warning shots that sent the police diving for cover. As the Canaa rose into the air, she saw the police removing Eli and Chloe from the battle zone. She prayed they would be okay. They'd been relatively close to the blast, but both seemed able to walk with assistance.

Baii crawled to the side to allow Harry access to Darlen. "I can't stabilise him out here," Harry said, frantically cutting away Darlen's jacket. "Shit, Darlen," he said in exasperation, "why do you wear so many clothes? Mer!" he shouted out to the black robot, then he turned back to Laurel. "Ava can take us up, we need to get Darlen to the med bay."

Mer released control of the ship to Ava and scooped Darlen up carefully, but his abdomen and chest had taken the force of the blast, and Harry could not keep the wound enclosed. Laurel tried to shield Scarlett from the spectacle of blood gushing to the floor, but it was too late. She saw everything. Angrily, she shook Laurel's hand away and followed them to the med bay.

CHAPTER FORTY-THREE _

Only Scarlett's soft weeping could be heard above the sound of the pandroscope's diagnostic probes. It took a moment for the equipment to discover what was already evident to everyone. There would be no coming back from this. There was no programming that either Laurel or Harry could give the pandroscope to make sense of the mess that was once Darlen's upper body. Even the painbots or healbots did not activate, given the futility of the situation. Darlen's life signs were fading fast—anyone else who suffered a blast like that would have died instantly, but Darlen would have been far too cussed to leave without comment.

Laurel made sure the first person he saw when he opened his eyes for the last time would be Scarlett. The girl stroked her father's bald head and smiled bravely through her tears.

"Daddy, I don't want you to leave me."

Darlen smiled weakly. "You know, my darling; I think there might be too much of me missing to stay. Maybe I'll go and see your mother."

Scarlett's lip trembled, but she nodded. "Tell her I love her." Scarlett leaned up to wrap her arms around her beloved daddy, feeling the breath struggling in his chest as he kissed her hair and held her close. Darlen focused briefly on Laurel and Harry.

"Take care of her."

Laurel couldn't help it. She covered her face with her hands and wept into Harry's shoulder. Harry was shaking but managed to answer, "We will."

Darlen painfully moved his arm and held up a bloodied Magen star. Somehow, he'd had the foresight and determination to remove it. "She'll need this."

Harry took it from him and wiped the blood away with a thumb. It sparkled brilliantly. Harry looked at Darlen. "How do we insert it?"

Darlen rested for a moment before answering. "Just give it to her, and the one I took from Enoch. She'll know what to do."

Harry nodded and stepped back, placing his arm around the still weeping Laurel. They heard Darlen's whispered final "I love you" to Scarlett, seconds before the pandroscope's alert that the patient's life was now extinct. A moment later, Ava rushed into the med bay, followed quickly by a hobbling Baii. She stopped in her tracks as the scene told its story.

"We're clear," she said, her voice breaking. "We've plotted a course back to the nebula." Her face crumpled. "Oh, Mom!" Without a word, Laurel gathered her into her arms.

Harry muted the pandroscope so they didn't have to listen to the incessant "life extinct" warning. He looked at the bloodied Scarlett, still draped across her father's chest, at Laurel and Ava sobbing gently in each other's arms, then at Baii, who had sunk to the floor, bleeding copiously from a wound in his shin. Harry grabbed a palm pandroscope and knelt beside him.

"I'm sorry, Harry, I wasn't quick enough," Baii said, pain and grief turning his voice to a mere whisper.

"The flight disruptor was booby-trapped," Harry told him. "They must have suspected Darlen might try to leave; we couldn't have known. And they knew how to affect Hebre cloaks, at least in the proximity of the disruptor." He looked over at the scene of heartbreak. Nothing would ever be the same. "No-one could survive those injuries."

"He was your friend," Baii said sadly. "You loved him."

Harry sighed. "It wasn't always like that, but, yes, he was my friend, and yes, I suppose I loved him."

"Will we take him back to Isilia? To lie beside his beloved?"

"I think that will be the plan." Harry flopped against the bulkhead and checked the palm pandroscope. "You're good to go. Nothing a healbot won't fix." Harry tilted back his head and caught sight of Mer, who stood eerily still beside Scarlett. His claws were covered in Darlen's blood, his gaze fixed on his master.

"Mer?" Harry got to his feet and stood in front of the black robot, but Mer didn't respond. Scarlett lifted a tear-stained face and stood back from her father's body. "Uncle Harry," she said in a small, wise voice, far beyond her tender years, "He serves those with the star."

Harry lifted the gem between his thumb and forefinger before handing it to Scarlett.

"Your father said you would know what to do with it."

Scarlett nodded and took the star. Lifting her shirt, she held the tiny gem against her lower rib and, without so much as a blink, pushed hard. Laurel looked for blood, but there was none, and she could see the star settled and shining in its new universe. Scarlett took a deep breath and smiled. "I'm a real Soul Monger now," she said, "and my daddy is always going to be with me."

Minutes later, Mer and Harry removed Darlen to stasis to await their arrival on Isilia. Mer initiated a cleaning cycle then offered himself to Laurel for a final polish, something she knew Helen used to do regularly, but Mer had never asked of her. Although she obliged, she wondered if the black robot was grieving. It seemed extraordinary that he could, but he had been with Darlen a long time. It was reasonable to assume that somewhere amongst Mer's circuits, he developed a close bond with his master.

As the sad day ended, they sat together in the common lounge. Darlen's presence was all around them, his love of this ship, the sleeping Scarlett, too big for Harry's lap but content there nonetheless and not wishing to be alone just yet. In her hand was the locket the Chaese had fashioned from Helen's heart; the locket Darlen had worn for years. The Canaa had been on autopilot since they left the orbit of Homeworld so Mer could remain with them. They hadn't encountered any surprises as they approached the planet and expected none on the route out. Just in case, they kept the ship cloaked.

"I can't believe Chloe," Ava said. "How could she do that?"

Harry knew. "She was a police officer. She took her oaths in the League Constabulary very seriously, and I expect it was no different here. She was following orders."

Laurel didn't blame Chloe. "It would have been difficult for her to have had to choose between us and her life on Homeworld. She couldn't help us escape. If she did, what would have happened to her life there?"

"I hope Eli's okay," Harry said. "Darlen really smashed his jaw."

"From the way the police were handling them, I don't believe they suspect Eli encouraged us to leave," Baii said. "And Chloe saw Darlen swipe him, so I don't think there's going to be any fallout."

Ava speculated that Eli's feelings about Homeworld and his relationship with Chloe would likely be forever changed. They all agreed.

"But he has a good life there," Harry reminded them, "and an enormous family. In time, things will return to normal."

"Why weren't you able to command time, Laurel?" Baii asked. Laurel knew he wasn't accusing her of not using her abilities; the truth was, the power was not there during their escape.

"All I had was my fighting abilities and senses. I didn't even suspect Chloe until the moments before she drew the weapon. Also, I think to change Time, I need to be either in direct contact with the nebula or possibly where Time is unstable, what Darlen used to call 'slips'. Earth is covered in them, so is Isilia, plus Isilia is in a Transcender picot. Maybe this planet isn't. I've still got a lot to learn. Maybe when I've fulfilled my purpose, I'll have all the answers."

Laurel hoped that wouldn't be for a long time.

CHAPTER FORTY-FOUR _

The woman stood on her stateroom balcony overlooking San Francisco Bay. The chilly night breeze whipped her long dark hair about her face, and she drew her wrap tightly around her shoulders, her thin, glamorous evening dress not suitable attire for standing outside on a winter's night. The full moon hung low in the sky, its brightness obscuring the stars and she missed her home, but if she had to be away, for her, this was one of the most beautiful and vibrant places in the universe. Now, there would be no need to come back, and this would be her final visit, so she would etch this view in her memory. The last whole soul was on board the Canaa. They'd searched every time period and made two trips back to Isilia. Now, in the year 2073, the covenant was about to be fulfilled. Not a single whole soul remained on Earth.

Ava had visited her mother's home, had walked down the streets that were not her own, yet felt so familiar from her mother's stories. She even visited the little park in Chicago with the lake that froze at the slightest sign of winter. She also went to France to take in the sights her mother shared in a psychic link with her father while she was his prisoner on Semevale 7. She had made memories of her own here.

A petite girl with a purple and gold-streaked bobbed haircut opened the door to the balcony.

"Hi, have you had dinner?" she called out. "I brought McDonald's just in case."

"Hi Scarlett, yes, earlier."

Seventeen-year-old Soul Monger Scarlett rested her arms on the balcony rail and looked out over the moonlit bay. "I don't know why you like this place so much; Isilia is far prettier."

"I feel a connection to Earth," Ava said. "Remember, my mother was born here, and so was my father's mother. Is Baii on his way up?"

Scarlett grinned. "He sure is! The crowd went wild! I tell you; he's going to be missed by this cruise line. To get a world-famous magician in return for an all-expenses-paid cruise was a good price!"

Ava laughed. "We don't actually need money, do we? And this world-famous magician is about to disappear off the face of the Earth. They'll never know he's not performing magic, that it's real." She stared out in the distance. "I'm looking forward to seeing everyone. It seems every time we go back, Marcel and Ilivi have added to their brood!"

"What about you and Baii?" Scarlett said. "Isn't it about time you gave Auntie Laurel and Harry another grandchild? You never know; it might be a whole soul."

Ava smiled. "Maybe, but I suspect Hebre have fulfilled their purpose. At least now you know you haven't got to have a whole soul to produce a Magen Bearer."

"Meh," Scarlett wrinkled up her nose, "plenty of time

for that. I can always come back. Baii might decide to do a revival tour, and there are heaps of direct line Sons of David on Earth." She gave her friend a mischievous grin. "I've checked a few out. I can always kidnap one, pop him into variance and take him home! And don't forget I've got an extra Magen."

Ava knew Scarlett was entirely capable of it. These trips had been liberating, and she wished her mother would have accompanied her, but Laurel never once expressed a desire to return to Earth.

As a whole soul in full recognition, Ava ignited the Hebre memory in the whole souls she and Scarlett collected. She learned that when separated from the Miran Forin, the source of their power, Hebre instinctively sought Edensai progeny on Earth and changed the gene to produce a host copy. While the instinct to remain alive until they returned home prevailed, on Earth, Hebre's memory of where they came from faded, until a Soul Monger's deliverance to the proximity of the nebula.

Ava communicated to the Hebre entity, and because of the bond, variance was no longer necessary. She also learned the truth about Canaa, the planet where the Hebre and Sons of David settled after fleeing Eden. The masters had indeed found them, and to protect Hebre, the Sons of David hid their children on other planets, with the sad consequence their covenant became corrupted by history and thus established the whole soul trade. To protect the remnants of their society, the Sons of David captured the sole Magen Bearer loyal to the masters and fled with the remaining Hebre to the Transcender.

Time also became more cooperative to Ava, and with practice, traversing the nebula had become second nature.

Baii caught Ava's eye as he tossed his top hat and cloak onto a chair. He was not only a world-famous magician, but he was also considered by Time magazine the most good-looking man on the planet. Ava had taken a copy back to Isilia on their last trip to show her mother. The fact it was in a "Time" magazine had amused Ava and the irony not lost on Laurel.

"Enjoying the view for the last time?" Baii said, giving Ava a brief peck on the lips, then changing his mind and turning the peck to a lingering kiss.

Scarlett coughed. "Why do you two do that in company?"

"We're not in company," Baii laughed. "Remember, it is *you* who is in *our* stateroom!"

"I came to see if Ava is ready to leave. I know I am."

Baii looked at Ava. She nodded. "Okay."

Scarlett put her arms around Baii. She could hop through the slip above San Francisco, and Ava was entirely capable of teleporting up. Baii blew a kiss as he and Scarlett disappeared. Ava stood for a moment longer to gaze at the view. In the morning, there would be questions as to how three people could vanish into thin air on a calm night in a harbour, even if one was the most accomplished magician of all time. But by then, the missing trio would already have entered the Transcender with their whole soul cargo and would be well on their way home.

END

ACKNOWLEDGEMENTS

Thank you so much for reading Testimony, the final instalment of The Soul Monger trilogy. If you enjoyed the adventures of Laurel and her friends, I would love for you to leave a review on Amazon. Good reviews are the life blood of Indie authors, and we thank you for your support.

I would also like to thank my awesome editors, Jo and Amy. I am so lucky to have them on the team.

If you would like to be kept informed of my new releases, you can sign up for my (very occasional) newsletter here:
https://matildascotneybooks.com/

Or connect with me on Facebook:
https://www.facebook.com/Offtheplanetbooks/

ALSO BY MATILDA SCOTNEY

The Afterlife of Alice Watkins: A Time Travel mystery, Book One
The Afterlife of Alice Watkins: Book Two
Joy in Four Parts: A quirky sci fi novella.
Myth of Origin: A Sci Fi adventure
The Monk's Gate" A historical time travel novel.
The Soul Monger: Book One
Revelations: The Soul Monger Book Two
Foresight: A Science Fiction short story (kindle only)
Rattlebones: A paranormal AI short story (kindle only)
We Unseen: A First Contact short story (kindle only)

ABOUT THE AUTHOR

When my mind isn't off on galactic imaginings with my trusty chihuahua sidekick Oggie, I can be found in Australia, sand between my toes, collecting teapots and nerding about all things Star Wars.

www.ingramcontent.com/pod-product-compliance
Lightning Source LLC
Chambersburg PA
CBHW022359110726
47903CB00004B/1054